PHILIP ROTH

PHILIP ROTH

NEMESES

Everyman
Indignation
The Humbling
Nemesis

THE LIBRARY OF AMERICA

Everyman copyright © 2006 by Philip Roth. *Indignation* copyright ©
2008 by Philip Roth. *The Humbling* copyright © 2009 by Philip Roth.
Nemesis copyright © 2010 by Philip Roth. Published by special
arrangement with Houghton Mifflin Harcourt
Publishing Company.

The paper used in this publication meets the
minimum requirements of the American National Standard for
Information Sciences—Permanence of Paper for Printed
Library Materials, ANSI Z39.48—1984.

Distributed to the trade in the United States
by Penguin Group (USA) Inc.
and in Canada by Penguin Books Canada Ltd.

Library of Congress Control Number: 2012904759
ISBN 978-1-59853-199-2

First Printing
The Library of America—237

Manufactured in the United States of America

Ross Miller
WROTE THE Chronology AND Notes
FOR THIS VOLUME

Contents

EVERYMAN

To J. C.

Here, where men sit and hear each other groan;
Where palsy shakes a few, sad, last grey hairs,
Where youth grows pale, and spectre-thin, and dies;
Where but to think is to be full of sorrow . . .

—JOHN KEATS, "Ode to a Nightingale"

AROUND THE grave in the rundown cemetery were a few of his former advertising colleagues from New York, who recalled his energy and originality and told his daughter, Nancy, what a pleasure it had been to work with him. There were also people who'd driven up from Starfish Beach, the residential retirement village at the Jersey Shore where he'd been living since Thanksgiving of 2001—the elderly to whom only recently he'd been giving art classes. And there were his two sons, Randy and Lonny, middle-aged men from his turbulent first marriage, very much their mother's children, who as a consequence knew little of him that was praiseworthy and much that was beastly and who were present out of duty and nothing more. His older brother, Howie, and his sister-in-law were there, having flown in from California the night before, and there was one of his three ex-wives, the middle one, Nancy's mother, Phoebe, a tall, very thin whitehaired woman whose right arm hung limply at her side. When asked by Nancy if she wanted to say anything, Phoebe shyly shook her head but then went ahead to speak in a soft voice, her speech faintly slurred. "It's just so hard to believe. I keep thinking of him swimming the bay—that's all. I just keep seeing him swimming the bay." And then Nancy, who had made her father's funeral arrangements and placed the phone calls to those who'd showed up so that the mourners wouldn't consist of just her mother, herself, and his brother and sister-in-law. There was only one person whose presence hadn't to do with having been invited, a heavyset woman with a pleasant round face and dyed red hair who had simply appeared at the cemetery and introduced herself as Maureen, the private duty nurse who had looked after him following his heart surgery years back. Howie remembered her and went up to kiss her cheek.

Nancy told everyone, "I can begin by saying something to you about this cemetery, because I've discovered that my father's grandfather, my great-grandfather, is not only buried in the original few acres alongside my great-grandmother but was one of its founders in 1888. The association that first financed and erected the cemetery was composed of the burial societies of Jewish benevolent organizations and congregations scattered across Union and Essex counties. My great-grandfather owned and ran a boarding house in Elizabeth that catered especially to newly arrived immigrants, and he was concerned with their well-being as more than a mere landlord. That's why he was among the original members who purchased the open field that was here and who themselves graded and landscaped it, and why he served as the first cemetery chairman. He was relatively young then but in his full vigor, and it's his name alone that is signed to the document specifying that the cemetery was for 'burying deceased members in accordance with Jewish law and ritual.' As is all too obvious, the maintenance of individual plots and of the fencing and the gates is no longer what it should be. Things have rotted and toppled over, the gates are rusted, the locks are gone, there's been vandalism. By now the place has become the butt end of the airport and what you're hearing from a few miles away is the steady din of the New Jersey Turnpike. Of course I thought first of the truly beautiful places where my father might be buried, the places where he and my mother used to swim together when they were young, and the places where he loved to swim at the shore. Yet despite the fact that looking around at the deterioration here breaks my heart—as it probably does yours, and perhaps even makes you wonder why we're assembled on grounds so badly scarred by time—I wanted him to lie close to those who loved him and from whom he descended. My father loved his parents and he should be near them. I didn't want him to be somewhere alone." She was silent for a moment to collect herself. A gentle-faced woman in her mid-thirties, plainly pretty as her mother had been, she looked all at once in no way authoritative or even brave but like a ten-year-old overwhelmed. Turning toward the coffin, she picked up a clod of dirt and, before dropping it onto the lid, said lightly, with the air still of a bewildered young girl, "Well, this is how it turns out. There's nothing more we can do, Dad." Then she remembered his own stoical maxim from decades back and began to cry. "There's no remaking reality," she told him. "Just take it as it comes. Hold your ground and take it as it comes."

The next to throw dirt onto the lid of the coffin was Howie, who'd been the object of his worship when they were children and in return had always treated him with gentleness and affection, patiently teaching him to ride a bike and to swim and to play all the sports in which Howie himself excelled. It still appeared as if he could run a football through the middle of the line, and he was seventy-seven years old. He'd never been hospitalized for anything and, though a sibling bred of the same stock, had remained triumphantly healthy all his life.

His voice was husky with emotion when he whispered to his wife, "My kid brother. It makes no sense." Then he too addressed everyone. "Let's see if I can do it. Now let's get to this guy. About my brother . . ." He paused to compose his thoughts so that he could speak sensibly. His way of talking and the pleasant pitch of his voice were so like his brother's that Phoebe began to cry, and, quickly, Nancy took her by the arm. "His last few years," he said, gazing toward the grave, "he had health problems, and there was also loneliness—no less a problem. We spoke on the phone whenever we could, though near the end of his life he cut himself off from me for reasons that were never clear. From the time he was in high school he had an irresistible urge to paint, and after he retired from advertising, where he'd made a considerable success first as an art director and then when he was promoted to be a creative director—after a life in advertising he painted practically every day of every year that was left to him. We can say of him what has doubtless been said by their loved ones about nearly everyone who is buried here: he should have lived longer. He should have indeed." Here, after a moment's silence, the resigned look of gloom on his face gave way to a sorrowful smile. "When I started high school and had team practice in the afternoons, he took over the errands that I used to run for my father after school. He loved being only nine years old and carrying the diamonds in an envelope in his jacket pocket onto the bus to Newark, where the setter and the sizer and the polisher and the watch repairman our father used each sat in a cubbyhole of his own, tucked away on Frelinghuysen Avenue. Those trips gave that kid enormous pleasure. I think watching these artisans doing their lonely work in those tight little places gave him the idea for using his hands to make art. I think looking at the facets of the diamonds through my father's jewelry loupe is something else that fostered his desire to make art." A

laugh suddenly got the upper hand with Howie, a little flurry
of relief from his task, and he said, "I was the conventional
brother. In me diamonds fostered a desire to make money."
Then he resumed where he'd left off, looking through the
large sunny window of their boyhood years. "Our father took
a small ad in the *Elizabeth Journal* once a month. During the
holiday season, between Thanksgiving and Christmas, he took
the ad once a week. 'Trade in your old watch for a new one.'
All these old watches that he accumulated—most of them
beyond repair—were dumped in a drawer in the back of the
store. My little brother could sit there for hours, spinning the
hands and listening to the watches tick, if they still did, and
studying what each face and what each case looked like. That's
what made that *boy* tick. A hundred, two hundred trade-in
watches, the entire drawerful probably worth no more than
ten bucks, but to his budding artist's eye, that backroom watch
drawer was a treasure chest. He used to take them and wear
them—he always had a watch that was out of that drawer. One
of the ones that worked. And the ones he tried to make work,
whose looks he liked, he'd fiddle around with but to no avail—
generally he'd only make them worse. Still, that was the beginning of his using his hands to perform meticulous tasks. My
father always had two girls just out of high school, in their late
teens or early twenties, helping him behind the counter in the
store. Nice, sweet Elizabeth girls, well-mannered, clean-cut girls,
always Christian, mainly Irish Catholic, whose fathers and
brothers and uncles worked for Singer Sewing Machine or for
the biscuit company or down at the port. He figured nice
Christian girls would make the customers feel more at home.
If asked to, the girls would try on the jewelry for the customers, model it for them, and if we were lucky, the women would
wind up buying. As my father told us, when a pretty young
woman wears a piece of jewelry, other women think that when
they wear the piece of jewelry they'll look like that too. The
guys off the docks at the port who came in looking for engagement rings and wedding rings for their girlfriends would sometimes have the temerity to take the salesgirl's hand in order to
examine the stone up close. My brother liked to be around the
girls too, and that was long before he could even begin to understand what it was he was enjoying so much. He would help

the girls empty the window and the showcases at the end of the day. He'd do anything at all to help them. They'd empty the windows and cases of everything but the cheapest stuff, and just before closing time this little kid would open the big safe in the backroom with the combination my father had entrusted to him. I'd done all these jobs before him, including getting as close as I could to the girls, especially to two blond sisters named Harriet and May. Over the years there was Harriet, May, Annmarie, Jean, there was Myra, Mary, Patty, there was Kathleen and Corine, and every one of them took a shine to that kid. Corine, the great beauty, would sit at the workbench in the backroom in early November and she and my kid brother would address the catalogues the store printed up and sent to all the customers for the holiday buying season, when my father was open six nights a week and everybody worked like a dog. If you gave my brother a box of envelopes, he could count them faster than anybody because his fingers were so dexterous and because he counted the envelopes by fives. I'd look in and, sure enough, that's what he'd be doing—showing off with the envelopes for Corine. How that boy loved doing everything that went along with being the jeweler's reliable son! That was our father's favorite accolade—'reliable.' Over the years our father sold wedding rings to Elizabeth's Irish and Germans and Slovaks and Italians and Poles, most of them young working-class stiffs. Half the time, after he'd made the sale, we'd be invited, the whole family, to the wedding. People liked him—he had a sense of humor and he kept his prices low and he extended credit to everyone, so we'd go—first to the church, then on to the noisy festivities. There was the Depression, there was the war, but there were also the weddings, there were our salesgirls, there were the trips to Newark on the bus with hundreds of dollars' worth of diamonds stashed away in envelopes in the pockets of our mackinaws. On the outside of each envelope were the instructions for the setter or the sizer written by our father. There was the five-foot-high Mosley safe slotted for all the jewelry trays that we carefully put away every night and removed every morning . . . and all of this constituted the core of my brother's life as a good little boy." Howie's eyes rested on the coffin again. "And now what?" he asked. "I think this had better be all there is. Going on and on, remembering still more . . . but why not remember? What's another gallon of tears between family and friends? When our father died my brother asked me if I minded if he took our father's watch. It was a Hamilton, made in Lancaster, P-A, and according to the expert, the boss, the best watch this country ever produced. Whenever he sold one, our father never failed to assure the customer that he'd made no mistake. 'See, I wear one myself. A very, very highly respected watch, the Hamilton. To my mind,' he'd say, 'the premier American-made watch, bar none.' Seventy-nine fifty, if I remember correctly. Everything for sale in those days had to end in fifty. Hamilton had a great reputation. It *was* a classy watch, my dad did love his, and when my brother said he'd like to own it, I couldn't have been happier. He could have taken the jeweler's loupe and our father's diamond carrying case. That was the worn old leather case that he would always carry with him in his coat pocket whenever he went to do business outside the store: with the tweezers in it, and the tiny screwdrivers and the little ring of sizers that gauge the size of a round stone and the folded white papers for holding the loose diamonds. The beautiful, cherished little things he worked with, which he held in his hands and next to his heart, yet we decided to bury the loupe and the case and all its contents in his grave. He always kept the loupe in one pocket and his cigarettes in the other, so we stuck the loupe inside his shroud. I remember my brother saying, 'By all rights we should put it in his eye.' That's what grief can do to you. That's how thrown we were. We didn't know what else to do. Rightly or wrongly, there didn't seem to us anything but that to do. Because they were not just his—they were *him* . . . To finish up about the Hamilton, my father's old Hamilton with the crown that you would turn to wind it every morning and that you would pull out on its stem to turn to move the hands . . . except while he was in swimming, my brother wore it day and night. He took it off for good only forty-eight hours ago. He handed it to the nurse to lock away for safekeeping while he was having the surgery that killed him. In the car on the way to the cemetery this morning, my niece Nancy showed me that she'd put a new notch in the band and now it's she who's wearing the Hamilton to tell time by."

Then came the sons, men in their late forties and looking, with their glossy black hair and their eloquent dark eyes and the sensual fullness of their wide, identical mouths, just like their father (and like their uncle) at their age. Handsome men beginning to grow beefy and seemingly as closely linked with each other as they'd been irreconcilably alienated from the dead father. The younger, Lonny, stepped up to the grave first. But once he'd taken a clod of dirt in his hand, his entire body began to tremble and quake, and it looked as though he were on the edge of violently regurgitating. He was overcome with a feeling for his father that wasn't antagonism but that his antagonism denied him the means to release. When he opened his mouth, nothing emerged except a series of grotesque gasps, making it appear likely that whatever had him in its grip would never be finished with him. He was in so desperate a state that Randy, the older, more decisive son, the scolding son, came instantly to his rescue. He took the clod of dirt from the hand of the younger one and tossed it onto the casket for both of them. And he readily met with success when he went to speak. "Sleep easy, Pop," Randy said, but any note of tenderness, grief, love, or loss was terrifyingly absent from his voice.

The last to approach the coffin was the private duty nurse, Maureen, a battler from the look of her and no stranger to either life or death. When, with a smile, she let the dirt slip slowly across her curled palm and out the side of her hand onto the coffin, the gesture looked like the prelude to a carnal act. Clearly this was a man to whom she'd once given much thought.

That was the end. No special point had been made. Did they all say what they had to say? No, they didn't, and of course they did. Up and down the state that day, there'd been five hundred funerals like his, routine, ordinary, and except for the thirty wayward seconds furnished by the sons—and Howie's resurrecting with such painstaking precision the world as it innocently existed before the invention of death, life perpetual in their father-created Eden, a paradise just fifteen feet wide by forty feet deep disguised as an old-style jewelry store—no more or less interesting than any of the others. But then it's the commonness that's most wrenching, the registering once more of the fact of death that overwhelms everything.

In a matter of minutes, everybody had walked away—wearily

and tearfully walked away from our species' least favorite activity—and he was left behind. Of course, as when anyone dies, though many were grief-stricken, others remained unperturbed, or found themselves relieved, or, for reasons good or bad, were genuinely pleased.

Though he had grown accustomed to being on his own and fending for himself since his last divorce ten years back, in his bed the night before the surgery he worked at remembering as exactly as he could each of the women who had been there waiting for him to rise out of the anesthetic in the recovery room, even remembering that most helpless of mates, the last wife, with whom recovering from quintuple bypass surgery had not been a sublime experience. The sublime experience had been the private nurse with the unassuming professional air who'd come home with him from the hospital and who tended him with a high-spirited devotion that promoted a slow, steady recovery and with whom, unknown to his wife, he conducted a sustained affair once he had recovered his sexual prowess. Maureen. Maureen Mrazek. He'd called all over trying to find Maureen. He'd wanted her to come and be his nurse, should he need a nurse, when he got home from the hospital this time. But sixteen years had passed, and the nursing agency at the hospital had lost track of her. She'd be forty-eight now, more than likely married and a mother, a shapely, energetic young woman grown into middle-aged stoutness while the battle to remain an unassailable man had by then been lost by him, time having transformed his own body into a storehouse for manmade contraptions designed to fend off collapse. Defusing thoughts of his own demise had never required more diligence and cunning.

A lifetime later, he remembered the trip to the hospital with his mother for his hernia operation in the fall of 1942, a bus ride lasting no more than ten minutes. Usually if he was traveling somewhere with his mother, it was in the family car and his father was driving. But now there were just the two of them alone together on the bus, and they were headed for the hospital where he had been born, and she was what calmed his apprehension and allowed him to be brave. As a small child he'd had his tonsils removed at the hospital, but otherwise he'd never been back there. Now he was to stay for four days and four nights. He was a sensible boy of nine with no conspicuous problems, but on the bus he felt much younger and found that he required his mother's proximity in ways he thought he'd outgrown.

His brother, a high school freshman, was in class, and his father had driven the car to work well before he and his mother left for the hospital. A small overnight case rested on his mother's lap. In it were a toothbrush, pajamas, a bathrobe and slippers, and the books he'd brought with him to read. He could still remember which books they were. The hospital was around the corner from the local branch library, so his mother could replenish his reading material should he read through the books he'd brought for his hospital stay. He was to spend a week convalescing at home before returning to school, and he was more anxious about all the school he was missing than he was as yet about the ether mask that he knew they would clamp over his face to anesthetize him. In the early forties hospitals didn't as yet permit parents to stay overnight with their children, and so he'd be sleeping without his mother, his father, or his brother anywhere nearby. He was anxious about that, too.

His mother was well-spoken and mannerly, as, in turn, were the women who registered him at the admissions office and the nurses at the nurses' station when he and his mother made their way by elevator to the children's wing of the surgical floor. His mother took his overnight case because, small as it was, he wasn't supposed to carry anything until after his hernia was repaired and he had fully recuperated. He had discovered the swelling in his left groin a few months earlier and had told no one but just tried pressing it down with his fingers to make it go away. He did not know exactly what a hernia was or what significance to give to swelling located so close to his genitals.

In those days a doctor could prescribe a stiff corset with metal stays if the family didn't want the child to undergo surgery or if they couldn't afford it. He knew of a boy at school who wore such a corset, and one of the reasons he'd told no one about the swelling was his fear that he too would have to wear a corset and reveal it to the other boys when he changed into his shorts for gym class.

Once he had finally confessed to his parents, his father took him to the doctor's office. Quickly the doctor examined him and made the diagnosis and, after conversing with his father for a few minutes, arranged for the surgery. Everything was done with astonishing speed, and the doctor—the very one who had delivered him into the world—assured him that he was going to be fine and then went on to joke about the comic strip *Li'l Abner*, which the two of them enjoyed reading in the evening paper.

The surgeon, Dr. Smith, was said by his parents to be the best in the city. Like the boy's own father, Dr. Smith, born Solly Smulowitz, had grown up in the slums, the son of poor immigrants.

He was in bed in his room within an hour of arriving at the hospital, though the surgery was not scheduled until the following morning—that's how patients were tended to then.

In the bed next to his was a boy who'd had stomach surgery and wasn't allowed to get up and walk yet. The boy's mother sat beside the bed holding her son's hand. When the father came to visit after work, the parents spoke in Yiddish, which made him think that they were too worried to speak understandable English in their son's presence. The only place where he heard Yiddish spoken was at the jewelry store when the war refugees came in search of Schaffhausen watches, a hard-to-find brand that his father would call around to try to locate for them—"Schaffhausen—I want a Schaffhausen," that would be the extent of their English. Of course Yiddish was spoken all but exclusively when the Hasidic Jews from New York traveled to Elizabeth once or twice a month to replenish the store's diamond inventory—for his father to have maintained a large inventory in his own safe would have been too expensive. There were far fewer Hasidic diamond merchants in America before the war than after, but his father, from the very beginning, preferred to deal with them rather than with the big diamond houses. The diamond merchant who came most frequently—and whose migration route had carried him and his family in only a few years from Warsaw to Antwerp to New York—was an older man dressed in a large black hat and a long black coat of a kind that you never saw on anyone else in Elizabeth's streets, not even other Jews. He wore a beard and sidelocks and kept the waist pouch that held his diamonds secreted beneath fringed undergarments whose religious significance eluded the nascent secularist—that, in fact, seemed ludicrous to him—even after his father explained why the Hasidim still wore what their ancestors had worn in the old country two hundred years before and lived much as they did then, though, as he pointed out to his father again and again, they were now in America, free to dress and to shave and to behave as they wished. When one of the seven sons of the diamond merchant got married, the merchant invited their entire family to the wedding in Brooklyn. All the men there had beards and all the women wore wigs and the sexes sat on different sides of the synagogue, separated by a wall—afterward the men and the women did not even dance together—and everything about that wedding he and Howie hated. When the diamond merchant arrived at the store he would remove his coat but leave on his hat, and the two men would sit behind the showcase chatting amiably together in Yiddish, the language that his father's parents, his own grandparents, had continued to speak in their immigrant households with their American-born children for as long as they lived. But when it was time to look at the diamonds, the two went into the backroom, where there was a safe and a workbench and a brown linoleum floor and, jammed together behind a door that never shut completely even when you had successfully struggled to hook it from within, a toilet and a tiny sink. His father always paid on the spot with a check.

After closing the store with Howie's help—pulling the lattice gate with the padlocks across the shop's display window, switching on the burglar alarm, and throwing all the locks on the front door—his father showed up in his younger son's hospital room and gave him a hug.

He was there when Dr. Smith came around to introduce himself. The surgeon was wearing a business suit rather than a white coat, and his father jumped to his feet as soon as he saw him enter the room. "It's Dr. Smith!" his father cried.

"So this is my patient," Dr. Smith said. "Well," he told him, coming to the side of the bed to take him firmly by the shoulder, "we're going to fix that hernia tomorrow and you'll be as good as new. What position do you like to play?" he asked.

"End."

"Well, you're going to be back playing end before you know it. You're going to play anything you want. You get a good night's sleep and I'll see you in the morning."

Daring to joke with the eminent surgeon, his father said, "And you get a good night's sleep too."

When his dinner came, his mother and father sat and talked to him as though they were all at home. They spoke quietly so as not to disturb the sick boy or his parents, who were silent now, the mother still seated beside him and the father incessantly pacing at the foot of the bed and then out into the corridor and back. The boy hadn't so much as stirred while they were there.

At five to eight a nurse stuck her head in to announce that visiting hours were over. The parents of the other boy again spoke together in Yiddish and, after the mother repeatedly kissed the boy's forehead, they left the room. The father had tears running down his face.

Then his own parents left to go home to his brother and eat a late dinner together in the kitchen without him. His mother kissed him and held him tightly to her. "You can do it, son," his father said, leaning over to kiss him as well. "It's like when I give you an errand to run on the bus or a job to do at the store. Whatever it is, you never let me down. Reliable—my two reliable boys! I pop my buttons when I think about my boys. Always, you do the work like the thorough, careful, hard-working boys you were brought up to be. Carrying precious jewels to Newark and back, quarter-carat, half-carat diamonds in your pocket, and at your age that doesn't faze you. You look to all the world like it's some junk you found in your Cracker Jacks. Well, if you can do that job, you can do this job. It's just another job of work as far as you're concerned. Do the work, finish the job, and by tomorrow the whole thing will be over. You hear the bell, you come out fighting. Right?"

"Right," the boy said.

"By the time I see you tomorrow, Dr. Smith will have fixed that thing, and that'll be the end of that."

"Right."

"My two terrific boys!"

Then they were gone and he was alone with the boy in the

next bed. He reached over to his bedside table, where his mother had piled his books, and began to read *The Swiss Family Robinson*. Then he tried *Treasure Island*. Then *Kim*. Then he put his hand under the covers to look for the hernia. The swelling was gone. He knew from past experience that there were days when the swelling would temporarily subside, but this time he was sure that it had subsided for good and that he no longer needed an operation. When a nurse came by to take his temperature, he didn't know how to tell her that the hernia had disappeared and that his parents should be called to come take him home. She looked approvingly at the titles of the books he'd brought and told him that he was free to get out of bed to use the bathroom but that otherwise he should make himself comfortable reading until she returned to put out the lights. She said nothing about the other boy, who he was sure was going to die.

At first he didn't fall asleep because of his waiting for the boy to die, and then he didn't because he couldn't stop thinking of the drowned body that had washed up on the beach that past summer. It was the body of a seaman whose tanker had been torpedoed by a German U-boat. The Coast Guard beach patrol had found the body amid the oil scum and shattered cargo cases at the edge of the beach that was only a block away from the house where his family of four rented a room for a month each summer. Most days the water was clear and he didn't worry that a drowned man would collide with his bare legs as he stepped out into the low surf. But when oil from torpedoed tankers clotted the sand and caked the bottom of his feet as he crossed the beach, he was terrified of stumbling upon a corpse. Or stumbling upon a saboteur, coming ashore to work for Hitler. Armed with rifles or submachine guns and often accompanied by trained dogs, the Coast Guardsmen patrolled day and night to prevent saboteurs from landing on the miles of deserted beaches. Yet some sneaked through without detection and, along with native-born Nazi sympathizers, were known to be in ship-to-shore communication with the U-boats that prowled the East Coast shipping lanes and had been sinking ships off New Jersey since the war began. The war was closer than most people imagined, and so was the horror. His father had read that the waters of New Jersey were "the worst ship graveyard" along the entire U.S. coastline, and now, in the hospital, he couldn't get the word "graveyard" to stop tormenting him, nor could he erase from his mind that bloated dead body the Coast Guard had removed from the few inches of surf in which it lay, while he and his brother looked on from the boardwalk.

Sometime after he'd fallen asleep he heard noises in the room and awakened to see that the curtain between the two beds had been pulled to screen off the other bed and that there were doctors and nurses at work on the other side—he could see their forms moving and could hear them whispering. When one of the nurses emerged from behind the curtain, she realized that he was awake and came over to his bed and told him softly, "Go back to sleep. You have a big day tomorrow." "What's the matter?" he asked. "Nothing," she said, "we're changing his bandages. Close your eyes and go to sleep."

He was awakened early the next morning for the operation, and there was his mother, already at the hospital and smiling at him from the foot of the bed.

"Good morning, darling. How's my brave boy?"

Looking across at the other bed, he saw that it was stripped of its bedding. Nothing could have made clearer to him what had happened than the sight of the bare mattress ticking and the uncovered pillows piled in the middle of the empty bed.

"That boy died," he said. Memorable enough that he was in the hospital that young, but even more memorable that he had registered a death. The first was the bloated body, the second was this boy. During the night, when he had awakened to see the forms moving behind the curtain, he couldn't help but think, The doctors are killing him.

"I believe he was moved, sweetheart. He had to be moved to another floor."

Just then two orderlies appeared to take him to the operating room. When he was told by one of them to use the bathroom, the first thing he did when the door was closed was to check if the hernia was gone. But the swelling had come back. There was no way out of the operation now.

His mother was allowed to walk alongside the gurney only as far as the elevator that was to take him to the operating room. There the orderlies pushed him into the elevator, and it descended until it opened onto a shockingly ugly corridor that led to an operating room where Dr. Smith was wearing a surgical gown and a white mask that changed everything about him—he might not even have been Dr. Smith. He could have been someone else entirely, someone who had not grown up the son of poor immigrants named Smulowitz, someone his father knew nothing about, someone nobody knew, someone who had just wandered into the operating room and picked up a knife. In that moment of terror when they lowered the ether mask over his face as though to smother him, he could have sworn that the surgeon, whoever he was, had whispered, "Now I'm going to turn you into a girl."

The malaise began just days after his return home from a monthlong vacation as happy as any he'd known since the family vacations at the Jersey Shore before the war. He'd spent August in a semi-furnished ramshackle house on an inland road on Martha's Vineyard with the woman whose constant lover he had been for two years. Until now they'd never dared to chance living together day in and day out, and the experiment had been a joyous success, a wonderful month of swimming and hiking and of easygoing sex at all times of the day. They'd swim across a bay to a ridge of dunes where they could lie out of sight and fuck in the sunshine and then rouse themselves to slip into their suits and swim back to the beach and collect clusters of mussels off the rocks to carry home for dinner in a pail full of seawater.

The only unsettling moments were at night, when they walked along the beach together. The dark sea rolling in with its momentous thud and the sky lavish with stars made Phoebe rapturous but frightened him. The profusion of stars told him unambiguously that he was doomed to die, and the thunder of the sea only yards away—and the nightmare of the blackest blackness beneath the frenzy of the water—made him want to run from the menace of oblivion to their cozy, lighted, underfurnished house. This was not the way he had experienced the vastness of the sea and the big night sky while he'd served manfully in the navy just after the Korean War—never were they the tolling bells. He could not understand where the fear was coming from and had to use all his strength to conceal it from Phoebe. Why must he mistrust his life just when he was more its master than he'd been in years? Why should he imagine himself on the edge of extinction when calm, straightforward thinking told him that there was so much more solid life to come? Yet it happened every night during their seaside walk beneath the stars. He was not flamboyant or deformed or extreme in any way, so why then, at his age, should he be haunted by thoughts of dying? He was reasonable and kindly, an amicable, moderate, industrious man, as everyone who knew him well would probably agree, except, of course, for the wife and two boys whose household he'd left and who, understandably, could not equate reasonableness and kindliness with his finally giving up on a failed marriage and looking elsewhere for the intimacy with a woman that he craved.

Most people, he believed, would have thought of him as square. As a young man, he'd thought of *himself* as square, so conventional and unadventurous that after art school, instead of striking out on his own to paint and to live on whatever money he could pick up at odd jobs—which was his secret ambition—he was too much the good boy, and, answering to his parents' wishes rather than his own, he married, had children, and went into advertising to make a secure living. He never thought of himself as anything more than an average human being, and one who would have given anything for his marriage to have lasted a lifetime. He had married with just that expectation. But instead marriage became his prison cell, and so, after much tortuous thinking that preoccupied him while he worked and when he should have been sleeping, he began fitfully, agonizingly, to tunnel his way out. Isn't that what an average human being would do? Isn't that what average human beings do every day? Contrary to what his wife told everyone, he hadn't hungered after the wanton freedom to do anything and everything. Far from it. He hungered for something stable all the while he detested what he had. He was not a man who wished to live two lives. He held no grudge against either the limitations or the comforts of conformity. He'd wanted merely to empty his mind of all the ugly thoughts spawned by the disgrace of prolonged marital warfare. He was not claiming to be exceptional. Only vulnerable and assailable and confused. And convinced of his right, as an average human being, to be pardoned ultimately for whatever deprivations he may have inflicted upon his innocent children in order not to live deranged half the time.

Terrifying encounters with the end? I'm thirty-four! Worry about oblivion, he told himself, when you're seventy-five! The remote future will be time enough to anguish over the ultimate catastrophe!

But no sooner did he and Phoebe return to Manhattan—where they lived in apartments some thirty blocks apart—than he mysteriously fell ill. He lost his appetite and his energy and found himself nauseated throughout the day, and he could not walk a city block without feeling weak and woozy.

The doctor could find nothing wrong with him. He had begun to see a psychoanalyst in the aftermath of his divorce, and the psychoanalyst attributed his condition to envy of a fellow art director who had just been promoted to a vice presidency in the agency.

"It makes you sick," the analyst said.

He maintained that his colleague was twelve years his senior and a generous coworker whom he only wished well, but the analyst continued to harp on "deep-seated envy" as the hidden reason for the malaise, and when circumstances proved him wrong, the analyst appeared unperturbed by his mistaken judgment.

He went to the medical doctor's office several more times in the succeeding weeks, whereas ordinarily he saw him only for a minor problem every couple of years. But he'd lost weight and the bouts of nausea were getting worse. He'd never before felt so rotten, not even after he'd left Cecilia and the two small boys and the court battle ensued over the terms of the separation and he was characterized to the court by Cecilia's attorney as "a well-known philanderer" because of the affair he was having with Phoebe, who was a new copywriter in the agency (and who was referred to in court by the plaintiff on the witness stand—aggrieved, overwrought, as though she found herself bringing charges against the Marquis de Sade—as "number thirty-seven in his parade of girlfriends," when in fact she was looking too far into the future and Phoebe was as yet number two). At least back then there'd been a recognizable cause for all the misery he felt. But this was his turning overnight from someone who was bursting with health into someone inexplicably losing his health.

A month passed. He couldn't concentrate on his work, he gave up his morning swim, and by now he couldn't look at food. On a Friday afternoon he left work early and took a taxi to the doctor's office without having made an appointment or even a phone call. The only one he phoned was Phoebe, to tell her what he was doing.

"Admit me to a hospital," he told the doctor. "I feel like I'm dying."

The doctor made the arrangements, and Phoebe was at the hospital's information desk when he arrived. By five o'clock he was settled into a room, and just before seven a tall, tanned, good-looking middle-aged man wearing a dinner jacket came into the room and introduced himself as a surgeon who had been called by his physician to take a look at him. He was on his way to some formal event but wanted to stop by first to do a quick examination. What he did was to press his hand down very hard just above the groin on the right side. Unlike the regular physician, the surgeon kept pressing and the pain was excruciating. He felt on the verge of vomiting. The surgeon said, "Haven't you had any stomach pain before?" "No," he said. "Well, it's your appendix. You need an operation." "When?" "Now."

He saw the surgeon next in the operating room. He'd changed out of the evening clothes into a surgical gown. "You've saved me from a very boring banquet," the surgeon said.

He didn't wake up until the next morning. Standing at the foot of the bed, along with Phoebe, were his mother and father, looking grim. Phoebe, whom they did not know (other than from Cecilia's denigrating descriptions, other than from the telephone tirades ending, "I pity this Little Miss Muffet coming after me—I honestly do pity the vile little Quaker slut!"), had phoned them and they'd immediately driven over from New Jersey. As best he could make out, a male nurse seemed to be having trouble feeding some sort of tube up his nose, or maybe the nurse was trying to extract it. He spoke his first words—"Don't fuck up!"—before falling back into unconsciousness.

His mother and father were seated in chairs when he came around again. They seemed still to be tormented and weighed down by fatigue as well.

Phoebe was in a chair beside the bed holding his hand. She was a pale, pretty young woman whose soft appearance belied her equanimity and steadfastness. She manifested no fear and allowed none in her voice.

Phoebe knew plenty about physical misery because of the severe headaches that she'd dismissed as nothing back in her twenties but that she realized were migraines when they became regular and frequent in her thirties. She was lucky enough to be able to sleep when she got one, but the moment she opened her eyes, the moment she was conscious, there it was —the incredible ache on one side of her head, the pressure in her face and her jaw, and back of her eye socket a foot on her eyeball crushing it. The migraines started with spirals of light, bright spots moving in a swirl in front of her eyes even when she closed them, and then progressed to disorientation, dizziness, pain, nausea, and vomiting. "It's nothing like being in this world," she told him afterward. "There's nothing in my body but the pressure in my head." All he could do for her was to remove the big cooking pot into which she vomited, and to clean it out in the bathroom, and then to tiptoe back into the bedroom and place it beside the bed for her to use when she was sick again. For the twenty-four or forty-eight hours that the migraine lasted, she could not stand another presence in the darkened room, any more than she could bear the thinnest sliver of light filtering in from beneath the drawn shades. And no drugs helped. None of them worked for her. Once the migraine started, there was no stopping it.

"What happened?" he asked her.

"A burst appendix. You had it for some time."

"How sick am I?" he asked weakly.

"There's a lot of peritonitis. There are drains in the wound. They're draining it. You're getting big doses of antibiotics. You're going to pull through. We're going to swim across the bay again."

That was hard to believe. Back in 1943 his father had come close to dying from undiagnosed appendicitis and severe peritonitis. He was forty-two with two young children, and he had been in the hospital—and away from his business—thirty-six days. When he got home, he was so weak he could barely make it up the one little flight to their flat, and after he'd been helped by his wife from the entryway into the bedroom, he sat on the edge of the bed, where, for the first time in the presence of his children, he broke down and cried. Eleven years earlier, his youngest brother, Sammy, the adored favorite of eight children, had died of acute appendicitis in his third year at engineering school. He was nineteen years old, having entered college at sixteen, and his ambition was to be an aeronautical engineer. Only three of the eight children had got as far as high school, and Sammy was the first and only one to go to college. His friends were the smartest boys in the neighborhood, all of them the children of Jewish immigrants who met regularly at one another's houses to play chess and to talk heatedly about politics and philosophy. He was their leader, a runner on the track team and a mathematics whiz with a sparkling personality. It was Sammy's name that his father intoned as he sobbed in the bedroom, astonished to find himself back among the family whose provider he was.

Uncle Sammy, his father, now him—the third of them to have been felled by a burst appendix and peritonitis. While he drifted in and out of consciousness for the next two days, it was not certain whether he would meet Sammy's fate or his father's.

His brother flew in from California on the second day, and when he opened his eyes and saw him at the side of the bed, a big and gentle presence, unperturbed, confident, jolly, he thought, I cannot die while Howie is here. Howie bent over to kiss his forehead, and then no sooner did he sit down in the bedside chair and take the patient's hand than time stopped, the present disappeared, and he was returned to childhood, a small boy again, preserved from worry and fear by the generous brother who slept in the bed beside his.

Howie stayed for four days. In four days he sometimes flew to Manila and Singapore and Kuala Lumpur and back. He had started at Goldman Sachs as a runner and quickly went from

relaying messages to top dog on the currency-trading desk and
began investing for himself in stocks. He had ended up in currency arbitrage for multinational and large foreign corporations
—winemakers in France and camera makers in West Germany
and automakers in Japan, for whom he turned francs and
deutsche marks and yen into dollars. He traveled frequently to
meet with his clients and continued investing in companies he
liked, and by thirty-two he had his first million.

Sending their parents home to rest, Howie joined with
Phoebe to see him through the worst of it and prepared to fly
out only after receiving the doctor's assurances that the crisis
was over. On the last morning, Howie quietly said to him,
"You've got a good girl this time. Don't screw it up. Don't let
her go."

He thought, in his joy at having survived, Was there ever a
man whose appetite for life was as contagious as Howie's? Was
there ever a brother as lucky as me?

He was in the hospital for thirty days. The nurses were mostly
agreeable, conscientious young women with Irish accents who
seemed always to have time to chat a little when they looked in
on him. Phoebe came directly from work to have dinner in his
room every night; he couldn't imagine what being needy and
infirm like this and facing the uncanny nature of illness would
have been like without her. His brother needn't have warned
him not to let her go; he was never more determined to keep
anyone.

Beyond his window he could see the leaves of the trees turning as the October weeks went by, and when the surgeon came
around he said to him, "When am I going to get out of here?
I'm missing the fall of 1967." The surgeon listened soberly, and
then, with a smile, he said, "Don't you get it yet? You almost
missed everything."

Twenty-two years passed. Twenty-two years of excellent health
and the boundless self-assurance that flows from being fit—
twenty-two years spared the adversary that is illness and the
calamity that waits in the wings. As he'd reassured himself
while walking under the stars on the Vineyard with Phoebe, he
would worry about oblivion when he was seventy-five.

*

He had been driving to New Jersey after work nearly every day for over a month to see his dying father when he wound up badly short of breath in the City Athletic Club swimming pool one August evening in 1989. He had gotten back from Jersey about half an hour earlier and decided to recover his equilibrium by taking a quick swim before heading home. Ordinarily he swam a mile at the club early each morning. He barely drank, had never smoked, and weighed precisely what he'd weighed when he got home from the navy in '57 and started his first job in advertising. He knew from the ordeal with appendicitis and peritonitis that he was as liable as anyone else to falling seriously ill, but that he, with a lifelong regimen of healthful living, would end up as a candidate for cardiac surgery seemed preposterous. It was simply not how things were going to turn out.

Yet he couldn't finish the first lap without pulling over to the side and hanging there completely breathless. He got out of the pool and sat with his legs in the water trying to calm down. He was sure that the breathlessness was the result of having seen how far his father's condition had deteriorated in just the past few days. But in fact it was his that had deteriorated, and when he went to the doctor the next morning, his EKG showed radical changes that indicated severe occlusion of his major coronary arteries. Before the day was out he was in a bed in the coronary care unit of a Manhattan hospital, having been given an angiogram that determined that surgery was essential. There were oxygen prongs in his nose and he was attached by numerous leads to a cardiac monitoring machine behind his bed. The only question was whether the surgery should take place immediately or the following morning. It was by then almost eight in the evening, and so the decision was made to wait. Sometime in the night, however, he was awakened to discover his bed surrounded by doctors and nurses, just as the bed of the boy in his room had been back when he was nine. All these years he had been alive while that boy was dead—and now he was that boy.

Some sort of medication was being administered through the IV and he vaguely understood that they were trying to avert a crisis. He could not make out what they were mumbling to one another and then he must have fallen asleep, because the next he knew it was morning and he was being rolled onto a gurney to take him to the operating room.

His wife at this time—his third and his last—bore no resemblance to Phoebe and was nothing short of a hazard in an emergency. She certainly didn't inspire confidence on the morning of the surgery, when she followed beside the gurney weeping and wringing her hands and finally, uncontrollably, cried out, "What about me?"

She was young and untried and maybe she had intended to say something different, but he took it that she meant what would happen to her should he fail to survive. "One thing at a time," he told her. "First let me die. Then I'll come help you bear up."

The operation went on for seven hours. Much of that time he was connected to a heart-lung machine that pumped his blood and breathed for him. The doctors gave him five grafts, and he emerged from the surgery with a long wound down the center of his chest and another extending from his groin to his right ankle—it was from his leg that they had removed the vein from which all but one of the grafts were fashioned.

When he came around in the recovery room there was a tube down his throat that felt as though it were going to choke him to death. Having it there was horrible, but there was no way he could communicate that to the nurse who was telling him where he was and what had happened to him. He lost consciousness then, and when he came around again the tube was still there choking him to death, but now a nurse was explaining that it would be removed as soon as it was determined that he could breathe on his own. Over him next was the face of his young wife, welcoming him back to the world of the living, where he could resume looking after her.

He had left her with a single responsibility when he went into the hospital: to see that the car was taken off the street where it was parked and put into the public garage a block away. It turned out to be a task that she was too frazzled to undertake, and so, as he later learned, she'd had to ask one of his friends to do it for her. He hadn't realized how observant his cardiologist was of nonmedical matters until the man came to see him midway through his hospital stay and told him that he could not be released from the hospital if his home care was to be provided by his wife. "I don't like to have to say these things, fundamentally she's not my business, but I've watched her when she's come to visit. The woman is basically an absence and not a presence, and I have no choice but to protect my patient."

By this time Howie had arrived. He had flown in from Europe, where he'd gone to do business and also to play polo. He could ski now, skeet-shoot, and play water polo as well as polo from atop a pony, having acquired virtuosity in these activities in the great world long after he'd left his lower-middle-class high school in Elizabeth, where, along with the Irish-Catholic and Italian boys whose fathers worked on the docks at the port, he'd played football in the fall and pole-vaulted in the spring, all the while garnering grades good enough to earn him a scholarship to the University of Pennsylvania and then admission to the Wharton School to earn an MBA. Though his father was dying in a hospital in New Jersey and his brother recovering from open-heart surgery in a hospital in New York —and though he spent the week traveling from the one bedside to the other—Howie's vigor never lapsed, nor did his capacity to inspire confidence. The sustenance the healthy thirty-year-old wife proved incapable of providing her ailing fifty-six-year-old husband was more than compensated for by Howie's jovial support. It was Howie who suggested hiring two private duty nurses—the daytime nurse, Maureen Mrazek, and the night nurse, Olive Parrott—to substitute for the woman he'd come to refer to as "the titanically ineffective cover girl," and then he insisted, over his brother's objections, on covering the costs himself. "You were dangerously ill, you went through hell," Howie said, "and so long as I'm around, nothing and nobody is going to impede your recovery. This is just a gift to ensure the speedy restoration of your health." They were standing together by the entrance to the room. Howie spoke with his brawny arms around his brother. Much as he preferred to appear breezily superior to the claims of sentiment, his face —a virtual replica of his brother's—could not disguise his emotions when he said, "Losing Mom and Dad I have to accept. I could never accept losing you." Then he left to find the limo that was waiting downstairs to drive him to the hospital in Jersey.

*

Olive Parrott, the night nurse, was a large black woman whose carriage and bearing and size reminded him of Eleanor Roosevelt. Her father owned an avocado farm in Jamaica, and her mother kept a dream book in whose pages, each morning, she recorded her children's dreams. On the nights when he was too uncomfortable to sleep, Olive sat in a chair at the foot of the bed and told him innocent tales about her life as a child on the avocado farm. She had a West Indian accent and a lovely voice, and her words soothed him as no woman's had since his mother sat and talked to him in the hospital after the hernia operation. Except for the questions that he asked Olive, he remained silent, deliriously contented to be alive. It turned out that they'd caught him just in time: when he was admitted to the hospital, his coronary arteries were anywhere from ninety to ninety-five percent occluded and he'd been on the verge of a massive and probably fatal heart attack.

Maureen was a buxom, smiling redhead who had grown up something of a roughneck in an Irish-Slavic family in the Bronx and had a blunt way of talking that was fueled by the self-possession of a working-class toughie. The mere sight of her raised his spirits when she arrived in the morning, even though the postsurgical exhaustion was so severe that merely shaving —and not even shaving standing up but while sitting in a chair—tired him out, and he had to return to bed for a long nap after taking his first walk down the hospital corridor with her at his side. Maureen was the one who called his father's doctor for him and kept him informed of the dying man's condition until he had the strength to talk to the doctor himself.

It had been decided peremptorily by Howie that when he left the hospital Maureen and Olive would look after him (again at Howie's expense) for at least his first two weeks at home. His wife was not consulted, and she resented the arrangement and the implication that she was unable to care for him on her own. She particularly resented Maureen, who herself did little to hide her contempt for the patient's wife.

At home it was more than three weeks before the exhaustion began to diminish and he felt ready even to consider returning to work. After dinner he had to go back to bed for the evening simply from the effort of eating sitting up in a chair, and in the morning he had to remain seated on a plastic stool to wash himself in the shower. He began to do mild calisthenics with Maureen and tried each day to add another ten yards to the afternoon walk he took with her. Maureen had a boyfriend whom she talked about—a TV cameraman whom she expected to marry once he found a permanent job—and when she got off work at the end of the day, she liked to have a couple of drinks with the neighborhood regulars in a bar around the corner from where she lived in Yorkville. The weather was beautiful, and so when they walked outdoors he got a good look at how she carried herself in her close-fitting polo shirts and short skirts and summer sandals. Men looked her over all the time, and she was not averse to staring someone down with mock belligerence if she was being ostentatiously ogled. Her presence at his side made him feel stronger by the day, and he would come home from the walks delighted with everything, except, of course, with the jealous wife, who would slam doors and sometimes barge out of the apartment only moments after he and Maureen had swept in.

He was not the first patient to fall in love with his nurse. He was not even the first patient to fall in love with Maureen. She'd had several affairs over the years, a few of them with men rather worse off than he was, who, like him, made a full recovery with the help of Maureen's vitality. Her gift was to make the ill hopeful, so hopeful that instead of closing their eyes to blot out the world, they opened them wide to behold her vibrant presence, and were rejuvenated.

Maureen came along to New Jersey when his father died. He was still not allowed to drive, so she volunteered and helped Howie make the arrangements with Kreitzer's Memorial Home in Union. His father had become religious in the last ten years of his life and, after having retired and having lost his wife, had taken to going to the synagogue at least once a day. Long before his final illness, he'd asked his rabbi to conduct his burial service entirely in Hebrew, as though Hebrew were the strongest answer that could be accorded death. To his father's younger son the language meant nothing. Along with Howie, he'd stopped taking Judaism seriously at thirteen—the Sunday after the Saturday of his bar mitzvah—and had not set foot since then in a synagogue. He'd even left the space for religion blank on his hospital admission form, lest the word "Jewish" prompt a visit to his room by a rabbi, come to talk in the way rabbis talk. Religion was a lie that he had recognized early in life, and he found all religions offensive, considered their superstitious folderol meaningless, childish, couldn't stand the complete unadultness—the baby talk and the righteousness and the sheep, the avid believers. No hocus-pocus about death and God or obsolete fantasies of heaven for him. There was only our bodies, born to live and die on terms decided by the bodies that had lived and died before us. If he could be said to have located a philosophical niche for himself, that was it—he'd come upon it early and intuitively, and however elemental, that was the whole of it. Should he ever write an autobiography, he'd call it *The Life and Death of a Male Body*. But after retiring he tried becoming a painter, not a writer, and so he gave that title to a series of his abstractions.

But none of what he did or didn't believe mattered on the day that his father was buried beside his mother in the rundown cemetery just off the Jersey Turnpike.

Over the gate through which the family entered into the original acreage of the old nineteenth-century cemetery was an arch with the cemetery association's name inscribed in Hebrew; at either end of the arch was carved a six-pointed star. The stone of the gate's two pillars had been badly broken and chipped away—by time and by vandals—and a crooked iron gate with a rusted lock hadn't to be pushed open in order to enter but was half off its hinges and embedded several inches in the ground. Nor had the stone of the obelisk that they passed—inscribed with Hebrew scripture and the names of the family buried at the foot of its plinth—weathered the decades well either. At the head of the crowded rows of upright gravestones stood the old section's one small brick mausoleum, whose filigreed steel door and original two windows—which, at the time of the interment of its occupants, would have been colored with stained glass—had been sealed with concrete blocks to protect against further vandalism, so that now the little square building looked more like an abandoned toolshed or an outdoor toilet no longer in operation than an eternal dwelling place in keeping with the renown, wealth, or status of

those who'd constructed it to house their family dead. Slowly
they passed between the upright gravestones that were mainly
inscribed with Hebrew but that in some cases also bore words
in Yiddish, Russian, German, even Hungarian. Most were engraved with the Star of David while others were more elaborately decorated, with a pair of blessing hands or a pitcher or a
five-branched candelabrum. At the graves of the young children and infants—and there were more than a handful, though
not as many as those of young women who'd died in their
twenties, more than likely during childbirth—they came upon
an occasional gravestone topped with the sculpture of a lamb
or decorated with an engraving in the shape of a tree trunk
with its upper half sawed away, and as they headed in single file
through the crooked, uneven, narrow pathways of the original
cemetery toward the newer, parklike northern spaces, where
the funeral was to take place, it was possible—in just this little
Jewish cemetery, founded in a field on the border of Elizabeth
and Newark by, among others, the community-minded father
of the late owner of Elizabeth's most beloved jewelry store—to
count how many had perished when influenza killed ten million in 1918.

Nineteen eighteen: only one of the terrible years among the
plethora of corpse-strewn *anni horribili* that will blacken the
memory of the twentieth century forever.

He stood at the graveside among some two dozen of his relatives, with his daughter at his right, clutching his hand, and his
two sons behind him and his wife to the side of his daughter.
Merely standing there absorbing the blow that is the death of
a father proved to be a surprising challenge to his physical
strength—it was a good thing Howie was beside him on the
left, one arm holding him firmly around his waist, to prevent
anything untoward from happening.

It had never been difficult to know what to make of either
his mother or his father. They were a mother and a father. They
were imbued with few other desires. But the space taken up by
their bodies was now vacant. Their lifelong substantiality
was gone. His father's coffin, a plain pine box, was lowered on
its straps into the hole that had been dug for him beside his
wife's coffin. There the dead man would remain for even more

hours than he'd spent selling jewelry, and that was in itself no number to sneer at. He had opened the store in 1933, the year his second son was born, and got rid of it in 1974, having by then sold engagement and wedding rings to three generations of Elizabeth families. How he scrounged up the capital in 1933, how he found *customers* in 1933, was always a mystery to his sons. But it was for them that he had left his job behind the watch counter at Abelson's Irvington store on Springfield Avenue, where he worked nine A.M. to nine P.M. Mondays, Wednesdays, Fridays, and Saturdays, and nine to five on Tuesdays and Thursdays, to open his own little Elizabeth store, fifteen feet wide, with the inscription in black lettering on the display window that read, from day one, "Diamonds—Jewelry —Watches," and in smaller letters beneath, "Fine watch, clock, and jewelry repair." At the age of thirty-two he finally set out to work sixty and seventy hours a week for his family instead of for Moe Abelson's. To lure Elizabeth's big working-class population and to avoid alienating or frightening away the port city's tens of thousands of churchgoing Christians with his Jewish name, he extended credit freely—just made sure they paid at least thirty or forty percent down. He never checked their credit; as long as he got his cost out of it, they could come in afterward and pay a few dollars a week, even nothing, and he really didn't care. He never went broke with credit, and the good will generated by his flexibility was more than worth it. He decorated the shop with a few silver-plated pieces to make it attractive—tea sets, trays, chafing dishes, candlesticks that he sold dirt cheap—and at Christmastime he always had a snow scene with Santa in the window, but the stroke of genius was to call the business not by his name but rather Everyman's Jewelry Store, which was how it was known throughout Union County to the swarms of ordinary people who were his faithful customers until he sold his inventory to the wholesaler and retired at the age of seventy-three. "It's a big deal for working people to buy a diamond," he told his sons, "no matter how small. The wife can wear it for the beauty and she can wear it for the status. And when she does, this guy is not just a plumber —he's a man with a wife with a diamond. His wife owns something that is imperishable. Because beyond the beauty and the status and the value, the diamond is imperishable. A piece of the earth that is imperishable, and a mere mortal is wearing it on her hand!"

The reason for leaving Abelson's, where he'd still been lucky enough to be collecting a paycheck through the crash and into the worst years of the Depression, the reason for daring to open a store of his own in such bad times, was simple: to everyone who asked, and even to those who didn't, he explained, "I had to have something to leave my two boys."

There were two upright shovels with their blades in the large pile of earth to one side of the grave. He had thought they had been left there by the gravediggers, who would use them later to fill the grave. He had imagined that, as at his mother's funeral, each mourner would step up to the hole to throw a clump of dirt onto the coffin's lid, after which they would all depart for their cars. But his father had requested of the rabbi the traditional Jewish rites, and those, he now discovered, called for burial by the mourners and not by employees of the cemetery or anyone else. The rabbi had told Howie beforehand, but Howie, for whatever reason, hadn't told him, and so he was surprised now when his brother, handsomely dressed in a dark suit, a white shirt, a dark tie, and shining black shoes, walked over to pull one of the shovels out of the pile, and then set out to fill the blade until it was brimming with dirt. Then he walked ceremoniously to the head of the grave, stood there a moment to think his thoughts, and, angling the shovel downward a little, let the dirt run slowly out. Upon landing on the wood cover of the coffin, it made the sound that is absorbed into one's being like no other.

Howie returned to plunge the blade of the shovel into the crumbling pyramid of dirt that stood about four feet high. They were going to have to shovel that dirt back into the hole until his father's grave was level with the adjacent cemetery grounds.

It took close to an hour to move the dirt. The elderly among the relatives and friends, unable to wield a shovel, helped by throwing fistfuls of dirt onto the coffin, and he himself could do no more than that, and so it fell to Howie and Howie's four sons and his own two—the six of them all strapping men in their late twenties and early thirties—to do the heavy labor. In

teams of two they stood beside the pile and, spadeful by spadeful, moved the dirt from the pile back into the hole. Every few
minutes another team took over, and it seemed to him, at one
point, as though this task would never end, as though they
would be there burying his father forever. The best he could
do to be as immersed in the burial's brutal directness as his
brother, his sons, and his nephews was to stand at the edge of
the grave and watch as the dirt encased the coffin. He watched
till it reached the lid, which was decorated only with a carving
of the Star of David, and then he watched as it began to cover
the lid. His father was going to lie not only in the coffin but
under the weight of that dirt, and all at once he saw his father's
mouth as if there were no coffin, as if the dirt they were throwing into the grave was being deposited straight down on him,
filling up his mouth, blinding his eyes, clogging his nostrils,
and closing off his ears. He wanted to tell them to stop, to
command them to go no further—he did not want them to
cover his father's face and block the passages through which he
sucked in life. I've been looking at that face since I was born—
stop burying my father's face! But they had found their
rhythm, these strong boys, and they couldn't stop and they
wouldn't stop, not even if he hurled himself into the grave and
demanded that the burial come to a halt. Nothing could stop
them now. They would just keep going, burying him, too, if
that was necessary to get the job done. Howie was off to the
side, his brow covered with sweat, watching the six cousins
athletically complete the job, with the goal in sight shoveling
at a terrific pace, not like mourners assuming the burden of an
archaic ritual but like old-fashioned workmen feeding a furnace
with fuel.

Many of the elderly were weeping now and holding on to
each other. The pyramid of dirt was gone. The rabbi stepped
forward and, after carefully smoothing the surface with his
bare hands, used a stick to delineate in the loose soil the dimensions of the grave.

He had watched his father's disappearance from the world
inch by inch. He had been forced to follow it right to the end.
It was like a second death, one no less awful than the first.
Suddenly he was remembering the rush of emotion that carried him down and down into the layers of his life when, at the

hospital, his father had picked up each of the three infant grandchildren for the first time, pondering Randy, then later Lonny, then finally Nancy with the same expressive gaze of baffled delight.

"Are you all right?" Nancy asked, putting her arms around him while he stood and looked at the lines the stick had made in the soil, drawn there as if for a children's game. He squeezed her tightly to him and said, "Yes, I'm all right." Then he sighed, even laughed, when he said, "Now I know what it means to be buried. I didn't till today." "I've never seen anything so chilling in my life," Nancy said. "Nor have I," he told her. "It's time to go," he said, and with him and Nancy and Howie in the lead, the mourners slowly departed, though he could not begin to empty himself of all that he'd just seen and thought, the mind circling back even as the feet walked away.

Because a wind had been blowing while the grave was being filled, he could taste the dirt coating the inside of his mouth well after they had left the cemetery and returned to New York.

For the next nine years his health remained stable. Twice he'd been blindsided by a crisis, but unlike the boy in the bed next to his, he'd been spared the disaster. Then in 1998, when his blood pressure began to mount and would not respond to changes in medication, the doctors determined that he had an obstruction of his renal artery, which fortunately had resulted so far in only a minor loss of kidney function, and he entered the hospital for a renal artery angioplasty. Yet again his luck held, and the problem was resolved with the insertion of a stent that was transported on a catheter maneuvered up through a puncture in the femoral artery and through the aorta to the occlusion.

He was sixty-five, newly retired, and by now divorced for the third time. He went on Medicare, began to collect Social Security, and sat down with his lawyer to write a will. Writing a will—that was the best part of aging and probably even of dying, the writing and, as time passed, the updating and revising and carefully reconsidered rewriting of one's will. A few years later he followed through on the promise he'd made to himself immediately after the 9/11 attacks and moved from

Manhattan to the Starfish Beach retirement village at the Jersey Shore, only a couple of miles from the seaside town where his family had vacationed for a portion of every summer. The Starfish Beach condominiums were attractive shingled one-story houses with big windows and sliding glass doors that led to rear outdoor decks; eight units were attached to form a semicircular compound enclosing a shrubbery garden and a small pond. The facilities for the five hundred elderly residents who lived in these compounds, spread over a hundred acres, included tennis courts, a large common garden with a potting shed, a workout center, a postal station, a social center with meeting rooms, a ceramics studio, a woodworking shop, a small library, a computer room with three terminals and a common printer, and a big room for lectures and performances and for the slide shows that were offered by couples who had just returned from their travels abroad. There was a heated Olympic-sized outdoor swimming pool in the heart of the village as well as a smaller indoor pool, and there was a decent restaurant in the modest mall at the end of the main village street, along with a bookstore, a liquor store, a gift shop, a bank, a brokerage office, a realtor, a lawyer's office, and a gas station. A supermarket was only a short drive away, and if you were ambulatory, as most residents were, you could easily walk the half mile to the boardwalk and down to the wide ocean beach, where a lifeguard was on duty all summer long.

As soon as he moved into the village, he turned the sunny living room of his three-room condo into an artist's studio, and now, after taking his daily hour-long four-mile walk on the boardwalk, he spent most of the remainder of each day fulfilling a long-standing ambition by happily painting away, a routine that yielded all the excitement he'd expected. He missed nothing about New York except Nancy, the child whose presence had never ceased to delight him, and who, as a divorced mother of two four-year-olds, was no longer protected in the way that he'd hoped. In the aftermath of their daughter's divorce, he and Phoebe—equally weighed down by anxiety—had stepped in and, separately, spent more time with Nancy than they had since she'd gone off to the Midwest to college. There she'd met the poetic husband-to-be, a graduate student openly disdainful of commercial culture and particularly of her father's

line of work, who, once he discovered himself no longer simply
half of a quiet, thoughtful couple who liked to listen to chamber music and read books in their spare time but a father of
twins, found the tumult of a young family's domestic existence
unbearable—especially for someone needing order and silence
to complete a first novel—and charged Nancy with fostering
this great disaster with her ongoing lament over his impeding
her maternal instinct. After work and on weekends he absented
himself more and more from the clutter created in their under-
sized apartment by the needs of the two clamoring tiny crea-
tures he had crazily spawned, and when he finally upped and
left his publishing job—and parenthood—he had to go clear
back to Minnesota to regain his sanity and resume his thinking
and evade as much responsibility as he possibly could.

If her father could have had his way, Nancy and the twins
would have moved to the shore too. She could have commuted to work on the Jersey line, leaving the kids with nannies
and babysitters costing half as much as help in New York, and
he would have been nearby to look after them as well, to take
them to and from preschool, to oversee them at the beach, and
so on. Father and daughter could have met to have dinner
once a week and to take a walk together on weekends. They'd
all be living beside the beautiful sea and away from the threat
of Al Qaeda. The day after the destruction of the Twin Towers
he'd said to Nancy, "I've got a deep-rooted fondness for survival. I'm getting out of here." And just ten weeks later, in late
November, he left. The thought of his daughter and her children falling victim to a terrorist attack tormented him during
his first months at the shore, though once there he no longer
had anxiety for himself and was rid of that sense of pointless
risk taking that had dogged him every day since the catastrophe had subverted everyone's sense of security and introduced
an ineradicable precariousness into their daily lives. He was
merely doing everything he reasonably could to stay alive. As
always—and like most everyone else—he didn't want the end
to come a minute earlier than it had to.

The year after the insertion of the renal stent, he had surgery
for another major obstruction, this one in his left carotid artery, one of the two main arteries that stretch from the aorta to

the base of the skull and supply blood to the brain and that if left obstructed could cause a disabling stroke or even sudden death. The incision was made in the neck, then the artery feeding the brain was clamped shut to stop the blood flowing through it. Then it was slit open and the plaque that was causing the blockage scraped out and removed. It would have been a help not to have to face this delicate an operation alone, but Nancy was swamped by her job and the demands of caring for the children without a mate, and at that time there was no one else in his life whom he could ask for assistance. Nor did he want to disrupt his brother's hectic schedule to tell him about the surgery and cause him to be concerned, especially as he would be out of the hospital the following morning, providing there were no complications. This wasn't the peritonitis crisis or the quintuple bypass surgery—from a medical point of view it was nothing extraordinary, or so he was led to believe by the agreeable surgeon, who assured him that a carotid endarterectomy was a common vascular surgical procedure and he would be back at his easel within a day or two.

So he drove off alone in the early morning to the hospital and waited in a glassed-in anteroom on the surgical floor along with another ten or twelve men in hospital gowns scheduled for the first round of operations that day. The room would probably be full like this until as late as four in the afternoon. Most of the patients would come out the other end, and, too, over the course of the weeks, a few might not; nonetheless, they passed the time reading the morning papers, and when the name of one of them was called and he got up to leave for the operating room, he gave his sections of the paper to whoever requested them. You would have thought from the calm in the room that they were going off to get their hair cut, rather than, say, to get the artery leading to the brain sliced open.

At one point, the man to his side, having handed him that day's sports section, quietly began talking to him. He was probably only in his late forties or early fifties, but his skin was pasty and his voice was not strong or assured. "First my mother died," he said, "six months later my father died, eight months after that my only sister died, a year later my marriage broke down and my wife took everything I had. And that's when I began to imagine someone coming to me and saying, 'Now we're going to cut off your right arm as well. Do you think you can take that?' And so they cut off my right arm. Then later they come around and they say, 'Now we're going to cut off your left arm.' Then, when that's done, they come back one day and they say, 'Do you want to quit now? Is that enough? Or should we go ahead and start in on your legs?' And all the time I was thinking, When, when do I quit? When do I turn on the gas and put my head in the oven? When is enough enough? That was how I lived with my grief for ten years. It took ten years. And now the grief is finally over and this shit starts up."

When his turn came, the fellow beside him reached over to take the sports section back, and he was shepherded to the operating room by a nurse. Inside, half a dozen people were moving about in the glare of the lights making preparations for his surgery. He could not locate the surgeon among them. It would have reassured him to see the surgeon's friendly face, but either the doctor hadn't entered the operating room yet or he was off in some corner where he couldn't quite be seen. Several of the younger doctors were already wearing surgical masks, and the look of them made him think of terrorists. One of them asked whether he wanted a general or a local anesthetic, the way a waiter might have asked if he preferred red or white wine. He was confused—why should the decision about anesthesia be made this late? "I don't know. Which is better?" he said. "For us, the local. We can monitor the brain function better if the patient is conscious." "You're telling me that's safer? Is that what you're saying? Then I'll do it."

It was a mistake, a barely endurable mistake, because the operation lasted two hours and his head was claustrophobically draped with a cloth and the cutting and scraping took place so close to his ear, he could hear every move their instruments made as though he were inside an echo chamber. But there was nothing to be done. No fight to put up. You take it and endure it. Just give yourself over to it for as long as it lasts.

He slept well that night, by the next day felt fine, and at noon, after he lied and said a friend was waiting downstairs to pick him up, he was released and went out to the parking lot and cautiously drove himself home. When he got to the condo and sat down in his studio to look at the canvas he could soon resume painting, he burst into tears, just as his father had after he'd got home from his near-fatal bout of peritonitis.

But now, instead of ending, it continued; now not a year went by when he wasn't hospitalized. The son of long-lived parents, the brother of a man six years his senior who was seemingly as fit as he'd been when he'd carried the ball for Thomas Jefferson High, he was still only in his sixties when his health began giving way and his body seemed threatened all the time. He'd married three times, had mistresses and children and an interesting job where he'd been a success, but now eluding death seemed to have become the central business of his life and bodily decay his entire story.

The year after he had carotid artery surgery he had an angiogram in which the doctor discovered that he'd had a silent heart attack on the posterior wall because of an obstructed graft. The news stunned him, though fortunately Nancy had come down by train to accompany him to the hospital and her reassurance helped restore his equanimity. The doctor then went on to perform an angioplasty, and inserted a stent in his left anterior descending artery, after ballooning the artery open where new deposits of plaque had formed. From the table he could watch the catheter being wiggled up into the coronary artery—he was under the lightest sedation and able to follow the whole procedure on the monitor as though his body were somebody else's. A year later he had another angioplasty and another stent installed in one of the grafts, which had begun to narrow. The following year he had to have three stents installed at one go—to repair arterial obstructions whose location, as the doctor told him afterward, made the procedure no picnic to perform.

As always, to keep his mind elsewhere he summoned up his father's store and the names of the nine brands of watches and seven brands of clocks for which his father was an authorized distributor; his father didn't make much money selling watches and clocks, but he loaded up on them because they were a steady item and brought window-shoppers in from the street. What he did with these seed memories during each of his angioplasties was this: he would tune out the badinage the doctors and nurses invariably exchanged while setting up, tune

out the rock music pumped into the chilly, sterile room where
he lay strapped to the operating table amid all the intimidating
machinery designed to keep cardiac patients alive, and from
the moment they got to work anesthetizing his groin and
puncturing the skin for the insertion of the arterial catheter, he
would distract himself by reciting under his breath the lists
he'd first alphabetized as a small boy helping at the store after
school—"Benrus, Bulova, Croton, Elgin, Hamilton, Helbros,
Ovistone, Waltham, Wittnauer"—focusing all the while on the
distinctive look of the numerals on the dial of the watch as he
intoned its brand name, sweeping from one through twelve
and back again. Then he'd start on the clocks—"General Electric, Ingersoll, McClintock, New Haven, Seth Thomas, Tele-
chron, Westclox"—remembering how the wind clocks ticked
and the electric clocks hummed until finally he heard the doctor announce that the procedure was over and that everything
had gone well. The doctor's assistant, after applying pressure
to the wound, placed a sandbag on the groin to prevent bleeding, and with the weight resting there, he had to lie motionless
in his hospital bed for the next six hours. His not being able to
move was the worst of it, strangely—because of the thousands
of involuntary thoughts that suffused the slow-moving time—
but the following morning, if all had gone well overnight, he
was brought a tray of inedible breakfast to look at and a sheaf
of post-angioplasty instructions to follow and by eleven A.M.
he would have been discharged. On three separate occasions
he'd arrived at home and was hurriedly undressing for a much-
needed shower when he'd found a couple of the EKG electrode
pads still stuck to him, because the nurse helping to discharge
him had forgotten to peel them from his chest and throw them
in the garbage. One morning he looked down in the shower to
find that no one had bothered to remove the IV feeding needle,
a gadget they called a heplock, from his black-and-blue forearm, and so he had to dress and drive over to his internist's
office in Spring Lake to have the heplock taken out before it
became a source of infection.

The year after the three stents he was briefly knocked out on
an operating table while a defibrillator was permanently inserted as a safeguard against the new development that endangered his life and that along with the scarring at the posterior

wall of his heart and his borderline ejection fraction made him a candidate for a fatal cardiac arrhythmia. The defibrillator was a thin metal box about the size of a cigarette lighter; it was lodged beneath the skin of his upper chest, a few inches from his left shoulder, with its wire leads attached to his vulnerable heart, ready to administer a shock to correct his heartbeat—and confuse death—if it became perilously irregular.

Nancy had been with him for this procedure too, and afterward, when he got back to his room and he lowered one side of his hospital gown to show her the visible bulge that was the embedded defibrillator, she had to turn away. "Darling," he said to her, "it's to protect me—there's nothing to be upset about." "I know that it's to protect you. I'm glad there is such a thing that's able to protect you. It's just a shock to see because," and finding herself too far along to come up with a comforting lie, she said, "because you've always been so youthful." "Well, I'm more youthful with it than I would be without it. I'll be able to do everything I like to do, only without having to worry about the arrhythmia putting me at serious risk." But she was pale with helplessness and couldn't stop the tears from running down her face: she wanted her father to be the way he was when she was ten and eleven and twelve and thirteen, without impediment or incapacity—and so did he. She couldn't possibly have wanted it as much as he did, but for that moment he found his own sorrow easier to accept than hers. The desire was strong to say something tender to alleviate her fears, as though, all over again, she were the more vulnerable of the two.

He never really stopped worrying about her, nor did he understand how it happened that such a child should be his. He hadn't necessarily done the right things to make it happen, even if Phoebe had. But there are such people, spectacularly good people—miracles, really—and it was his great fortune that one of these miracles was his own incorruptible daughter. He was amazed when he looked around himself and saw how bitterly disappointed parents could be—as he was with his own two sons, who continued to act as if what had happened to them had never happened before or since to anyone else—and then to have a child who was number one in every way. Sometimes it seemed that everything was a mistake except Nancy. So he

worried about her, and he still never passed a women's clothing shop without thinking of her and going in to find something she'd like, and he thought, I'm very lucky, and he
thought, Some good has to come out somewhere, and it has in
her.

He was remembering now her brief period as a track star.
When Nancy was thirteen she'd placed second in a race at her
all-girls school, a run of about two miles, and she saw the possibility of something in which she could be exceptional. She
was good in everything else, but this was another kind of star-
dom. For a while he gave up swimming at the club first thing
so they could run together in the early morning and sometimes, too, in the day's waning hours. They'd go to the park
and it would be just the two of them and the shadows and the
light. She was running for the school team by then, and during
a meet she was rounding a bend when her leg gave way and
she fell to the track in agony. What had happened was something that can happen to a girl in early puberty—because the
bones don't fully harden by that age, what would have been in
a mature woman merely a strained tendon was more dramatic
for Nancy: the tendon held but a piece of bone in the hip
pulled away. Along with the track coach, he rushed Nancy to
the hospital emergency room, where she was in great pain and
very fearful, especially when she heard there was nothing to be
done, though at the same time she was told, correctly enough,
that the injury would heal by itself over a period of time. But
that was the end of her track career, not just because recovery
would take the rest of the season but because puberty was
upon her, and soon her breasts enlarged and her hips widened
and the speed that was hers when she had her childish body
disappeared. And then, as if the end of her championship running and the alteration of her physique weren't enough to
leave her reeling, that very year delivered the misery of her
parents' divorce.

When she sat on his hospital bed and wept in his arms it was
for many reasons, not least for his having left her when she was
thirteen. She'd come to the shore to assist him and all his cool-
headed and sensible daughter could do was relive the difficulties that had resulted from the divorce and confess to the
undying fantasy of a parental reconciliation that she had spent

more than half of her life hoping for. "But there's no remaking reality," he said softly, rubbing her back and stroking her hair and rocking her gently in his arms. "Just take it as it comes. Hold your ground and take it as it comes. There's no other way."

That was the truth and the best he could do—and exactly what he'd told her many years earlier, when he held her in his arms in the taxi coming home from the emergency room while she shook with sobs because of the inexplicable turn of events.

All these procedures and hospitalizations had made him a decidedly lonelier, less confident man than he'd been during the first year of retirement. Even his cherished peace and quiet seemed to have been turned into a self-generated form of solitary confinement, and he was hounded by the sense that he was headed for the end. But instead of moving back to attackable Manhattan, he decided to oppose the sense of estrangement brought on by his bodily failings and to enter more vigorously into the world around him. He did this by organizing two weekly painting classes for the village residents, an afternoon class for beginners and an evening class for those already somewhat familiar with paints.

There were about ten students in each class, and they loved meeting in his bright studio room. By and large, learning to paint was a pretext for their being there, and most of them were taking the class for the same reason he was giving it: to find satisfying contact with other people. All but two were older than he, and though they assembled each week in a mood of comradely good cheer, the conversation invariably turned to matters of sickness and health, their personal biographies having by this time become identical with their medical biographies and the swapping of medical data crowding out nearly everything else. At his studio, they more readily identified one another by their ailments than by their painting. "How is your sugar?" "How is your pressure?" "What did the doctor say?" "Did you hear about my neighbor? It spread to the liver." One of the men came to class with his portable oxygen unit. Another had Parkinson's tremors but was eager to learn to paint anyway. All of them without exception complained—sometimes jokingly, sometimes not—about increasing memory loss, and they spoke of how rapidly the months and the seasons and the years went by, how life no longer moved at the same speed. A couple of the women were being treated for cancer. One had to leave halfway through the course to return to the hospital for treatment. Another woman had a bad back and occasionally had to lie on the floor at the edge of the room for ten or fifteen minutes before she could get up and resume working in front of her easel. After the first few times, he told her she should go into his bedroom instead and lie down for as long as she liked on his bed—it had a firm mattress and she would be more comfortable. Once when she did not come out of the bedroom for half an hour, he knocked and, when he heard her crying inside, opened the door and went in.

She was a lean, tall, gray-haired woman, within a year or two of his age, whose appearance and gentleness reminded him of Phoebe. Her name was Millicent Kramer, and she was the best of his students by far and, coincidentally, the least messy. She alone, in what he charitably called "Advanced Painting," managed to finish each class without having dripped paint all over her running shoes. He never heard her say, as others did, "I can't get the paint to do what I want it to do," or "I can picture it in my mind but I can't seem to get it on the canvas," nor did he ever have to tell her, "Don't be intimidated, don't hold back." He tried to be generous to them all, even the hopeless ones, usually those very ones who came in and said right off, "I had a great day—I feel inspired today." When finally he'd heard enough of that, he repeated to them something he vaguely remembered Chuck Close's having said in an interview: amateurs look for inspiration; the rest of us just get up and go to work. He didn't start them with drawing, because barely a one of them was able to draw, and a figure would have set up all sorts of problems of proportion and scale, so instead, after they'd finished a couple of sessions going over the rudiments (how to lay their paints out and arrange their palettes, and so on) and familiarizing themselves with the medium itself, he set up a still life on a table—a vase, some flowers, a piece of fruit, a teacup—and encouraged them to use it as a reference point. He told them to be creative in order to try to get them to loosen up and use their whole arm and paint, if possible, without fear. He told them they didn't have to worry about what the arrangement actually looked like: "Interpret it," he told them, "this is a creative act." Unfortunately, saying that sometimes led to his having to tell someone, "You know, maybe you shouldn't make the vase six times larger than the teacup." "But you told me I should interpret it" was invariably the reply, to which, as kindly as he could, he in turn replied, "I didn't want that much interpretation." The art-class misery he least wished to deal with was their painting from imagination; yet because they were very enthusiastic about "creativity" and the idea of letting yourself go, those remained the common themes from one session to the next. Sometimes the worst occurred and a student said, "I don't want to do flowers or fruit, I want to do abstraction like you do." Since he knew there was no way to discuss what a beginner is doing when he does what he calls an abstraction, he told the student, "Fine— why don't you just do whatever you like," and when he walked around the studio, dutifully giving tips, he would find, as expected, that after looking at an attempt at an abstract painting, he had nothing to say except "Keep working." He tried to link painting to play rather than to art by quoting Picasso to them, something along the lines of their having to regain the child in order to paint like a grownup. Mainly what he did was to replicate what he'd heard as a kid when he started taking classes and his teachers were telling him the same things.

He was only called upon to be at all specific when he stood beside Millicent and saw what she could do and how fast she got better. He could sense right off that she had a knack that was innate and that far exceeded what little gift some of the others began to demonstrate as the weeks went by. It was never a question with her of combining the red and the blue right off the palette but rather of modifying the mixture with a little black or with just a bit of the blue so that the colors were interestingly harmonious, and her paintings had coherence instead of falling apart everywhere, which was what he confronted much of the time when he went from easel to easel and, for lack of anything else he could think of, heard himself saying, "That's coming along well." Millicent did need to be reminded "Don't overwork it," but otherwise nothing he suggested was wasted on her and she would look for the slightest shade of meaning in whatever he told her. Her way of painting seemed to arise directly from her instincts, and if her painting didn't look like anyone else's in the class, it wasn't solely because of stylistic distinction but because of the way she felt and perceived things. Others varied in their neediness; though the class was largely full of good will, some still resented it when they needed help at all, and even inadvertent criticism could make one of the men, a former CEO of a manufacturing company, frighteningly touchy. But never Millicent: she would have been the teacher's most rewarding pupil in anyone's amateur painting class.

Now he sat beside her on the bed and took her hand in his, thinking: When you are young, it's the outside of the body that matters, how you look externally. When you get older, it's what's inside that matters, and people stop caring how you look.

"Don't you have some medication you can take?" he asked her.

"I took it," she said. "I can't take any more. It doesn't help but for a few hours anyway. Nothing helps. I've had three operations. Each one is more extensive than the last and more harrowing than the last, and each one makes the pain worse. I'm sorry I'm in such a state. I apologize for this."

Near her head on the bed was a back brace she'd removed in order to lie down. It consisted of a white plastic shell that fit across the lower spine and attached to a web of elasticized cloth and Velcro straps that fastened snugly over the stomach an oblong piece of felt-lined canvas. Though she remained in her white painting smock, she had removed the brace and tried to push it out of sight under a pillow when he opened the door and walked in, which was why it was up by her head and impossible not to be continually mindful of while they talked. It was only a standard back brace, worn under the outer clothing, whose plastic posterior section was no more than eight or nine inches high, and yet it spoke to him of the perpetual nearness in their affluent retirement village of illness and death.

"Would you like a glass of water?" he asked her.

He could see by looking into her eyes how difficult the pain was to bear. "Yes," she said weakly, "yes, please."

Her husband, Gerald Kramer, had been the owner, publisher, and editor of a county weekly, the leading local paper, that did not shy away from exposing corruption in municipal government up and down the shore. He remembered Kramer, who'd grown up a slum kid in nearby Neptune, as a compact, bald, opinionated man who walked with considerable swagger, played aggressive, ungainly tennis, owned a little Cessna, and ran a discussion group once a week on current events—the most popular evening event on the Starfish Beach calendar along with the screenings of old movies sponsored by the film society—until he was felled by brain cancer and was to be seen being pushed around the village streets in a wheelchair by his wife. Even in retirement he'd continued to have the air of an omnipotent being dedicated all his life to an important mission, but in those eleven months before he died he seemed pierced by bewilderment, dazed by his diminishment, dazed by his helplessness, dazed to think that the dying man enfeebled in a wheelchair—a man no longer able to smash a tennis ball, to sail a boat, to fly a plane, let alone to edit a page of the *Monmouth County Bugle*—could answer to his name. One of his dashing eccentricities was, for no special reason, to dress up from time to time in his tuxedo to partake of the veal scaloppine at the village restaurant with his wife of fifty-odd years. "Where the hell else am I going to wear it?" was the gruffly engaging explanation that went out to one and all—he could sometimes woo people with an unexpected charm. After the surgery, however, his wife had to sit beside him and wait for him to crookedly open his mouth and then feed him gingerly, the swaggering husband, the roughneck gallant, with a spoon. Many people knew Kramer and admired him and out on the street wanted to say hello and ask after his health, but often his wife had to shake her head to warn them away when he was in the depths of his despondency—the vitriolic despondency of one once assertively in the middle of everything who was now in the middle of nothing. Was himself now nothing, nothing but a motionless cipher angrily awaiting the blessing of an eradication that was absolute.

"You can continue to lie here if you like," he said to Millicent Kramer after she had drunk some of the water.

"I can't be lying down all the time!" she cried. "I just cannot do it anymore! I was so agile, I was so active—if you were Gerald's wife, you had to be. We went everywhere. I felt so free.

We went to China, we went all over Africa. Now I can't even take the bus to New York unless I'm laced to the gills with painkillers. And I'm not good with the painkillers—they make me completely crazy. And by the time I get there I'm in pain anyway. Oh, I'm sorry about this. I'm terribly sorry. Everybody here has their ordeal. There's nothing special about my story and I'm sorry to burden you with it. You probably have a story of your own."

"Would a heating pad help?" he asked.

"You know what would help?" she said. "The sound of that voice that's disappeared. The sound of the exceptional man I loved. I think I could take all this if he were here. But I can't without him. I never saw him weaken once in his life—then came the cancer and it crushed him. I'm not Gerald. He would just marshal all his forces and do it—marshal all his everything and do whatever it was that had to be done. But I can't. I can't take the pain anymore. It overrides everything. I think sometimes that I can't go on another hour. I tell myself to ignore it. I tell myself it doesn't matter. I tell myself, 'Don't engage it. It's a specter. It's an annoyance, it's nothing more than that. Don't accord it power. Don't cooperate with it. Don't take the bait. Don't respond. Muscle through. Barrel through. Either you're in charge or it's in charge—the choice is yours!' I repeat this to myself a million times a day, as though I'm Gerald speaking, and then suddenly it's so awful I have to lie down on the floor in the middle of the supermarket and all the words are meaningless. Oh, I'm sorry, truly. I abhor tears."

"We all do," he told her, "but we cry anyway."

"This class has meant so much to me," she said. "I spend the whole week waiting for it. I'm like a schoolkid about this class," she confessed, and he found her looking at him with a childish trust, as though she were indeed a little one being put to sleep—and he, like Gerald, could right anything.

"Do you have any of your medication with you?" he asked.

"I already took one this morning."

"Take another," he told her.

"I have to be so careful with those pills."

"I understand. But do yourself a favor and take another now. One more can't do much harm, and it'll get you over the hump. It'll get you back to the easel."

"It takes an hour for it to work. The class will be over."

"You're welcome to stay and keep painting after the others go. Where is the medication?"

"In my purse. In the studio. By my easel. The old brown bag with the worn shoulder strap."

He brought it to her, and with what was left of the water in the glass, she took the pill, an opiate that killed pain for three or four hours, a large, white lozenge-shaped pill that caused her to relax with the anticipation of relief the instant she swallowed it. For the first time since she'd begun the class he could see unmistakably how attractive she must have been before the degeneration of an aging spine took charge of her life.

"Lie here until it starts to work," he said. "Then come join the class."

"I do apologize for all this," she said as he was leaving. "It's just that pain makes you so alone." And here the fortitude gave way again and left her sobbing into her hands. "It's so shameful."

"There's nothing shameful about it."

"There is, there is," she wept. "The not being able to look after oneself, the pathetic need to be comforted . . ."

"In the circumstances, none of that is remotely shameful."

"You're wrong. You don't know. The dependence, the helplessness, the isolation, the dread—it's all so ghastly and shameful. The pain makes you frightened of yourself. The utter otherness of it is awful."

She's embarrassed by what she's become, he thought, embarrassed, humiliated, humbled almost beyond her own recognition. But which of them wasn't? They were all embarrassed by what they'd become. Wasn't he? By the physical changes. By the diminishment of virility. By the errors that had contorted him and the blows—both those self-inflicted and those from without—that deformed him. What lent a horrible grandeur to the process of reduction suffered by Millicent Kramer—and miniaturized by comparison the bleakness of his own—was, of course, the intractable pain. Even those pictures of the grandchildren, he thought, those photographs that grandparents have all over the house, she probably doesn't even look at anymore. Nothing anymore but the pain.

"Shhh," he said, "shhh, quiet down," and he returned to the

bed to momentarily take her hand again before heading back to the class. "You wait for the painkiller to work and come back in when you're ready to paint."

Ten days later she killed herself with an overdose of sleeping pills.

At the end of the twelve-week session virtually everyone wanted to sign up for a second one, but he announced that a change of plans would make it impossible for him to resume giving the courses until the following fall.

When he'd fled New York, he'd chosen the shore as his new home because he'd always loved swimming in the surf and battling the waves, and because of the happy childhood associations he had with this stretch of Jersey beach, and because, even if Nancy wouldn't join him, he'd be just over an hour away from her, and because living in a relaxing, comfortable environment was bound to be beneficial to his health. There was no woman in his life other than his daughter. She never failed to call before leaving for work each morning, but otherwise his phone seldom rang. The affection of the sons of his first marriage he no longer pursued; he had never done the right thing by their mother or by them, and to resist the repetitiveness of these accusations and his sons' version of family history would require a measure of combativeness that had vanished from his arsenal. The combativeness had been replaced by a huge sadness. If he yielded in the solitude of his long evenings to the temptation to call one or the other of them, he always felt saddened afterward, saddened and beaten.

Randy and Lonny were the source of his deepest guilt, but he could not continue to explain his behavior to them. He had tried often enough when they were young men—but then they were too young and angry to understand, now they were too old and angry to understand. And what was there to understand? It was inexplicable to him—the excitement they could seriously persist in deriving from his denunciation. He had done what he did the way that he did it as they did what they did the way they did it. Was their steadfast posture of unforgivingness any more forgivable? Or any less harmful in its effect? He was one of the millions of American men who were party to a divorce that broke up a family. But did he beat their mother? Did he beat them? Did he fail to support their mother or fail to support them? Did any one of them ever have to beg money from him? Was he ever once severe? Had he not made every overture toward them that he could? What could have been avoided? What could he have done differently that would have made him more acceptable to them other than what he could not do, which was to remain married and live with their mother? Either they understood that or they didn't—and sadly for him (and for them), they didn't. Nor could they ever understand that he had lost the same family they did. And no doubt there were things he still failed to understand. If so, that was no less sad. No one could say there wasn't enough sadness to go around or enough remorse to prompt the fugue of questions with which he attempted to defend the story of his life.

He told them nothing about his string of hospitalizations for fear that it might inspire too much vindictive satisfaction. He was sure that when he died they would rejoice, and all because of those earliest recollections they'd never outgrown of his leaving his first family to start a second. That he had eventually betrayed his second family for a beauty twenty-six years his junior who, according to Randy and Lonny, anyone other than their father could have spotted as a "nutcase" a mile away —a model, no less, "a brainless model" he'd met when she was hired by his agency for a job that carried the entire crew, including the two of them, to the Caribbean for a few days' work —had only reinforced their view of him as an underhanded, irresponsible, frivolously immature sexual adventurer. As a father, he was an impostor. As a husband, even to the incomparable Phoebe, for whom he jettisoned their mother, he was an impostor. As anything but a cunthound, he was a fake through and through. And as for his becoming an "artist" in his old age, that, to his sons, was the biggest joke of all. Once he took up painting in earnest every day, the derisive nickname coined by Randy for their father was "the happy cobbler."

In response he did not claim either moral rectitude or perfect judgment. His third marriage had been founded on boundless desire for a woman he had no business with but a desire that never lost its power to blind him and lead him, at fifty, to play a young man's game. He had not slept with Phoebe for the previous six years, yet he could not offer this intimate fact of their life as an explanation to his sons for his second divorce. He didn't think that his record as Phoebe's husband for fifteen years, as Nancy's live-in father for thirteen years, as Howie's brother and his parents' son since birth, required him to make such an explanation. He did not think that his record as an advertising man for over twenty years required him to make such an explanation. He did not think that his record as father to *Lonny* and *Randy* required such an explanation!

Yet their description of how he'd conducted himself over a lifetime was not even a caricature but, in his estimation, a portrayal of what he was not, a description with which they persisted in minimizing everything worthwhile that he believed was apparent to most everyone else. Minimized his decency, then magnified his defects, for a reason that surely could not continue to carry such great force at this late date. Into their forties they remained with their father the children that they'd been back when he'd first left their mother, children who by their nature could not understand that there might be more than one explanation to human behavior—children, however, with the appearance and aggression of men, and against whose undermining he could never manage to sustain a solid defense. They elected to make the absent father suffer, and so he did, investing them with that power. Suffering his wrongdoing was all he could ever do to please them, to pay his bill, to indulge like the best of dads their maddening opposition.

You wicked bastards! You sulky fuckers! You condemning little shits! Would everything be different, he asked himself, if I'd been different and done things differently? Would it all be less lonely than it is now? Of course it would! But this is what I did! I am seventy-one. This is the man I have made. This is what I did to get here, and there's nothing more to be said!

Over the years, luckily, he heard regularly from Howie. In his late fifties Howie, like almost all the partners who reached that age except for the top three or four, had retired from Goldman Sachs; by then he was worth easily fifty million dollars. He was soon sitting on numerous corporate boards, eventually being named chairman of Procter & Gamble, for whom he'd done arbitrage in his early days. In his seventies, still vigorous and eager to be working, he'd become a consultant to a Boston buyout firm specializing in financial institutions and traveled to look for potential acquisitions. Yet despite the continuing responsibilities and the demands on Howie's time, the two brothers exchanged phone calls a couple of times a month, calls that could sometimes go on for as long as half an hour, with one of them laughingly entertaining the other with recollections of their years growing up and of comical moments from their days at school and in the jewelry store.

Now, though, when they spoke, an unwarranted coldness came over him, and to his brother's joviality his response was silence. The reason was ridiculous. He hated Howie because of his robust good health. He hated Howie because he'd never in his life been a patient in a hospital, because disease was unknown to him, because nowhere was his body scarred from the surgical knife, nor were there six metal stents lodged in his arteries along with a cardiac alarm system tucked into the wall of his chest that was called a defibrillator, a word that when he first heard it pronounced by his cardiologist was unknown to him and sounded, innocuously enough, as if it had something to do with the gear system of a bicycle. He hated him because, though they were offspring of the same two parents and looked so very much alike, Howie had inherited the physical impregnability and he the coronary and vascular weaknesses. It was ridiculous to hate him, because there was nothing Howie could do about his good health other than to enjoy it. It was ridiculous to hate Howie for nothing other than having been born himself and not someone else. He'd never envied him for his athletic or academic prowess, for his financial wizardry and his wealth, never envied him even when he thought of his own sons and wives and then of Howie's—four grown boys who continued to love him and the devoted wife of fifty years who clearly was as important to him as he to her. He was proud of the muscular, athletic brother who rarely got less than an A in school, and had admired him since earliest childhood. Himself a youngster with an artistic talent whose single noteworthy physical skill was swimming, he'd loved Howie unabashedly and followed him everywhere. But now he hated him and he envied him and he was poisonously jealous of him and, in his thoughts, all but rose up in rage against him because the force that Howie brought to bear on life had in no way been impeded.

Though on the phone he suppressed as best he could everything irrational and indefensible that he felt, as the months
passed their calls took up less time and became less frequent,
and soon they were hardly speaking at all.

He did not retain for long the spiteful desire for his brother
to lose his health—that far he could not go as an envier, since
his brother's losing his health would not result in his regaining
his own. Nothing could restore his health, his youth, or in-
vigorate his talent. He could, nonetheless, in a frenzied mood,
almost reach a point where he could believe that Howie's good
health was responsible for his own compromised health, even
though he knew better, even though he was not without a
civilized person's tolerant understanding of the puzzle of in-
equality and misfortune. Back when the psychoanalyst had
glibly diagnosed the symptoms of severe appendicitis as a case
of envy, he was still very much his parents' son and barely ac-
quainted with the feelings that come with believing that the
possessions of another might better belong to you. But now
he knew; in his old age he had discovered the emotional state
that robs the envier of his serenity and, worse, his realism—he
hated Howie for that biological endowment that should have
been his as well.

Suddenly he could not stand his brother in the primitive,
instinctual way that his sons could not stand him.

He had been hoping there would be a woman in the painting
classes in whom he might take an interest—that was half the
reason for giving them. But pairing up with one of the widows
his age toward whom he felt no attraction proved to be beyond
him, though the robustly healthy young women he saw jogging along the boardwalk when he took his morning walk, still
all curves and gleaming hair and, to his eyes, seemingly more
beautiful than their counterparts of an earlier era had ever been,
were not sufficiently lacking in common sense to exchange
with him anything other than a professionally innocent smile.
Following their speedy progress with his gaze was a pleasure,
but a difficult pleasure, and at bottom the mental caress was a
source of biting sadness that only intensified an unbearable
loneliness. True, he had chosen to live alone, but not unbearably alone. The worst of being unbearably alone was that you

had to bear it—either that or you were sunk. You had to work hard to prevent your mind from sabotaging you by its looking hungrily back at the superabundant past.

And he'd become bored with his painting. For many years he'd dreamed of the uninterrupted span of time that his retirement would afford him to paint—as had thousands and thousands of other art directors who'd also earned their livelihood working in ad agencies. But after painting almost every day since moving to the shore, he had run out of interest in what he was doing. The urgent demand to paint had lifted, the enterprise designed to fill the rest of his life fizzled out. He had no more ideas. Every picture he worked on came out looking like the last one. His brightly colored abstractions had always been prominently displayed in the Starfish Beach show of local artists, and of the three that were taken by a gallery in the nearby seaside tourist town, all had been sold to the gallery's best customers. But that was nearly two years ago. Now he had nothing to show. It had all come to nothing. As a painter he was and probably always had been no more than the "happy cobbler" he happened to know he'd been dubbed by the satirical son. It was as though painting had been an exorcism. But designed to expel what malignancy? The oldest of his self-delusions? Or had he run to painting to attempt to deliver himself from the knowledge that you are born to live and you die instead? Suddenly he was lost in nothing, in the sound of the two syllables "nothing" no less than in the nothingness, lost and drifting, and the dread began to seep in. Nothing comes without risk, he thought, nothing, nothing—there's nothing that doesn't backfire, not even painting stupid pictures!

He explained to Nancy, when she asked about his work, that he'd had "an irreversible aesthetic vasectomy."

"Something will start you again," she said, accepting the hyperbolic language with an absolving laugh. She had been permeated by the quality of her mother's kindness, by the inability to remain aloof from another's need, by the day-to-day earthborn soulfulness that he had disastrously undervalued and thrown away—thrown away without beginning to realize all he would subsequently live without.

"I don't think it will," he was saying to their daughter.

"There's a reason I was never a painter. I've run smack up against it."

"The reason you weren't a painter," Nancy explained, "is because you've had wives and children. You had mouths to feed. You had responsibilities."

"The reason I wasn't a painter was because I'm not a painter. Not then and not now."

"Oh, Dad—"

"No, listen to me. All I've been doing is doodling away the time."

"You're just upset right now. Don't insult yourself—it's not so. I know it's not so. I have your paintings all over my apartment. I look at them every day, and I can promise you I'm not looking at doodlings. People come over—they look at them. They ask me who the artist is. They pay attention to them. They ask if the artist is living."

"What do you tell them?"

"Listen to *me* now: they're not responding to doodlings. They're responding to work. To work that is beautiful. And of course," she said, and now with that laugh that left him feeling washed clean and, in his seventies, infatuated with his girl-child all over again, "of course I tell them you're living. I tell them my father painted these, and I'm so proud to say that."

"Good, sweetie."

"I've got a little gallery going here."

"That's good—that makes me feel good."

"You're just frustrated now. It's just that simple. You're a wonderful painter. I know what I'm talking about. If there's anybody in this world equipped to know if you're a wonderful painter or not, it's me."

After all he'd put her through by betraying Phoebe, she still wanted to praise him. From the age of ten she'd been like that —a pure and sensible girl, besmirched only by her unstinting generosity, harmlessly hiding from unhappiness by blotting out the faults of everyone dear to her and by overloving love. Baling forgiveness as though it were so much hay. The harm inevitably came when she concealed from herself just a little too much that was wanting in the makeup of the ostentatiously brilliant young crybaby she had fallen for and married.

"And it's not just me, Dad. It's everybody who comes. I was interviewing babysitters the other day, because Molly can't do it anymore. I was interviewing for a new babysitter and this wonderful girl I ended up hiring, Tanya—she's a student looking to earn some extra money, she's at the Art Students League just like you were—she couldn't take her eyes off the one I have in the dining room, over the sideboard, the yellow one—you know the one I mean?"

"Yes."

"She couldn't take her eyes off it. The yellow and black one. It was really quite something. I was asking her these questions and she was focused over the sideboard. She asked when it was painted and where I had bought it. There's something very compelling about your work."

"You're very sweet to me, darling."

"No. I'm candid with you, that's all."

"Thank you."

"You'll get back to it. It'll happen again. Painting isn't through with you yet. Just enjoy yourself in the meantime. It's so beautiful where you are. Just be patient. Just take your time. Nothing's vanished. Enjoy the weather, enjoy your walks, enjoy the beach and the ocean. Nothing's vanished and nothing's altered."

Strange—all the comfort he was taking from her words and yet he wasn't convinced for a second that she knew what she was talking about. But the wish to take comfort, he realized, is no small thing, particularly from the one who miraculously still loves you.

"I don't go in the surf anymore," he told her.

"You don't?"

It was only Nancy, but he felt humiliated nonetheless by the confession. "I've lost the confidence for the surf."

"You can swim in the pool, can't you?"

"I can."

"Okay, so swim in the pool."

He asked her then about the twins, thinking if only he were still with Phoebe, if only Phoebe were with him now, if only Nancy hadn't to work so hard to shore him up in the absence of a devoted wife, if only he hadn't wounded Phoebe the way that he had, if only he hadn't wronged her, if only he hadn't lied! If only she hadn't said, "I can never trust you to be truthful again."

It didn't begin until he was nearly fifty. The young women were everywhere—photographers' reps, secretaries, stylists, models, account executives. Lots of women, and you worked and traveled and had lunch together, and what was astonishing wasn't what happened—the acquisition by a husband of "someone else"—but that it took so long to happen, even after the passion had dwindled and disappeared from his marriage. It began with a pretty, darkhaired young woman of nineteen whom he hired to work as his secretary and who, within two weeks of taking the job, was kneeling on his office floor with her ass raised and him fucking her fully clothed, with just his fly unzipped. He had not possessed her by coercion, though he had indeed taken her by surprise—but then he, who was conscious of having no peculiarities to flaunt and who believed himself content to live by the customary norms, to behave more or less the same as others, had taken himself no less by surprise. It was an easy entry because she was so moist and, in those daredevil circumstances, it took no time for each of them to achieve a vigorous orgasm. One morning just after she had gotten up from the floor and returned to her desk in the outer office, and while he was still standing, face flushed, in the middle of the room and adjusting his clothing, his boss, Clarence, the group management supervisor and an executive vice president, opened the door and came in. "Where is her apartment?" Clarence asked him. "I don't know," he replied. "Use her apartment," Clarence said severely and left. But they couldn't stop what they were doing where and how they were doing it, even though theirs was one of those office trapeze acts in which everyone has everything to lose. They were too close to each other all day to stop. All either of them could think about was her kneeling on his office floor and him hurling her skirt up over her back and grabbing her by the hair and, after pushing aside her underpants, penetrating her as forcefully as he could and with an utter disregard for discovery.

Then came the shoot in Grenada. He was running the show, and he and the photographer he hired picked the models, ten of them for a towel ad that would be set beside a small natural pool in the tropical forest, with each model clad in a short summer robe, her head turbaned in the client's towel as though she'd just washed her hair. The arrangements had been made, the ad okayed, and he was on the plane sitting alone away from everyone else so he could read a book and fall asleep and fly there unperturbed.

They had a stop in the Caribbean, and he got off the plane and went into the waiting room and looked around, saw all the models, and said hello to them before everyone got onto another, smaller plane and took a short hop to their destination, where they were picked up by several cars and by a small jeep-like vehicle, which he decided to ride in with one of the models whom he'd taken note of when she was hired. She was the only foreign model on the shoot, a Dane named Merete and probably, at twenty-four, the oldest of the ten; the rest were American girls, eighteen and nineteen years old. There was somebody driving, Merete was in the middle, and he was on the outside. It was nighttime and very dark. They were squeezed in tightly together and he had his arm around the top of her seat. Only moments after the car took off his thumb was in her mouth, and without his knowing it, his marriage had come under assault. The young man who started out hoping never to live two lives was about to cleave himself open with a hatchet.

When they got to the hotel and he went to his room, he lay there most of the night thinking only of Merete. The next day when they met, she said to him, "I waited for you." The whole thing was so quick and so intense. They shot all day in the middle of the forest with the small natural pool, worked hard and seriously for the entire day, and when they got back he found that the photographer's rep who was along on the job had rented a house on the beach just for him—he had thrown a lot of work her way, and so the rep rented it for him and he moved out of the hotel and Merete came with him and they lived there on the beach together for three days. In the early morning when he was coming back up the beach from his swim, she would be waiting on the veranda wearing just her bikini underpants. They would start then and there, while he was still wet from his long swim. For the first two days he was always diddling around her ass with his fingers while she went down on him, until finally she looked up and said, "If you like that little hole, why don't you use it?"

Of course he saw her back in New York. Every day that she was free he would go to her place at lunchtime. Then one Saturday he, Phoebe, and Nancy were walking down Third Avenue when he saw Merete walking on the other side of the street with that easy, upright, somnambulant gait whose feral assuredness always slayed him, as if she were not approaching the Seventy-second Street light carrying a bag of groceries but serenely traversing the Serengeti, Merete Jespersen of Copenhagen grazing the grasses of the savanna amid a thousand African antelope. Models didn't all have to be needle-thin in those days, and even before he spotted her by her glide and saw the sheaf of golden hair down her back, he identified her as his very own treasure, the white hunter's prize, by the weight of her breasts inside her blouse and the light heft of the behind whose little hole had come to afford them such delight. He displayed neither fear nor excitement upon seeing her, though he felt extremely ill and had to get to a phone alone to call her—getting to the phone was all he thought about for the rest of the afternoon. This wasn't ravishing the secretary on the office floor. This was the raw supremacy of her creatureliness over his instinct for survival, itself a force to be reckoned with. This was the wildest venture of his life, the one, as he was only faintly beginning to understand, that could wipe out everything. Only in passing did it occur to him that it might be somewhat delusional at the age of fifty to think that he could find a hole that would substitute for everything else.

A few months later he flew to Paris to see her. She had been working in Europe for six weeks, and though they spoke secretly on the phone as often as three times a day, that wasn't sufficient to satisfy the longing in either of them. A week before the Saturday when he and Phoebe were to drive to New Hampshire to bring Nancy home from summer camp, he told Phoebe that he would have to fly to Paris for a shoot that weekend. He'd leave on Thursday night and be home by Monday morning. Ezra Pollock, the account executive, would be going with him and they would meet up with a European crew over there. He knew that Ez was with his family until after Labor Day, unreachable on a tiny phoneless island several miles out to sea from South Freeport, Maine, so far from everything that seals could be seen socializing on the ledges of the rocky island nearby. He gave Phoebe the name and number of the Paris hotel and then reconsidered ten times a day his risking the chance of being discovered by her just so he and Merete could spend a long weekend together in the lovers' capital of the world. But Phoebe remained unsuspicious and seemed to be looking forward to picking up Nancy by herself. She was eager to have her home after a summer away, just as he was dying to see Merete after a month and a half apart, and so he flew off on Thursday night, his mind on that little hole and what she liked him to do with it. Yes, fixed dreamily on no more than that all the way across the Atlantic on Air France.

What went wrong was the weather. High winds and blustery storms swept through Europe, and no planes were able to take off all day Sunday and into Monday. Both days he sat at the airport with Merete, who had come along to cling to him until the last possible moment, but when it was clear that there would be no departures from de Gaulle until Tuesday at the earliest, they took a taxi back to the Rue des Beaux Arts, to Merete's favorite swank little Left Bank hotel, where they were able to rebook their room, the room mirrored with smoked glass. During every night ride they took by taxi in Paris, they performed the same impudent playlet, always as though inadvertently and for the first time: he'd drop his hand onto her knee and she'd let her legs fall open just far enough so that he could reach up under her silk slip of a dress—nothing more, really, than a piece of deluxe lingerie—and finger her while she adjusted her head to look idly out of the taxi at the illuminated shop windows and he, leaning back in his seat, pretended to be anything but riveted by the way she could continue to behave as if no one were touching her even as he sensed her beginning to come. Merete carried everything erotic to the limit. (Earlier, in a discreet antique jewelry shop down the street from their hotel, he'd adorned her throat with a stunning trinket, a pendant necklace set with diamonds and demantoid garnets and strung on its original gold chain. Like the knowledgeable son of his father that he was, he'd asked to examine the stones through the jeweler's loupe. "What are you looking for?" Merete asked. "Flaws, cracks, the coloring—if nothing appears under a ten-power magnification the diamond can be certified as flawless. You see? My father's words issue from my mouth whenever I speak about jewelry." "But not about anything else," she said. "Not about anything about you. Those words are mine." Not while shopping, not while walking the streets, not while taking an elevator or having coffee together in a booth around the corner from her apartment, could they ever stop seducing each other. "How do you know how to do that, to hold the thing—?" "The loupe." "How do you know how to hold the loupe in your eye like that?" "My father taught me. You just tighten your socket around it. Rather like you do." "So what color is it?" "Blue. Blue-white. That was the best in the old days. My father would say it still is. My father would say, 'Beyond the beauty and the status and the value, the diamond is imperishable.' 'Imperishable' was a word he loved to savor." "Who doesn't?" Merete said. "What is it in Danish?" he asked her. "'*Uforgængelig.*' It's just as wonderful." "Why don't we take it?" he told the saleswoman, who in turn, speaking in perfect English and with a touch of French—and with perfect cunning—told the young companion of the older gentleman, "Mademoiselle is very lucky. *Une femme choyée*," and the cost was about as much as the entire inventory of the Elizabeth store, if not more, back when he was running one-hundred-dollar engagement rings of a quarter or a half carat to be sized for his father's customers by a man working on a bench in a cubbyhole on Frelinghuysen Avenue circa 1942.) And now he withdrew the finger sticky with her slime, perfumed her lips with it, then pressed it between her teeth for her tongue to caress, reminding her of their first meeting and what they'd dared to do as strangers, an American adman of fifty and a Danish model of twenty-four, crossing a Caribbean island in the dark, transfixed. Reminding her that she was his and he hers. A cult of two.

There was a message from Phoebe waiting for him at the hotel: "Contact me immediately. Your mother gravely ill."

When he phoned he learned that his eighty-year-old mother had had a stroke at five A.M. Monday, New York time, and was not expected to live.

He explained to Phoebe about the weather conditions and

learned that Howie was already on his way east and that his father was keeping vigil beside his mother's bed. He wrote down the telephone number of his mother's room at the hospital, and Phoebe told him that as soon as she hung up, she would be heading over to Jersey herself, to be with his father at the hospital until Howie arrived. She had only been waiting for him to call her back. "I missed you by a few minutes this morning. The desk clerk told me, 'Madame and monsieur have just departed for the airport.'"

"Yes," he said, "I shared a cab with the photographer's rep."

"No, you shared a cab with the Danish twenty-four-year-old with whom you are having an affair. I'm sorry, but I can no longer look the other way. I looked the other way with that secretary. But the humiliation has now gone too far. Paris," she said with disgust. "The planning. The premeditation. The tickets and the travel agent. Tell me, which of you romantic cornballs dreamed up Paris for your sneaky little undertaking? Where did you two eat? What charming restaurants did you go to?"

"Phoebe, I don't know what you're talking about. You're not making any sense. I'll get the first plane back that I possibly can."

His mother died an hour before he was able to reach the hospital in Elizabeth. His father and his brother were sitting beside the body that lay beneath the covers of the bed. He had never before seen his mother in a hospital bed, though of course she had seen him there more than once. Like Howie, she had enjoyed perfect health all her life. It was she who would rush to the hospital to comfort others. Howie said, "We haven't told the staff she died. We waited. We wanted you to be able to see her before they took her away." What he saw was the high-relief contour of an elderly woman asleep. What he saw was a stone, the heavy, sepulchral, stonelike weight that says, Death is just death—it's nothing more.

He hugged his father, who patted his hand and said, "It's best this way. You wouldn't have wanted her to live the way that thing left her."

When he took his mother's hand and held it to his lips, he realized that in a matter of hours he had lost the two women whose devotion had been the underpinning of his strength.

With Phoebe he lied and lied and lied, but to no avail. He

told her that he had gone to Paris to break off the affair with Merete. He'd had to see her face to face to do it, and that's where she was working.

"But in the hotel, while you were breaking off the affair, didn't you sleep with her at night in the same bed?"

"We didn't sleep. She cried all night long."

"For four whole nights? That's a lot of crying for a twenty-four-year-old Dane. I don't think even Hamlet cried that much."

"Phoebe, I went to tell her it was over—and it *is* over."

"What did I do so wrong," Phoebe asked, "that you should want to humiliate me like this? Why should you want to un-hinge *everything*? Has it all been so hideous? I should get over being dumbstruck, but I can't. I, who never doubted you, to whom it rarely occurred even to question you, and now I can never believe another word you say. I can never trust you to be truthful again. Yes, you wounded me with the secretary, but I kept my mouth shut. You didn't even know I knew, did you? Well, did you?"

"I didn't, no."

"Because I hid my thoughts from you—unfortunately I couldn't hide them from myself. And now you wound me with the Dane and you humiliate me with the lying, and now I will *not* hide my thoughts and keep my mouth shut. A mature, intelligent woman comes along, a mate who understands what reciprocity is. She rids you of Cecilia, gives you a phenomenal daughter, changes your entire life, and you don't know what to do for her except to fuck the Dane. Every time I looked at my watch I kept figuring what time it was in Paris and what you two would be doing. That went on for the whole weekend. The basis of everything is trust, is it not? Is it not?"

She had only to say Cecilia's name to instantaneously recall the vindictive tirades visited on his mother and father by his first wife, who, fifteen years later, to his horror, turned out to have been not merely abandoned Cecilia but his Cassandra: "I pity this little Miss Muffet coming after me—I genuinely do pity the vile little Quaker slut!"

"You can weather anything," Phoebe was telling him, "even if the trust is violated, if it's owned up to. Then you become life partners in a different way, but it's still possible to remain partners. But lying—lying is cheap, contemptible control over the other person. It's watching the other person acting on incomplete information—in other words, humiliating herself. Lying is so commonplace and yet, if you're on the receiving end, it's such an astonishing thing. The people you liars are betraying put up with a growing list of insults until you really can't help but think less of them, can you? I'm sure that liars as skillful and persistent and devious as you reach the point where it's the one you're lying to, and not you, who seems like the one with the serious limitations. You probably don't even think you're lying—you think of it as an act of kindness to spare the feelings of your poor sexless mate. You probably think your lying is in the nature of a virtue, an act of generosity toward the dumb cluck who loves you. Or maybe it's just what it is— a fucking lie, one fucking lie after another. Oh, why go on—all these episodes are so well known," she said. "The man loses the passion for the marriage and he cannot live without. The wife is pragmatic. The wife is realistic. Yes, passion is gone, she's older and not what she was, but to her it's enough to have the physical affection, just being there with him in the bed, she holding him, he holding her. The physical affection, the tenderness, the comradery, the closeness . . . But he cannot accept that. Because he is a man who *cannot live without*. Well, you're going to live without now, mister. You're going to live without plenty. You're going to find out what living without is all about! Oh, go away from me, please. I can't bear the role you've reduced me to. The pitiful middle-aged wife, embittered by rejection, consumed by rotten jealousy! Raging! Repugnant! Oh, I hate you for that more than anything. Go away, leave this house. I can't bear the sight of you with that satyr-on-his-good-behavior look your face! You'll get no absolution from me—never! I will not be trifled with any longer! Go, please! Leave me alone!"

"Phoebe—"

"No! Don't you dare call me by my name!"

But these episodes are indeed well known and require no further elaboration. Phoebe threw him out the night after his mother's burial, they were divorced after negotiating a financial settlement, and because he did not know what else to do to make sense of what had happened or how else to appear responsible—and to rehabilitate himself particularly in Nancy's eyes—a few months later he married Merete. Since he had broken everything up because of this person half his age, it seemed only logical to go ahead and tidy everything up again by making her his third wife—never was he clever enough as a married man to fall into adultery or to fall in love with a woman who was not free.

It was not long afterward that he discovered that Merete was something more than that little hole, or perhaps something less. He discovered her inability to think anything through without all her uncertainties intruding and skewing her thought. He discovered the true dimensions of her vanity and, though she was only in her twenties, her morbid fear of aging. He discovered her green card problems and her long-standing tax mess with the IRS, the result of years of failing to file a return. And when he required emergency coronary artery surgery, he discovered her terror of illness and her uselessness in the face of danger. Altogether he was a little late in learning that all her boldness was encompassed in her eroticism and that her carrying everything erotic between them to the limit was their only overpowering affinity. He had replaced the most helpful wife imaginable with a wife who went to pieces under the slightest pressure. But in the immediate aftermath, marrying her had seemed the simplest way to cover up the crime.

Passing the time was excruciating without painting. There was the hour-long morning walk, in the late afternoon there was twenty minutes of working out with his light weights and a half hour of doing easy laps at the pool—the daily regime his cardiologist encouraged—but that was it, those were the events of his day. How much time could you spend staring out at the ocean, even if it was the ocean you'd loved since you were a boy? How long could he watch the tides flood in and flow out without his remembering, as anyone might in a sea-gazing reverie, that life had been given to him, as to all, randomly, fortuitously, and but once, and for no known or knowable reason? On the evenings he drove over to eat broiled bluefish on the back deck of the fish store that perched at the edge of the inlet where the boats sailed out to the ocean under the old drawbridge, he sometimes stopped first at the town where his family had vacationed in the summertime. He got out of the car on the ocean road and went up onto the boardwalk and sat on one of the benches that looked out to the beach and the sea, the stupendous sea that had been changing continuously without ever changing since he'd been a bony sea-battling boy. This was the very bench where his parents and grandparents used to sit in the evenings to catch the breeze and enjoy the boardwalk promenade of neighbors and friends, and this was the very beach where his family had picnicked and sunned themselves and where he and Howie and their pals went swimming, though it was now easily twice as wide as it had been then because of a reclamation project recently engineered by the army. Yet wide as it was, it was still his beach and at the center of the circles in which his mind revolved when he remembered the best of boyhood. But how much time could a man spend remembering the best of boyhood? What about enjoying the best of old age? Or was the best of old age just that—the longing for the best of boyhood, for the tubular sprout that was then his body and that rode the waves from way out where they began to build, rode them with his arms pointed like an arrowhead and the skinny rest of him following behind like the arrow's shaft, rode them all the way in to where his rib cage scraped against the tiny sharp pebbles and jagged clamshells and pulverized seashells at the edge of the shore and he hustled to his feet and hurriedly turned and went lurching through the low surf until it was knee high and deep enough for him to plunge in and begin swimming madly out to the rising breakers—into the advancing, green Atlantic, rolling unstoppably toward him like the obstinate fact of the future— and, if he was lucky, make it there in time to catch the next big wave and then the next and the next and the next until from the low slant of inland sunlight glittering across the water he knew it was time to go. He ran home barefoot and wet and salty, remembering the mightiness of that immense sea boiling in his own two ears and licking his forearm to taste his skin fresh from the ocean and baked by the sun. Along with the ecstasy of a whole day of being battered silly by the sea, the taste and the smell intoxicated him so that he was driven to the brink of biting down with his teeth to tear out a chunk of himself and savor his fleshly existence.

Quickly as he could on his heels he crossed the concrete sidewalks still hot from the day and when he reached their rooming house headed around back to the outdoor shower with the soggy plywood walls, where wet sand plopped out of his suit when he kicked it off over his feet and held it up to the cold water beating down on his head. The level force of the surging tide, the ordeal of the burning pavement, the bristling shock of the ice-cold shower, the blessing of the taut new muscles and the slender limbs and the darkly suntanned flesh marked by just a single pale scar from the hernia surgery hidden down by his groin—there was nothing about those August days, after the German submarines had been destroyed and there were no more drowned sailors to worry about, that wasn't wonderfully clear. And nothing about his physical perfection that he had any reason not to take for granted.

When he returned from dinner he would try to settle in and read. He had a library of oversized art books filling one wall of the studio; he had been accumulating and studying them all his life, but now he couldn't sit in his reading chair and turn the pages of a single one of them without feeling ridiculous. The delusion—as he now thought of it—had lost its power over him, and so the books only magnified his sense of the hopelessly laughable amateur he was and of the hollowness of the pursuit to which he had dedicated his retirement.

Trying to pass more than a little time in the company of the Starfish Beach residents was also unendurable. Unlike him, many were able not merely to construct whole conversations that revolved around their grandchildren but to find sufficient grounds for existence in the existence of their grandchildren. Caught in their company, he sometimes experienced loneliness in what felt like its purest form. And even those among the village residents who were thoughtful, well-spoken people were not interesting to be with more than once in a while. Most of the elderly residents had been settled into their marriages for decades and were sufficiently connected still to whatever was left of their marital felicity that only rarely could he get the husband to go off by himself for lunch without the wife. However wistfully he might sometimes look at such couples as dusk approached or on Sunday afternoons, there were the rest of the hours of the week to think about, and theirs wasn't a life for him when he was on top of his melancholy. The upshot was that he should never have moved into such a community in the first place. He had displaced himself just when what age most demanded was that he be rooted as he'd been for all those years he ran the creative department at the agency. Always he had been invigorated by stability, never by stasis. And this was stagnation. There was an absence now of all forms of solace, a barrenness under the heading of consolation, and no way to return to what was. A sense of otherness had overtaken him— "otherness," a word in his own language to describe a state of being all but foreign to him till his art student Millicent Kramer had jarringly used it to bemoan her condition. Nothing any longer kindled his curiosity or answered his needs, not his painting, not his family, not his neighbors, nothing except the young women who jogged by him on the boardwalk in the morning. My God, he thought, the man I once was! The life that surrounded me! The force that was mine! No "otherness" to be felt anywhere! Once upon a time I was a full human being.

There was one particular girl whom he never failed to wave to when she jogged by, and one morning he set out to meet her. Always she waved back and smiled, and then forlornly he watched her run on. This time he stopped her. He called out, "Miss, miss, I want to talk to you," and instead of shaking her head no and breezing by with a "Can't now," as he fully imagined her doing, she turned and jogged back to where he was waiting, by the plank stairs that led down to the beach, and stood with her hands on her hips only a foot away from him, damp with perspiration, a tiny creature perfectly formed. Until she fully relaxed, she pawed the boardwalk with one running shoe like a pony while looking up at this unknown man in the sunglasses who was six feet three and had a full head of wavy gray hair. It turned out, fortuitously, that she had been working for seven years at an ad agency in Philadelphia, lived here at the shore, and was currently on her two-week vacation. When he told her the name of the New York agency where he'd worked for nearly a lifetime she was terrifically impressed; his employer was legendary, and for the next ten minutes they made the kind of advertising talk that had never interested him. She would have to be in her late twenties and yet, with her long, crinkly auburn hair tied back and in her running shorts and tank top, and small as she was, she might have been taken for fourteen. He tried repeatedly to prevent his gaze from falling to the swell of the breasts that rose and fell with her breathing. This was torment to walk away from. The idea was an affront to common sense and a menace to his sanity. His excitement was disproportionate to anything that had happened or that possibly could happen. He had not just to hide his hunger; so as not to go mad he had to annihilate it. Yet he doggedly continued on as he had planned, still half believing that there was some combination of words that would somehow save him from defeat. He said, "I've noticed you jogging." She surprised him by responding, "I've noticed you noticing me." "How game are you?" he heard himself asking her, but feeling that the encounter was now out of his control and that everything was going much too fast—feeling, if it were possible, even more reckless than when he'd draped that pendant necklace costing a small fortune around Merete's neck in Paris. Phoebe the devoted wife and Nancy the cherished child were home in New York, awaiting his return—he'd spoken to Nancy the day before, within only hours of her getting back from summer camp—and still he'd told the saleswoman, "We'll take it. You needn't wrap it. Here, Merete, let me do it. I teethed on these clasps. It's called a tubular box clasp. In the thirties, it would have been the safest one around for a piece like this. Come, give me your throat." "What do you have in mind?" the jogger boldly replied, so boldly that he felt at a disadvantage and did not know how forthright to make his answer. Her belly was tanned and her arms were thin and her prominent buttocks were round and firm and her slender legs were strongly muscled and her breasts were substantial for someone not much more than five feet tall. She had the curvaceous lusciousness of a Varga Girl in the old 1940s magazine illustrations, but a miniaturized, childlike Varga Girl, which was why he had begun waving to her in the first place.

He'd said, "How game are you?" and she'd replied, "What do you have in mind?" Now what? He removed his sunglasses so she could see his eyes when he stared down at her. Did she understand what she was implying by answering him like that? Or was it something she said just to be saying something, just to be sounding in charge of herself even as she was feeling frightened and out of her depth? Thirty years ago he wouldn't have doubted the result of pursuing her, young as she was, and the possibility of humiliating rejection would never have occurred to him. But lost was the pleasure of the confidence, and with it the engrossing playfulness of the exchange. He did his best to conceal his anxiety—and the urge to touch—and the craving for just one such body—and the futility of it all—and his insignificance—and apparently succeeded, for when he took a piece of paper from his wallet and wrote down his phone number, she didn't make a face and run off laughing at him but took it with an agreeable little catlike smile that could easily have been accompanied by a purr. "You know where I am," he said, feeling himself growing hard in his pants unbelievably, magically quickly, as though he were fifteen. And feeling, too, that sharp sense of individualization, of sublime singularity, that marks a fresh sexual encounter or love affair and that is the opposite of the deadening depersonalization of serious illness. She scanned his face with two large, lively blue eyes. "There's something in you that's unusual," she said thoughtfully. "Yes, there is," he said and laughed, "I was born in 1933." "You look pretty fit to me," she told him. "And you look pretty fit to me," he replied. "You know where to find me," he said. Engagingly she swung the piece of paper in the air as though it were a tiny bell and to his delight shoved it deep into her damp tank top before taking off down the boardwalk again.

She never called. And when he took his walks he never saw her again. She must have decided to do her jogging along another stretch of the boardwalk, thereby thwarting his longing for the last great outburst of everything.

Shortly after the folly with the childlike Varga Girl in the running shorts and the tank top, he decided to sell the condominium and move back to New York. He considered his giving up on the shore a failure, almost as painful a failure as what had happened to him as a painter in the past half year. Even before 9/11 he had contemplated a retirement of the kind he'd been living for three years now; the disaster of 9/11 had appeared to accelerate his opportunity to make a big change, when in fact it had marked the beginning of his vulnerability and the origin of his exile. But now he'd sell the condo and try to find a place in New York close to Nancy's apartment on the Upper West Side. Because the condo's value had almost doubled in the short time he'd owned it, he might be able to shell out enough cash down to buy a place up by Columbia big enough for all of them to live together under one roof. He'd pay the household expenses and she could meet her own expenses with the child support. She could cut back to working three days a week and spend four full days with the children, as she'd been wanting to do—but couldn't afford to do—since she'd returned to her job from maternity leave. Nancy, the twins, and himself. It was a plan worth proposing to her. She might not mind his assistance, and he was hungering for the company of an intimate to whom he could give and from whom he could receive, and who better in all the world than Nancy?

He allowed himself a couple of weeks to determine how workable the plan was and to gauge how desperate he might seem presenting it. Finally, when he'd decided that for the time being he would propose nothing to Nancy but rather go into New York for a day to begin on his own to investigate the possibility of finding an apartment in his price range that could comfortably accommodate the four of them, the rush of bad news came over the phone, first about Phoebe and the next day about three of his former colleagues.

He learned of Phoebe's stroke when the phone rang a little after six-thirty in the morning. It was Nancy calling from the hospital. Phoebe had phoned her about an hour earlier to tell her that something was happening to her, and by the time Nancy got her to the emergency room her speech was so thick she could barely make herself understood and she'd lost movement in her right arm. They had just finished the MRI and Phoebe was now resting in her room.

"But a stroke, someone as youthful and healthy as your mother? Was it something to do with the migraines? Is that possible?"

"They think it was from the medication she was taking for the migraines," Nancy said. "It was the first drug that had ever helped. She realized the medication posed a minute danger of causing a stroke. She knew that. But once she found that it worked, once she was rid of that pain for the first time in fifty years, she decided it was worth the risk. She'd had three miraculous years pain free. It was bliss."

"Till now," he said sadly. "Till this. Do you want me to drive up?"

"I'll let you know. Let's see how things go. They believe she's out of trouble."

"Will she recover? Will she be able to speak?"

"The doctor says so. He thinks she'll recover one hundred percent."

"Wonderful," he said, but thought, Let's see what he thinks a year from now.

Without his even asking her, Nancy told him, "When she leaves the hospital, she's going to come to stay with me. Matilda will be there during the day and I'll be there the rest of the time." Matilda was the Antiguan nanny who'd begun looking after the children once Nancy had gone back to work.

"That's good," he said.

"It's going to be a total recovery, but the rehab will take a long time."

He was to have driven into New York that very day to begin the search for an apartment for all of them; instead, after consulting Nancy, he went into the city to visit Phoebe at the hospital and then drove back to the shore that evening to resume his life there alone. Nancy, the twins, and himself—it had been a ridiculous idea to begin with, and unfair as well, an abdication of the pledge he'd made to himself after having moved to the shore, which was to insulate his all too responsive daughter from the fears and vulnerabilities of an aging man. Now that Phoebe was so ill, the change he'd imagined for them was impossible anyway, and he determined never to entertain any such plan for Nancy again. He could not let her see him as he was.

At the hospital, Phoebe lay there looking stunned. In addition to the slurred speech caused by the stroke, her voice was barely audible, and she was having difficulty swallowing. He had to sit right up against the hospital bed in order to understand what she was saying. They hadn't been this close to each other's limbs in over two decades, not since he'd gone off to Paris and was there with Merete when his own mother had the stroke that killed her.

"Paralysis is terrifying," she told him, staring down at the lifeless right arm by her side. He nodded. "You look at it," she said, "you tell it to move . . ." He waited while the tears rolled down her face and she struggled to finish the sentence. When she couldn't, he finished it for her. "And it doesn't," he said softly. Now she nodded, and he remembered the heated eruption of fluency that had come in the wake of his betrayal. How he wished she could scald him in that lava now. Anything, anything, an indictment, a protest, a poem, an ad campaign for American Airlines, a one-page ad for the *Reader's Digest*— anything as long as she could recover her speech! Playfully-full-of-words Phoebe, frank and open Phoebe, muzzled! "It's everything you can imagine," she painstakingly told him.

Her beauty, frail to begin with, was smashed and broken, and tall as she was, under the hospital sheets she looked shrunken and already on the way to decomposing. How could the doctor dare to tell Nancy that the mercilessness of what had befallen her mother would leave no enduring mark? He leaned forward to touch her hair, her soft white hair, doing his best not to cry himself and remembering again—the migraines, Nancy's birth, the day he'd come upon Phoebe Lambert at the agency, fresh, frightened, intriguingly innocent, a properly raised girl and, unlike Cecilia, unclouded by a crushing history of childhood chaos, everything about her sound and sane, blessedly not prone to outbursts, and yet without her being at all simple: the very best in the way of naturalness that Quaker Pennsylvania and Swarthmore College could produce. He remembered her reciting from memory for him, unostentatiously and in flawless Middle English, the prologue to *The Canterbury Tales* and, too, the surprising antique locutions she'd picked up from her starchy father, things like "We must be at pains to understand this" and "It is not going too far to say," which could have made him fall for her even without that first glimpse of her striding single-mindedly by his open office door, a mature young woman, the only one in the office who wore no lipstick, tall and bosomless, her fair hair pulled back to reveal the length of her neck and the delicate small-lobed ears of a child. "Why do you laugh sometimes at what I say," she asked him the second time he took her to dinner, "why do you laugh when I'm being perfectly serious?" "Because you charm me so, and you're so unaware of your charm." "There's so much to learn," she said while he accompanied her home in the taxi; when he replied softly, without a trace of the urgency he felt, "I'll teach you," she had to cover her face with her hands. "I'm blushing. I blush," she said. "Who doesn't?" he told her, and he believed that she'd blushed because she thought he was referring not to the subject of their conversation—all the art she'd never seen—but to sexual ardor, as indeed he was. He wasn't thinking in the taxi of showing her the Rembrandts at the Metropolitan Museum but of her long fingers and her wide mouth, though soon enough he'd take her not just to the Metropolitan but to the Modern, the Frick, and the Guggenheim. He remembered her removing her bathing suit out of sight in the dunes. He remembered them, later in the afternoon, swimming back together across the bay. He remembered how everything about this candid, unaffected woman was so unpredictably exciting. He remembered the nobility of her straightness. Against her own grain, she sparkled. He recalled telling her, "I can't live without you," and Phoebe's replying, "Nobody has ever said that to me before," and his admitting, "I've never said it before myself."

The summer of 1967. She was twenty-six.

Then the next day came news of the former colleagues, the same men he worked with and often ate lunch alongside while they were all with the agency. One was a creative supervisor named Brad Karr, who'd been hospitalized for suicidal depression; the second was Ezra Pollock, who had terminal cancer at seventy; and the third, his boss, was a gentle, lucid bigwig who walked around with the company's most profitable accounts in his pocket, who was almost maternal toward his favorites, who had been suffering for years with heart trouble and the aftereffects of a stroke, and whose picture he was stunned to see in the obituary section of the *Times*: "Clarence Spraco, Wartime Eisenhower Aide and Advertising Innovator, Dies at 84."

He immediately called Clarence's wife at their retirement home up in the Berkshires.

"Hello, Gwen," he said.

"Hi, dear. How are you?"

"I'm okay. How are you doing?" he asked.

"I'm doing all right. My kids came. I have a lot of company. And a lot of help. There are so many things I could tell you. In a sense, I was prepared, and in a way one never is. When I came home I found him dead on the floor, and that was a terrible shock. He had been dead for a couple of hours at that point. He seemed to have died at lunchtime. I had gone out for lunch, and so forth. You know, for him it was a good end. It was sudden, and he didn't have another stroke that would have debilitated him and put him in the hospital."

"Was it a stroke or was it a heart attack?" he asked her.

"It was a myocardial infarct."

"Had he been feeling ill?"

"Well, his blood pressure had been—well, he had a lot of trouble with his blood pressure. And then this past weekend he wasn't feeling so great. His blood pressure had gone up again."

"They couldn't control that with drugs?"

"They did. He took all kinds of drugs. But he probably had a lot of arterial damage. You know, bad old arteries, and there's a point at which the body wears out. And he was so weary at that point. He said to me just a couple of nights ago, 'I'm so weary.' He wanted to live, but there wasn't anything anybody could do to keep him alive any longer. Old age is a battle, dear, if not with this, then with that. It's an unrelenting battle, and just when you're at your weakest and least able to call up your old fight."

"That was a very nice tribute to him in the obituary today. They recognized that he was someone special. I wish I'd had a chance to tell them a few things about his wonderful ability to recognize the value of the people who worked with him. I saw his picture today," he said, "and I remembered a day years ago when a client had taken me to lunch at the Four Seasons, and we were heading down those stairs into the lobby there, and we bumped into Clarence. And my client was feeling expansive and he said, 'Clarence, how are you? Do you know this young art director?' And Clarence said, 'I do. Thank God I do. Thank

God the agency does.' He did this again and again, and not just with me."

"He had the highest regard for you, dear. He meant every word of that. I remember," she said, "how he plucked you out of the bullpen when you weren't at the agency even a year. He came home and told me about you. Clarence had an eye for creative talent, and he plucked you out of the bullpen and made you into an art director before you'd even completed your penal servitude working on brochures."

"He was good to me. I always thought of him as the general."

"He'd only been a colonel under Eisenhower."

"He was a general to me. I could tell you dozens of things that are in my mind now." Clarence's suggestion that he fuck his secretary in her apartment rather than in his office wasn't among them.

"Please do. When you talk about him, it's as if he's still here," Gwen said.

"Well, there was the time when we worked and worked every night for two or three weeks until after midnight, sometimes until two or three in the morning, for the Mercedes-Benz pitch. This was really one of the big ones, and we worked like hell, and we didn't get it. But when it was over Clarence said to me, 'I want you and your wife to go to London for a long weekend. I want you to stay at the Savoy because it's my favorite hotel, and I want you and Phoebe to have dinner at the Connaught. And it's on me.' In those days, this was a huge gift, and he gave it even though we'd lost the account. I wish I could have told that to the papers, and all the stories like it."

"Well, the press has been superb," Gwen said. "Even up here. There was an article about him in today's *Berkshire Eagle*. It was long, with a wonderful picture, and very laudatory. They made much of what he'd done in the war and about his being the army's youngest full colonel. I think Clarence would have been amused and contented by the recognition he's gotten."

"Look, you sound, for the moment, okay."

"Well, of course, it's okay now—I'm busy and I've got lots of company. The hard part is going to be when I'm alone."

"What are you going to do? Are you going to stay on in Massachusetts?"

"Yes, I am, for now. I discussed it with Clarence. I said, 'If I'm the one who's left, I'm going to sell the house and go back to New York.' But the kids want me not to do that, because they think I ought to give myself a year."

"Probably they're right. People regret, sometimes, the actions they take right off."

"I think so," she said. "And how is Nancy?"

"She's fine."

"Whenever I think of Nancy as a child, a smile comes to my face. She was pure life. I remember the two of you singing 'Smile' together at our house. We were living in Turtle Bay. It was an afternoon so long ago. You'd taught it to her. She must have been all of six. 'Smile, tho' your heart is aching'—how does it go?—'smile even tho' it's breaking—' You bought her the Nat 'King' Cole record. Remember? I do."

"I do too."

"Does she? Does Nancy?"

"I'm sure she does. Gwen, my heart and thoughts are with you."

"Thank you, dear. So many people have called. The phone has been going steadily for two days. So many people have wept, so many people have told me what he meant to them. If Clarence could only see all this. He knew his value to the company, but you know he also needed the same reassurances that everyone needs in this world."

"Well, he was awfully important to all of us. Look, we'll talk more," he said.

"Okay, dear. I so appreciate your calling."

It took him a while to go back to the phone with a voice he could trust. Brad Karr's wife told him the Manhattan hospital where Brad was a psychiatric patient. He was able to dial Brad's room directly, remembering as he did the time they'd done that slice-of-life commercial for Maxwell House coffee, when they were kids in their twenties, just starting out together, teamed up as a copywriter and an art director, and they broke the bank on the day-after recall score. They got a 34, the highest score in the history of Maxwell House. It was the day of the group Christmas party, and Brad, knowing Clarence would be coming, had his sidekick make cardboard buttons saying "34," and everybody wore them, and Clarence stopped by just to congratulate Brad and him and even put on a button, and they were on their way.

"Hello, Brad? Your old buddy calling from the Jersey Shore."

"Hi. Hello there."

"What's up, kid? I called your house a few minutes ago. I just had a yen to talk to you after all this time, and Mary told me you were in the hospital. That's how I've reached you. How are you doing?"

"Well, I'm doing all right. As such things go."

"How are you feeling?"

"Well, there are better places to be."

"Is it awful?"

"It could be worse. I mean, this happens to be a pretty good one. It's okay. I don't recommend it for a holiday, but it's been all right."

"How long have you been there?"

"Oh, about a week." Mary Karr had just told him that it had been a month at this point, and that it was his second stay in a year, and that things hadn't been so great in between. Brad's speech was very slow and faltering—probably from the medication—and heavy with hopelessness. "I expect I'll be out soon," he said.

"What do you do all day?"

"Oh, you cut out paper dolls. Things like that. I wander up and down the hallways. Try to keep my sanity."

"What else?"

"Take therapy. Take drugs. I feel like I'm a depository for every drug you can name."

"In addition to the antidepressant, there's other stuff?"

"Yeah. It's mostly a downer. It's not the tranquilizers, it's the antidepressants. They're working, I think."

"Are you able to sleep?"

"Oh yeah. At first there was a little problem, but now they've gotten that part straightened out."

"Do you talk to a doctor during the day?"

"Yeah." Brad laughed, and for the first time sounded something like himself. "He doesn't do any good. He's nice. He tells you to buck up and everything's going to be all right."

"Bradford, remember when you were pissed at Clarence about something and gave him two weeks' notice? I told you not to leave. You said, 'But I've resigned.' 'Rescind your resignation,' I said. And you did. Who else but Clarence and what other agency would have put up with that crap from a copywriter? You did it twice, as I remember. And stayed another ten years."

He'd gotten Brad to laugh again. "Yeah, I was always nuts," Brad said.

"We worked together for a lot of years. Endless silent hours together, hundreds and hundreds, maybe thousands and thousands of silent hours together in your office or mine trying to figure things out."

"That was something," Brad said.

"You bet it was. *You* were something. And don't forget it."

"Thanks, buddy."

"And so what about leaving?" he asked Brad. "When do you think that's going to happen?"

"Well, I don't really know. I imagine it's a matter of a couple of weeks. Since I've been here I've been far less depressed than when I was out. I feel almost composed. I think I'm going to recover."

"That's good news. I'll call you again. I hope to speak to you under better circumstances very shortly."

"Okay. Thanks for calling," Brad said. "Thanks a lot. I'm awfully glad you called."

After hanging up, he wondered: Did he know it was me? Did he truly remember what I remembered? From the voice alone I can't imagine he'll ever get out of there.

Then the third call. He couldn't stop himself from making it, though learning of Brad's hospitalization and Clarence's death and seeing the damage caused by Phoebe's stroke had given him enough to ponder for a while. As did Gwen's reminding him of his teaching Nancy to sing "Smile" like Nat "King" Cole. This call was to Ezra Pollock, who wasn't expected to live out the month but who, astonishingly, when he answered the phone, sounded like someone happy and fulfilled and no less cocky than usual.

"Ez," he said, "what's cookin'? You sound elated."

"I rise to conversation because conversation is my only recreation."

"And you're not depressed?"

"Not at all. I don't have time to be depressed. I'm all concentration." Laughing, Ezra said, "I see through everything now."

"Yourself included?"

"Yes, believe it or not. I've stripped away my bullshit and I'm getting down to brass tacks at last. I've begun my memoir of the advertising business. Before you go, you've got to face the facts, Ace. If I live, I'll write some good stuff."

"Well, don't forget to include how you'd walk into my office and say, 'Okay, here's your panic deadline—first thing tomorrow I need that storyboard in my hand.'"

"It worked, didn't it?"

"You were diligent, Ez. I asked you one time why that fucking detergent *was* so gentle to a lady's delicate hands. You gave me twenty pages on aloes. I got the art director's award for that campaign, and it was because of those pages. It should have been yours. When you get better we'll have lunch and I'll bring you the statue."

"That's a deal," Ez said.

"And how's the pain? Is there pain?"

"Yes, there is, I have it. But I've learned how to handle it. I've got special medicines and I've got five doctors. Five. An oncologist, a urologist, an internist, a hospice nurse, and a hypnotist to help me overcome the nausea."

"The nausea from what, from therapy?"

"Yeah, and the cancer gives you nausea too. I throw up liberally."

"Is that the worst of it?"

"Sometimes my prostate feels like I'm trying to excrete it."

"Can't they take it out?"

"It wouldn't do any good. It's too late for that. And it's a big operation. My weight is down. My blood is down. It would make me so weak and I'd have to give up the treatment, too.

It's a big lie that it moves slowly," Ezra said. "It moves like lightning. I didn't have anything in my prostate in the middle of June, but by the middle of August it had spread too far to cut it out. It really moves. So look to your prostate, my boy."

"I'm sorry to hear all this. But I'm glad to hear that you sound as you do. You're yourself, only more so."

"All I want is to write this memoir," Ez said. "I've talked about it long enough, now I have to write it. All that happened to me in that business. If I can write this memoir, I will have told people who I am. If I can write that, I'll die with a grin on my face. How about you, are you working happily? Are you painting? You always said you would. Are you?"

"Yes, I do it. I do it every day. It's fine," he lied.

"Well, I could never write this book, you know. Once I retired I immediately had blocks. But as soon as I got cancer most of my blocks fell away. I can do whatever I want now."

"That's a brutal therapy for writer's block."

"Yeah," Ez said, "I think it is. I don't advise it. You know, I may make it. Then we'll have that lunch and you'll give me the statue. If I make it, the doctors say I can have a normal life."

If he already had a hospice nurse, it seemed unlikely that the doctors would have said such a thing. Though maybe they had to lift his spirits, or maybe he'd imagined they had, or maybe it was just arrogance speaking, that wonderful, ineradicable arrogance of his. "Well, I'm rooting for you, Ez," he said. "If you should want to speak to me, here's my number." He gave it to him.

"Good," Ezra said.

"I'm here all the time. If you feel in the mood, do it, call me. Anytime. Will you?"

"Great. I will."

"All right. Very good. Bye."

"Bye. Bye for now," Ezra said. "Polish up the statue."

For hours after the three consecutive calls—and after the predictable banality and futility of the pep talk, after the attempt to revive the old esprit by reviving memories of his colleagues' lives, by trying to find things to say to buck up the hopeless and bring them back from the brink—what he wanted to do was not only to phone and speak to his daughter, whom he found in the hospital with Phoebe, but to revive his own esprit by phoning and talking to his mother and father. Yet what he'd learned was nothing when measured against the inevitable onslaught that is the end of life. Had he been aware of the mortal suffering of every man and woman he happened to have known during all his years of professional life, of each one's painful story of regret and loss and stoicism, of fear and panic and isolation and dread, had he learned of every last thing they had parted with that had once been vitally theirs and of how, systematically, they were being destroyed, he would have had to stay on the phone through the day and into the night, making another hundred calls at least. Old age isn't a battle; old age is a massacre.

When he next went to the hospital for the annual checkup on his carotids, the sonogram revealed that the second carotid was now seriously obstructed and required surgery. This would make the seventh year in a row that he would have been hospitalized. The news gave him a jolt—particularly as he'd heard by phone that morning of Ezra Pollock's death—but at least he would have the same vascular surgeon and the operation in the same hospital, and this time he would know enough not to put up with a local anesthetic and instead to ask to be unconscious throughout. He tried so hard to convince himself from the experience of the first carotid surgery that there was nothing to worry about, he did not bother to tell Nancy about the pending operation, especially while she still had her mother to tend to. He did, however, make a determined effort to locate Maureen Mrazek, though within only hours he had exhausted any clues he might have had to her whereabouts.

That left Howie, whom by then he hadn't phoned in some time. It was as though once their parents were long dead all sorts of impulses previously proscribed or just nonexistent had been loosed in him, and his giving vent to them, in a sick man's rage—in the rage and despair of a joyless sick man unable to steer clear of prolonged illness's deadliest trap, the contortion of one's character—had destroyed the last link to the dearest people he'd known. His first love affair had been with his brother. The one solid thing throughout his life had been his admiration for this very good man. He'd made a mess of all his marriages, but throughout their adult lives he and his brother had been truly constant. Howie never had to be asked for anything. And now he'd lost him, and in the same way he'd lost Phoebe—by doing it to himself. As if there weren't already fewer and fewer people present who meant anything to him, he had completed the decomposition of the original family. But decomposing families was his specialty. Hadn't he robbed three children of a coherent childhood and the continuous loving protection of a father such as he himself had cherished, who had belonged exclusively to him and Howie, a father they and no one else had owned?

At the realization of all he'd wiped out, on his own and for seemingly no good reason, and what was still worse, against his every intention, *against his will*—of his harshness toward a brother who had never once been harsh to him, who'd never failed to soothe him and come to his aid, of the effect his leaving their households had had on his children—at the humiliating realization that not only physically had he now diminished into someone he did not want to be, he began striking his chest with his fist, striking in cadence with his self-admonition, and missing by mere inches his defibrillator. At that moment, he knew far better than Randy or Lonny ever could where he was insufficient. This ordinarily even-tempered man struck furiously at his heart like some fanatic at prayer, and, assailed by remorse not just for this mistake but for all his mistakes, all the ineradicable, stupid, inescapable mistakes—swept away by the misery of his limitations yet acting as if life's every incomprehensible contingency were of his making—he said aloud, "Without even Howie! To wind up like this, without even him!"

At Howie's ranch in Santa Barbara there was a comfortable guest cottage nearly as large as his condo. Years back he, Phoebe, and Nancy had stayed there for two weeks one summer while Howie and his family were vacationing in Europe. The pool was just outside the door, and Howie's horses were off in the hills, and the staff had made their meals and looked after them. Last he knew, one of Howie's kids—Steve, the oceanographer—was temporarily living there with a girlfriend. Did he dare to ask? Could he come right out and tell his brother that he'd like to stay at the guest house for a couple of months until he could figure out where and how to live next? If he could fly out to

California after the surgery and enjoy his brother's company while beginning to recover . . .

He picked up the phone and dialed Howie. He got an answering machine and left his name and number. About an hour later he was called by Howie's youngest son, Rob. "My folks," Rob said, "are in Tibet." "Tibet? What are they doing in Tibet?" He believed they were in Santa Barbara and Howie just didn't want to take his call. "Dad went on business to Hong Kong, I believe to a board meeting, and my mother went with him. Then they went off to see Tibet." "Are Westerners allowed in Tibet?" he asked his nephew. "Oh, sure," Rob said. "They'll be gone another three weeks. Is there a message? I can e-mail them. That's what I've been doing when people call." "No, no need," he said. "How are all your brothers, Rob?" "Everybody's doing okay. How about you?" "I'm coming along," he said, and hung up.

Well, he was thrice divorced, a one-time serial husband distinguished no less by his devotion than by his misdeeds and mistakes, and he would have to continue to manage alone. From here on out he would have to manage everything alone. Even in his twenties, when he'd thought of himself as square, and on into his fifties, he'd had all the attention from women he could have wanted; from the time he'd entered art school it never stopped. It seemed as though he were destined for nothing else. But then something unforeseen happened, unforeseen and unpredictable: he had lived close to three quarters of a century, and the productive, active way of life was gone. He neither possessed the productive man's male allure nor was capable of germinating the masculine joys, and he tried not to long for them too much. On his own he had felt for a while that the missing component would somehow return to make him inviolable once again and reaffirm his mastery, that the entitlement mistakenly severed would be restored and he could resume where he'd left off only a few years before. But now it appeared that like any number of the elderly, he was in the process of becoming less and less and would have to see his aimless days through to the end as no more than what he was —the aimless days and the uncertain nights and the impotently putting up with the physical deterioration and the terminal sadness and the waiting and waiting for nothing. This is how it works out, he thought, this is what you could not know.

The man who swam the bay with Nancy's mother had arrived at where he'd never dreamed of being. It was time to worry about oblivion. It was the remote future.

One Saturday morning less than a week before the scheduled surgery—after a night of horrible dreaming when he'd awakened struggling to breathe at three A.M. and had to turn on all the lights in the apartment to calm his fears and was only able to fall back to sleep with the lights still burning—he decided it would do him good to go to New York to see Nancy and the twins and to visit Phoebe again, who was now at home with a nurse. Normally his deliberate independence constituted his bedrock strength; it was why he could take up a new life in a new place unconcerned over leaving friends and family behind. But ever since he'd abandoned any hope of living with Nancy or staying with Howie, he felt himself turning into a childlike creature who was weakening by the day. Was it the imminence of the seventh annual hospitalization that was crushing his confidence? Was it the prospect of coming steadily to be dominated by medical thoughts to the exclusion of everything else? Or was it the realization that with each hospital stay, going back to childhood and proceeding on up to his imminent surgery, the number of presences at his bedside diminished and the army he'd begun with had dwindled to none? Or was it simply the foreboding of helplessness to come?

What he had dreamed was that he was lying naked beside Millicent Kramer, from his art class. He was holding her cold dead body in bed the way he'd held Phoebe the time the migraine had got so bad that the doctor came to give her a morphine shot, which suppressed the pain but produced terrifying hallucinations. When he'd awakened in the night and turned on all the lights, he drank some water and threw open a window and paced the apartment to restore his stability, but despite himself he was thinking about only one thing: how it had been for her to kill herself. Did she do it in a rush, gobbling down the pills before she changed her mind? And after she'd finally taken them, did she scream that she didn't want to die, that she

just couldn't face any more crippling pain, that all she wanted
was for the pain to stop—scream and cry that all she wanted was
for Gerald to be there to help her and to tell her to hang on
and to assure her that she could bear it and that they were in it
together? Did she die in tears, mumbling his name? Or did she
do it all calmly, convinced at long last that she was not making
a mistake? Did she take her time, contemplatively holding the
pill bottle in her two hands before emptying the contents into
her palm and slowly swallowing them with her last glass of
water, with the last taste of water ever? Was she resigned and
thoughtful, he wondered, courageous about everything she was
leaving behind, perhaps smiling while she wept and remembered all the delights, all that had ever excited her and pleased
her, her mind filled with hundreds of ordinary moments that
meant little at the time but now seemed to have been especially
intended to flood her days with commonplace bliss? Or had
she lost interest in what she was leaving behind? Did she show
no fear, thinking only, At last the pain is over, the pain is finally
gone, and now I have merely to fall asleep to depart this amazing thing?

But how does one voluntarily choose to leave our fullness
for that endless nothing? How would he do it? Could he lie
there calmly saying goodbye? Had he Millicent Kramer's
strength to eradicate everything? She was his age. Why not? In
a bind like hers, what's a few years more or less? Who would
dare to challenge her with leaving life precipitously? I must, I
must, he thought, my six stents tell me I must one day soon
fearlessly say goodbye. But leaving Nancy—I can't do it! The
things that could happen to her on the way to school! His
daughter left behind with no more of him for protection than
their biological bond! And he bereft for eternity of her morning phone calls! He saw himself racing in every direction at
once through downtown Elizabeth's main intersection—the
unsuccessful father, the envious brother, the duplicitous husband, the helpless son—and only blocks from his family's jewelry store crying out for the cast of kin on whom he could not
gain no matter how hard he pursued them. "Momma, Poppa,
Howie, Phoebe, Nancy, Randy, Lonny—if only I'd known
how to do it! Can't you hear me? I'm leaving! It's over and I'm
leaving you all behind!" And those vanishing as fast from him

as he from them turned just their heads to cry out in turn, and all too meaningfully, "Too late!"

Leaving—the very word that had conveyed him into breathless, panic-filled wakefulness, delivered alive from embracing a corpse.

He never made it to New York. Traveling north on the Jersey Turnpike, he remembered that just south of Newark Airport was the exit to the cemetery where his parents were buried, and when he reached there, he pulled off the turnpike and followed the road that twisted through a decrepit residential neighborhood and then past a grim old elementary school until it ended at a beat-up truck thoroughfare that bordered the five or so acres of Jewish cemetery. At the far end of the cemetery was a vacant street where driving instructors took their students to learn to make a U-turn. He edged the car slowly through the open, spiked gate and parked opposite a small building that must once have been a prayer house and was now a dilapidated, hollowed-out ruin. The synagogue that had administered the cemetery's affairs had been disbanded years ago when its congregants had moved to the Union, Essex, and Morris County suburbs, and it didn't look as if anyone was taking care of anything anymore. The earth was giving way and sinking around many of the graves, and footstones everywhere had tumbled onto their sides, and all this was not even in the original graveyard where his grandparents were buried, amid hundreds of darkened tombstones packed tightly together, but in the newer sections where the granite markers dated from the second half of the twentieth century. He had noticed none of this when they had assembled to bury his father. All he'd seen then was the casket resting on the belts that spanned the open grave. Plain and modest though it was, it took up the world. Then followed the brutality of the burial and the mouth full of dust.

In just the past month he had been among the mourners at two funerals in two different cemeteries in Monmouth County, both rather less dreary than this one, and less dangerous, too. During recent decades, aside from vandals who damaged and destroyed the stones and the outbuildings where his parents were buried, there were muggers who worked the cemetery as well. In broad daylight they preyed upon the elderly who would occasionally show up alone or in pairs to spend time visiting a family gravesite. At his father's burial he had been informed by the rabbi that, if he was on his own, it would be wisest to visit his mother and father during the High Holy Day period, when the local police department, at the request of a committee of cemetery chairmen, had agreed to provide protection for the observant who turned out to recite the appropriate psalms and remember their dead. He had listened to the rabbi and nodded his head, but as he did not number himself among the believers, let alone the observant, and had a decided aversion to the High Holy Days, he would never choose to come to the cemetery then.

The dead were the two women in his class who'd had cancer and who'd died within a week of each other. There were many people from Starfish Beach at these funerals. As he looked around he could not help speculating about who among them would be killed off next. Everyone thinks at some time or other that in a hundred years no one now alive will be on earth—the overwhelming force will sweep the place clean. But he was thinking in terms of days. He was musing like a marked man.

There was a short, plump elderly woman at both the funerals who wept so uncontrollably that she seemed more than a mere friend of the dead and instead, impossibly, the mother of both. At the second funeral, she stood and sobbed only a few feet from him and the overweight stranger next to him, who he assumed was her husband, even though (or perhaps because), with his arms crossed and his teeth clenched and his chin in the air, he remained strikingly aloof and apart from her, an indifferent spectator who refused any longer to put up with this person. If anything, her tears would seem to have aroused bitter contempt rather than sympathetic concern, because in the midst of the funeral, as the rabbi was intoning in English the words of the prayer book, the husband turned unbidden and impatiently asked, "You know why she's carrying on like that?" "I believe I do," he whispered back, meaning by this, It's because it is for her as it's been for me ever since I was a boy. It's because it is for her as it is for everyone. It's because life's most disturbing intensity is death. It's because death is so unjust. It's because once one has tasted life, death does not even seem natural. I had thought—*secretly I was certain*—that life goes on and on. "Well, you're wrong," the man said flatly, as though having read his mind. "She's like that all the time. That has been the story for fifty years," he added with an unforgiving scowl. "She's like that because she isn't eighteen anymore."

His parents were situated close to the perimeter of the cemetery, and it was a while before he found their graves by the iron fence that separated the last row of burial plots from a narrow side street that appeared to be a makeshift rest stop for truckers taking a break from their turnpike run. In the years since he'd last been here, he'd forgotten the effect the first sight of the headstone had on him. He saw their two names carved there, and he was incapacitated by the kind of sobbing that overpowers babies and leaves them limp. He elicited easily enough his last recollection of each of them—the hospital recollection —but when he tried to call up the earliest recollection, the effort to reach as far back as he could in their common past caused a second wave of feeling to overwhelm him.

They were just bones, bones in a box, but their bones were his bones, and he stood as close to the bones as he could, as though the proximity might link him up with them and mitigate the isolation born of losing his future and reconnect him with all that had gone. For the next hour and a half, those bones were the things that mattered most. They were all that mattered, despite the impingement of the neglected cemetery's environment of decay. Once he was with those bones he could not leave them, couldn't not talk to them, couldn't but listen to them when they spoke. Between him and those bones there was a great deal going on, far more than now transpired between him and those still clad in their flesh. The flesh melts away but the bones endure. The bones were the only solace there was to one who put no stock in an afterlife and knew without a doubt that God was a fiction and this was the only life he'd have. As young Phoebe might have put it back when they first met, it was not going too far to say that his deepest pleasure now was at the cemetery. Here alone contentment was attainable.

He did not feel as though he were playing at something. He did not feel as though he were trying to make something come true. This *was* what was true, this intensity of connection with those bones.

His mother had died at eighty, his father at ninety. Aloud he said to them, "I'm seventy-one. Your boy is seventy-one." "Good. You lived," his mother replied, and his father said, "Look back and atone for what you can atone for, and make the best of what you have left."

He couldn't go. The tenderness was out of control. As was the longing for everyone to be living. And to have it all all over again.

He was walking back through the cemetery to his car when he came upon a black man digging a grave with a shovel. The man was standing about two feet down in the unfinished grave and stopped shoveling and hurling the dirt out to the side as the visitor approached him. He wore dark coveralls and an old baseball cap, and from the gray in his mustache and the lines in his face he looked to be at least fifty. His frame, however, was still thick and strong.

"I thought they did this with a machine," he said to the gravedigger.

"In big cemeteries, where they do many graves, a lot of times they use machines, that's right." He spoke like a Southerner, but very matter-of-factly, very precisely, more like a pedantic schoolteacher than a physical laborer. "I don't use a machine," the gravedigger continued, "because it can sink the other graves. The soil can give and it can crush in on the box. And you have the gravestones you have to deal with. It's just easier in my case to do everything by hand. Much neater. Easier to take the dirt away without ruining anything else. I use a real small tractor that I can maneuver easily, and I dig by hand."

Now he noticed the tractor in the grassy pathway between the graves. "The tractor's for what?"

"Use that to haul the dirt away. I've been doing it long enough that I know how much dirt to take away and how much dirt to leave. The first ten trailers of dirt I take away. Whatever's left I throw up on boards. I put down plywood boards. You can see 'em. I lay down three plywood boards so

the dirt doesn't sit on the grass itself. The last half of the dirt I
throw out onto the boards. To fill in afterwards. Then I cover
everything with this green carpet. Try to make it nice for the
family. So it looks like grass."

"How do you dig it? Mind if I ask?"

"Nope," said the gravedigger, still a couple feet down,
standing where he'd been digging. "Most folks don't care.
With most folks, the less they know the better."

"I want to know," he assured him. And he did. He did not
want to go.

"Well, I have a map. Shows every grave that's ever been sold
or laid out in the cemetery. With the map you locate the plot,
purchased who knows when, fifty years ago, seventy-five years
ago. Once I got it located I come here with a probe. There it
is. That seven-foot spike on the ground. I take this probe and
I go down two or three feet, and that's how I locate the next
grave over. Bang—you hit it and you hear it. And then I take a
stick and I mark on the ground where the new grave is. Then
I have a wood frame that I lay down on the ground and that's
what I cut the soil to. I take an edger first and I cut the sod to
the size of the frame. Then I size it down, make one-foot-
square pieces of sod, and put them back of the grave, out of
sight—because I don't want to make any kind of mess where
the funeral will be. The less dirt, the easier it is to clean up. I
don't ever want to leave a mess. I lay down a board back of the
grave next to it, where I can carry the squares of sod to it on
the fork. I lay 'em like a grid so it looks like where I took 'em
out. That takes about an hour. It's a hard part of the job. Once
I've done that, then I dig. I bring the tractor over, and my
trailer attached. What I do is, I dig first. That's what I'm doing
now. My son digs the hard part. He's stronger than I am now.
He likes to come in after I'm done. When he's busy or not
around I dig the whole thing myself. But when he's here I always let him dig the harder part. I'm fifty-eight. I don't dig like
I used to. When he started I had him here all the time, and
we'd take turns digging. That was fun because he was young
and it gave me time to talk to him, just the two of us alone."

"What did you talk to him about?"

"Not about graveyards," he said, laughing hard. "Not like
I'm talking to you."

"What then?"

"Things in general. Life in general. Anyway, I dig the first half. I use two shovels, a square shovel when the digging is easy and you can take more dirt, and then I use just a round pointed shovel, just a standard shovel. That's what you use for basic digging, a regular common shovel. If it's easy digging, especially in the spring when the ground isn't real solid, when the ground is wet, I use the big shovel and I can take out big shovelfuls and heave 'em into the trailer. I dig front to back, and I dig a grid, and as I go I use my edger to square the hole. I use that and a straight fork—they call it a spading fork. I use that to edge too, to bang down, cut the edges, and keep it square. You've got to keep it square as you go. The first ten loads go into the trailer and I take it over to an area in the cemetery where it's low and where we're filling that area, and I dump the trailer, come back, fill it up again. Ten loads. At that point I'm about halfway. That's about three foot."

"So from start to finish, how long does it take?"

"It'll take about three hours to do my end. Could even take four hours. Depends on the dig. My son's a good digger— takes him about two and a half hours more. It's a day's work. I usually come in about six in the morning, and my son comes in around ten. But he's busy now and I tell him he can do it when he wants. If the weather's hot, he'll come at night when it's cooler. With Jewish people we only get a day's notice, and we got to do it quick. At the Christian cemetery"—he pointed to the large, sprawling cemetery that lay across the road—"the undertakers will give us two or three days' notice."

"And you been doing this work how long?"

"Thirty-four years. A long time. It's good work. It's peaceful. Gives you time to think. But it's a lot of work. Starting to hurt my back. One day soon I'm turning it all over to my son. He'll take over and I'm moving back to where it's warm year round. Because, don't forget, I only told you about digging it. You got to come back and fill it up. That takes you three hours. Put the sod back, and so on. But let's go back to when the grave is dug. My son has finished up. He's squared it up, it's flat on the bottom. It's six foot deep, it looks good, you could jump down in the hole. Like the old guy used to say who I first dug with, it's got to be flat enough to lay a bed out on it. I used to laugh at him when he said that. But it's so: you've got this hole, six foot deep, and it's got to be right for the sake of the family and right for the sake of the dead."

"Mind if I stand here and watch?"

"Not at all. This is nice diggin'. No rocks. Straight in."

He watched him dig down with the shovel and then hoist up the dirt and heave it easily onto the plywood. Every few minutes he would use the tines of the fork to loosen up the sides and then choose one of the two shovels to resume the digging. Once in a while a small rock would strike the plywood, but mostly what came up out of the grave was moist brown soil that broke apart easily on leaving the shovel.

He was watching from beside the gravestone to the rear of which the gravedigger had laid out the square patches of sod that he would return to the plot after the funeral. The sod was fitted perfectly to the piece of plywood on which the patches rested. And still he did not want to go, not while by merely turning his head he could catch a glimpse of his parents' stone. He never wanted to go.

Pointing to the gravestone, the gravedigger said, "This guy here fought in World War Two. Prisoner of war in Japan. Helluva nice guy. Know him from when he used to come visit his wife. Nice guy. Always a decent guy. Got stuck with your car, the kind of guy who'd pull you out."

"So you know some of these people."

"Sure I do. There's a boy here, seventeen. Killed in a car crash. His friends come by and put beer cans on his grave. Or a fishing pole. He liked to fish."

He cleaned a clump of dirt from his shovel by banging it down on the plywood and then resumed digging. "Oops," he said, looking out across the cemetery to the street, "here she comes," and he instantly put aside the shovel and pulled off his soiled yellow work gloves. For the first time he stepped up out of the grave and banged each of his battered work shoes against the other to dislodge the dirt that was clinging to them.

An elderly black woman was approaching the open grave carrying a small plaid cooler in one hand and a thermos in the other. She was wearing running shoes, a pair of nylon slacks the color of the gravedigger's work gloves, and a blue, zippered New York Yankees team jacket.

The gravedigger said to her, "This is a nice gentleman who's been visiting with me this morning."

She nodded and handed him the cooler and the thermos, which he set down beside his tractor.

"Thank you, honey. Arnold still sleeping?"

"He's up," she said. "I made you two meat loaf and one baloney."

"That's good. Thank you."

She nodded again and then turned and went out of the cemetery, where she got into her car and drove away.

"That your wife?" he asked the gravedigger.

"That is Thelma." Smiling, he added, "She nourishes me."

"She isn't your mother."

"Oh, no, no—no, sir," said the gravedigger with a laugh, "not Thelma."

"And she doesn't mind coming out here?"

"You gotta do what you gotta do. That's her philosophy in a nutshell. What it comes down to for Thelma is just diggin' a hole. This is nothing special to her."

"You want to eat your lunch, so I'm going to leave you. But I want to ask—I wonder if you dug my parents' graves. They're buried over here. Let me show you."

The gravedigger followed him a ways until they could see clearly the site of his family stone.

"Did you dig those?" he asked him.

"Sure, I did them," the gravedigger said.

"Well, I want to thank you. I want to thank you for everything you've told me and for how clear you've been. You couldn't have made things more concrete. It's a good education for an older person. I thank you for the concreteness, and I thank you for being so careful and considerate when you dug my parents' graves. I wonder if I might give you something."

"I received my fee at the time, thank you."

"Yes, but I'd like to give you something for you and your son. My father always said, 'It's best to give while your hand is still warm.'" He slipped him two fifties, and as the gravedigger's large, roughened palm closed around the bills, he looked at him closely, at the genial, creased face and the pitted skin of the mustached black man who might someday soon be digging a hole for him that was flat enough at the bottom to lay a bed on.

*

In the days that followed he had only to yearn for them to conjure them up, and not merely the bone parents of the aging man but the flesh parents of the boy still in bud, off to the hospital on the bus with *Treasure Island* and *Kim* in the bag his mother balanced on her knees. A boy still in bud but because of her presence showing no fear and shoving aside all his thoughts about the bloated body of the seaman that he'd watched the Coast Guard remove from the edge of the oil-clotted beach.

He went in early on a Wednesday morning for the surgery on his right carotid artery. The routine was exactly as it had been for the surgery on the left carotid. He waited his turn in the anteroom with everyone else on the surgical schedule until his name was called, and in his flimsy gown and paper slippers he was accompanied by a nurse into the operating room. This time when he was asked by the masked anesthesiologist if he wanted the local or the general anesthetic, he requested the general so as to make the surgery easier to bear than it had been the first time around.

The words spoken by the bones made him feel buoyant and indestructible. So did the hard-won subjugation of his darkest thoughts. Nothing could extinguish the vitality of that boy whose slender little torpedo of an unscathed body once rode the big Atlantic waves from a hundred yards out in the wild ocean all the way in to shore. Oh, the abandon of it, and the smell of the salt water and the scorching sun! Daylight, he thought, penetrating everywhere, day after summer day of that daylight blazing off a living sea, an optical treasure so vast and valuable that he could have been peering through the jeweler's loupe engraved with his father's initials at the perfect, priceless planet itself—at his home, the billion-, the trillion-, the quadrillion-carat planet Earth! He went under feeling far from felled, anything but doomed, eager yet again to be fulfilled, but nonetheless, he never woke up. Cardiac arrest. He was no more, freed from being, entering into nowhere without even knowing it. Just as he'd feared from the start.

INDIGNATION

ACKNOWLEDGMENTS

The Chinese national anthem appears here in a World War Two translation of a song composed by Tian Han and Nieh Erh after the Japanese invasion of 1931; there are other translations of the song extant. During World War Two it was sung around the world by those allied with China in their struggle against the Empire of Japan. In 1949 it was adopted as the national anthem of the People's Republic of China.

Much of the dialogue attributed to Marcus Messner on pages 154–156 is taken almost verbatim from Bertrand Russell's lecture "Why I Am Not a Christian," delivered on March 6, 1927, at Battersea Town Hall, London, and collected by Simon and Schuster in 1957 in a volume of essays of the same name, edited by Paul Edwards and largely devoted to the subject of religion.

The quotations on pages 188–189 are taken from chapter 19 of *The Growth of the American Republic*, fifth edition, by Samuel Eliot Morison and Henry Steele Commager (Oxford University Press, 1962).

Olaf (upon what were once knees)
   does almost ceaselessly repeat
   "there is some shit I will not eat"

      —E. E. Cummings,
         "i sing of Olaf glad and big"

CONTENTS

Under Morphine

ABOUT TWO and a half months after the well-trained divisions of North Korea, armed by the Soviets and Chinese Communists, crossed the 38th parallel into South Korea on June 25, 1950, and the agonies of the Korean War began, I entered Robert Treat, a small college in downtown Newark named for the city's seventeenth-century founder. I was the first member of our family to seek a higher education. None of my cousins had gone beyond high school, and neither my father nor his three brothers had finished elementary school. "I worked for money," my father told me, "since I was ten years old." He was a neighborhood butcher for whom I'd delivered orders on my bicycle all through high school, except during baseball season and on the afternoons when I had to attend interschool matches as a member of the debating team. Almost from the day that I left the store—where I'd been working sixty-hour weeks for him between the time of my high school graduation in January and the start of college in September— almost from the day that I began classes at Robert Treat, my father became frightened that I would die. Maybe his fear had something to do with the war, which the U.S. armed forces, under United Nations auspices, had immediately entered to bolster the efforts of the ill-trained and underequipped South Korean army; maybe it had something to do with the heavy casualties our troops were sustaining against the Communist firepower and his fear that if the conflict dragged on as long as World War Two had, I would be drafted into the army to fight and die on the Korean battlefield as my cousins Abe and Dave had died during World War Two. Or maybe the fear had to do with his financial worries: the year before, the neighborhood's first supermarket had opened only a few blocks from our family's kosher butcher shop, and sales had begun steadily falling off, in part because of the supermarket's meat and poultry section's undercutting my father's prices and in part because of a general postwar decline in the number of families bothering to maintain kosher households and to buy kosher meat and chickens from a rabbinically certified shop whose owner was a member of the Federation of Kosher Butchers of New Jersey. Or maybe his fear for me began in fear for himself, for at the age of fifty, after enjoying a lifetime of robust good health, this sturdy little man began to develop the persistent racking cough that, troubling as it was to my mother, did not stop him from keeping a lit cigarette in the corner of his mouth all day long. Whatever the cause or mix of causes fueling the abrupt change in his previously benign paternal behavior, he manifested his fear by hounding me day and night about my whereabouts. Where were you? Why weren't you home? How do I know where you are when you go out? You are a boy with a magnificent future before you—how do I know you're not going to places where you can get yourself killed?

The questions were ludicrous since, in my high school years, I had been a prudent, responsible, diligent, hardworking A student who went out with only the nicest girls, a dedicated debater, and a utility infielder for the varsity baseball team, living happily enough within the adolescent norms of our neighborhood and my school. The questions were also infuriating—it was as though the father to whom I'd been so close during all these years, practically growing up at his side in the store, had no idea any longer of who or what his son was. At the store, the customers would delight him and my mother by telling them what a pleasure it was to watch the little one to whom they used to bring cookies—back when his father used to let him play with some fat and cut it up like "a big butcher," albeit using a knife with a dull blade—to watch him mature under their eyes into a well-mannered, well-spoken youngster who put their beef through the grinder to make chopped meat and who scattered and swept up the sawdust on the floor and who dutifully yanked the remaining feathers from the necks of the dead chickens hanging from hooks on the wall when his father called over to him, "Flick two chickens, Markie, will ya, for Mrs. So-and-So?" During the seven months before college he did more than give me the meat to grind and a few chickens to flick. He taught me how to take a rack of lamb and cut lamb chops out of it, how to slice each rib, and, when I got down to the bottom, how to take the chopper and chop off the rest of it. And he taught me always in the most easygoing way. "Don't hit your hand with the chopper and everything will be okay,"

he said. He taught me how to be patient with our more demanding customers, particularly those who had to see the
meat from every angle before they bought it, those for whom
I had to hold up the chicken so they could literally look up the
asshole to be sure that it was clean. "You can't believe what
some of those women will put you through before they buy
their chicken," he told me. And then he would mimic them:
"'Turn it over. No, *over*. Let me see the bottom.'" It was my
job not just to pluck the chickens but to eviscerate them. You
slit the ass open a little bit and you stick your hand up and you
grab the viscera and you pull them out. I hated that part.
Nauseating and disgusting, but it had to be done. That's what
I learned from my father and what I loved learning from him:
that you do what you have to do.

Our store fronted on Lyons Avenue in Newark, a block up
the street from Beth Israel Hospital, and in the window we
had a place where you could put ice, a wide shelf tilted slightly
down, back to front. An ice truck would come by to sell us
chopped ice, and we'd put the ice in there and then we'd put
our meat in so people could see it when they walked by. During the seven months I worked in the store full time before
college I would dress the window for him. "Marcus is the artist," my father said when people commented on the display. I'd
put everything in. I'd put steaks in, I'd put chickens in, I'd put
lamb shanks in—all the products that we had I would make
patterns out of and arrange in the window "artistically." I'd
take some ferns and dress things up, ferns that I got from the
flower shop across from the hospital. And not only did I cut
and slice and sell meat and dress the window with meat; during those seven months when I replaced my mother as his
sidekick I went with my father to the wholesale market early in
the morning and learned to buy it too. He'd be there once a
week, five, five-thirty in the morning, because if you went to
the market and picked out your own meat and drove it back to
your place yourself and put it in the refrigerator yourself, you
saved on the premium you had to pay to have it delivered.
We'd buy a whole quarter of the beef, and we'd buy a fore-
quarter of the lamb for lamb chops, and we'd buy a calf, and
we'd buy some beef livers, and we'd buy some chickens and
chicken livers, and since we had a couple of customers for

them, we would buy brains. The store opened at seven in the
morning and we'd work until seven, eight at night. I was
seventeen, young and eager and energetic, and by five I'd be
whipped. And there he was, still going strong, throwing
hundred-pound forequarters on his shoulders, walking in and
hanging them in the refrigerator on hooks. There he was, cutting and slicing with the knives, chopping with the cleaver,
still filling out orders at seven P.M. when I was ready to collapse. But my job was to clean the butcher blocks last thing
before we went home, to throw some sawdust on the blocks
and then scrape them with the iron brush, and so, marshaling
the energy left in me, I'd scrape out the blood to keep the
place kosher.

I look back at those seven months as a wonderful time—
wonderful except when it came to eviscerating chickens. And
even that was wonderful in its way, because it was something
you did, and did well, that you didn't care to do. So there was
a lesson in doing it. And lessons I loved—bring them on! And
I loved my father, and he me, more than ever before in our
lives. In the store, I prepared our lunch, his and mine. Not only
did we eat our lunch there but we cooked our lunch there, on
a small grill in the backroom, right next to where we cut up
and prepared the meat. I'd grill chicken livers for us, I'd grill
little flank steaks for us, and never were we two happier together. Yet only shortly afterward the destructive struggle between us began: Where were you? Why weren't you home?
How do I know where you are when you go out? You are a
boy with a magnificent future before you—how do I know
you're not going to places where you can get yourself killed?

During that fall I began Robert Treat as a freshman, whenever my father double-locked our front and back doors and I
couldn't use my keys to open either and I had to pound on one
or the other door to be let in if I came home at night twenty
minutes later than he thought I ought to, I believed he had
gone crazy.

And he had: crazy with worry that his cherished only child
was as unprepared for the hazards of life as anyone else entering manhood, crazy with the frightening discovery that a little
boy grows up, grows tall, overshadows his parents, and that

you can't keep him then, that you have to relinquish him to the world.

I left Robert Treat after only one year. I left because suddenly my father had no faith even in my ability to cross the street by myself. I left because my father's surveillance had become insufferable. The prospect of my independence made this otherwise even-tempered man, who only rarely blew up at anyone, appear as if he were intent on committing violence should I dare to let him down, while I—whose skills as a cool-headed logician had made me the mainstay of the high school debating team—was reduced to howling with frustration in the face of his ignorance and irrationality. I had to get away from him before I killed him—so I wildly told my distraught mother, who now found herself as unexpectedly without influence over him as I was.

One night I got home on the bus from downtown about nine-thirty. I'd been at the main branch of the Newark Public Library, as Robert Treat had no library of its own. I had left the house at eight-thirty that morning and been away attending classes and studying, and the first thing my mother said was "Your father's out looking for you." "Why? Where is he looking?" "He went to a pool hall." "I don't even know how to shoot pool. What is he thinking about? I was studying, for God's sake. I was writing a paper. I was reading. What else does he think I do night and day?" "He was talking to Mr. Pearlgreen about Eddie, and it got him all riled up about you." Eddie Pearlgreen, whose father was our plumber, had graduated from high school with me and gone on to college at Panzer, in East Orange, to learn to become a high school phys-ed teacher. I'd played ball with him since I was a kid. "I'm not Eddie Pearlgreen," I said, "I'm me." "But do you know what he did? Without telling anybody, he drove all the way to Pennsylvania, to Scranton, in his father's car to play pool in some kind of special pool hall there." "But Eddie's a pool shark. I'm not surprised he went to Scranton. Eddie can't brush his teeth in the morning without thinking about pool. I wouldn't be surprised if he went to the moon to play pool. Eddie pretends with guys who don't know him that he's only at their level of skill, and then they play and he beats the pants off them for as

much as twenty-five dollars a game." "He'll end up stealing
cars, Mr. Pearlgreen said." "Oh, Mother, this is ridiculous.
Whatever Eddie does has no bearing on me. Will *I* end up
stealing cars?" "Of course not, darling." "I don't like this game
Eddie likes, I don't like the atmosphere he likes. I'm not interested in the low life, Ma. I'm interested in things that matter. I
wouldn't so much as stick my head in a pool hall. Oh, look,
this is as far as I go explaining what I am and am not like. I will
not explain myself one more time. I will not make an inventory
of my attributes for people or mention my goddamn sense of
duty. I will not take one more round of his ridiculous, nonsen-
sical crap!" Whereupon, as though following a stage direction,
my father entered the house through the back door, still all
charged up, reeking of cigarette smoke, and angry now not
because he'd found me in a pool hall but because he hadn't
found me there. It wouldn't have dawned on him to go downtown and look for me at the public library—the reason being
that you can't get cracked over the head with a pool cue at the
library for being a pool shark or have someone pull a knife on
you because you are sitting there reading a chapter assigned
from Gibbon's *Decline and Fall of the Roman Empire*, as I'd
been doing since six that night.

"So *there* you are," he announced. "Yeah. Strange, isn't it? At
home. I sleep here. I live here. I am your son, remember?"
"Are you? I've been everywhere looking for you." "Why?
Why? Somebody, please, tell me why 'everywhere.'" "Because if
anything were to happen to you—if something were ever to
happen to you—" "But nothing will happen. Dad, I am not
this terror of the earth who plays pool, Eddie Pearlgreen!
Nothing is going to happen." "I know that you're not him, for
God's sake. I know better than anybody that I'm lucky with
my boy." "Then what is this all about, Dad?" "It's about life,
where the tiniest misstep can have tragic consequences." "Oh,
Christ, you sound like a fortune cookie." "Do I? Do I? Not
like a concerned father but like a fortune cookie? That's what I
sound like when I'm talking to my son about the future he has
ahead of him, which any little thing could destroy, the tiniest
thing?" "Oh, the hell with it!" I cried, and ran out of the house,
wondering where I could find a car to steal to go to Scranton
to play pool and maybe pick up the clap on the side.

Later I learned from my mother the full circumstances of that day, about how Mr. Pearlgreen had come to see about the toilet at the back of the store that morning and left my father brooding over their conversation from then until closing time. He must have smoked three packs of cigarettes, she told me, he was so upset. "You don't know how proud of you he is," my mother said. "Everybody who comes into the store—'My son, all A's. Never lets us down. Doesn't even have to look at his books—automatically, A's.' Darling, when you're not present you are the focus of all his praise. You must believe that. He boasts about you all the time." "And when I *am* present I'm the focus of these crazy new fears, and I'm sick and tired of it, Ma." My mother said, "But I heard him, Markie. He told Mr. Pearlgreen, 'Thank God I don't have to worry about these things with my boy.' I was there with him in the store when Mr. Pearlgreen came because of the leak. That's exactly what he said when Mr. Pearlgreen was telling him about Eddie. Those were his words: 'I don't have to worry about these things with my boy.' But what does Mr. Pearlgreen say back to him—and this is what started him off—he says, 'Listen to me, Messner. I like you, Messner, you were good to us, you took care of my wife during the war with meat, listen to somebody who knows from it happening to him. Eddie is a college boy too, but that doesn't mean he knows enough to stay away from the pool hall. How did we lose Eddie? He's not a bad boy. And what about his younger brother—what kind of example is he to his younger brother? What did we do wrong that the next thing we know he's in a pool hall in Scranton, three hours from home! With my car! Where does he get the money for the gas? From playing pool! Pool! Pool! Mark my words, Messner: the world is waiting, it's licking its chops, to take your boy away.'" "And my father believes him," I said. "My father believes not what he sees with his eyes for an entire lifetime, instead he believes what he's told by the plumber on his knees fixing the toilet in the back of the store!" I couldn't stop. He'd been driven crazy by the chance remark of a plumber! "Yeah, Ma," I finally said, storming off to my room, "the tiniest, littlest things *do* have tragic consequences. He proves it!"

*

I had to get away but I didn't know where to go. I didn't know one college from another. Auburn. Wake Forest. Ball State. SMU. Vanderbilt. Muhlenberg. They were nothing but the names of football teams to me. Every fall I eagerly listened to the results of the college games on Bill Stern's Saturday evening sports roundup, but I had little idea of the academic differences between the contending schools. Louisiana State 35, Rice 20; Cornell 21, Lafayette 7; Northwestern 14, Illinois 13. *That* was the difference I knew about: the point spread. A college was a college—that you attended one and eventually earned a degree was all that mattered to a family as unworldly as mine. I was going to the one downtown because it was close to home and we could afford it.

And that was fine with me. At the outset of my mature life, before everything suddenly became so difficult, I had a great talent for being satisfied. I'd had it all through childhood, and in my freshman year at Robert Treat it was in my repertoire still. I was thrilled to be there. I'd quickly come to idolize my professors and to make friends, most of them from working families like my own and with little, if any, more education than my own. Some were Jewish and from my high school, but most were not, and it at first excited me to have lunch with them *because* they were Irish or Italian and to me a new category, not only of Newarker but of human being. And I was excited to be taking college courses; though they were rudimentary, something was beginning to happen to my brain akin to what had happened when I first laid eyes on the alphabet. And, too—after the coach had gotten me to choke up a few inches on the bat and to punch the ball over the infield and into the outfield instead of my mightily swinging as blindly as I had in high school—I had gained a first-string position on the tiny college's freshman baseball team that spring and was playing second base alongside a shortstop named Angelo Spinelli.

But primarily I was learning, discovering something new every hour of the school day, which was why I even enjoyed Robert Treat's being so small and unobtrusive, more like a neighborhood club than a college. Robert Treat was tucked away at the northern end of the city's busy downtown of office buildings, department stores, and family-owned specialty shops, squeezed between a triangular little Revolutionary War park where the bedraggled bums hung out (most of whom we knew by name) and the muddy Passaic. The college consisted of two undistinguished buildings: an old abandoned smoke-stained brick brewery down near the industrial riverfront that had been converted into classrooms and science labs and where I took my biology course and, several blocks away, across from the city's major thoroughfare and facing the little park that was what we had instead of a campus—and where we sat at noontime to eat the sandwiches we'd packed at dawn while the bums down the bench passed the muscatel bottle—a small four-story neoclassical stone building with a pillared entrance that from the outside looked just like the bank it had been for much of the twentieth century. The building's interior housed the college administrative offices and the makeshift classrooms where I took history, English, and French courses taught by professors who called me "Mr. Messner" rather than "Marcus" or "Markie" and whose every written assignment I tried to anticipate and complete before it was due. I was eager to be an adult, an educated, mature, independent adult, which was just what was terrifying my father, who, even as he was locking me out of our house to punish me for beginning to sample the minutest prerogatives of young adulthood, could not have been any more proud of my devotion to my studies and my unique family status as a college student.

My freshman year was the most exhilarating and most awful of my life, and that was why I wound up the next year at Winesburg, a small liberal arts and engineering college in the farm country of north-central Ohio, eighteen miles from Lake Erie and five hundred miles from our back door's double lock. The scenic Winesburg campus, with its tall, shapely trees (I learned later from a girlfriend they were elms) and its ivy-covered brick quadrangles set picturesquely on a hill, could have been the backdrop for one of those Technicolor college movie musicals where all the students go around singing and dancing instead of studying. To pay for my going to a college away from home, my father had to let go of Isaac, the polite, quiet Orthodox young fellow in a skullcap who'd begun to apprentice as an assistant after I started my first year of school, and my mother, whose job Isaac was supposed to have absorbed in time, had to take over again as my father's full-time partner. Only in this way could he make ends meet.

I was assigned to a dormitory room in Jenkins Hall, where I discovered that the three other boys I was to live with were Jews. The arrangement struck me as odd, first because I'd been expecting to have one roommate, and second because part of the adventure of going away to college in far-off Ohio was the chance it offered to live among non-Jews and see what that was like. Both my parents thought this a strange if not danger-ous aspiration, but to me, at eighteen, it made perfect sense. Spinelli, the shortstop—and a pre-law student like me—had become my closest friend at Robert Treat, and his taking me home to the city's Italian First Ward to meet his family and eat their food and sit around and listen to them talk with their accents and joke in Italian had been no less intriguing than my two-semester survey course in the history of Western civiliza-tion, where at each class the professor laid bare something more of the way the world went before I existed.

The dormitory room was long, narrow, smelly, and poorly lit, with double-decker bunk beds at either end of the worn floorboards and four clunky old wooden desks, scarred by use, pushed against the drab green walls. I took the lower bunk under an upper already claimed by a lanky, raven-haired boy in glasses named Bertram Flusser. He didn't bother to shake my hand when I tried to introduce myself but looked at me as though I were a member of a species he'd been fortunate enough never to have come upon before. The other two boys looked me over too, though not at all with disdain, so I intro-duced myself to them, and they to me, in a way that half con-vinced me that, among my roommates, Flusser was one of a kind. All three were junior English majors and members of the college drama society. None of them was in a fraternity.

There were twelve fraternities on the campus, but only two admitted Jews, one a small all-Jewish fraternity with about fifty members and the other a nonsectarian fraternity about half that size, founded locally by a group of student idealists, who took in anyone they could get their hands on. The remaining ten were reserved for white Christian males, an arrangement that no one could have imagined challenging on a campus that so prided itself on tradition. The imposing Christian fraternity

houses with their fieldstone façades and castlelike doors dominated Buckeye Street, the tree-lined avenue bisected by a small
green with a Civil War cannon that, according to the risqué
witticism repeated to newcomers, went off whenever a virgin
walked by. Buckeye Street led from the campus through the
residential streets of big trees and neatly kept-up old frame
houses to the one business artery in town, Main Street, which
was four blocks long, stretching from the bridge over Wine
Creek at one end to the railroad station at the other. Main was
dominated by the New Willard House, the inn in whose taproom alumni gathered on football weekends to drunkenly
relive their college days and where, through the college place-
ment office, I got a job Friday and Saturday nights, working as
a waiter for the minimum wage of seventy-five cents an hour
plus tips. The social life of the college of some twelve hundred
students was conducted largely behind the fraternities' massive
black studded doors and out on their expansive green lawns—
where, in virtually any weather, two or three boys could always
be seen tossing a football around.

My roommate Flusser had contempt for everything I said
and mocked me mercilessly. When I tried being agreeable with
him, he called me Prince Charming. When I told him to leave
me alone, he said, "Such thin skin for such a big boy." At night
he insisted on playing Beethoven on his record player after I
got into bed, and at a volume that didn't seem to bother my
other two roommates as much as it did me. I knew nothing
about classical music, didn't much like it, and besides, I needed
my sleep if I was to continue to hold down a weekend job and
get the kind of grades that had put me on the Robert Treat
Dean's List both semesters I was there. Flusser himself never
got up before noon, even if he had classes, and his bunk was
always unmade, the bedding hanging carelessly down over one
side, obscuring the view of the room from my bunk. Living in
close quarters with him was worse even than living with my
father during my freshman year—my father at least went off all
day to work in the butcher shop and, albeit fanatically, cared
about my well-being. All three of my roommates were going
to act in the college's fall production of *Twelfth Night*, a play
I'd never heard of. I had read *Julius Caesar* in high school,
Macbeth in my English literature survey course my first year of

college, and that was it. In *Twelfth Night*, Flusser was to play a character called Malvolio, and on the nights when he wasn't listening to Beethoven after hours he would lie in the bunk above me reciting his lines aloud. Sometimes he would strut about the room practicing his exit line, which was "I'll be revenged on the whole pack of you." From my bed I would plead, "Flusser, please, could you quiet it down," to which he would respond—by shouting or cackling or menacingly whispering—"I'll be revenged on the whole pack of you" once again.

Within only days of arriving on the campus, I began to look around the dormitory for somebody with an empty bunk in his room who would agree to have me as a roommate. That took several more weeks, during which time I reached the peak of my frustration with Flusser and, about an hour after I'd gone to bed one night, rose screaming from my bunk to yank a phonograph record of his from the turntable and, in the most violent act I'd ever perpetrated, to smash it against the wall.

"You have just destroyed Quartet Number Sixteen in F Major," he said, without moving from where he was smoking in the upper bunk, fully clothed and still in his shoes.

"I don't care! I'm trying to get to sleep!"

The bare overhead lights had been flipped on by one of the other two boys. Both of them were out of their bunk beds and standing in their Jockey shorts waiting to see what would happen next.

"Such a nice polite little boy," Flusser said. "So clean-cut. So upright. A bit rash with the property of others, but otherwise so ready and willing to be a human being."

"What's wrong with being a human being!"

"Everything," Flusser replied with a smile. "Human beings stink to high heaven."

"*You* stink!" I shouted. "You do, Flusser! You don't shower, you don't change your clothes, you never make your bed—you have got no consideration for *anyone*! You're either emoting your head off at four in the morning or playing music as loud as you can!"

"Well, I am not a nice boy like you, Marcus."

Here at last one of the others spoke up. "Take it easy," he

said to me. "He's just a pain in the ass. Don't take him so seriously."

"But I've got to get my sleep!" I cried. "I can't do my work without getting my sleep! I don't want to wind up getting sick, for Christ's sake!"

"Getting sick," said Flusser, adding to the smile a small derisive laugh, "would do you a world of good."

"He's crazy!" I shouted at the other two. "Everything he says is crazy!"

"You destroy Beethoven's Quartet in F Major," said Flusser, "and *I'm* the one who's crazy."

"Knock it off, Bert," said one of the other boys. "Shut up and let him go to sleep."

"After what the barbarian has done to my record?"

"Tell him you'll replace the record," the boy said to me. "Tell him you'll go downtown and buy him a new one. Go ahead, tell him, so we can all go back to bed."

"I'll buy you a new one," I said, seething at the injustice of it all.

"Thank you," Flusser said. "Thank you so much. You really are a nice boy, Marcus. Irreproachable. Marcus the well-washed, neatly dressed boy. You do the right thing in the end, just like Mama Aurelius taught you."

I replaced the record out of what I earned waiting tables in the taproom of the inn. I did not like the job. The hours were far shorter than those I put in for my father at the butcher shop and yet, because of the din and the excessive drinking and the stink of beer and cigarette smoke that pervaded the place, the work turned out to be more tiring and, in its way, as disgusting as the worst things I had to do at the butcher shop. I myself didn't drink beer or anything else alcoholic, I'd never smoked, and I'd never tried by shouting and singing at the top of my voice to make a dazzling impression on girls—as did any number of inebriates who brought their dates to the inn on Friday and Saturday nights. There were "pinning" parties held almost weekly in the taproom to celebrate the informal engagement of a Winesburg boy to a Winesburg girl by his presenting her with his fraternity pin for her to wear to class on the front of her sweater or blouse. Pinned as a junior, engaged as a senior, and married upon graduation—those were the innocent ends pursued by most of the Winesburg virgins during my own virginal tenure there.

There was a narrow cobblestone alleyway that ran back of the inn and the neighboring shops that fronted on Main Street, and students were in and out of the inn's rear door all evening long either to vomit or to be off alone to try to feel up their girlfriends and dry-hump them in the dark. To break up the necking sessions, every half hour or so one of the town's police cars would cruise slowly along the alleyway with its brights on, sending those desperate for an outdoor ejaculation scurrying for cover inside the inn. With rare exceptions, the girls at Winesburg were either wholesome-looking or homely, and they all appeared to know how to behave properly to perfection (which is to say, they appeared not to know how to misbehave or how to do anything that was considered improper), so when they got drunk, instead of turning raucous the way the boys did, they wilted and got sick. Even the ones who dared to step through the doorway into the alley to neck with their dates came back inside looking as though they'd gone out to the alley to have their hair done. Occasionally I would see a girl who attracted me, and while running back and forth with my pitchers of beer, I would turn my head to try to get a good look at her. Almost always I discovered that her date was the evening's most aggressively obnoxious drunk. But because I was being paid the minimum wage plus tips, I arrived promptly at five every weekend to begin setting up for the night and worked till after midnight, cleaning up, and throughout tried to maintain a professional waiterly air despite people's snapping their fingers at me to get my attention or whistling at me sharply with their fingers in their mouths and treating me more like a lackey than a fellow student who needed the work. More than a few times during the first weeks, I thought I heard myself being summoned to one of the rowdier tables with the words "Hey, Jew! Over here!" But, preferring to believe the words spoken had been simply "Hey, you! Over here!" I persisted with my duties, determined to abide by the butcher-shop lesson learned from my father: slit the ass open and stick your hand up and grab the viscera and pull them out; nauseating and disgusting, but it had to be done.

Invariably, after my nights of working at the inn, there would be beer sloshing about me in all my dreams: dripping from the tap in my bathroom, filling the bowl of my toilet when I flushed it, flowing into my glass from the cartons of milk that I drank with my meals at the student cafeteria. In my dreams, nearby Lake Erie, which bordered to the north on Canada and to the south on the United States, was no longer the tenth-largest freshwater lake on earth but the largest body of beer in the world, and it was my job to empty it into pitchers to serve to fraternity boys bellowing belligerently, "Hey, Jew! Over here!"

Eventually I found an empty bunk in a room on the floor below the one where Flusser had been driving me crazy and, after filing the appropriate papers with the secretary to the dean of men, moved in with a senior in the engineering school. Elwyn Ayers Jr. was a strapping, laconic, decidedly non-Jewish boy who studied hard, took his meals at the fraternity house where he was a member, and owned a black four-door LaSalle Touring Sedan built in 1940, the last year, as he explained to me, that GM manufactured that great automobile. It had been a family car when he was a kid, and now he kept it parked out back of the fraternity house. Only seniors were allowed to have cars, and Elwyn seemed to have his largely so as to spend his weekend afternoons tinkering with its impressive engine. After we'd come back from dinner—I took my macaroni and cheese in the cheerless student cafeteria with the other "independents" while he ate roast beef, ham, steak, and lamb chops with his fraternity brothers—he and I sat at separate desks facing the same blank wall and we did not speak all evening long. When we were finished studying, we washed up at the bank of sinks in the communal bathroom down the hall, got into our pajamas, muttered to each other, and went to sleep, I in the bottom bunk and Elwyn Ayers Jr. in the top.

Living with Elwyn was much like living alone. All I ever heard him talk about with any enthusiasm was the virtues of the 1940 LaSalle, with its wheel-base lengthened over previous models and with a larger carburetor that provided edged-up horsepower. In his quiet, flat Ohio accent, he'd make a dry crack that would cut off conversation when I felt like taking a break from studying to talk for a few minutes. But, lonely as it might sometimes be as Elwyn's roommate, I had at least rid myself of the destructive nuisance who was Flusser and could get on with getting my A's; the sacrifices my family was making to send me away to college made it imperative that I continue to get only A's.

As a pre-law student majoring in political science, I was taking The Principles of American Government and American History to 1865, along with required courses in literature, philosophy, and psychology. I was also enrolled in ROTC and had every expectation that when I graduated I would be sent to serve as a lieutenant in Korea. The war was by then into a second horrible year, with three-quarters of a million Chinese Communist and North Korean troops regularly staging massive offensives and, after taking heavy casualties, the U.S.-led United Nations forces responding by staging massive counter-offensives. All the previous year, the front line had moved up and down the Korean peninsula, and Seoul, the South Korean capital, had been captured and liberated four times over. In April 1951 President Truman had relieved General MacArthur of his command after MacArthur threatened to bomb and blockade Communist China, and by September, when I entered Winesburg, his replacement, General Ridgway, was in the difficult first stages of armistice negotiations with a Communist delegation from North Korea, and the war looked as though it could go on for years, with tens of thousands more Americans killed, wounded, and captured. American troops had never fought in any war more frightening than this one, facing as they did wave after wave of Chinese soldiers seemingly impervious to our firepower, often fighting them in the foxholes with bayonets and their bare hands. U.S. casualties already totaled more than one hundred thousand, any number of them fatalities of the frigid Korean winter as well as of the Chinese army's mastery of hand-to-hand combat and night fighting. Chinese Communist soldiers, attacking sometimes by the thousands, communicated not by radio and walkie-talkie—in many ways theirs was still a premechanized army—but by bugle call, and it was said that nothing was more terrifying than those bugles sounding in the pitch dark and swarms of the enemy, having stealthily infiltrated American lines, cascading with

weapons ablaze down on our weary men, prostrate from cold
and huddled for warmth in their sleeping bags.

The clash between Truman and MacArthur had resulted,
the previous spring, in a Senate investigation into Truman's
firing of the general that I followed in the paper along with the
war news, which I read obsessively from the moment I understood what might befall me if the conflict continued seesawing
back and forth with neither side able to claim victory. I hated
MacArthur for his right-wing extremism, which threatened to
widen the Korean conflict into an all-out war with China, and
perhaps even the Soviet Union, which had recently acquired
the atomic bomb. A week after being fired, MacArthur addressed a joint session of Congress; he argued for bombing
Chinese air bases in Manchuria and using Chiang Kai-shek's
Chinese nationalist troops in Korea, before concluding the
speech with his famous farewell, vowing himself to "just fade
away, an old soldier who tried to do his duty as God gave him
the light to see that duty." After the speech, some in the Republican Party began to promote the vainglorious general with
the patrician airs, who was already by then in his seventies, as
their nominee in the '52 presidential election. Predictably,
Senator Joseph McCarthy announced that the Democrat Truman's firing of MacArthur was "perhaps the greatest victory
the Communists have ever won."

One semester of ROTC—or "Military Science," as the program was designated in the catalogue—was a requirement for
all male students. To qualify as an officer and to enter the army
as a second lieutenant for a two-year stint in the Transportation Corps after graduation, a student had to take no fewer
than four semesters of ROTC. If you took only the one required semester, on graduating you would be just another guy
caught in the draft and, after basic training, could well wind up
as a lowly infantry private with an M-1 rifle and a fixed bayonet
in a freezing Korean foxhole awaiting the bugles' blare.

My Military Science class met one and a half hours a week.
From an educational perspective, it seemed to me a childish
waste of time. The captain who was our teacher appeared
dimwitted compared with my other teachers (who were themselves slow to impress me), and the material we read was of no
interest at all. "Rest the butt of your rifle on the ground with

the barrel to the rear. Hold the toe of the butt against your right shoe and on line with the toe. Hold the rifle between the thumb and fingers of your right hand . . ." Nonetheless, I applied myself on tests and answered questions in class so as to be sure I would be invited to take advanced ROTC. Eight older cousins—seven on my father's side and one on my mother's—had seen combat in World War Two, two of them lowly riflemen who'd been killed less than a decade back, one at Anzio in '43 and the other in the Battle of the Bulge in '44. I thought my chances for survival would be far better if I entered the army as an officer, especially if, on the basis of my college grades and my class standing—I was determined to become valedictorian—I was able to get transferred out of transportation (where I could wind up serving in a combat zone) and into army intelligence once I was in the service.

I wanted to do everything right. If I did everything right, I could justify to my father the expense of my being at college in Ohio rather than in Newark. I could justify to my mother her having to work full time in the store again. At the heart of my ambition was the desire to be free of a strong, stolid father suddenly stricken with uncontrollable fear for a grown-up son's well-being. Though I was enrolled in a pre-law program, I did not really care about becoming a lawyer. I hardly knew what a lawyer did. I wanted to get A's, get my sleep, and not fight with the father I loved, whose wielding of the long, razor-sharp knives and the hefty meat cleaver had made him my first fascinating hero as a little boy. I envisioned my father's knives and cleavers whenever I read about the bayonet combat against the Chinese in Korea. I knew how murderously sharp sharp could be. And I knew what blood looked like, encrusted around the necks of the chickens where they had been ritually slaughtered, dripping out of the beef onto my hands when I was cutting a rib steak along the bone, seeping through the brown paper bags despite the wax paper wrappings within, settling into the grooves crosshatched into the chopping block by the force of the cleaver crashing down. My father wore an apron that tied around the neck and around the back and it was always bloody, a fresh apron always smeared with blood within an hour after the store opened. My mother too was covered in blood. One day while slicing a piece of liver—which can slide or wiggle under your hand if you don't hold it down firmly enough—she cut her palm and had to be rushed to the hospital for twelve painful stitches. And, careful and attentive as I tried to be, I had nicked myself dozens of times and had to be bandaged up, and then my father would upbraid me for letting my mind wander while I was working with the knife. I grew up with blood—with blood and grease and knife sharpeners and slicing machines and amputated fingers or missing parts of fingers on the hands of my three uncles as well as my father—and I never got used to it and I never liked it. My father's father, dead before I was born, had been a kosher butcher (he was the Marcus I was named for, and he, because of his hazardous occupation, was missing half of one thumb), as were my father's three brothers, Uncle Muzzy, Uncle Shecky, and Uncle Artie, each of whom had a shop like ours in a different part of Newark. Blood on the slotted, raised wooden flooring back of the refrigerated porcelain-and-glass showcases, on the weighing scales, on the sharpeners, fringing the edge of the roll of wax paper, on the nozzle of the hose we used to wash down the refrigerator floor—the smell of blood the first thing that would hit me whenever I visited my uncles and aunts in their stores. That smell of carcass after it's slaughtered and before it's been cooked would hit me every time. Then Abe, Muzzy's son and heir apparent, was killed at Anzio, and Dave, Shecky's son and heir apparent, was killed in the Battle of the Bulge, and the Messners who lived on were steeped in *their* blood.

All I knew about becoming a lawyer was that it was as far as you could get from spending your working life in a stinking apron covered with blood—blood, grease, bits of entrails, everything was on your apron from constantly wiping your hands on it. I had gladly accepted working for my father when it was expected of me, and I had obediently learned everything about butchering that he could teach me. But he never could teach me to like the blood or even to be indifferent to it.

One evening two members of the Jewish fraternity knocked on the door of the room while Elwyn and I were studying and asked if I could come out to have a talk with them at the Owl, the student hangout and coffee shop. I stepped into the corridor and closed the door behind me so as not to disturb Elwyn. "I don't think I'm going to join a fraternity," I told them. "Well, you don't have to," one of them replied. He was the taller of the two and stood several inches taller than me and had that smooth, confident, easygoing way about him that reminded me of all those magically agreeable, nice-looking boys who'd served as president of the Student Council back in high school and were worshiped by girlfriends who were star cheerleaders or drum majorettes. Humiliation never touched these youngsters, while for the rest of us it was always buzzing overhead like the fly or the mosquito that won't go away. What did evolution have in mind by making but one out of a million look like the boy standing before me? What was the function of such handsomeness except to draw attention to everyone else's imperfection? I hadn't been wholly disregarded by the god of appearances, yet the brutal standard set by this paragon turned one, by comparison, into a monstrosity of ordinariness. While talking to him I had deliberately to look away, his features were so perfect and his looks that humbling, that shaming—that *significant*. "Why don't you have dinner at the house some night?" he asked me. "Come tomorrow night. It's roast beef night. You'll have a good meal, and you'll meet the brothers, and there's no obligation to do anything else." "No," I said. "I don't believe in fraternities." "Believe in them? What is there to believe in or not believe in? A group of like-minded guys come together for friendship and camaraderie. We play sports together, we hold parties and dances, we take our meals together. It can be awfully lonely here otherwise. You know that out of twelve hundred students on this campus, less than a hundred are Jewish. That's a pretty small percentage. If you don't get into our fraternity, the only other house that'll have a Jew is the nonsectarian house, and they don't have much going for them in the way of facilities or a social calendar. Look, to introduce myself—my name is Sonny Cottler." A mere mortal's name, I thought. How could that be, with those flashing black eyes and that deeply cleft chin and that helmet of wavy dark hair? And so confidently fluent besides. "I'm a senior," he said. "I don't want to pressure you. But our brothers have noticed you and seen you around, and they think you'd make a great addition to the house. You know, Jewish boys have only been coming here in any numbers since just before the war, so we're a relatively new fraternity on campus, and still we've won the Interfraternity Scholarship Cup more times than any other house at Winesburg. We have a lot of guys who study hard and go on to med school and law school. Think about it, why don't you? And give me a ring at the house if you decide you want to come over and say hello. If you want to stay for dinner, all the better."

The following night I had a visit from two members of the nonsectarian fraternity. One was a slight, blond-haired boy who I did not know was homosexual—like most heterosexuals my age, I didn't quite believe that anyone was homosexual—and the other a heavyset, friendly Negro boy, who did the talking for the pair. He was one of three Negroes in the whole student body—there were none on the faculty. The other two Negroes were girls, and they were members of a small nonsectarian sorority whose membership was drawn almost entirely from the tiny population of Jewish girls on the campus. There was no face deriving from the Orient to be seen anywhere; everyone was white and Christian, except for me and this colored kid and a few dozen more. As for the student homosexuals among us, I had no idea how many there were. I didn't understand, even while he was sleeping directly above me, that Bert Flusser was homosexual. That realization would arrive later.

The Negro said, "I'm Bill Quinby, and this is the other Bill, Bill Arlington. We're from Xi Delta, the nonsectarian fraternity."

"Before you go any further," I said, "I'm not joining a fraternity. I'm going to be an independent."

Bill Quinby laughed. "Most of the guys in our fraternity are guys who weren't going to join a fraternity. Most of the guys in our fraternity aren't guys who think like the ordinary male student on campus. They're against discrimination and unlike the guys whose consciences can tolerate their being members of fraternities that keep people out because of their race or their religion. You seem to me to be the sort of person who thinks that way yourself. Am I wrong?"

"Fellas, I appreciate your coming around, but I'm not going to join any fraternity."

"Might I ask why?" he said.

"I'd rather be on my own and study," I said.

Again Quinby laughed. "Well, there too, most of the guys in our fraternity are guys who prefer to be on their own and study. Why not come around and pay us a visit? We're not in any way Winesburg's conventional fraternity. We're a distinctive group, if I say so myself—a bunch of outsiders who have banded together because we don't belong with the insiders or share their interests. You seem to me to be somebody who'd be at home in a house like ours."

Then the other Bill spoke up, and with words pretty much like those uttered to me the night before by Sonny Cottler. "You can get awfully lonely on this campus living entirely on your own," he said.

"I'll take my chances," I said. "I'm not afraid of being alone. I've got a job and I've got my studies, and that doesn't leave much time for loneliness."

"I like you," Quinby said, laughing good-naturedly. "I like your certainty."

"And half the guys in your fraternity," I said, "have the same kind of certainty." The three of us laughed together. I liked these two Bills. I even liked the idea of belonging to a fraternity with a Negro in it—that *would* be distinctive, especially when I brought him home to Newark for the Messner family's big Thanksgiving dinner—but nonetheless I said, "I've got to tell you, I'm not in the market for anything more than my studies. I can't afford to be. Everything rides on my studies." I was thinking, as I often thought, especially on days when the news from Korea was particularly dire, of how I would go about maneuvering from the Transportation Corps into military intelligence after graduating as valedictorian. "That's what I came for and that's what I'm going to do. Thanks anyway."

That Sunday morning, when I made my weekly collect call home to New Jersey, I was surprised to learn that my parents knew about my visit from Sonny Cottler. To prevent my father's intruding in my affairs, I told the family as little as possible when I phoned. Mostly I assured them that I was feeling well and everything was fine. This sufficed with my mother, but my father invariably would ask, "So what else is going on? What else are you doing?" "Studying. Studying and working weekends at the inn." "And what are you doing to divert your-self?" "Nothing, really. I don't need diversions. I haven't the time." "Is there a girl in the picture yet?" "Not yet," I'd say. "You be careful," he'd say. "I will be." "You know what I mean," he'd say. "Yep." "You don't want to get in any trouble." I'd laugh and say, "I won't." "On your own like that—I don't like the sound of it," my father said. "I'm fine on my own." "And if you make a mistake," he said, "with nobody there to give you advice and see what you're up to—then what?"

That was the standard conversation, permeated throughout with his hacking cough. On this Sunday morning, however, no sooner did I call than he said, "So we understand you met the Cottler boy. You know who he is, don't you? His aunt lives here in Newark. She's married to Spector, who owns the office supply store on Market Street. His uncle is Spector. When we said where you were, she told us that her maiden name was Cottler, and her brother's family lives in Cleveland, and her nephew goes to the same college and is president of the Jewish fraternity. And president of the Interfraternity Council. A Jew and president of the Interfraternity Council. How about that? Donald. Donald Cottler. They call him Sonny, isn't that right?" "That's right," I said. "So he came around—wonderful. He's a basketball star, I understand, and a Dean's List student. So what did he tell you?" "He made a pitch for his fraternity." "And?" "I said I wasn't interested in fraternity life." "But his aunt says he's a wonderful boy. All A's, like you. And a hand-some boy, I understand." "Extremely handsome," I said wea-rily. "A dreamboat." "What's that supposed to mean?" he replied. "Dad, stop sending people to visit me." "But you're off there all by yourself. They gave you three Jewish room-mates when you arrived, and the first thing you do, you move out on them to find a Gentile and you room with him." "Elwyn is the perfect roommate. Quiet, considerate, neat, and he's studious. I couldn't ask for anyone better." "I'm sure, I'm sure, I have nothing against him. But then the Cottler boy comes around—" "Dad, I can't take any more of this." "But how do I know what's going on with you? How do I know what you're doing? You could be doing anything." "I do one thing," I said firmly. "I study and I go to class. And I make about eighteen bucks at the inn on the weekend." "And what would be wrong with having some Jewish friends in a place like that? Somebody to eat a meal with, to go to a movie with—" "Look, I know what I'm doing." "At eighteen years of age?" "Dad, I'm hanging up now. Mom?" "Yes, dear." "I'm hanging up. I'll speak to you next Sunday." "But what about the Cottler boy—" were the last of his words that I heard.

There *was* a girl, if not yet in the picture, one that I had my eye on. She was a sophomore transfer student like me, pale and slender, with dark auburn hair and with what seemed to me an aloofly intimidating, self-confident manner. She was enrolled in my American history class and sometimes sat right next to me, but because I didn't want to run the risk of her telling me to leave her alone, I hadn't worked up the courage to nod hello, let alone speak to her. One night I saw her at the library. I was sitting at a desk up in the stacks that overlooked the main reading room; she was at one of the long tables on the reading room floor, diligently taking notes out of a reference book. Two things captivated me. One was the part in her exquisite hair. Never before had I been so vulnerable to the part in someone's hair. The other was her left leg, which was crossed over her right leg and rhythmically swaying up and down. Her skirt fell midway down her calf, as was the style, but still, from where I was seated I could see beneath the table the unceasing movement of that leg. She must have remained there like that for two hours, steadily taking notes without a break, and all I did during that time was to look at the way that hair was parted in an even line and the way she never stopped moving her leg up and down. Not for the first time, I wondered what moving a leg like that felt like for a girl. She was absorbed in her homework, and I, with the mind of an eighteen-year-old boy, was absorbed in wanting to put my hand up her skirt. The strong desire to rush off to the bathroom was quelled by my fear that if I did so, I might get caught by a librarian or a teacher or even by an honorable student, be expelled from school, and wind up a rifleman in Korea.

That night, I had to sit at my desk until two A.M.—and with the gooseneck lamp twisted down to keep the glare of my light clear of Elwyn, asleep in the upper bunk—in order to finish the homework that I'd failed to do because of my being preoccupied with the auburn-haired girl's swinging leg.

What happened when I took her out exceeded anything I could have imagined in the library bathroom, had I the daring to retreat to one of the stalls there to relieve myself temporarily of my desire. The rules regulating the lives of the girls at Winesburg were of the sort my father wouldn't have minded their imposing on me. All female students, including seniors, had to sign in and out of their dormitories whenever they left in the evening, even to go to the library. They couldn't stay out past nine on weekdays or past midnight on Fridays and Saturdays, nor, of course, were they ever allowed in male dormitories or in fraternity houses except at chaperoned events, nor were men allowed inside the women's dorms other than to wait on a florally upholstered chintz sofa in the small parlor to pick up a date whom the attendant downstairs would summon on the house phone; the attendant would have gotten the young man's name from his student ID card, which he was required to show her. Since students other than seniors were prohibited from having cars on campus—and in a college with a preponderantly middle-class student body, only a few seniors had families who could provide for a car or its upkeep—there was almost no place where a student couple could be alone together. Some went out to the town cemetery and conducted their sex play against the tombstones or even down on the graves themselves; others got away with what little they could at the movies; but mostly, after evening dates, girls were thrust up against the trunks of trees in the dark of the quadrangle containing the three women's dorms, and the misdeeds that the parietal regulations were intended to curb were partially perpetrated among the elms that beautified the campus. Mainly there was no more than fumbling and groping through layers of clothing, but among the male students the passion for satisfaction even that meager was boundless. Since evolution abhors unclimactic petting, the prevailing sexual code could be physically excruciating. Prolonged excitation that failed to result in orgasmic discharge could set strapping young men to hobbling about like cripples until the searing, stabbing, cramping pain of the widespread testicular torture known as blue balls would slowly diminish and pass away. On a weekend night at Winesburg, blue balls constituted the norm, striking down dozens between, say, ten and midnight, while ejaculation, that most pleasant and natural of remedies, was the ever-elusive, unprecedented event in the erotic career of a student libidinally at his lifetime's peak of performance.

My roommate, Elwyn, loaned me his black LaSalle the night I took out Olivia Hutton. It was a weeknight, when I wasn't working, and so we had to start out early to get her back to her dormitory by nine. We drove to L'Escargot, the fanciest restaurant in Sandusky County, about ten miles down Wine Creek from the college. She ordered snails, the featured dish, and I didn't, not only because I'd never had them and couldn't imagine eating them, but because I was trying to keep the cost down. I took her to L'Escargot because she seemed far too sophisticated for a first date at the Owl, where you could get a hamburger, french fries, and a Coke for under fifty cents. Besides, as out of place as I felt at L'Escargot, I felt more so at the Owl, whose patrons were usually jammed into booths together alongside members of their own fraternities or sororities and, as far as I could tell, spoke mostly about social events of the previous weekend or those of the weekend to come. I had enough of them and their socializing while waiting tables at the Willard.

She ordered the snails and I didn't. She was from wealthy suburban Cleveland and I wasn't. Her parents were divorced and mine weren't, nor could they possibly be. She'd transferred from Mount Holyoke back to Ohio for reasons having to do with her parents' divorce, or so she said. And she was even prettier than I had realized in class. I'd never before looked her in the eyes long enough to see the size of them. Nor had I noticed the transparency of her skin. Nor had I dared to look at her mouth long enough to realize how full her upper lip was and how provocatively it protruded when she spoke certain words, words beginning with "m" or "w" or "wh" or "s" or "sh," as in the commonplace affirmation "Sure," which Olivia pronounced as though it rhymed with "purr" and I as though it rhymed with "cure."

After we'd been speaking for some ten or fifteen minutes, she surprisingly reached across the table to touch the back of my hand. "You're so intense," she said. "Relax."

"I don't know how to," I said, and though I meant it as a lighthearted, self-effacing joke, it happened to be true. I was always working on myself. I was always pursuing a goal. Delivering orders and flicking chickens and cleaning butcher blocks and getting A's so as never to disappoint my parents. Shortening up on the bat to just meet the ball and get it to drop between the infielders and the outfielders of the opposing team. Transferring from Robert Treat to get away from my father's unreasonable strictures. Not joining a fraternity in order to concentrate exclusively on my studies. Taking ROTC dead seriously in an attempt not to wind up dead in Korea. And now the goal was Olivia Hutton. I'd taken her to a restaurant whose cost came to nearly half of a weekend's earnings because I wanted her to think I was, like her, a worldly sophisticate, and simultaneously I wanted dinner to end almost before it had begun so that I could get her into the car's front seat and park somewhere and touch her. To date, the limit of my carnality was touching. I'd touched two girls in high school. Each had been a girlfriend for close to a year. Only one had been willing to touch me back. I had to touch Olivia because touching her was the only path to follow if I was to lose my virginity before I graduated from college and went into the army. There—yet another goal: despite the trammels of convention still rigidly holding sway on the campus of a middling little midwestern college in the years immediately after World War Two, I was determined to have intercourse before I died.

After dinner, I drove out beyond the campus to the edge of town to park on the road alongside the town cemetery. It was already a little after eight, and I had less than an hour to get her back to the dormitory and inside the doors before they were locked for the night. I didn't know where else to park, even though I was fearful of the police car that patrolled the alley back of the inn pulling up behind Elwyn's car with its brights on and one of the cops coming around on foot to shine a flashlight into the front seat and to ask her, "Everything all right, Miss?" That's what the cops said when they did it, and in Winesburg they did it all the time.

So I had the cops to worry about, and the late hour—8:10—when I cut off the engine of the LaSalle and turned to kiss her. Without a fuss she kissed me back. I instructed myself, "Avoid rejection—stop here!" but the advice was fatuous, and my erection concurred. I delicately slipped my hand under her coat and unbuttoned her blouse and moved my fingers onto her bra. In response to my beginning to fondle her through the cloth cup of her bra, she opened her mouth wider and continued kissing me, now with the added enticement of the stimulus of her tongue. I was alone in a car on an unlit road with my hand moving around inside someone's blouse and her tongue moving around inside my mouth, the very tongue that lived alone down in the darkness of her mouth and that now seemed the most promiscuous of organs. Till that moment I was wholly innocent of anyone's tongue in my mouth other than my own. That alone nearly made me come. That alone was surely enough. But the rapidity with which she had allowed me to proceed—and that darting, swabbing, gliding, teeth-licking tongue, the tongue, which is like the body stripped of its skin—prompted me to attempt to delicately move her hand onto the crotch of my pants. And again I met with no resistance. *There was no battle.*

What happened next I had to puzzle over for weeks afterward. And even dead, as I am and have been for I don't know how long, I try to reconstruct the mores that reigned over that campus and to recapitulate the troubled efforts to elude those mores that fostered the series of mishaps ending in my death at the age of nineteen. Even now (if "now" can be said to mean anything any longer), beyond corporeal existence, alive as I am here (if "here" or "I" means anything) as memory alone (if "memory," strictly speaking, is the all-embracing medium in which I am being sustained as "myself"), I continue to puzzle over Olivia's actions. Is that what eternity is for, to muck over a lifetime's minutiae? Who could have imagined that one would have forever to remember each moment of life down to its tiniest component? Or can it be that this is merely the afterlife that is mine, and as each life is unique, so too is each afterlife, each an imperishable fingerprint of an afterlife unlike anyone else's? I have no means of telling. As in life, I know only what is, and in death what is turns out to be what was. You are not just shackled to your life while living it, you continue to be stuck with it after you're gone. Or, again, maybe I do, I alone.

Who could have told me? And would death have been any less terrifying if I'd understood that it wasn't an endless nothing but consisted instead of memory cogitating for eons on itself? Though perhaps this perpetual remembering is merely the anteroom to oblivion. As a nonbeliever, I assumed that the afterlife was without a clock, a body, a brain, a soul, a god—without anything of any shape, form, or substance, decomposition absolute. I did not know that it was not only *not* without remembering but that remembering would *be* the everything. I have no idea, either, whether my remembering has been going on for three hours or for a million years. It's not memory that's obliviated here—it's time. There is no letup—for the afterlife is without sleep as well. Unless it's all sleep, and the dream of a past forever gone is with the deceased one forever. But dream or no dream, here there is nothing to think about but the bygone life. Does that make "here" hell? Or heaven? Better than oblivion or worse? You would imagine that at least in death uncertainty would vanish. But inasmuch as I have no idea where I am, what I am, or how long I am to remain in this state, uncertainty appears to be enduring. This is surely not the spacious heaven of the religious imagination, where all of us good people are together again, happy as can be because the sword of death is no longer hanging over our heads. For the record, I have a strong suspicion that you can die here too. You can't go forward here, that's for sure. There are no doors. There are no days. The direction (for now?) is only back. And the judgment is endless, though not because some deity judges you, but because your actions are naggingly being judged for all time by yourself.

If you ask how this can be—memory upon memory, nothing but memory—of course I can't answer, and not because neither a "you" nor an "I" exists, any more than do a "here" and a "now," but because all that exists is the recollected past, not recovered, mind you, not relived in the immediacy of the realm of sensation, but merely replayed. And how much more of my past can I take? Retelling my own story to myself round the clock in a clockless world, lurking disembodied in this memory grotto, I *feel* as though I've been at it for a million years. Is this really to go on and on—my nineteen little years forever while everything else is absent, my nineteen little

years inescapably here, persistently present, while everything
that went into making real the nineteen years, while everything that put one squarely *in the midst of*, remains a phantasm
far, far away?

I could not believe then—ridiculously enough, I cannot still—
that what happened next happened because Olivia wanted it to
happen. That was not the way it went between a convention-
ally brought-up boy and a nice well-bred girl when I was alive
and it was 1951 and, for the third time in just over half a century, America was at war again. I certainly could never believe
that what happened might have anything to do with her finding me attractive, let alone desirable. What girl found a boy
"desirable" at Winesburg College? I for one had never heard
of such feelings existing among the girls of Winesburg or
Newark or anywhere else. As far as I knew, girls didn't get fired
up with desire like that; they got fired up by limits, by prohibi-
tions, by outright taboos, all of which helped to serve what
was, after all, the overriding ambition of most of the coeds
who were my contemporaries at Winesburg: to reestablish
with a reliable young wage earner the very sort of family life
from which they had temporarily been separated by attending
college, and to do so as rapidly as possible.

Nor could I believe that what Olivia did she did because she
enjoyed doing it. The thought was too astonishing even for an
open-minded, intelligent boy like me. No, what happened
could only be a consequence of something being wrong with
her, though not necessarily a moral or intellectual failing—in
class she struck me as mentally superior to any girl I'd ever
known, and nothing at dinner had led me to believe that her
character was anything but solid through and through. No,
what she did would have to have been caused by an abnormality. "It's because her parents are divorced," I told myself. There
was no other explanation for an enigma so profound.

When I got to the room later, Elwyn was still studying. I gave
him back the keys to the LaSalle, and he accepted them while
continuing to underline the text in one of his engineering
books. He was wearing his pajama bottoms and a T-shirt, and
four empty Coke bottles stood upright beside him on the desk.
He'd go through another four at least before packing it in

around midnight. I wasn't surprised by his not asking me about my date—he himself never went on dates and never attended his fraternity's social events. He had been a high school wrestler in Cincinnati but had given up sports in college to pursue his engineering degree. His father owned a tugboat company on the Ohio River, and his plan was to succeed his father someday as head of the firm. In pursuit of that goal he was even more single-minded than I was.

But how could I wash and get into my pajamas and go to sleep and say nothing to anyone about something so extraordinary having happened to me? Yet that's what I set out to do, and almost succeeded in doing, until, after lying in my bunk for about a quarter of an hour while Elwyn remained studying at his desk, I bolted upright to announce, "She blew me."

"Uh-huh," Elwyn said without turning his head from the page he was studying.

"I got sucked off."

"Yep," said Elwyn in due time, teasing out the syllable to signal that his attention was going to remain on his work regardless of what I might take it in my head to start going on about.

"I didn't even ask for it," I said. "I wouldn't have dreamed of asking for it. I don't even know her. And she blew me. Did you ever hear of that happening?"

"Nope," replied Elwyn.

"It's because her parents are divorced."

Now he turned to look at me. He had a round face and a large head and his features were so basic that they might have been modeled on those carved by a child for a Halloween pumpkin. Altogether he was constructed on completely utilitarian lines and did not look as though he had, like me, to keep a sharp watch over his emotions—if, that is, he had any of an unruly nature that required monitoring. "She tell you that?" he asked.

"She didn't say anything. I'm only guessing. She just did it. I pulled her hand onto my pants, and on her own, without my doing anything more, she unzipped my fly and took it out and did it."

"Well, I'm very happy for you, Marcus, but if you don't mind, I've got work to do."

"I want to thank you for the car. It wouldn't have happened without the car."

"Run all right?"

"Perfect."

"Should. Just greased 'er."

"She must have done it before," I said to Elwyn. "Don't you think?"

"Could be," Elwyn replied.

"I don't know what to make of it."

"That's clear."

"I don't know if I should see her again."

"Up to you," he said with finality, and so, in silence, I lay atop my bunk bed barely able to sleep for trying to figure out on my own what to think of Olivia Hutton. How could such bliss as had befallen me also be such a burden? I who should have been the most satisfied man in all of Winesburg was instead the most bewildered.

Strange as Olivia's conduct was when I thought about it on my own, it was more impenetrable still when she and I showed up at history class and, as usual, sat beside each other and I immediately resumed remembering what she had done—and what I had done in response. In the car, I had been so taken by surprise that I had sat straight up in the seat and looked down at the back of her head moving in my lap as if I were watching someone doing it to somebody other than me. Not that I had seen such a thing done before, other than in the stray "dirty picture"—always raggedy-edged and ratty-looking from being passed back and forth between so many hundreds of horny boys' hands—that would invariably be among the prized possessions of the renegade kid at the bottom of one's high school class. I was as transfixed by Olivia's complicity as by the diligence and concentration she brought to the task. How did she know what to do or how to do it? And what would happen if I came, which seemed a strong likelihood from the very first moment? Shouldn't I warn her—if there was time enough to warn her? Shouldn't I shoot politely into my handkerchief? Or fling open the car door and spray the cemetery street instead of one or the other of us? Yes, do that, I thought, come into the street. But, of course, I couldn't. The sheer unimaginableness of coming into her mouth—of coming into anything other than the air or a tissue or a dirty sock—was an allurement too stupendous for a novice to forswear. Yet Olivia said nothing.

All I could figure was that for a daughter of divorced parents, whatever she did or whatever was done to her was okay with her. It would be some time before it would dawn on me, as it has finally (millennia later, for all I know), that whatever I did might be okay with me, too.

Days passed and I didn't ask her out again. Nor after class, when we were all drifting into the hallway, did I try to talk to her again. Then, one chilly fall morning, I ran into her at the student bookstore. I can't say that I hadn't been hoping to run into her somewhere, despite the fact that when we met in class I didn't even acknowledge her presence. Every time I turned a corner on that campus, I was hoping not only to see her but to hear myself saying to her, "We have to go on another date. I have to see you. You have to become mine and no one else's!"

She was wearing a camel's hair winter coat and high woolen socks and over her auburn hair a snug white wool hat with a fleecy, red woven ball at the top. Directly in from the out-of-doors, with red cheeks and a slightly runny nose, she looked like the last girl in the world to give anyone a blowjob.

"Hello, Marc," she said.

"Oh, yes, hi," I said.

"I did that because I liked you so much."

"Pardon?"

She pulled off her hat and shook out her hair—thick and long and not cut short with a little crimp of curls over the forehead, as was the hairdo worn by most every other coed on the campus.

"I said I did that because I liked you," she told me. "I know you can't figure it out. I know that's why I haven't heard from you and why you ignore me in class. So I'm figuring it out for you." Her lips parted in a smile, and I thought, With those lips, she, without my urging, completely voluntarily . . . And yet I was the one who felt shy! "Any other mysteries?" she asked.

"Oh, no, that's okay."

"It's *not*," she said, and now she was frowning, and every time her expression changed her beauty changed with it. She wasn't one beautiful girl, she was twenty-five different beautiful girls. "You're a hundred miles away from me. No, it's not okay with you," she said. "I liked your seriousness. I liked your maturity at dinner—or what I took to be maturity. I made a joke about it, but I liked your intensity. I've never met anyone so intense before. I liked your looks, Marcus. I still do."

"Did you ever do that with someone else?"

"I did," she said, without hesitation. "Has no one ever done it with you?"

"No one's come close."

"So you think I'm a slut," she said, frowning again.

"Absolutely not," I rushed to assure her.

"You're lying. That's why you won't speak to me. Because I'm a slut."

"I was surprised," I said, "that's all."

"Did it ever occur to you that I was surprised too?"

"But you've done it before. You just told me you did."

"This was the second time."

"Were you surprised the first time?"

"I was at Mount Holyoke. It was at a party at Amherst. I was drunk. The whole thing was awful. I didn't know anything. I was drinking all the time. That's why I transferred. They suspended me. I spent three months at a clinic drying out. I don't drink anymore. I don't drink anything alcoholic and I won't ever again. This time when I did it I wasn't drunk. I wasn't drunk and I wasn't crazy. I wanted to do it to you not because I'm a slut but because I wanted to do it to you. I wanted to give you that. Can't you understand that I wanted to give you that?"

"It seems as though I can't."

"I–wanted–to–give–you–what–you–wanted. Are those words impossible to understand? They're almost all of one syllable. God," she said crossly, "what's wrong with *you*?"

The next time we were together in history class, she chose to sit in a chair at the back of the room so I couldn't see her. Now that I knew that she had had to leave Mount Holyoke because of drinking and that she'd had then to enter a clinic for three months to stop drinking, I had even stronger reasons to keep away from her. I didn't drink, my parents drank barely at all, and what business did I have with somebody who, not even twenty years old, already had a history of having been hospitalized for drinking? Yet despite my being convinced that I must have nothing further to do with her, I sent her a note through the campus mail:

Dear Olivia,

You think I've spurned you because of what happened in the car that night. I haven't. As I explained, it's because nothing approaching that had ever happened to me before. Just as no girl ever before has said to me anything resembling what you said in the bookstore. I had girlfriends whose looks I've liked and who I told how pretty they were, but no girl till you has ever said to me that she liked my looks or expressed admiration for anything else about me. That isn't the way it worked with any girl I've known before or that I've ever heard of—which is something that I've realized about my life only since you spoke your mind in the bookstore. You are different from anyone I've known, and the last thing you could ever be called is a slut. I think you're a wonder. You're beautiful. You're mature. You are, I admit, vastly more experienced than I am. That's what threw me. I was thrown. Forgive me. Say hello to me in class.

Marc

But she didn't say anything; she wouldn't even look my way. *She* wanted nothing further to do with *me*. I'd lost her, and not, I realized, because her parents were divorced but because mine were not.

No matter how often I told myself I was better off without her and that she drank for the same reason she'd given me the blowjob, I couldn't stop thinking about her. I was afraid of her. I was as bad as my father. I *was* my father. I hadn't left him back in New Jersey, hemmed in by his apprehension and unhinged by fearful premonitions; I had become him in Ohio.

When I phoned the dormitory, she wouldn't take my calls. When I tried to get her to talk with me after class, she walked away. I wrote again:

Dear Olivia,

Speak to me. See me. Forgive me. I'm ten years older than when we met. I'm a man.

Marc

Because of something puerile in those last three words—puerile and pleading and false—I carried the letter in my pocket for close to a week before I dropped it into the slotted box for campus mail in the dormitory basement.

I got this in return:

Dear Marcus,

I can't see you. You'll only run away from me again, this time when you see the scar across the width of my wrist. Had you seen it the night of our date I would have honestly explained it to you. I was prepared to do that. I didn't try to cover it up, but as it happened you failed to notice it. It's a scar from a razor. I tried to kill myself at Mount Holyoke. That's why I went for three months to the clinic. It was the Menninger Clinic in Topeka, Kansas. The Menninger Sanitarium and Psychopathic Hospital. There's the full name for you. My father is a doctor and he knows people there and that's where the family hospitalized me. I used the razor when I was drunk but I had been thinking about doing it for a long time, all that while I wasn't living but went from class to class acting as though I were living. Had I been sober I would have succeeded. So three cheers for ten rye and gingers—they're why I'm alive today. That, and my incapacity to carry anything out. Even suicide is beyond me. I cannot justify my existence even that way. Self-accusation is my middle name.

I don't regret doing what we did, but we mustn't do anything more. Forget about me and go on your way. There's no one around here like you, Marcus. You didn't just become a man—you've more than likely been one all your life. I can't ever imagine you as a "kid" even when you were one. And certainly never a kid like the kids around here. You are not a simple soul and have no business being here. If you survive the squareness of this hateful place, you're going to have a sterling future. Why did you come to Winesburg to begin with? I'm here *because* it's so square—that's supposed to make me a normal girl. But you? You should be studying philosophy at the Sorbonne and living in a garret in Montparnasse. We both should. Farewell, beauticious man!

Olivia

I read the letter twice over, then, for all the good it did me, shouted, "There's no one around here like you! You're no simple soul either!" I had seen her using her Parker 51 fountain pen to take notes in class—a brown-and-red tortoiseshell pen

—but I had never before seen her handwriting or how she signed her name with the nib of that pen, the narrow way she formed the "O," the strange height at which she dotted the two "i"s, the long graceful upswept tail at the end of the concluding "a." I put my mouth to the page and kissed the "O." Kissed it and kissed it. Then, impulsively, with the tip of my tongue I began to lick the ink of the signature, patiently as a cat at his milk bowl I licked away until there was no longer the "O," the "l," the "i," the "v," the second "i," the "a"— licked until the upswept tail was completely gone. I had drunk her writing. I had eaten her name. I had all I could do not to eat the whole thing.

That night I couldn't concentrate on my homework but remained riveted by her letter, read it again and again, read it from top to bottom, then from bottom to top, starting with "beauticious man" and ending with "I can't see you." Finally I interrupted Elwyn at his desk and asked him if he would read it and tell me what he thought. He was my roommate, after all, in whose company I spent hours studying and sleeping. I said, "I've never gotten a letter like this." That was the bewildering refrain all through that last year of my life: never before anything like this. Giving such a letter to Elwyn—Elwyn who wanted to operate a tugboat company on the Ohio River—was, of course, a big and very stupid mistake.

"This the one that blew you?" he said when he finished.

"Well—yes."

"In the car?"

"Well, you know that—yes."

"Great," he said. "All I need is for a cunt like that to slit her wrists in my LaSalle."

I was enraged by his calling Olivia a cunt and determined then and there to find a new room and a new roommate. It took a week for me to discover a vacancy on the top floor of Neil Hall, the oldest residence on the campus, dating from the school's beginnings as a Baptist seminary, and despite its exterior fire escapes, a building commonly referred to as The Firetrap. The room I found had been vacant for years before I again filed the appropriate papers with the secretary of the dean of men and moved in. It was tiny, at the far end of a hallway with a creaky wooden floor and a high, narrow dormer window that looked as though it hadn't been washed since Neil Hall was built, the year after the Civil War.

I had wanted to pack and leave my Jenkins Hall room without having to see Elwyn and explain to him why I was going. I wanted to disappear and never endure those silences of his again. I couldn't stand his silence and I couldn't stand what little he said—and how grudgingly he said it—when he deigned to speak. I hadn't realized how much I had disliked him even before he had called Olivia a cunt. The unbroken silences would make me think that he disapproved of me for some reason—because I was a Jew, because I wasn't an engineering student, because I wasn't a fraternity boy, because I wasn't interested in tinkering with car engines or manning tugboats, because I wasn't whatever else I wasn't—or that he just didn't care if I existed. Yes, he had loaned me his treasured LaSalle when I'd asked, which did momentarily seem to suggest that there was more fellow feeling between us than he was able or willing to make visible to me, or maybe just that he was sufficiently human to sometimes do something expansive and unexpected. But then he'd called Olivia a cunt, and I despised him for it. Olivia Hutton was a wonderful girl who'd somehow become a drunk at Mount Holyoke and had tragically tried to end her life with a razor blade. She wasn't a cunt. She was a heroine.

I was still packing my two suitcases when Elwyn unexpectedly appeared in the room in the middle of the day, walked right by me, gathered up two books from the end of his desk, and turned and started back out the door, as usual without saying anything.

"I'm moving," I told him.

"So?"

"Oh, fuck you," I said.

He set down the books and punched me in the jaw. I felt as if I were going to collapse, then as if I were going to be sick, then, holding my face where he'd struck me, to see whether I was bleeding or the bone was broken or the teeth were knocked out, I watched as he picked up the two books and made his exit.

I didn't understand Elwyn, didn't understand Flusser, didn't understand my father, didn't understand Olivia—I understood no one and nothing. (Another big theme of my life's last year.)

Why had a girl so pretty and so intelligent and so sophisticated wanted to die at the age of nineteen? Why had she become a drunk at Mount Holyoke? Why had she wanted to blow me? To "give" me something, as she put it? No, there was more than that to what she'd done, but what that might be I couldn't grasp. Everything couldn't be accounted for by her parents' divorce. And what difference would it make if it could? The more chagrined I became thinking about her, the more I wanted her; the more my jaw hurt, the more I wanted her. Defending her honor, I had been punched in the face for the first time in my life, and she didn't know it. I was moving into Neil Hall because of her, and she didn't know that either. I was in love with her, and she didn't know that—I had only just found out myself. (Another theme: only just finding things out.) I had fallen in love with an ex–teenage drunk and inmate of a psychiatric sanitarium who'd failed at suicide with a razor blade, a daughter of divorced parents, and a Gentile to boot. I had fallen in love with—or I had fallen in love with the folly of falling in love with—the very girl my father must have been imagining me in bed with on that first night he'd locked me out of the house.

> Dear Olivia,
>   I did see the scar at dinner. It wasn't hard to figure out how it got there. I didn't say anything, because if you didn't care to talk about it, why should I? I also surmised, when you told me that you didn't want anything to drink, that you were someone who once used to drink too much. Nothing in your letter comes as a surprise.
>   I would very much like it if we could at least get together to take a walk—

I was going to write "to take a walk down by Wine Creek" but didn't, for fear that she would think I was perversely suggesting that she might want to jump in. I didn't know what I was doing by lying to her about noticing the scar and then compounding the lie by saying I'd doped out her drinking all on my own. Until she'd told me of the drinking in her letter, and despite the drunkenness I witnessed each weekend while working at the Willard, I'd had no idea that anyone that young could even be an alcoholic. And as for accepting with equanimity the scar on her wrist—well, that scar, which I had not noticed the night of our date, was now all I could think about.

Was this moment to mark the beginning of a lifetime's accumulation of mistakes (had I been given a lifetime in which to make them)? I thought then that it marked, if anything, the beginning of my manhood. Then I wondered if the two had coincided. All I knew was that the scar did it. I was transfixed. I'd never been so worked up over anyone before. The history of drinking, the scar, the sanitarium, the frailty, the fortitude— I was in bondage to it all. To the heroism of it all.

I finished the letter:

> If you'd resume sitting next to me in History it would enable me to keep my mind on the class. I keep thinking of you sitting behind my back instead of thinking about what we're studying. I look over at the space previously occupied by your body, and the temptation to turn is a perpetual source of distraction— because, beauticious Olivia, I want nothing more than to be close to you. I love your looks and am nuts about your exquisite frame.

I debated whether to write "am nuts about your exquisite frame, scar and all." Would it appear insensitive of me to be making light of her scar, or would it appear a sign of my maturity to be making light of the scar? To play it safe, I didn't write "scar and all" but added a cryptic P.S.—"I am moving to Neil Hall because of a disagreement with my roommate"—and sent the letter off through the campus mail.

She did not return to sit beside me in class but chose to remain at the back of the classroom, out of my sight. I nonetheless ran off every day at noon to my mailbox in the basement of Jenkins to see if she had answered me. Every day for a week I looked into an empty box, and when a letter finally appeared it was from the dean of men.

> Dear Mr. Messner:
> It has come to my attention that you have taken up residence in Neil Hall after having already briefly occupied two separate rooms in Jenkins. I am concerned about so many changes of residence on the part of a transfer student who has been at Winesburg as a sophomore for less than a semester. Will you

please arrange with my secretary to come to my office sometime this week? A short meeting is in order, one that I'm sure
will prove useful to both of us.

> Yours sincerely,
> Hawes D. Caudwell,
> Dean of Men

The meeting with Dean Caudwell was scheduled for the following Wednesday, fifteen minutes after chapel ended at noon.
Though Winesburg became a nonsectarian college only two
decades after it was founded as a seminary, one of the last ves-
tiges of the early days, when attending religious services was a
daily practice, lay in the strict requirement that a student attend chapel, between eleven and noon on Wednesdays, forty
times before he or she graduated. The religious content of the
sermons had been diluted into—or camouflaged as—a talk on
a high moral topic, and the speakers were not always clergy-
men: there were occasional religious luminaries like the president of the United Lutheran Church in America, but once or
twice a month the speakers were faculty members from
Winesburg or nearby colleges, or local judges, or legislators
from the state assembly. More than half the time, however,
chapel was presided over and the lectern occupied by Dr.
Chester Donehower, the chairman of Winesburg's religion
department and a Baptist minister himself, whose continuing
topic was "How to Take Stock of Ourselves in the Light of
Biblical Teachings." There was a robed choir of some fifty students, about two-thirds of whom were young women, and
every week they sang a Christian hymn to open and close the
hour; the Christmas and Easter programs featured the choir
singing renditions of seasonal music and were the most popular chapels of the year. Despite the school's having by then
been secularized for nearly a century, chapel was held not in
any of the college's public halls but in a Methodist church, the
most imposing church in town, located halfway between Main
Street and the campus, and the only one large enough to accommodate the student body.

I objected strongly to everything about attending chapel,
beginning with the venue. I didn't think it fair to have to sit in
a Christian church and listen for forty-five or fifty minutes to

Dr. Donehower or anyone else preach to me against my will in order for me to qualify for graduation from a secular institution. I objected not because I was an observant Jew but because I was an ardent atheist.

Consequently, at the end of my first month at Winesburg, after having listened to a second sermon from Dr. Donehower even more cocksure about "Christ's example" than the first, I went directly from the church back up to the campus and headed for the library's reference section to sift through the college catalogues collected there, to look for another college to transfer to, one where I could continue to be free of my father's surveillance but where I would not be forced to compromise my conscience by listening to biblical hogwash that I could not bear being subjected to. So as to be free of my father, I'd chosen a school fifteen hours by car from New Jersey, difficult to reach by bus or train, and more than fifty miles from the nearest commercial airport—but with no understanding on my part of the beliefs with which youngsters were indoctrinated as a matter of course deep in the heart of America.

To make it through Dr. Donehower's second sermon, I had found it necessary to evoke my memory of a song whose fiery beat and martial words I had learned in grade school when World War Two was raging and our weekly assembly programs, designed to foster the patriotic virtues, consisted of us children singing in unison the songs of the armed services: the navy's "Anchors Aweigh," the army's "The Caissons Go Rolling Along," the air corps' "Off We Go into the Wild Blue Yonder," the marine corps' "From the Halls of Montezuma," along with the songs of the Seabees and the WACs. We also sang what we were told was the national anthem of our Chinese allies in the war begun by the Japanese. It went as follows:

> Arise, ye who refuse to be bondslaves!
> With our very flesh and blood
> We will build a new Great Wall!
> China's masses have met the day of danger.
> Indignation fills the hearts of all of our countrymen,
> Arise! Arise! Arise!
> Every heart with one mind,

Brave the enemy's gunfire,
March on!
Brave the enemy's gunfire,
March on! March on! March on!

I must have sung this verse to myself fifty times during the course of Dr. Donehower's second sermon, and then another fifty during the choir's rendering of their Christian hymns, and every time giving special emphasis to each of the four syllables that melded together form the noun "indignation."

The office of the dean of men was among a number of administrative offices lining the corridor of the first floor of Jenkins Hall. The men's dormitory, where I had slept in a bunk bed first beneath Bertram Flusser and then beneath Elwyn Ayers, occupied the second and third floors. When I entered his office from the anteroom, the dean came around from behind his desk to shake my hand. He was lean and broad-shouldered, with a lantern jaw, sparkling blue eyes, and a heavy crest of silver hair, a tall man probably in his late fifties who still moved with the agility of the young athletic star he'd been in three sports at Winesburg just before World War One. There were photos of championship Winesburg athletic teams on his walls, and a bronzed football was displayed on a stand back of his desk. The only books in the office were the volumes of the college's yearbook, the *Owl's Nest*, arranged in chronological order in a glass-enclosed case behind him.

He motioned for me to take a seat in the chair across from his, and while returning to his side of the desk, he said amiably, "I wanted you to come in so we could meet and find out if I can be of any help to you in adjusting to Winesburg. I see by your transcript"—he lifted from his desk a manila folder he'd been riffling through when I entered—"that you earned straight A's for your freshman year. I wouldn't want anything at Winesburg to interfere in the slightest with such a stellar record of academic achievement."

My undershirt was saturated with perspiration before I even sat down to stiffly speak my first few words. And, of course, I was still overwrought and agitated from just having left chapel, not only because of Dr. Donehower's sermon but because of my own savage interior vocalizations of the Chinese national anthem. "Neither do I, sir," I replied.

I had not expected to hear myself saying "sir" to the dean, though it was not that unusual for timidity—taking the form of great formality—to all but overwhelm me whenever I first had to confront a person of authority. Though my impulse wasn't exactly to grovel, I had to fight off a strong sense of intimidation, and invariably I would manage this only by speaking with somewhat more bluntness than the interview required. Repeatedly I'd leave such encounters scolding myself for the initial timidity and then for the unnecessary candor by which I overcame it and swearing in the future to answer with the utmost brevity any questions put to me and otherwise to keep myself calm by shutting my mouth.

"Do you see any potential difficulties on the horizon here?" the dean asked me.

"No, sir. I don't, sir."

"How are things going with your classwork?"

"I believe well, sir."

"You're getting all you hoped for from your courses?"

"Yes, sir."

This wasn't strictly speaking true. My professors were either too starchy or too folksy for my taste, and during these first months on campus, I hadn't as yet found any as spellbinding as those I'd had during my freshman year at Robert Treat. The teachers I'd had at Robert Treat nearly all commuted the twelve miles from New York City to Newark to teach, and they seemed to me bristling with energy and opinions—some of them decidedly and unashamedly left-wing opinions, despite prevailing political pressures—in ways these midwesterners were not. A couple of my Robert Treat teachers were Jews, excitable in a manner hardly foreign to me, but even the three who weren't Jews talked a lot faster and more combatively than the professors at Winesburg, and brought with them into the classroom from the hubbub across the Hudson an attitude that was sharper and harder and more vital all around and that didn't necessarily hide their aversions. In bed at night, with Elwyn asleep in the top bunk, I thought often of those wonderful teachers I was lucky enough to have had there and whom I eagerly embraced and who first introduced me to real knowledge, and, with feelings of tenderness that were unforeseen and that nearly overwhelmed me, I thought of the friends from the freshman team, like my Italian buddy Angelo Spinelli, now all lost to me. I'd never felt at Robert Treat that there was some old way of life that everyone on the faculty was protecting, which was decidedly different from what I thought at Winesburg whenever I heard the boosters intoning the virtues of their "tradition."

"You're socializing enough?" Caudwell asked. "You're getting around and meeting the other students?"

"Yes, sir."

I waited for him to ask me to list those I had met so far, expecting he would then record their names on the legal pad in front of him—which had my name written in his script across the top—and bring them into his office to find out if I'd been telling the truth. But his response was only to pour a glass of water from a pitcher on a small table behind his desk and hand it across the desk to me.

"Thank you, sir." I sipped at the water so it wouldn't go down the wrong way and set me to coughing uncontrollably. I also flushed fiercely from realizing that just by listening to my first few answers he had been able to surmise how parched my mouth had become.

"Then the only problem is that you seem to be having some trouble settling into dormitory life," he said. "Is that so? As I said in my letter, I'm a bit concerned about your having already resided in three different dormitory rooms in just your first weeks here. Tell me in your own words, what seems to be the trouble?"

The night before I had worked out an answer, knowing as I did that my moving was to be the meeting's main subject. Only now I couldn't remember what I'd planned to say.

"Could you repeat your question, sir?"

"Calm down, son," Caudwell said. "Try a little more water."

I did as he told me. I am going to be thrown out of school, I thought. For moving too many times I am going to be asked to leave Winesburg. That's how this is going to wind up. Thrown out, drafted, sent to Korea, and killed.

"What's the problem with your accommodations, Marcus?"

"In the room to which I was initially assigned"—yes, there

they were, the words that I'd written out and memorized—
"one of my three roommates was always playing his phonograph after I went to bed and I wasn't able to get my night's
sleep. And I need my sleep in order to do my work. The situation was insupportable." I had decided at the last minute on
"insupportable" instead of "insufferable," the adjective with
which I'd rehearsed the previous night.

"But couldn't you sit down and work out a time for his playing the phonograph that was agreeable to the two of you?"
Caudwell asked me. "You had to move out? There was no
other choice?"

"Yes, I had to move out."

"No way of reaching a compromise."

"Not with him, sir." That's as far as I went, hoping that he
might find me admirable for protecting Flusser from exposure
by not mentioning his name.

"Are you often unable to reach a compromise with people
whom you don't see eye to eye with?"

"I wouldn't say 'often,' sir. I wouldn't say that anything like
that has happened before."

"How about your second roommate? Living with him doesn't
appear to have worked out either. Am I correct?"

"Yes, sir."

"Why do you think that was so?"

"Our interests weren't compatible."

"So there was no room for compromise there either."

"No, sir."

"And now you're living alone, I see. Living by yourself under
the eaves in Neil Hall."

"This far into the semester, that was the only empty room I
could find, sir."

"Drink some more water, Marcus. It'll help."

But my mouth was no longer dry. I was no longer sweating
either. I was angered, in fact, by his saying "It'll help," when I
considered myself over the worst of my nervousness and performing as well as anybody my age could be expected to in this
situation. I was angered, I was humiliated, I was resentful, and
I would not even look in the direction of the glass. Why should
I have to go through this interrogation simply because I'd
moved from one dormitory room to another to find the peace

of mind I required to do my schoolwork? What business was it of his? Had he nothing better to do than interrogate me about my dormitory accommodations? I was a straight-A student—why wasn't that enough for *all* my unsatisfiable elders (by whom I meant two, the dean and my father)?

"What about the fraternity you're pledging? You're eating your meals there, I take it."

"I'm not pledging a fraternity, sir. I'm not interested in fraternity life."

"What would you say your interests are, then?"

"My studies, sir. Learning."

"That's admirable, to be sure. But nothing more? Have you socialized with anyone at all since you've come to Winesburg?"

"I work on weekends, sir. I work at the inn as a waiter in the taproom. It's necessary for me to work to assist my father in meeting my expenses, sir."

"You don't have to do that, Marcus—you can stop calling me sir. Call me Dean Caudwell, or call me Dean, if you like. Winesburg isn't a military academy, and it's not the turn of the century either. It's 1951."

"I don't mind calling you sir, Dean." I did, though. I hated it. That's why I was doing it! I wanted to take the word "sir" and stick it up his ass for singling me out to come to his office to be grilled like this. I was a straight-A student. Why wasn't that good enough for everybody? I worked on weekends. Why wasn't that good enough for everybody? I couldn't even get my first blowjob without wondering while I was getting it what had gone wrong to allow me to get it. Why wasn't *that* good enough for everybody? What more was I supposed to do to prove my worth to people?

Promptly the dean mentioned my father. "It says here your father is a kosher butcher."

"I don't believe so, sir. I remember writing down just 'butcher.' That's what I'd write on any form, I'm sure."

"Well, that's what you did write. I'm merely assuming that he's a kosher butcher."

"He is. But that's not what I wrote down."

"I acknowledged that. But it's not inaccurate, is it, to identify him more precisely as a kosher butcher?"

"But neither is what I wrote down inaccurate."

"I'd be curious to know why you didn't write down 'kosher,' Marcus."

"I didn't think that was relevant. If some entering student's father was a dermatologist or an orthopedist or an obstetrician, wouldn't he just write down 'physician'? Or 'doctor'? That's my guess, anyway."

"But kosher isn't in quite the same category."

"If you're asking me, sir, if I was trying to hide the religion into which I was born, the answer is no."

"Well, I certainly hope that's so. I'm glad to hear that. Everyone has a right to openly practice his own faith, and that holds true at Winesburg as it does everywhere else in this country. On the other hand, under 'religious preference' you didn't write 'Jewish,' I notice, though you are of Jewish extraction and, in accordance with the college's attempt to assist students in residing with others of the same faith, you were originally assigned Jewish roommates."

"I didn't write *anything* under religious preference, sir."

"I can see that. I'm wondering why that is."

"Because I have none. Because I don't prefer to practice one religion over another."

"What then provides you with spiritual sustenance? To whom do you pray when you need solace?"

"I don't need solace. I don't believe in God and I don't believe in prayer." As a high school debater I was known for hammering home my point—and that I did. "I am sustained by what is real and not by what is imaginary. Praying, to me, is preposterous."

"Is it now?" he replied with a smile. "And yet so many millions do it."

"Millions once thought the earth was flat, sir."

"Yes, that's true. But may I ask, Marcus, merely out of curiosity, how you manage to get by in life—filled as our lives inevitably are with trial and tribulation—lacking religious or spiritual guidance?"

"I get straight A's, sir."

That prompted a second smile, a smile of condescension that I liked even less than the first. I was prepared now to despise Dean Caudwell with all my being for putting me through *this* tribulation.

"I didn't ask about your grades," he said. "I know your grades. You have every right to be proud of them, as I've already told you."

"If that is so, sir, then you know the answer to your question about how I get along without any religious or spiritual guidance. I get along just fine."

I had begun to rile him up, I could see, and in just the ways that could do me no good.

"Well, if I may say so," the dean said, "it doesn't look to me like you get along just fine. At least you don't appear to get along just fine with the people you room with. It seems that as soon as there's a difference of opinion between you and a roommate, you pick up and leave."

"Is there anything wrong with finding a solution in quietly leaving?" I asked, and within I heard myself beginning to sing, "Arise, ye who refuse to be bondslaves! With our very flesh and blood we will build a new Great Wall!"

"Not necessarily, no more than there is anything wrong with finding a solution in quietly working it out and staying. Look where you've wound up—in the least desirable room on this entire campus. A room where no one has chosen to live or has had to live for many years now. Frankly, I don't like the idea of you up there alone. It's the worst room at Winesburg, bar none. It's been the worst room on the worst floor of the worst dorm for a hundred years. In winter it's freezing and by early spring it's already a hotbox, full of flies. And that's where you've chosen to spend your days and nights as a sophomore student here."

"But I'm not living there, sir, because I don't have religious beliefs—if that is what you are suggesting in a roundabout way."

"Why is it, then?"

"It's as I explained it—" I said, meanwhile, in full voice, in my head, singing, "China's masses have met the day of danger" —"in my first room I couldn't get sufficient sleep because of a roommate who insisted on playing his phonograph late into the night and reciting aloud in the middle of the night, and in my second room I found myself living with someone whose conduct I considered intolerable."

"Tolerance appears to be something of a problem for you, young man."

"I never heard that said about me before, sir," said I at the very instant I inwardly sang out the most beautiful word in the English language: "In-dig-*na*-tion!" I suddenly wondered what it was in Chinese. I wanted to learn it and go around the campus shouting it at the top of my lungs.

"There appear to be several things you've never heard about yourself before," he replied. "But 'before' you were living at home, in the bosom of your childhood family. Now you're living as an adult on his own with twelve hundred others, and what there is for you to master here at Winesburg, aside from mastering your studies, is to learn how to get along with people and how to extend tolerance to people who are not carbon copies of yourself."

Stirred up now by my stealthy singing, I blurted out, "Then how about extending some tolerance to me? I'm sorry, sir, I don't mean to be brash or insolent. But," and, to my own astonishment, leaning forward, I hammered the side of my fist on his desk, "exactly what is the crime I've committed? So I've moved a couple of times, I've moved from one dorm room to another—is that considered a crime at Winesburg College? That makes me into a culprit?"

Here he poured some water and himself took a long drink. Oh, if only I could have graciously poured it for him. If only I could have handed him the glass and said, "Calm down, Dean. Try this, why don't you?"

Smiling generously, he said, "Has anyone said it is a crime, Marcus? You display a fondness for dramatic exaggeration. It doesn't serve you well and is a characteristic you might want to reflect upon. Now tell me, how do you get along with your family? Is everything all right at home between your mother and your father and you? I see from the form here, where you say you have no religious preference, that you also say you have no siblings. There's the three of you at home, if I'm to take what you've written here to be accurate."

"Why wouldn't it be accurate, sir?" Shut up, I told myself. Shut up, and from here on out, stop marching on! Only I couldn't. I couldn't because the fondness for exaggeration wasn't mine but the dean's: this meeting was itself based on his giving a ridiculously exaggerated importance to where I chose to live. "I was accurate when I wrote that my father was a butcher," I said. "He is a butcher. It isn't I alone who would describe him as a butcher. He would describe himself as a butcher. It's you who described him as a kosher butcher. Which is fine with me. But that's not grounds for intimating that I've been in any way inaccurate in filling out my application form for Winesburg. It was not inaccurate for me to leave the religious-preference slot blank—"

"If I may interrupt, Marcus. How do you three get along, from your perspective? That's the question I asked. You, your mother, and your father—how do you get along? A straight answer, please."

"My mother and I get along perfectly well. We always have. So have my father and I gotten along perfectly well for most of my life. From my last year in grade school until I started at Robert Treat, I worked part time for him at the butcher shop. We were as close as a son and father could be. Of late there's been some strain between us that's made us both unhappy."

"Strain over what, may I ask?"

"He's been unnecessarily worried about my independence."

"Unnecessarily because he has no reason to be?"

"None at all."

"Is he worried, for instance, about your inability to adjust to your roommates here at Winesburg?"

"I haven't told him about my roommates. I didn't think it was that important. Nor is 'inability to adjust' a proper way to describe the difficulty, sir. I don't want to be distracted from my studies by superfluous problems."

"I wouldn't consider your moving twice in less than two months a superfluous problem, and neither would your father, I'm sure, if he were apprised of the situation—as he has every right to be, by the way. I don't think you would have bothered moving to begin with if you yourself saw it merely as a 'superfluous problem.' But be that as it may, Marcus, have you gone on any dates since you've been at Winesburg?"

I flushed. "Arise, ye who refuse—" "Yes," I said.

"A few? Some? Many?"

"One."

"Just one."

Before he could dare to ask me with whom, before I had to speak her name and be pressed to answer a single question about what had transpired between the two of us, I rose from my chair. "Sir," I said, "I object to being interrogated like this. I don't see the purpose of it. I don't see why I should be expected to answer questions about my relations with my roommates or my association with my religion or my appraisal of anyone else's religion. Those are my own private affair, as is my social life and how I conduct it. I am breaking no laws, my behavior is causing no one any injury or harm, and in nothing that I've done have I impinged on anyone's rights. If anyone's rights are being impinged on, they are mine."

"Sit down again, please, and explain yourself."

I sat, and this time, on my own initiative, drank deeply from my glass of water. This was now beginning to be more than I could take, yet how could I capitulate when he was wrong and I was right? "I object to having to attend chapel forty times before I graduate in order to earn a degree, sir. I don't see where the college has the right to force me to listen to a clergyman of whatever faith even once, or to listen to a Christian hymn invoking the Christian deity even once, given that I am an atheist who is, to be truthful, deeply offended by the practices and beliefs of organized religion." Now I couldn't stop myself, weakened as I felt. "I do not need the sermons of professional moralists to tell me how I should act. I certainly don't need any God to tell me how. I am altogether capable of leading a moral existence without crediting beliefs that are impossible to substantiate and beyond credulity, that, to my mind, are nothing more than fairy tales for children held by adults, and with no more foundation in fact than a belief in Santa Claus. I take it you are familiar, Dean Caudwell, with the writings of Bertrand Russell. Bertrand Russell, the distinguished British mathematician and philosopher, was last year's winner of the Nobel Prize in Literature. One of the works of literature for which he was awarded the Nobel Prize is a widely read essay first delivered as a lecture in 1927 entitled, 'Why I Am Not a Christian.' Are you familiar with that essay, sir?"

"Please sit down again," said the dean.

I did as he told me, but said, "I am asking if you are familiar with this very important essay by Bertrand Russell. I take it that the answer is no. Well, I am familiar with it because I set myself the task of memorizing large sections of it when I was captain of my high school debating team. I haven't forgotten it yet, and I have promised myself that I never will. This essay and others like it contain Russell's argument not only against the Christian conception of God but against the conceptions of God held by all the great religions of the world, every one of which Russell finds both untrue and harmful. If you were to read his essay, and in the interest of open-mindedness I would urge you to do so, you would find that Bertrand Russell, who is one of the world's foremost logicians as well as a philosopher and a mathematician, undoes with logic that is beyond dispute the first-cause argument, the natural-law argument, the argument from design, the moral arguments for a deity, and the argument for the remedying of injustice. To give you two examples. First, as to why there cannot be any validity to the first-cause argument, he says, 'If everything must have a cause, then God must have a cause. If there can be anything without a cause, it may just as well be the world as God.' Second, as to the argument from design, he says, 'Do you think that, if you were granted omnipotence and omniscience and millions of years in which to perfect your world, you could produce nothing better than the Ku Klux Klan or the Fascists?' He also discusses the defects in Christ's teaching as Christ appears in the Gospels, while noting that historically it is quite doubtful that Christ ever existed. To him the most serious defect in Christ's moral character is his belief in the existence of hell. Russell writes, 'I do not myself feel that any person who is really profoundly humane can believe in everlasting punishment,' and he accuses Christ of a vindictive fury against those people who would not listen to his preaching. He discusses with complete candor how the churches have retarded human progress and how, by their insistence on what they choose to call morality, they inflict on all sorts of people undeserved and unnecessary suffering. Religion, he declares, is based primarily and mainly on fear—fear of the mysterious, fear of defeat, and fear of death. Fear, Bertrand Russell says, is the parent of cruelty, and it is therefore no wonder that cruelty and religion have gone hand in hand throughout the centuries. Conquer the world by intelligence, Russell says, and not by being slavishly subdued by the terror that comes from living in it. The whole conception of God, he concludes, is a conception unworthy of free men. These are the thoughts of a Nobel Prize winner renowned for his contributions to philosophy and for his mastery of logic and the theory of knowledge, and I find myself in total agreement with them. Having studied them and having thought them through, I intend to live in accordance with them, as I'm sure you would have to admit, sir, I have every right to do."

"Please sit down," said the dean once more.

I did. I hadn't realized I had again gotten up. But that's what the exhortation "Arise!," stirringly repeated three successive times, can do to someone in a crisis.

"So you and Bertrand Russell don't tolerate organized religion," he told me, "or the clergy or even a belief in the divinity, any more than you, Marcus Messner, tolerate your roommates —as far as I can make out, any more than you tolerate a loving, hardworking father whose concern for the well-being of his son is of the highest importance to him. His financial burden in paying to send you away from home to college is not inconsiderable, I'm sure. Isn't that so?"

"Why else would I be working at the New Willard House, sir? Yes, that's so. I believe I told you that already."

"Well, tell me now, and this time leaving out Bertrand Russell—do you tolerate *anyone's* beliefs when they run counter to your own?"

"I would think, sir, that the religious views that are more than likely intolerable to ninety-nine percent of the students and faculty and administration of Winesburg are mine."

Here he opened my folder and began slowly turning pages, perhaps to renew his recollection of my record, perhaps (I hoped) to prevent himself from expelling me on the spot for the charge I had so forcefully brought against the entire college. Perhaps merely to pretend that, esteemed and admired as he was at Winesburg, he was nonetheless someone who could bear to be contradicted.

"I see here," he said to me, "that you are studying to be a lawyer. On the basis of this interview, I think you are destined to be an outstanding lawyer." Unsmilingly now, he said, "I can see you one day arguing a case before the Supreme Court of the United States. And winning it, young man, winning it. I admire your directness, your diction, your sentence structure— I admire your tenacity and the confidence with which you hold to everything you say. I admire your ability to memorize and retain abstruse reading matter even if I don't necessarily admire whom and what you choose to read and the gullibility with which you take at face value rationalist blasphemies spouted by an immoralist of the ilk of Bertrand Russell, four times married, a blatant adulterer, an advocate of free love, a self-confessed socialist dismissed from his university position for his antiwar campaigning during the First War and imprisoned for that by the British authorities."

"But what about the Nobel Prize!"

"I even admire you now, Marcus, when you hammer on my desk and stand up to point at me so as to ask about the Nobel Prize. You have a fighting spirit. I admire that, or would admire it should you choose to harness it to a worthier cause than that of someone considered a criminal subversive by his own national government."

"I didn't mean to point, sir. I didn't even know I did it."

"You did, son. Not for the first time and probably not for the last. But that is the least of it. To find that Bertrand Russell is a hero of yours comes as no great surprise. There are always one or two intellectually precocious youngsters on every campus, self-appointed members of an elite intelligentsia who need to elevate themselves and feel superior to their fellow students, superior even to their professors, and so pass through the phase of finding an agitator or iconoclast to admire on the order of a Russell or a Nietzsche or a Schopenhauer. Nonetheless, these views are not what we are here to discuss, and it is certainly your prerogative to admire whomever you like, however deleterious the influence and however dangerous the consequences of such a so-called freethinker and self-styled reformer may seem to me. Marcus, what brings us together today, and what is worrying me today, is not your having memorized word for word as a high school debater the contrarianism of a Bertrand Russell that is designed to nurture malcontents and rebels. What worries me are your social skills as exhibited here at Winesburg College. What worries me is your isolation. What worries me is your outspoken rejection of long-standing Winesburg tradition, as witness your response to chapel attendance, a simple undergraduate requirement which amounts to little more than one hour of your time each week for about

three semesters. About the same as the physical education requirement, and no more insidious, either, as you and I well
know. In all my experience at Winesburg I have never come
across a student yet who objected to either of those requirements as infringements on his rights or comparable to his
being condemned to laboring in the salt mines. What worries
me is how poorly you are fitting into the Winesburg community. To me it seems something to be attended to promptly
and nipped in the bud."

I'm being expelled, I thought. I'm being sent back home to
be drafted and killed. He didn't comprehend a single word I
repeated to him from "Why I Am Not a Christian." Or he did,
and *that's* why I'm going to be drafted and killed.

"I have both a personal and a professional responsibility to
the students," Caudwell said, "to their families—"

"Sir, I can't stand any more of this. I feel as though I'm going
to vomit."

"Excuse me?" His patience exhausted, Caudwell's startlingly
brilliant, crystal-blue eyes were staring at me now with a lethal
blend of disbelief and exasperation.

"I feel sick," I said. "I feel as though I'm going to vomit. I
can't bear being lectured to like this. I am not a malcontent. I
am not a rebel. Neither word describes me, and I resent the
use of either one of them, even if it's only by implication that
they were meant to apply to me. I have done nothing to deserve this lecture except to find a room in which I can devote
myself to my studies without distraction and get the sleep I
need to do my work. I have committed no infraction. I have
every right to socialize or not to socialize to whatever extent
suits me. That is the long and the short of it. I don't care if the
room is hot or cold—that's my worry. I don't care if it's full of
flies or not full of flies. That isn't the point! Furthermore, I
must call to your attention that your argument against Bertrand Russell was not an argument against his ideas based on
reason and appealing to the intellect but an argument against
his character appealing to prejudice, i.e., an *ad hominem* attack, which is logically worthless. Sir, I respectfully ask your
permission to stand up and leave now because I am afraid I am
going to be sick if I don't."

"Of course you may leave. That's how you cope with all

your difficulties, Marcus—you leave. Has that never occurred to you before?" With another of those smiles whose insincerity was withering, he added, "I'm sorry if I wasted your time."

He got up from behind his desk and so, with his seeming consent, I got up from my chair as well, this time to go. But not without a parting shot to set the record straight. "Leaving is *not* how I cope with my difficulties. Think back only to my trying to get you to open your mind to Bertrand Russell. I strongly object to your saying that, Dean Caudwell."

"Well, at least we got over the 'sir,' finally . . . Oh, Marcus," he said as he was seeing me to the door, "what about sports? It says here you played for your freshman baseball team. So at least, I take it, you believe in baseball. What position?"

"Second base."

"And you'll be going out for our baseball team?"

"I played freshman ball at a very tiny city college back home. Virtually anybody who went out for the team made it. There were guys on that team, like our catcher and our first baseman, who didn't even play high school ball. I don't think I'd be good enough to make the team here. The pitching will be faster than I'm used to, and I don't think choking up on the bat, the way I did for the freshman team back home, is going to solve my hitting problem at this level of competition. Maybe I could hold my own in the field, but I doubt I'd be worth much at the plate."

"So what I understand you to be saying is that you're not going out for baseball because of the competition?"

"*No, sir!*" I exploded. "I'm not going out for the team because I'm realistic about my chances of *making* the team! And I don't want to waste the time trying when I have all this studying to do! Sir, I'm going to vomit. I told you I would. It's not my fault. Here it comes—sorry!"

I vomited then, though luckily not onto the dean or his desk. Head down, I robustly vomited onto the rug. Then, when I tried to avoid the rug, I vomited onto the chair in which I'd been sitting, and, when I spun away from the chair, vomited onto the glass of one of the framed photographs hanging on the dean's wall, the one of the Winesburg undefeated championship football team of 1924.

I hadn't the stomach to do battle with the dean of men any

more than I had the stomach to do battle with my father or with my roommates. Yet battle I did, despite myself.

The dean had his secretary accompany me down the corridor to the door of the men's room, where, once inside and alone, I washed my face and gargled with water that I cupped into my hands from beneath the spigot. I spat the water into the sink until I couldn't taste a trace of vomit in my mouth or my throat, and then, using paper towels doused with hot water, I rubbed away as best I could at whatever had spattered onto my sweater, my trousers, and my shoes. Then I leaned on the sink and looked into the mirror at the mouth that I couldn't shut. I clamped my teeth together so tightly that my bruised jawbone began throbbing with pain. Why did I have to mention chapel? Chapel is a discipline, I informed my eyes—eyes that, to my astonishment, looked unbelievably fearful. Treat their chapel as part of the job that you have to do to get through this place as valedictorian—treat it the way you treat eviscerating the chickens. Caudwell was right, wherever you go there will always be something driving you nuts—your father, your roommates, your having to attend chapel forty times—so stop thinking about transferring to yet another school and just graduate first in your class!

But when I was ready to leave the bathroom for my American government class, I got a whiff of vomit again and, looking down, saw the minutest specks of it clinging to the edges of the soles of both my shoes. I took off the shoes and with soap and water and paper towels stood at the sink in my stocking feet, washing away the last of the vomit and the last of the smell. I even took my socks off and held them up to my nose. Two students came in to use the urinals just as I was smelling my socks. I said nothing, explained nothing, put my socks back on, pushed my feet into my shoes, tied the laces, and left. *That's how you cope with all your difficulties, Marcus—you leave. Has that never occurred to you before?*

I went outside and found myself on a beautiful midwestern college campus on a big, gorgeous, sunlit day, another grand fall day, everything around me blissfully proclaiming, "Delight yourselves in the geyser of life! You are young and exuberant and the rapture is yours!" Enviously I looked at the other students walking the brick paths that crisscrossed the green quadrangle. Why couldn't I share the pleasure they took in the splendors of a little college that answered all their needs? Why instead am I in conflict with everyone? It began at home with my father, and from there it has doggedly followed me here. First there's Flusser, then there's Elwyn, then there's Caudwell. And whose fault is it, theirs or mine? How had I gotten myself in trouble so fast, I who'd never before been in trouble in my life? And why was I looking for more trouble by writing fawning letters to a girl who only a year before had attempted suicide by slitting a wrist?

I sat on a bench and opened my three-ring binder and on a blank piece of lined paper I started in yet again. "Please answer me when I write to you. I can't bear your silence." Yet the weather was too beautiful and the campus too beautiful to find Olivia's silence unbearable. Everything was too beautiful, and I was too young, and my only job was to become valedictorian! I continued writing: "I feel on the verge of picking up and leaving here because of the chapel requirement. I would like to talk to you about this. Am I being foolish? You ask how did I get here in the first place? Why did I choose Winesburg? I'm ashamed to tell you. And now I just had a terrible interview with the dean of men, who is sticking his nose into my business in a way that I'm convinced he has no right to do. No, it was nothing about you, or us. It was about my moving into Neil Hall." Then I yanked the page out of the notebook as furiously as if I were my own father and tore it in pieces that I stuffed into my pants pocket. Us! There was no us!

I was wearing pleated gray flannel trousers and a check sport shirt and a maroon V-neck pullover and white buckskin shoes. It was the same outfit I'd seen on the boy pictured on the cover of the Winesburg catalogue that I'd sent away for and received in the mail, along with the college application forms. In the photo, he was walking beside a girl wearing a two-piece sweater set and a long, full dark skirt and turned-down white cotton socks and shiny loafers. She was smiling at him while they walked together as though he'd said to her something amusingly clever. Why had I chosen Winesburg? Because of that picture! There were big leafy trees on either side of the two happy students, and they were walking down a grassy hill with ivy-clad, brick buildings in the distance behind them, and the girl was smiling so appreciatively at the boy, and the boy looked so confident and carefree beside her, that I filled out the application and sent it off and within only weeks was accepted. Without telling anyone, I took from my savings account one hundred of the dollars that I'd diligently squirreled away of the wages I'd been paid as my father's employee, and after my classes one day I walked over to Market Street and went into the city's biggest department store and in their College Shop bought the pants and shirt and shoes and sweater that were worn by the boy in the photo. I had brought the Winesburg catalogue with me to the store; a hundred dollars was a small fortune, and I didn't want to make a mistake. I also bought a College Shop herringbone tweed jacket. In the end I had just enough change left to take the bus home.

I was careful to bring the boxes of clothing into the house when I knew my parents were off working at the store. I didn't want them to know about my buying the clothes. I didn't want anybody to know. These were nothing like the clothes that the guys at Robert Treat wore. We wore the same clothes we'd worn in high school. You didn't get a new outfit to go to Robert Treat. Alone in the house, I opened the boxes and laid the clothes out on the bed to see how they looked. I laid them out in place, as you would wear them—shirt, sweater, and jacket up top, trousers below, and shoes down near the foot of the bed. Then I pulled off everything I had on and dropped it at my feet like a pile of rags and put on the new clothes and went into the bathroom and stood on the lowered toilet seat lid so I was able to see more of myself in the medicine chest mirror than I would be able to see standing on the tile floor in my new white buckskin shoes with the pinkish rubber heels and soles. The jacket had two short slits, one on either side at the back. I'd never owned such a jacket before. Previously I'd owned two sport jackets, one bought for my bar mitzvah in 1945 and the other for my graduation from high school in 1950. Careful to take the tiniest steps, I rotated on the toilet seat lid to try to catch a look at my backside in that jacket with the slits. I put my hands in my pants pockets so as to look nonchalant. But there was no way of looking nonchalant standing on a toilet, so I climbed down and went into the bedroom and took off the clothes and put them back in their boxes, which I hid at the back of my bedroom closet, behind my bat, spikes, mitt, and a bruised old baseball. I had no intention of telling my parents about the new clothes, and I certainly wasn't going to wear them in front of my friends at Robert Treat. I was going to keep them a secret till I got to Winesburg. The clothes I'd bought to leave home in. The clothes I'd bought to start a new life in. The clothes I'd bought to be a new man in and to end my being the butcher's son.

Well, those were the very clothes on which I had vomited in Caudwell's office. Those were the clothes that I wore when I sat in chapel trying how not to learn to lead a good life in accordance with biblical teachings and singing to myself instead the Chinese national anthem. Those were the clothes I'd been wearing when my roommate Elwyn had thrown the punch that had nearly broken my jaw. Those were the clothes I was wearing when Olivia went down on me in Elwyn's LaSalle. Yes, *there's* the picture of the boy and girl that should adorn the cover of the Winesburg catalogue: me in those clothes being blown by Olivia and having no idea what to make of it.

You don't look yourself, Marcus. You all right? May I sit down?"

It was Sonny Cottler standing over me, wearing the same clothes that I was wearing, except that his wasn't an ordinary maroon pullover sweater but a maroon and gray Winesburg letter sweater that he'd earned playing varsity basketball. That too. The ease with which he wore his clothes seemed an extension somehow of the deep voice that was so rich with authority and confidence. A quiet kind of carefree vigor, an invulnerability that he exuded, repelled me and attracted me at once, perhaps because it struck me, unreasonably or not, as being rooted in condescension. His seemingly being deficient in nothing left me oddly with the impression of someone who was actually deficient in everything. But then these impressions could have been no more than the offshoot of a sophomore's envy and awe.

"Of course," I answered. "Sure. Sit."

"You look like you've been through the wringer," he said.

He, of course, looked like he'd just finished shooting a scene on the MGM lot opposite Ava Gardner. "The dean called me in. We had a disagreement. We had an altercation." Keep your mouth shut! I told myself. Why tell him? But I had to tell someone, didn't I? I had to talk to someone at this place, and Cottler wasn't necessarily a bad guy because my father had arranged for him to come to visit me in my room. Anyway, I felt so misunderstood all around that I might have looked up at the sky and howled like a dog if he hadn't happened by.

As calmly as I could, I told him about the dispute over chapel attendance between the dean and me.

"But," Cottler asked, "who goes to chapel? You pay somebody to go for you and you never have to go anywhere near chapel."

"Is that what *you* do?"

He laughed softly. "What else *would* I do? I went one time. I went in my freshman year. It was when they had a rabbi. They have a Catholic priest once each semester, and they have a rabbi over from Cleveland once a year. Otherwise it's Dr. Donehower and other great Ohio thinkers. The rabbi's passionate devotion to the concept of kindness was enough to cure me of chapel for good."

"How much do you have to pay?"

"For a proxy? Two bucks a pop. It's nothing."

"Forty times two is eighty dollars. That's not nothing."

"Look," he said, "figure you spend fifteen minutes getting down off the Hill and over to the church. And if you're you, serious you, you don't laugh off being there. You don't laugh off anything. Instead you spend an hour at chapel seething with rage. Then you spend another fifteen minutes seething with rage while getting back up the Hill to wherever you're going next. That's ninety minutes. Ninety times forty equals sixty hours of rage. That's not nothing either."

"How do you find the person to pay? Explain to me how it works."

"The person you hire takes the card the usher hands him at the door when he goes in, then he hands it back signed with your name when he goes out. That's it. You think a handwriting specialist pores over each card back in the little office where they keep the records? They tick off your name in some ledger, and that's it. In the old days they used to assign you a

seat and have a proctor who got to know everyone's face walk
up and down the aisles to see who was missing. Back then you
were screwed. But after the war they changed it, so now all you
have to do is pay someone to take your place."

"But who?"

"Anyone. Anyone who's done his forty chapels. It's work.
You work waiting tables at the taproom of the inn, someone
else works proxying at the Methodist church. I'll find you
somebody if you want me to. I can even try to find somebody
for less than two bucks."

"And if this person shoots off his mouth? Then you're out of
here on your ass."

"I've never heard yet of anybody shooting off his mouth. It's
a business, Marcus. You make a simple business arrangement."

"But surely Caudwell knows this is going on."

"Caudwell's the biggest Christer around. He can't imagine
why students don't *love* listening to Dr. Donehower instead of
having the hour free every Wednesday to jack off in their
rooms. Oh, that was a big mistake you made, bringing up
chapel with Caudwell. Hawes D. Caudwell is the idol of this
place. Winesburg's greatest halfback in football, greatest slug-
ger in baseball, greatest center in basketball, greatest exponent
on the planet of 'the Winesburg tradition.' Meet this guy
head-on about upholding the Winesburg tradition and he'll
make you into mush. Remember the drop kick, the old vintage
drop kick? Caudwell holds the Winesburg record for drop-
kicking points in a single season. And you know what he called
each of those drop kicks? 'A drop kick for Christ.' You go
around such creeps, Marcus. A little detachment goes a long
way at Winesburg. Keep your mouth shut, your ass covered,
smile—and then do whatever you like. Don't take it all person-
ally, don't take everything so seriously, and you might find this
is not the worst place in the world to spend the best years of
your life. You already located the Blowjob Queen of 1951.
That's a start."

"I don't know what you're talking about."

"You mean she *didn't* blow you? You *are* unique."

Angrily, I said, "I still don't know what you're referring to."

"To Olivia Hutton."

Fury swiftly mounted in me, the very fury that I'd felt toward Elwyn when he called Olivia a cunt. "Now why do you
say that about Olivia Hutton?"

"Because blowjobs are at a premium in north-central Ohio.
News of Olivia has traveled fast. Don't look so puzzled."

"I don't believe this."

"You should. Miss Hutton is a bit of a nutcase."

"Now why do you say *that*? I took her out."

"So did I."

That stunned me. I jumped up from the bench and, in a
dizzying state of confusion about what there was (or wasn't) in
me that made relations with others so wretchedly disappointing, fled Sonny Cottler and sped off to my government class,
and the last words of his I heard were "Withdraw 'nutcase.'
Okay? Let's say she's the kind of oddball who's exceptionally
good at sex, and it's a function of being disturbed—all right?
Marcus? Marc?"

The vomiting resumed that night, accompanied by stabbing
stomach pain and diarrhea, and when finally I realized I was ill
because of something other than my interview with Dean
Caudwell, I made my way through the dawn light to the Student Health Office, where before I could even be interviewed
by the on-duty nurse, I had to make a run for the toilet. I was
then given a cot to lie down on, at seven I was examined by the
college doctor, by eight I was in an ambulance bound for the
community hospital twenty-five miles away, and by noon my
appendix had been removed.

My first visitor was Olivia. She came the next day, having
learned of my operation in history class the previous afternoon.
She rapped on the half-open door to my room, arriving only
seconds after I had got off the telephone with my parents, who
had been contacted by Dean Caudwell after it was determined
at the hospital that I needed emergency surgery. "Thank God
you had the sense to go to the doctor," my father said, "and
they caught it in time. Thank God nothing terrible happened."
"Dad, it was my appendix. They took out my appendix. That's
all that happened." "But suppose they hadn't diagnosed it."
"But they *did*. Everything went perfectly. I'll be out of the
hospital in four or five days." "You had an emergency appen-

dectomy. You understand what an emergency is?" "But the emergency's *over*. There's no need for any more worrying." "There's plenty of need for worrying when it comes to you."

Here my father had to pause because of his hacking cough. It sounded worse than ever. When he was able to resume speaking, he asked, "Why are they letting you out so soon?" "Four or five days is normal. There's no need for me to be hospitalized longer." "I'm going to take the train out there after they discharge you. I'm shutting the store and I'm coming out there." "Don't, Dad. Don't talk that way. I appreciate the offer, but I'll be fine in the dorm." "Who will look after you in the dorm? You should recuperate in your house, where you belong. I don't understand why the college doesn't insist on this. How can you recuperate away from your home with nobody looking after you?" "But I'm up and walking already. I'm fine already." "How far is the hospital from the college?" I was tempted to say "Seventeen thousand miles," but he was coughing too painfully for me to be satirizing him. "Less than half an hour by ambulance," I said. "It's an excellent hospital." "There's no hospital there in Winesburg itself? Am I understanding you correctly?" "Dad, put Mother on. This isn't helping me any. And it isn't helping you. You sound awful." "I sound awful? You're the one in a hospital hundreds of miles away from home." "Please let me talk to Mother." When my mother came on, I told her to do something to contain him or next I'd transfer to the University of the North Pole, where there were no phones, hospitals, or doctors, just polar bears who stalk the ice floes where the undergraduates, naked in subzero temperatures—"Marcus, that's enough. I'm coming to see you." "But you don't have to come—neither of you has to come. It was an easy operation, it's over, and I'm fine." Whispering, she said, "*I* know that. But your father will not let up. I'm leaving here on the Saturday night train. Otherwise nobody in this house will sleep ever again."

Olivia. I hung up from speaking to my mother and there she was. In her arms she had a bouquet of flowers. She carried them over to where I lay propped up in the bed.

"It's no fun being in a hospital alone," she said. "I brought these to keep you company."

"It was worth the appendicitis," I replied.

"I doubt it," she said. "Were you very ill?"

"For less than a day. The best part came in Dean Caudwell's office. He called me in to grill me about changing my dorm room and I puked on his trophies. Then you turn up. It's been a great case of appendicitis all around."

"Let me get a vase for these."

"What are they?"

"You don't know?" she said, holding the bouquet to my nose.

"I know concrete. I know asphalt. I don't know flowers."

"They're called roses, dear."

When she came back into the room, she'd taken the roses out of their paper wrapping and arranged them in a glass vase half filled with water.

"Where will you be able to see them best?" she asked me, looking around the room, which, though small, was still larger and certainly brighter than the one I occupied in Neil Hall. At Neil Hall there was only a small dormer window up in the eaves, while here two good-sized windows looked out onto a well-tended lawn where somebody was trailing a rake along the ground, gathering the fallen leaves into a heap to burn. It was Friday, October 26, 1951. The Korean War was one year, four months, and one day old.

"I see them best," I said, "in your two hands. I see them best with you standing there. Just stay like that and let me look at you and your roses. That's what I came for." Yet by saying "hands," I caused myself to remember what Sonny Cottler had said about her, and again the fury rose in me, directed at both Cottler *and* Olivia. But so too did my penis rise.

"What are they giving you to eat?" she asked.

"Jell-O and ginger ale. Tomorrow they begin with the snails."

"You seem very chipper."

She was so beautiful! How could she blow Sonny Cottler? But then how could she blow me? If he took her out only once, then she would have blown him on the first date too. Too, the torment of that "too"!

"Look," I said, and pulled back the sheets.

Demurely, she lowered her lashes. "What happens, my master, should someone walk in?"

I couldn't believe that's what she had said, but then I couldn't believe what I had just done. Was it she who emboldened me, or I who emboldened her, or we two who emboldened each other?

"Is the wound draining?" she asked. "Is that tube dangling down there a drain?"

"I don't know. I can't tell. I suppose so."

"What about stitches?"

"This is a hospital. Where better to be when they come undone?"

There was a gently erotic sway to her gait as she slowly approached the bed pointing a finger at my erection. "You are odd, you know. Very odd," she told me, once she'd at last arrived at my side. "Odder than I think you realize."

"I'm always odd after I have my appendix out."

"Do you always get as huge as this after you've had your appendix out?"

"Never fails." Huge. She'd said huge. *Was* it?

"Of course we shouldn't," she whispered mischievously while wrapping my dick in her hand. "We could both get thrown out of school for this."

"Then stop!" I whispered back, realizing that, of course, she was right—that's exactly what would happen: caught and thrown out of school, she to slouch back home in shame to Hunting Valley, I to be drafted and killed.

But then she hadn't to stop, she hadn't even really to begin, because I had already ejaculated high in the air, and down over the bedsheets the semen showered, while Olivia recited sweetly, "I shot an arrow into the air / It fell to earth I knew not where" and just as my nurse walked through the door to take my temperature.

She was a round, gray-haired, middle-aged spinster named Miss Clement, the epitome of the thoughtful, soft-spoken, old-fashioned nurse—she even wore a starched white bonnet, unlike most of the younger nurses on the hospital staff. When I'd had to use the bedpan for the first time after the surgery, she'd quietly reassured me, saying, "I'm here to help you while you need help, and this is the help you now need, and there's nothing to be embarrassed about," and all the while she was gently positioning me over the bedpan and then cleaning me

with moist toilet tissue and finally removing the pan containing my slime and settling me back under the sheets.

And this was her reward for ever so tenderly wiping my ass.
And mine? For that one quick stroke of Olivia's hand, my reward would be Korea. Miss Clement must already be on the
phone to Dean Caudwell, who'd himself be on the phone to
my father following that. And easily enough I could envision my
father, after receiving the news, swinging the meat cleaver with
such force as to split wide open the four-foot-thick freestand-
ing butcher block on which he ordinarily cracked open the
carcasses of cows.

"Excuse me," murmured Miss Clement and, pulling the
door closed, disappeared. Quickly Olivia went into my bathroom and returned with hand towels, one for the bed linens,
another for me.

Struggling to feign a manly calm, I asked Olivia, "What's
she going to do now? What's going to happen next?"

"Nothing," Olivia replied.

"You're awfully poised about this. Is it all the practice you've
had?"

Her voice was husky when she replied. "It wasn't necessary
to say that."

"I apologize. I'm sorry. But this is all new to me."

"You don't think it's new to *me*?"

"What about Sonny Cottler?"

"I don't see where that's your business," she shot back.

"Isn't it?"

"*No.*"

"You're awfully poised about *everything*," I said. "How do
you know the nurse is going to do nothing?"

"She's too embarrassed to."

"Look, how did you get like this?"

"Like what?" asked Olivia, in anger now.

"So—expert."

"Oh, yes, Olivia the expert," she said sourly. "That's what
they called me at the Menninger Clinic."

"But you are. You're so under control."

"You really think so, do you? I, who have eight thousand
moods a minute, whose every emotion is a tornado, who can

be thrown by a *word*, by a *syllable*, am 'under control'? God, you *are* blind," she said and went back to the bathroom with the towels.

Olivia came by bus to the hospital the next day—a fifty-minute bus ride in either direction—and in my room the same delightful business transpired, after which she cleaned up and, while in the bathroom disposing of the towels, changed the water in the vase to keep the flowers fresh.

Miss Clement now tended to me without speaking. Despite Olivia's reassurance, I couldn't believe that she hadn't told someone, and that the payoff would come when I left the hospital and was back at school. I was as sure as my own father would have been that as a result of my having been caught having sexual contact with Olivia in my hospital room, full-scale disaster would shortly ensue.

Olivia was fascinated by my being a butcher's son. It seemed far more interesting to her that I should be a butcher's son than what was of no little interest to me, that she should be a doctor's daughter. I'd never before dated a doctor's daughter. Mostly the girls I'd known were girls whose fathers owned a neighborhood store, like my father did, or were salesmen who sold neckties or aluminum siding or life insurance, or were tradesmen—electricians, plumbers, and so forth. At the hospital, after I'd had my orgasm, she almost immediately began asking me about the store, and very quickly I got the idea: I was to her something on the order of the child of a snake charmer or of a circus performer raised in the big top. "Tell me more," she said. "I want to hear more." "Why?" I asked. "Because I know nothing about such things and because I like you so much. I want to learn everything about you. I want to know what made you you, Marcus."

"Well, the store made me me, if anything did, though what exactly was made I can't say I entirely know anymore. I've been in a very confused state of mind since I hit this place."

"It made you hardworking. It made you honest. It gave you integrity."

"Oh, did it?" I said. "The butcher shop?"

"Absolutely."

"Well, let me tell you about the fat man, then," I said. "Let me tell you what he gave me in the way of integrity. We'll start with him."

"Goodie. Story time. The fat man and how he gave Marcus integrity." She laughed in anticipation. The laugh of a child being tickled. Nothing exceptional, and still it enchanted me as much as everything else.

"Well, a fat man used to come every Friday and pick up all the fat. It's possible he had a name, though it's equally possible that he didn't. He was just the fat man. He would come in once a week, announce, 'Fat man here,' weigh all the fat, pay my father for it, and take it away. The fat was in a garbage pail, a regular fifty-five-gallon pail about this high, and while we were cutting we were tossing the fat into the pail there. Before the big Jewish holidays, when people loaded up with meat, there could be a couple of pailfuls waiting for him. It couldn't have been a lot of money that the fat man paid. A couple of bucks a week, no more than that. Well, our store was right near the corner where the bus to downtown stopped, the number eight Lyons Avenue bus. And on Fridays, after the fat man picked up the fat, he left behind the garbage cans, and I had the job of washing them out. I remember once one of the pretty girls from my class saying to me, 'Oh, when I stopped at the bus stop in front of your father's store, I saw you there cleaning out the garbage cans.' So I went to my father and said, 'This is ruining my social life. I can't clean these garbage cans anymore.' "

"You cleaned them in front of the store?" Olivia asked. "Right out on the street?"

"Where else?" I said. "I had a scrub brush, Ajax, threw a little water in with the Ajax, and I'd scrub the inside of it. If you didn't get it clean, it would start to smell. Become rancid. But you don't want to hear this stuff."

"I do. I do."

"I had you down for a great woman of the world, but in many ways you're a child, aren't you?"

"But of course. Isn't it a triumph at my age? Would you have it any other way? Continue. Washing the garbage cans after the fat man left."

"Well, you'd get a pail of water, pour it in, swish it around, and empty it into the gutter, and from there it would flow down along the curbstone, carrying with it all the street-side debris, and then drain into the sewer grate at the corner. Then you'd do the whole thing a second time, and that would get the can clean."

"And so," said Olivia, laughing—no, not laughing, nibbling rather at the bait of a laugh—"you figured you weren't going to pick up a lot of girls like that."

"No, I wasn't. That's why I said to the boss—I always referred to my father as the boss in the store—I said, 'Boss, I cannot do these garbage cans anymore. These girls from school are coming by, they stop in front of the store because of the bus, they see me cleaning garbage cans, and the next day I'm supposed to ask them to go out to a Saturday night movie with me? Boss, I can't do it.' And he said to me, 'You're ashamed? Why? What are you ashamed of? The only thing you have to be ashamed of is stealing. Nothing else. You clean the garbage cans.'"

"How terrific," she said, and captivated me now with a different laugh entirely, a laugh that was laden with the love of life for all its unexpected charms. At that moment you would have thought the whole of Olivia lay in her laughter, when in fact it lay in her scar.

It was also "terrific" and amused her greatly when I told her about Big Mendelson, who worked for my father when I was a little kid. "Big Mendelson had a nasty mouth on him," I said. "He really belonged in the back, in the refrigerator, and not in front waiting on customers. But I was seven or eight, and because he had this nasty kind of humor and because they called him Big Mendelson, I thought he was the funniest man on earth. Finally my father had to get rid of him."

"What did Big Mendelson do that he had to get rid of him?"

"Well, on Thursday mornings," I told her, "my father would come back from the chicken market and he would dump all the chickens in a pile and people would pick whatever chicken they wanted for the weekend. Dumped them on a table. Anyway, one woman, a Mrs. Sklon, she used to pick up a chicken and smell the mouth and then smell the rear end. Then she'd pick up another chicken, and again she'd smell the mouth and then smell the rear end. She did the same thing every week, and she did it so many times every week that Big Mendelson couldn't contain himself, and one day he said, 'Mrs. Sklon, can *you* pass that inspection?' She got so mad at him, she picked up a knife from the counter and said, 'If you ever talk to me that way again, I'll stab you.'"

"And that's why your father let him go?"

"Had to. By then he'd said lots of things like that. But about Mrs. Sklon Big Mendelson was right. Mrs. Sklon was no picnic even for me, and I was the nicest boy in the world."

"I never doubted that," Olivia said.

"Well, for good or bad, that's what I was."

"Am. Are."

"Mrs. Sklon was the only one of the customers who didn't want to fix me up with their daughters. I couldn't trick Mrs. Sklon," I said. "No one could. I would deliver to her. And every time I delivered she would take the order apart. And it was always a big order. And she would take it out of the bag and undo the wax paper and take everything out and weigh everything to make sure the weight was correct. I had to stand there and watch this show. I was always in a rush because I was always looking to deliver the orders as fast as I could and then get back to the schoolyard to play ball. So at a certain point I'd bring her order around to the back door, plop it down on the top step, knock on the door once, and run like hell. And she would catch me. Every time. 'Messner! Marcus Messner! The butcher's son! Come back here!' I always felt, when I was with Mrs. Sklon, that I was at the heart of things. I felt that with Big Mendelson. I mean what I'm saying, Olivia. I felt that with people in the butcher shop. I got enjoyment out of that butcher shop." But only before, I thought, before his thoughts made my father defenseless.

"And she had a scale in the kitchen, Mrs. Sklon—was that it?" Olivia asked me.

"In the kitchen, yes. But it was not an accurate scale. It was a baby scale. Besides, she never found that there was anything wrong. But she always weighed the meat, and she always caught me when I tried to run away. I could never escape this woman. She used to give me a quarter tip. A quarter was a good tip. Most were nickels and dimes."

"You had humble origins. Like Abe Lincoln. Honest Marcus."

"Insatiate Olivia."

"What about the war, when meat was rationed? What about the black market? Was your father in the black market?"

"Did he bribe the owner of the slaughterhouse? He did. But his customers didn't have ration stamps sometimes, and they were having company, they were having family over, and he wanted them to have meat, so he would give the slaughter-house owner some cash each week, and he was able to get more meat. It wasn't a big deal. It was as easy as that. But otherwise my father was a man who never broke the law. I think that was the only law he ever broke in his life, and in those days every-one broke that one, more or less. You know kosher meat has to be washed every three days. My father would take a whisk broom with a bucket of water and wash all the meat down. But sometimes you had a Jewish holiday, and though we ourselves weren't strictly observant, we were Jews in a Jewish neighbor-hood, and what's more, kosher butchers, and so the store was closed. And one Jewish holiday, my father told me, he forgot. Say the Passover Seder was going to be on a Monday and a Tuesday, and he washed the meat on the previous Friday. He would have to come back on Monday or Tuesday to do it again, and this one time he forgot. Well, nobody knew he'd forgotten, but he knew, and he would not sell that meat to anyone. He took it all and sold it at a loss to Mueller, who had a nonkosher butcher store on Bergen Street. Sid Mueller. But he would not sell it to his customers. He took the loss instead."

"So you did learn to be honest from him in the store."

"Probably. I certainly can't say I ever learned anything bad from him. That would have been impossible."

"Lucky Marcus."

"You think so?"

"I know so," Olivia said.

"Tell me about being a doctor's daughter."

All color passed out of her face when she replied, "There's nothing to tell."

"You—"

She let me get no further. "Practice *tact*," she said coldly, and with that, as though a switch had been thrown or a plug pulled—as though gloom had swept through her like a storm —her face simply shut down. For the first time in my pres-ence, so too did the beauty. Gone. The play and the luster suddenly gone, the fun of the butcher shop stories gone, and replaced by a terrible, sick-looking pallor the instant I wanted to know more about her.

I feigned indifference but I was shocked, so shocked that I blotted out the moment almost immediately. It was as if I'd been spun round and round till I was giddy and needed first to regain my balance, before I could reply, "Tact it is, then, and tact it shall be." But I wasn't happy, and earlier I'd been *so* happy, not just because of my raising Olivia's laughter but because of my remembering my father as he'd once been—as he'd always been—back in those unimperiled, unchanging days when everybody felt safe and settled in his place. I'd been remembering my father as if that's the way he still was and our lives had never taken this freakish turn. I'd been remembering him when he was anything but defenseless—when he was, without dispute, untyrannically, reassuringly, matter-of-factly boss, and I, his child and beneficiary, had felt so astonishingly free.

Why wouldn't she answer me when I asked what it was like to be a doctor's daughter? At first I blotted out that moment, but later it returned and wouldn't go away. Was it the divorce she didn't want to talk about? Or was it something worse? "Practice tact." Why? What did that mean?

On Sunday, in the late morning, my mother arrived and we went to speak alone together in the solarium at the end of the corridor. I wanted to show her how steady I was on my feet and how far I could walk and how well I felt altogether. I was thrilled to see her here, away from New Jersey, in a part of the country unknown to her—nothing like that had ever happened before—but knew that when Olivia came I would have to introduce the two of them and that my mother, who missed nothing, would see the scar on Olivia's wrist and ask me what I was doing with a girl who had tried to commit suicide, a question whose answer I didn't yet know. Rarely an hour went by when I didn't ask it of myself.

I thought at first to tell Olivia not to visit on the day that my mother was coming. But I'd already hurt her enough by stupidly alluding to her blowing Cottler and then again when I'd asked in all innocence for her to tell me about being a doctor's daughter. I didn't want to hurt her again, and so did nothing to keep her slashed wrist out of the range of my hawk-eyed mother. I did nothing—which is to say, I did exactly the wrong thing. Again.

My mother was exhausted from her overnight train journey —followed by an hourlong bus ride—and though it was only a couple of months since I'd seen her at home, she struck me as a much older, more haggard mother than the one I'd left behind. A harried look I was unaccustomed to seeing deepened her wrinkles and pervaded her features and seemed ingrained in her very skin. Though I kept reassuring her about me—and trying to reassure myself about her—and though I lied about how happy I was with everything at Winesburg, she emanated a sadness so uncharacteristic of her that finally I had to ask, "Ma, is there something wrong that I don't know?"

"Something's wrong that you do know. Your father," she said and startled me further by beginning to cry. "Something is very wrong with your father, and I don't know what it is."

"Is he sick? Does he have something?"

"Markie, I think he's losing his mind. I don't know what else to call it. You know how he was with you on the phone about the operation? That's how he is now about everything. Your father, who could confront any hardship in the family, survive any ordeal with the store, be pleasant to the worst of the customers—even after we were robbed that time and the thieves locked him in the refrigerator and emptied the register, you remember how he said, 'The money we can replace. Thank God nothing happened to any of us.' The same man who could say that, and *believe* that, now he can't do anything without a million worries. This is the man who when Abe got killed in the war held Uncle Muzzy and Aunt Hilda together, who when Dave got killed in the war held Uncle Shecky and Aunt Gertie together, who to this day has held together the whole Messner family, with all of their tragedies—and now you should see what happens when all he's doing is driving the truck. He's been driving around Essex County all his life and now suddenly he's delivering orders as though everyone on the road is a maniac except him. 'Look at the guy—look what he did. Did you see that woman—is she crazy? Why must people cross with the yellow light? Do they want to get run down, do they not want to live to see their grandchildren grow up and go to school and get married?' I serve him his dinner and he sniffs at his food as if I'm trying to poison him. This is true. 'Is this fresh?' he says. 'Smell this.' Food prepared by me in my own spotless kitchen and he won't eat it for fear that it's spoiled and will poison him. We're at the table, just the two of us, and I'm eating and he's not. It's horrible. He sits there not taking a bite and waiting to see if I keel over."

"And is he like that at the store?"

"Yes. Fearful all the time. 'We're losing customers. The supermarket is ruining our business. They're selling choice for prime, don't think I don't know it. They don't give customers an honest weight, they're charging them seventeen cents a pound for chicken, and then they turn around and get it up to twenty on the scale. I know how they work it, I know for a fact that they're cheating the customer—' On it goes, darling, night and day. It is true that our business is off, but everybody's business is off in Newark. People are moving to the suburbs and the businesses are following behind. The neighborhood is undergoing a revolution. Newark's not the same as it was during the war. Many people in the city are hurting suddenly, but still, it isn't as though we're starving to death. We have expenses to meet, but who doesn't? Do I complain about working again? No. Never. Yet that's how he acts. I prepare and wrap an order the same way I've been preparing and wrapping orders for twenty-five years, and he tells me, 'Not like that—the customers don't like it like that! You're in such a hurry to go home, look how you wrap it!' He even complains how I take orders on the phone. The customers always love to talk to me, to give the orders to me, because I show some concern. Now I talk too much to the customers. He has no patience anymore for me to be nice to our customers! I'm on the phone taking an order, and I say, 'Oh, so your grandchildren are going to be coming. That's nice. How do they like school?' And your father will pick up the other phone and tell the customer, 'You want to talk to my wife, you call at night, not during business hours,' and he hangs up. If this goes on, if he keeps this up, if I have to keep watching him push the peas around the plate with his fork, looking like a crazy man for the cyanide pill . . . Darling, is this what they call a personality change or has something terrible happened to him? Is it something new—is that possible? Out of nowhere? At fifty? Or is it something long buried that has come to the surface? Have I been living all these years with a time bomb? All I know is that something has made my husband into a different person. My own dear husband, and now I am completely confused about whether he is one man or two!"

She ended there, in tears again, the mother who never cried, never faltered, a well-spoken American-born girl who picked up Yiddish from him so as to speak it to the elderly customers, a South Side High graduate who'd taken the commercial course there and could have easily worked as a bookkeeper at a desk in an office but who learned to butcher and prepare meat from him in order to work beside him in the store instead, whose bedrock dependability, whose sensible words and coherent thoughts, had filled me with confidence throughout a childhood that was unembattled. And she became a bookkeeper in the end anyway—a bookkeeper *also*, I should say, who after coming home from working all day at the store kept the accounts at night and spent the last day of each month sending out the bills on our own lined "Messner Kosher Meat" billing stationery with the little drawing of a cow on the upper left side and the drawing of a chicken on the upper right. When I was a child, what could buoy me up more than the sight of those drawings at the top of our billing stationery and the fortitude of the two of them? Once upon a time an admirable, well-organized, hardworking family, emanating unity, and now he was frightened of everything and she was out of her mind with grief over what she wasn't entirely sure whether or not to label a "personality change"—and I had as good as run away from home.

"Maybe you should have told me," I said. "Why didn't you tell me it was so extensive?"

"I didn't want to bother you at school. You had your studies."

"But when do you think this began?"

"The first night he locked you out of the house, that's when. That night changed everything. You don't know how I fought with him before you got home that night. I never told you. I didn't want to embarrass him further. 'What are you accomplishing by double-locking the door?' I asked him. 'Do you really want your son not to come into the house, is that why you're double-locking it? You think you're teaching him a les-son,' I told him. 'What will you do if he teaches *you* a lesson and goes somewhere else to sleep? Because that's what a person with any sense does when he finds himself locked out—he doesn't stand around in the cold, waiting to get pneumonia. He gets up and he goes where it's warm and he's welcome. He'll go to a friend, you'll see. He'll go to Stanley's house. He'll go to Alan's house. And their parents will let him in. He won't take this sitting down, not Markie.' But your father refused to budge. 'How do I know where he is at this hour? How do I know he's not in some whorehouse?' We're lying in bed and that's what he's hollering—about whether my son is in a whorehouse or not. 'How do I know,' he asks me, 'that he's not out at this hour ruining his life?' I couldn't control him, and this is the result."

"What is the result?"

"You are now living in the middle of Ohio and he's running around the house shouting, 'Why is he having his appendix out in a hospital five hundred miles from home? There aren't hospitals in New Jersey to take out an appendix? The best hos-pitals in the world are right here in this state! What is he doing out there in the first place?' Fear, Marcus, fear leaking out at every pore, anger leaking out at every pore, and I don't know how to stop either one."

"Take him to a doctor, Mom. Take him to one of those wonderful hospitals in New Jersey and get them to find out what is wrong with him. Maybe they can give him something to settle him down."

"Don't make fun of this, Markie. Don't make fun of your father. This has all the earmarks of a tragedy."

"But I *meant* it. It sounds like he should see a doctor. See *somebody*. It all can't fall on you like this."

"But your father is your father. He won't take an aspirin for a headache. He won't give in. He won't even go to see the doctor about the cough. People coddle themselves, in his eyes. 'It's smoking,' he says, and saying that settles it. 'My father smoked all his life. I've been smoking all my life. Shecky, Muzzy, and Artie have smoked all their lives. Messners smoke. I don't need a doctor to tell me how to cut a shoulder steak, and I don't need a doctor to tell me about smoking.' He can't drive in traffic now without blowing his horn at everybody who comes anywhere near him, and when I tell him there's no need for the horn, he shouts, 'There *isn't*? With madmen out driving cars on the roads?' But it's him—he's the madman on the roads. And I can't take anymore."

Concerned as I was for my mother's well-being, disturbed as I was to see her so shaken—she who was the anchor and the mainstay of our home, who, behind the counter of the butcher shop, was every bit the artist with a meat cleaver that he was—I remembered from listening to her why I was at Winesburg. Forget chapel, forget Caudwell, forget Dr. Donehower's sermons and the girls' convent curfew hours and everything else wrong with this place—endure what is and make it work. Because by leaving home you saved your life. You saved his. Because I would have shot him to shut him up. I could shoot him now for what he was doing to her. Yet what he was doing to himself was worse. And how do you shoot someone whose onset of craziness at the age of fifty wasn't just disrupting his wife's life and irreparably altering his son's life but devastating his own?

"Mom, you've got to get him to Dr. Shildkret. He trusts Dr. Shildkret. He swears by Dr. Shildkret. Let's hear what Dr. Shildkret thinks." I did not myself have a high regard for Shildkret, least of all for his thinking; he was our doctor only because he'd gone to grade school with my father and grown up penniless on the same Newark slum street. Because Shildkret's father was "a lazy bastard" and his mother a long-suffering woman who, in my father's kindly estimation, qualified as "a saint," their moron of a son was our family doctor. Woe unto us, but I didn't know who or what else to recommend other than Shildkret.

"He won't go," my mother said. "I already suggested it. He refuses to go. There's nothing wrong with him—it's the rest of the world that's in the wrong."

"Then *you* see Shildkret. Tell him what's happening. Hear what he says. Maybe he can send him to a specialist."

"A specialist in driving around Newark without honking the horn at every car nearby? No. I could not do that to your father."

"Do what?"

"Embarrass him like that in front of Dr. Shildkret. If he

knew I went and talked about this behind his back, it would
crush him."

"So instead he crushes you? Look at you. You're a wreck.
You, as strong as a person can be, and you have become a
wreck. The kind of wreck I would have become had I stayed
with him in that house another day."

"Darling"—here she grasped at my hand—"darling, should
I? Can I possibly? I came all this way to ask you. You're the
only one I can talk to about this."

"Could you possibly what? What are you asking?"

"I can't say the word."

"What word?" I asked.

"Divorce." And then, my hand still in hers, she used both of
our hands together to cover her mouth. Divorce was unknown
in our Jewish neighborhood. I was led to believe it was all but
unknown in the Jewish world. Divorce was shameful. Divorce
was scandalous. Breaking up a family with a divorce was virtually a criminal act. Growing up, I'd never known of a single
household among my friends or my schoolmates or our family's
friends where the parents were divorced or were drunks or, for
that matter, owned a dog. I was raised to think all three repugnant. My mother could have stunned me more only if she'd
told me she'd gone out and bought a Great Dane.

"Oh, Ma, you're trembling. You're in a state of shock." As
was I. *Would* she? Why not? I'd run off to Winesburg—why
shouldn't she get a divorce? "You've been married to him for
twenty-five years. You love him."

Vigorously, she shook her head. "I don't! I hate him! I sit in
the car while he's driving and screaming to me about how everybody is in the wrong except him, and I hate and I loathe
him from the bottom of my heart!"

By such vehemence we were both astonished. "That is not
true," I said. "Even if it seems true now, it's not a permanent
condition. It's only because I'm gone and you're all on your
own with him and you don't know what to do with him. Please
go see Dr. Shildkret. At least as a start. Ask his advice." Meanwhile, I was afraid of Shildkret's saying, "He's right. People don't
know how to drive anymore. I've noticed this myself. You get
into your car these days, you take your life into your hands."
Shildkret was a dope and a lousy doctor, and it was my good

luck that I had come down with appendicitis nowhere in his vicinity. He would have prescribed an enema and killed me.

Killed me. I'd caught it from my father. All I could think about were the ways I could be killed. *You are odd, you know. Very odd. Odder than I think you realize.* And Olivia should know how to spot oddness, should she not?

"I'm seeing a lawyer," my mother then told me.

"No."

"Yes. I've already seen him. I have an attorney," she said, the helpless way one would say, "I've gone bankrupt" or "I'm going in for a lobotomy." "I went on my own," she said. "I can't live any longer with your father in that house. I cannot work with him in the store. I cannot drive with him in the car. I cannot sleep beside him in the bed anymore. I don't want him near me like that—he's too angry a person to lie next to. It frightens me. That's what I came to tell you." Now she was no longer crying. Now suddenly she was herself, ready and able to do battle, and I was the one at the edge of tears, knowing that none of this would be happening had I remained at home.

It takes muscle to be a butcher, and my mother had muscles, and I felt them when she took me in her arms while I cried.

When we walked from the solarium back to the room—passing on the way Miss Clement, who, like the saint *she* was, kindly kept her gaze averted—Olivia was there arranging a second bouquet of flowers she'd brought with her on her arrival a few minutes earlier. Her sweater sleeves were pushed up so as not to get them wet with the water she'd put into a second vase she'd found, and so there was her scar, the scar on the wrist of the very hand with which she had driven Miss Clement into silence, the very hand with which we pursued our indecent ends in a hospital room while around us in the other rooms people were behaving according to rules that didn't even allow for loud talking. Now Olivia's scar looked to me as prominent as if she had cut herself open only days before.

As a child, I had sometimes been taken by my father to the slaughterhouse on Astor Street in Newark's Ironbound section. And I had been taken to the chicken market at the far end of Bergen Street. At the chicken market I saw them killing the chickens. I saw them kill hundreds of chickens according to the kosher laws. First my father would pick out the chickens he wanted. They were in a cage, maybe five tiers high, and he would reach in to pull one out, hold on to its head so it didn't bite him, and feel the sternum. If it wiggled, the chicken was young and was not going to be tough; if it was rigid, more than likely the chicken was old and tough. He would also blow on its feathers so he could see the skin—he wanted the flesh to be yellow, a little fatty. Whichever ones he picked, he put into one of the boxes that they had, and then the *shochet*, the slaughterer, would ritually slaughter them. He would bend the neck backward—not break it, just arc it back, maybe pull a few of the feathers to get the neck clear so he could see what he was doing—and then with his razor-sharp knife he would cut the throat. For the chicken to be kosher he had to cut the throat in one smooth, deadly stroke. One of the strangest sights I remember from my early youth was the slaughtering of the nonkosher chickens, where they lopped the head right off. Swish! Plop! Whereupon they put the headless chicken down into a funnel. They had about six or seven funnels in a circle. There the blood could drain from the body into a big barrel. Sometimes the chickens' legs were still moving, and occasionally a chicken would fall out of the funnel and, as the saying has it, begin running around with its head cut off. Such chickens might bump into a wall but they ran anyway. They put the kosher chickens in the funnels too. The bloodletting, the killing—my father was hardened to these things, but at the beginning I was of course unsettled, much as I tried not to show it. I was a little one, six, seven years old, but this was the business, and soon I accepted that the business was a mess. The same at the slaughterhouse, where to kosher the animal, you have to get the blood out. In a nonkosher slaughterhouse they can shoot the animal, they can knock it unconscious, they can kill it any way they want to kill it. But to be kosher they've got to bleed it to death. And in my days as a butcher's little son, learning what slaughtering was about, they would hang the animal by its foot to bleed it. First a chain is wrapped around the rear leg—they trap it that way. But that chain is also a hoist, and quickly they hoist it up, and it hangs from its heel so that all the blood will run down to the head and the upper body. Then they're ready to kill it. Enter *shochet* in skullcap. Sits in a little sort of alcove, at least at the Astor Street slaughterhouse he did, takes the head of the animal, lays it over his knees, takes a pretty big blade, says a *bracha*—a blessing— and he cuts the neck. If he does it in one slice, severs the trachea, the esophagus, and the carotids, and doesn't touch the backbone, the animal dies instantly and is kosher; if it takes two slices or the animal is sick or disabled or the knife isn't perfectly sharp or the backbone is merely nicked, the animal is not kosher. The *shochet* slits the throat from ear to ear and then lets the animal hang there until all the blood flows out. It's as if he took a bucket of blood, as if he took several buckets, and poured them out all at once, because that's how fast blood gushes from the arteries onto the floor, a concrete floor with a drain in it. He stands there in boots, in blood up to his ankles despite the drain—and I saw all this when I was a boy. I witnessed it many times. My father thought it was important for me to see it—the same man who now was afraid of everything for me and, for whatever reason, afraid for himself.

My point is this: that is what Olivia had tried to do, to kill herself according to kosher specifications by emptying her body of blood. Had she been successful, had she expertly completed the job with a single perfect slice of the blade, she would have rendered herself kosher in accordance with rabbinical law. Olivia's telltale scar came from attempting to perform her own ritual slaughter.

It was from my mother that I got my height. She was a big, heavyset woman, only one inch under six feet, towering not just over my father but over every mother in the neighborhood. With her dark bushy eyebrows and coarse gray hair (and, at the store, with her coarse gray clothes beneath a bloody white apron), she embodied the role of the laborer as convincingly as any Soviet woman in the propaganda posters about America's overseas allies that hung in the halls of our grade school during the years of World War Two. Olivia was slender and fair, and even at five-seven or -eight seemed diminutive beside my mother, so when the woman who was used to working in a bloody white apron wielding long knives as sharp as swords and opening and shutting the heavy refrigerator door gave Olivia her hand to shake, I saw not only what Olivia must have looked like as a small child but also what little protection she had against confusion when it came at her full force. Her delicate hand wasn't just clasped like a baby lamb chop in the big, bearish paw of my mother; she herself was still in the grip of whatever had driven her, only a few years beyond childhood, first to drink and then to the edge of destruction. She was yielding and fragile to the marrow of her bones, a *wounded* small child, and I finally grasped that only because my mother, even under assault from my father and prepared to go so far as to divorce him, which would be tantamount to killing him—yes, I now saw him dead too—was anything but fragile and yielding. That my father could have gotten my mother to go on her own to see a lawyer about a divorce was a measure not of her weakness but of the crushing power of his inexplicable transformation, of his all at once having been turned inside out by unrelenting intimations of catastrophe.

My mother called Olivia "Miss Hutton" throughout the twenty minutes they were together with me in my hospital room. Otherwise her behavior was impeccable, as was Olivia's. She asked Olivia no embarrassing questions, did not pry into her background or into what her arranging my flowers might signify about our acquaintance—*she* practiced tact. I introduced Olivia as the fellow student who was bringing my homework out to me and who was carrying back with her the written assignments I completed in order to keep abreast of my classes. I didn't once catch her looking at Olivia's wrists, nor did she register suspicion or disapproval of her in any way. If my mother hadn't married my father, she could, without difficulty, have held down any number of jobs far more demanding of the skills of diplomacy and the functioning of intelligence than what was required for work in a butcher shop. Her formidable figure belied the finesse she could marshal when circumstances required an astuteness in the ways of life of which my father was ignorant.

Olivia, as I said, didn't let me down either. She did not even wince at finding herself repeatedly being called Miss Hutton, though I did, each time. What was the something about her that necessitated such formality? It couldn't be because she wasn't Jewish. Though my mother was a Newark Jewish provincial of her class and time and background, she wasn't a stupid provincial, and she knew very well that by his living in the heart of the American Midwest in the middle of the twentieth century, her son was more than likely going to seek out the company of girls born into the predominant, ubiquitous, all but official American faith. Was it Olivia's appearance that put her off then, the look of privilege that she had, as though she'd never known a single hardship? Was it the slender young female body? Was my mother unprepared for that supple physical delicacy crowned by the auburn abundance of that hair? Why again and again "Miss Hutton" to a mannerly girl of nineteen who had done nothing as far as she knew except to help her recuperating son while he was a postoperative hospital patient? What had affronted her? What had alarmed her? It couldn't have been the flowers, though they didn't help. It could only be a quick glimpse of the scar that had made unspeakable and unsayable Olivia's given name. It was the scar *together* with the flowers.

The scar had taken possession of my mother, and Olivia knew it, and so did I. We all knew it, which made nearly unendurable listening to whatever words were spoken about anything else. Olivia's having lasted in the room with my mother for twenty minutes was a heartbreaking feat of gallantry and strength.

As soon as Olivia had left to take the bus back to Winesburg, my mother went into my bathroom, not to wash up but to clean out the sink, the tub, and the toilet bowl with soap and paper towels.

"Ma, don't," I called in to her. "You just got off a train. Everything is clean enough."

"I'm here, it needs it, I'll do it," she said.

"It *doesn't* need it. They did it this morning first thing."

But she needed it more than the bathroom needed it. Work—certain people yearn for work, any work, harsh or unsavory as it may be, to drain the harshness from their lives and drive from their minds the killing thoughts. By the time she came out, she was my mother again, scrubbing and scouring having restored the womanly warmth she'd always had at her disposal to give me. I remembered that when I was a child in school, *Ma at work* would always come to my mind whenever

I thought of my mother, *Ma at work*, but not because work was her burden. To me her maternal grandeur stemmed from her being no less a powerhouse of a butcher than my father.

"So tell me about your studies," she said, settling into the chair in the corner of the room while I propped myself up against the pillows in my bed. "Tell me about what you're learning here."

"American History to 1865. From the first settlements in Jamestown and Massachusetts Bay to the end of the Civil War."

"And you like that?"

"I like it, Mom, yes."

"What else do you study?"

"The Principles of American Government."

"What is that about?"

"How the government works. Its foundations. Its laws. The Constitution. The separation of powers. The three branches. I had civics in high school, but never the government stuff this thoroughly. It's a good course. We read documents. We read some of the famous Supreme Court cases."

"That's wonderful for you. That's right up your alley. And the teachers?"

"They're all right. They're not geniuses, but they're good enough. They're not what's uppermost anyway. I've got the books to study, I've got the library to use—I've got everything a brain requires for an education."

"And you're happier away from home?"

"I'm better off, Ma," I said, and better off, I thought, because you're not.

"Read me something, darling. Read me something from one of your school books. I want to hear what you're learning."

I took the first volume of *The Growth of the American Republic* that Olivia had brought me from my room and, opening it at random, hit upon the beginning of a chapter I'd already studied, "Jefferson's Administration," subtitled "1. The 'Revolution of 1800.'" "'Thomas Jefferson,'" I began, "'ruminating years later on the events of a crowded lifetime, thought that his election to the Presidency marked as real a revolution as that of 1776. He had saved the country from monarchy and militarism, and brought it back to republican simplicity. But there never had been any danger of monarchy; it was John Adams who saved the country from militarism; and a little simplicity cannot be deemed revolutionary.' "

I read further: " 'Fisher Ames predicted that, with a "Jacobin" President, America would be in for a real reign of terror. Yet the four years that followed were one of the most tranquil of the Republican Olympiads, marked not by radical reforms or popular tumults . . .' " And when I looked up, midway through that sentence, I saw that my mother had fallen half asleep in her chair. There was a smile on her face. Her son was reading aloud to her what he was studying in college. It was worth the train ride and the bus ride and maybe even the sight of Miss Hutton's scar. For the first time in months, she was happy.

To keep her that way, I kept going. " '. . . but by the peaceful acquisition of territory as large again as the United States. The election of 1800–1801 brought a change of men more than of measures, and a transfer of federal power from the latitude of Massachusetts to that of Virginia . . .' " Now she was fully asleep, but I did not stop. Madison. Monroe. J. Q. Adams. I'd read right on through to Harry Truman if that was what it took to ease the woes of my having left her behind alone with a husband now out of control.

She spent the night in a hotel not far from the hospital and came again to visit me the next morning, Monday, before she left by bus for the train to take her home. I was to leave the hospital myself after lunch that day. Sonny Cottler had phoned me the night before. He had only just heard about my appendectomy, and despite the unpleasantness of our last meeting out on the quad—to which neither of us alluded—he insisted on coming out in his car to drive me from the hospital back to school, where arrangements had already been made by Dean Caudwell's office for me to spend the next week sleeping in a bed in the small infirmary adjacent to the Student Health Office. I could rest there when I needed to during the day and resume attending all my classes other than gym. I should be ready after that to climb the three flights to my room at the top of Neil Hall. And a couple of weeks after that to return to my job at the inn.

That Monday morning my mother looked herself again, unbroken and unbreakable. After I'd finished assuring her about the helpful arrangements the college had made for my return, the first thing she said was "I won't divorce him, Marcus. I made up my mind. I'll bear him. I'll do all I can to help him, if anything *can* help him. If that's what you want from me, that's what I want too. You don't want divorced parents, and I don't want you to have divorced parents. I'm sorry now that I even allowed myself such thoughts. I'm sorry that I told them to you. The way that I did it, here at the hospital, with you just out of bed and starting to walk around on your own —that wasn't right. That wasn't fair. I apologize. I will stay with him, Marcus, through thick and thin."

I filled up with tears and immediately put my hand over my eyes as though I could either hide my tears that way or manage with my fingers to hold them back.

"You can cry, Markie. I've seen you cry before."

"I know you have. I know I can. I don't want to. I'm just very happy . . ." I had to stop for a while to find my voice and to recover from having been reduced by her words to being the tiny creature who is nothing but its need of perpetual nurture. "I'm just very happy to hear what you said. This behavior of his could be a temporary thing, you know. Things like this happen, don't they, when people hit a certain age?"

"I'm sure they do," she said soothingly.

"Thank you, Ma. This is a great relief to me. I could not imagine him living alone. With only the store and his work and nothing to come home to at night, on his own on the weekends . . . it was unimaginable."

"It is worse than unimaginable," she said, "so don't imagine it. But now I must ask for something in return. Because something is unimaginable to me. I never asked anything of you before. I never asked anything of you before because I never had to. Because you are perfect where sons are concerned. All you've ever wanted to be is a boy who does well. You have been the best son any mother could have. But I am going to ask you to have nothing more to do with Miss Hutton. Because for you to be with her is unimaginable to *me*. Markie, you are here to be a student and to study the Supreme Court and to study Thomas Jefferson and to prepare to go to law school. You are here so someday you will become a person in the community that other people look up to and that they come to for help. You are here so you don't have to be a Messner like your grandfather and your father and your cousins and work in a butcher shop for the rest of your life. You are not here to look for trouble with a girl who has taken a razor and slit her wrists."

"Wrist," I said. "She slit one wrist."

"One is enough. We have only two, and one is too much. Markie, I will stay with your father and in return I will ask you to give her up before you get in over your head and don't know how to get out. I want to make a deal. Will you make that deal with me?"

"Yes," I replied.

"That's my boy! That's my tall, wonderful boy! The world is full of young women who have not slit any wrists—who have slit *nothing*. They exist by the millions. Find one of *them*. She can be a Gentile, she can be anything. This is 1951. You don't live in the old world of my parents and their parents and their parents before them. Why should you? That old world is far, far away and everything in it long gone. All that is left is the kosher meat. That's enough. That suffices. It has to. Probably it should. All the rest can go. The three of us never lived like people in a ghetto, and we're not starting now. We are Americans. Date anyone you want, marry anyone you want, do whatever you want with whoever you choose—as long as she's never put a razor to herself in order to end her life. A girl so wounded as to do such a thing is not for you. To want to wipe out everything before your life has even begun—absolutely not! You have no business with such a person, you don't need such a person, no matter what kind of goddess she looks like and how many beautiful flowers she brings you. She is a beautiful young woman, there is no doubt about that. Obviously she is well brought up. Though maybe there is more to her upbringing than meets the eye. You never know about those things. You never know the truth of what goes on in people's houses. When the child goes wrong, look first to the family. Regardless, my heart goes out to her. I have nothing against her. I wish the girl luck. I pray, for her sake, that her life does not come to nothing. But you are my only son and my only child, and my responsibility is not to her but to you. You must sever the connection completely. You must look elsewhere for a girlfriend."

"I understand," I said.

"Do you? Or are you saying so to avoid a fight?"

"I'm not afraid of a fight, Mother. You know that."

"I know you are strong. You stood up to your father and he is no weakling. And you were right to stand up to him; between the two of us, I was proud of you for standing up to him. But I hope that doesn't mean that when I leave here, you will change your mind. You won't, will you, Markie? When you get back to school, when she comes to see you, when she begins to cry and you see her tears, you won't change your mind? This is a girl full of tears. You see that the moment you look at her. Inside she is all tears. Can you stand up to her tears, Marcus?"

"Yes."

"Can you stand up to hysterical screaming, if it should come to that? Can you stand up to desperate pleading? Can you look the other way when someone in pain begs and begs you for what she wants that you won't give her? Yes, to a father you could say, 'It's none of your business—leave me alone!' But do you have the kind of strength that *this* requires? Because you also have a conscience. A conscience that I'm proud that you have, but a conscience that can be your enemy. You have a conscience and you have compassion and you have sweetness in you too—so tell me, do you know how to do such things as may be required of you with this girl? Because other people's weakness can destroy you just as much as their strength can. Weak people are not harmless. Their weakness can *be* their strength. A person so unstable is a menace to you, Markie, and a trap."

"Mom, you don't have to go on. Stop right here. We have a deal."

Here she took me in those arms of hers, arms as strong as mine, if not stronger, and she said, "You are an emotional boy. Emotional like your father and all of his brothers. You are a Messner like all the Messners. Once your father was the sensible one, the reasonable one, the only one with a head on his shoulders. Now, for whatever reason, he's as crazy as the rest.

The Messners aren't just a family of butchers. They're a family of shouters and a family of screamers and a family of putting their foot down and banging their heads against the wall, and now, out of the blue, your father is as bad as the rest of them. Don't you be. You be *greater* than your feelings. I don't demand this of you—*life* does. Otherwise you'll be washed away by feelings. You'll be washed out to sea and never seen again. Feelings can be life's biggest problem. Feelings can play the most terrible tricks. They played them on me when I came to you and said I was going to divorce your father. Now I have dealt with those feelings. Promise me you will deal the same with yours."

"I promise you. I will."

We kissed, and thinking in unison of my father, we were as though welded together by our desperate passion for a miracle to occur.

At the infirmary, I was shown to the narrow hospital bed— one of three in a smallish, bright room looking onto the campus woods—that would be mine for the next week. The nurse showed me how to pull the curtain to encircle the bed for privacy, though, as she told me, the two other beds were unoccupied, so for the time being I'd have the place to myself. She pointed out the bathroom across the hall, where there was a sink, a toilet, and a shower. The sight of each made me remember my mother cleaning the bathroom at the hospital after Olivia had left us to return to the campus—after Olivia had left, never to be invited into my life again, should I go ahead and keep the promise I'd made to my mother.

Sonny Cottler was with me at the infirmary and helped me move my belongings—textbooks and a few toilet items—so that, in keeping with the parting instructions from the doctor, I didn't have to carry or lift anything. Driving back from the hospital in the car, Sonny had said I could call on him for whatever I might need and invited me to the fraternity house for dinner that night. He was as kind and attentive as he could be, and I wondered if my mother had spoken to him about Olivia and if he was being so solicitous to prevent me from pining for her and breaking my deal with my mother or if he was secretly planning on calling her himself and taking her out again now that I had forsworn her. Even with him helping me, I couldn't get over my suspiciousness.

Everything I saw or heard caused my thoughts to turn to Olivia. I declined going to the fraternity house with Sonny and instead ate my first meal back on campus alone at the student cafeteria, hoping to find Olivia eating by herself at one of the smaller tables. To return to the infirmary, I took the long way around, passing the Owl, where I put my head inside to see if she might be eating by herself at the counter, even though I knew she disliked the place as much as I did. And all the while I went looking for an opportunity to run into her, and all the while I was discovering that everything, starting with the bathroom at the infirmary, reminded me of her, I was addressing her inside my head: "I miss you already. I'll always miss you. There'll never be anybody like you!" And intermittently, in response, came her melodic, lighthearted "I shot an arrow into the air / It fell to earth I knew not where." "Oh, Olivia," I thought, beginning to write her another letter, this too in my head, "you are so wonderful, so beautiful, so smart, so dignified, so lucid, so uniquely sexed-up. What if you did slit your wrist? It's healed, isn't it? And so are you! So you blew me— where's the crime? So you blew Sonny Cottler—where's . . ." But that thought, and the snapshot accompanying it, was not so easy to manage successfully and took more than one effort to erase. "I want to be with you. I want to be near you. You *are* a goddess—my mother was right. And who deserts a goddess because his mother tells him to? And my mother won't divorce my father no matter what I do. There is no way that she would send him to live with the cats in back of the store. Her announcing that she was divorcing him and had engaged an attorney was merely the ploy by which she tricked me. But then it couldn't be a ploy, since she'd already told me about divorcing him before she'd even known of you. Unless she'd already learned of you through Cottler's relatives in Newark. But my mother would never deceive me like that. Nor could I deceive her. I'm caught—I've made her a promise I can never break, whose keeping is going to break me!"

Or perhaps, I thought, I could fail to keep the promise without her finding out . . . But when I got to history class on Tuesday, any possibility of betraying my mother's trust disappeared, because Olivia wasn't there. She was absent from class on Thursday as well. Nor did I see her seated anywhere at chapel when I attended on Wednesday. I checked every seat in every row, and she wasn't there. And I had thought, We'll sit side by side through chapel, and everything that drives me crazy will suddenly be a source of amusement with Olivia enchantingly laughing beside me.

But she'd left school entirely. I had known it the moment I saw she was absent from history class, and had then confirmed it by calling her dormitory and asking to speak to her. Whoever picked up said, "She's gone home," politely, but in such a way as to make me think something had happened beyond Olivia's simply having "gone home"—something that none of them were supposed to talk about. When I did not call or contact her, she had tried again to kill herself—that had to be what had happened. After being called "Miss Hutton" a dozen times in twenty minutes by my mother, after waiting in vain for me to phone once I was back and settled into the infirmary, she had taken measures of just the kind my mother had warned me about. So I was lucky, was I not? Spared a suicidal girlfriend, was I not? Yes, and never before so devastated.

And what if she had not merely tried to kill herself—suppose she'd succeeded? What if she had slit both wrists this time, and bled to death in the dormitory—what if she had done it out at the cemetery where we had parked that night? Not only would the college do everything to keep it a secret, but so would her family. That way no one at Winesburg would ever know what happened, and no one but me would know why. Unless she'd left a note. Then everyone would blame her suicide on me—on my mother and on me.

I had to walk back to Jenkins and down to the basement, across from the post office, to find a pay phone with a folding door that I could tightly shut in order to make my call without anyone overhearing it. There was no note from her at the post office—that was what I'd checked first after Sonny had installed me in the infirmary. Before making my call, I checked again, and this time found there a college envelope containing a handwritten letter from Dean Caudwell:

Dear Marcus:

We're all glad to have you back on campus and to be assured by the doctor that you came through in top-notch shape. I hope now you'll reconsider your decision not to go out for baseball when spring comes. This coming year's team needs a rangy infielder, à la Marty Marion of the Cards, and you look to me as if you might well fill the bill. I suspect you're fast on your feet, and as you know, there are ways to get on base and help score runs that don't necessitate hitting the ball over the fence. A bunt dropped for a base hit can be one of the most beautiful things to behold in all of sports. I've already put in a word with Coach Portzline. He is eager to see you at tryouts when they're held on March I. Welcome back rejuvenated to the Winesburg community. I like to think of this moment as your return to the fold. I hope you're thinking that way too. If I can be of any help to you, please do not hesitate to stop by the office.

> Yours sincerely,
> Hawes D. Caudwell,
> Dean of Men

I changed a five-dollar bill into quarters at the post office window, and then, after pulling shut the heavy glass door, I settled into the phone booth, where I arranged the quarters in stacks of four on the curved shelf beneath the phone in which a "G.L." had dared to carve his initials. Immediately I wondered how G.L. was disciplined when he was caught.

I was prepared for I didn't know what, and already as drenched in sweat as I had been in Caudwell's office. I dialed long-distance information and asked for Dr. Hutton in Hunting Valley. And there was such a one, a Dr. Tyler Hutton. I took down two numbers, for Dr. Hutton's office and for his residence. It was still daytime, and, having already convinced myself that Olivia was dead, I decided on calling the office, figuring that her father wouldn't be at work because of the death in the family, and that by speaking to a receptionist or a nurse I could get some idea of what had happened. I didn't want to speak to either of her parents for fear of hearing one or the other of them say, "So you're the one, you're the boy—you're the Marcus from her suicide note." After the long-distance operator reached the office number, and I had deposited a stream of quarters into the appropriate slot, I said, "Hello, I'm a friend of Olivia's," but didn't know what to say next. "This is Dr. Hutton's office," I was informed by the woman at the other end. "Yes, I want to find out about Olivia," I said. "This is the office," she said, and I hung up.

I walked directly down the Hill from the main quadrangle to the women's residence halls and up the stairs to Dowland Hall, where Olivia had lived and where I'd picked her up in Elwyn's LaSalle the night of the date that sealed her doom. I went inside, and at the desk blocking access to the first floor and the staircase was the student on duty. I showed her my ID and asked if she'd phone Olivia's floor to tell her that I was waiting downstairs. I'd already called Dowland on Thursday, when for the second time Olivia had failed to attend history class, and asked to speak to her. That's when I'd been told, "She's gone home." "When will she be back?" "She's gone home." So now I had asked for her again, this time in person, and again I was given the brushoff. "Has she gone for good?" I asked. The on-duty girl simply shrugged. "Is she all right, do you know?" She was a long time working up a response, only to decide in the end not to make one.

It was Friday, November 2. I was now five days out of the hospital and scheduled to resume climbing the three flights of stairs to my Neil Hall room on Monday, yet I felt weaker than I had when they got me up from bed to take my first few steps after the operation. Whom could I call to confirm that Olivia was dead without my also being accused of being the one who killed her? Would news of the death by her own hand of a Winesburg coed be in the papers? Shouldn't I go over to the library and comb through the Cleveland dailies to find out? The news surely wouldn't have been carried in the town paper, the *Winesburg Eagle*, or in the undergraduate paper, the *Owl's Eye*. You could commit suicide twenty times over on that campus and never make it into that insipid rag. What was I doing at a place like Winesburg? Why wasn't I back eating my lunch out of a paper bag down from the drunks in the city park with Spinelli and playing second for Robert Treat and taking all those great courses from my New York teachers? If only my father, if only Flusser, if only Elwyn, if only Olivia—!

Next I rushed from Dowland back to Jenkins and hurried

down the first-floor corridor to Dean Caudwell's office and asked his secretary if I could see him. She had me wait in a chair across from her desk in the outer office until the dean had finished meeting with another student. That student turned out to be Bert Flusser, whom I hadn't seen since I'd moved from the first of my rooms. What was he in with the dean for? Rather, why wasn't he with the dean every day? He must be in contention with him all the time. He must be in contention with *everybody* all the time. Provocation and rebellion and censure. How do you keep that drama going day in and day out? And who but a Flusser would want to be continually in the wrong, scolded and judged, contemptibly singular, disgusted by everyone and abominably unique? Where better than at Winesburg for a Bertram Flusser to luxuriate without abatement in an abundance of rebuke? Here in the world of the righteous, the anathema was in his element—more than could be said for me.

With no regard for the presence of the secretary, Flusser said to me, "The puking—good work." Then he proceeded toward the door to the hallway, where he turned and hissed, "I'll be revenged on the whole pack of you." The secretary pretended to have heard nothing but merely rose to escort me to the dean's door, where she knocked and said, "Mr. Messner."

He came around from behind his desk to shake my hand. The stink I'd left behind me had long been eradicated by now. So how did Flusser know about it? Because everyone knew about it? Because the secretary to the dean of men had made it her business to tell them? This sanctimonious little pisshole of a college—how I hated it.

"You look well, Marcus," the dean said. "You've lost a few pounds but otherwise you look fine."

"Dean Caudwell, I don't know who else to turn to about something that's very important to me. I never meant to throw up here, you know."

"You fell ill and you were sick and that's that. Now you're on the mend and soon will be yourself again. What can I do for you?"

"I'm here about a female student," I began. "She was in my history class. And now she's gone. When I told you I'd had

one date, it had been with her. Olivia Hutton. Now she's disappeared. Nobody will tell me where or why. I would like to
know what happened to her. I'm afraid something terrible has
happened to her. I'm afraid," I added, "that I may have had
something to do with it."

You should never have said that, I told myself. They'll throw
you out for contributing to a suicide. They could even turn
you over to the police. They probably turned G.L. over to the
police.

I still had in my pocket the dean's letter welcoming me back
"rejuvenated" to the college. I'd only just picked it up. That's
what had drawn me to his office—that's how foolishly I'd been
taken in.

"What is it you did," he asked, "that makes you think this?"

"I took her out on a date."

"Did something happen on the date that you want to tell
me about?"

"No, sir." He'd lured me in with no more than a kindly
handwritten letter. *A bunt dropped for a base hit can be one of
the most beautiful things to behold in all of sports. I've already
put in a word about you with Coach Portzline. He's eager to see
you at tryouts* . . . No, it was Caudwell who was eager to see
me about Olivia. I had stepped directly into his trap.

"Dean," he said kindly. "I'm 'Dean' to you, please."

"The answer is no, Dean," I repeated. "Nothing happened
that I want to tell you about."

"Are you sure?"

"Absolutely," and now I could imagine the suicide note and
understood how I'd just been bamboozled into perjuring myself: "Marcus Messner and I had sexual contact and then he
dropped me as though I were a slut. I'd prefer to be dead than
live with that shame."

"Did you impregnate this young lady, Marcus?"

"Why—*no*."

"You're sure?"

"Absolutely sure."

"She wasn't pregnant as far as you know."

"No."

"You're telling the truth."

"Yes!"

"And you didn't force yourself on her. You didn't force yourself on Olivia Hutton."

"No, sir. Never."

"She visited you in your hospital room, did she not?"

"Yes, Dean."

"According to a member of the hospital staff, something occurred between the two of you at the hospital, something sordid occurred that was observed and duly recorded. Yet you say you didn't force yourself on her in your room."

"I'd just had my appendix out, Dean."

"That doesn't answer my question."

"I've never used force in my life, Dean Caudwell. On anyone. I've never had to," I added.

"You didn't have to. May I ask what that means?"

"No, no, sir, you can't. Dean Caudwell, this is very hard to talk about. I do think I have the right to believe that whatever may have happened in the privacy of my hospital room was strictly between Olivia and myself."

"Perhaps and perhaps not. I think everyone would agree that if it ever was strictly between the two of you, in the light of circumstances it isn't any longer. I think we would agree that's why you came to see me."

"Why?"

"Because Olivia is no longer here."

"Where is she?"

"Olivia had a nervous breakdown, Marcus. She had to be taken away by ambulance."

She who looked the way she looked was taken away in an ambulance? That girl so blessed with that brain and that beauty and that poise and that charm and that wit? This was almost worse than her being dead. The smartest girl around goes off in an ambulance because of a nervous breakdown while everybody else on this campus is taking stock of themselves in the light of biblical teachings and coming out feeling just fine!

"I don't really know what goes into a nervous breakdown," I admitted to Caudwell.

"You lose control over yourself. Everything is too much for you and you give way, you collapse in every conceivable way. You have no more control over your emotions than an infant, and you have to be hospitalized and cared for like an infant until you recover. If you ever do recover. The college took a chance with Olivia Hutton. We knew the mental history. We knew the history of electroshock treatment and we knew the sad history of relapse after relapse. But her father is a Cleveland surgeon and a distinguished alumnus of Winesburg, and we took her in at Dr. Hutton's request. It didn't work out well either for Dr. Hutton or for the college, and it especially didn't work out for Olivia."

"But is she all right?" And when I asked the question I felt as though I were myself on the brink of collapsing. Please, I thought, please, Dean Caudwell, let us speak sensibly about Olivia and not about "relapse after relapse" and "electro-shock"! Then I realized that was what he was doing.

"I told you," he said, "the girl had a breakdown. No, she is not all right. Olivia is pregnant. Despite her history, someone went ahead and impregnated her."

"Oh, no," I said. "And she's where?"

"At a hospital specializing in psychiatric care."

"But she can't possibly be pregnant too."

"She can and she is. A helpless young woman, a deeply un-happy person suffering from long-standing mental and emo-tional problems, unable adequately to protect herself against the pitfalls of a young woman's life, has been taken advantage of by someone. By someone with a lot of explaining to do."

"It's not me," I said.

"What was reported to us about your conduct as a patient at the hospital suggests otherwise, Marcus."

"I don't care what it 'suggests.' I will not be condemned on the basis of no evidence. Sir, I resent once again your portrayal of me. You falsify my motives and you falsify my deeds. I did not have sexual intercourse with Olivia." Flushing furiously I said, "I have never had sexual intercourse with anyone. No-body in this world can be pregnant because of me. It's impos-sible!"

"Given all we now know," the dean said, "that's also hard to believe."

"Oh, fuck you it is!" Yes, belligerently, angrily, impulsively, and for the second time at Winesburg. But I *would* not be condemned on no evidence. I was sick of that from everyone.

He stood, not to rear back like Elwyn and take a shot at me but to let himself be seen in all his office's majesty. Nothing moved except for his eyes, which scanned my face as if in itself it were a moral scandal.

I left, and the wait to be expelled began. I couldn't believe Olivia was pregnant, just as I couldn't believe she'd sucked off Cottler or anyone else at Winesburg other than me. But whether or not it was true that she was pregnant—pregnant without telling me; pregnant, as it were, overnight; pregnant perhaps before she even got to Winesburg; pregnant, quite impossibly, like their Virgin Mary—I'd myself been drawn into the vapidity not merely of the Winesburg College mores but of the rectitude tyrannizing my life, the constricting rectitude that, I was all too ready to conclude, was what had driven Olivia crazy. Don't look to the family for the cause, Ma—look to what the conventional world deems impermissible! Look to me, so pathetically conventional upon his arrival here that he could not trust a girl because she blew him!

My room. My room, my home, my hermitage, my tiny Winesburg haven—when I reached it that Friday after a trek more laborious than I'd been expecting up a mere three and a half flights of stairs, I found the bedsheets and blankets and pillows strewn in every direction and the mattress and the floor overspread with the contents of my dresser drawers, all of which were flung wide open. Undershirts, undershorts, socks, and handkerchiefs were wadded up and scattered across the worn wooden floor along with shirts and trousers that had been pulled with their hangers from my tiny alcove of a closet and hurled everywhere. Then I saw—in the corner under the room's high little window—the garbage: apple cores, banana skins, Coke bottles, cracker boxes, candy wrappers, jelly jars, partially eaten sandwiches, and torn-off chunks of packaged bread smeared with what at first I took to be shit but was mercifully only peanut butter. A mouse appeared from amid the pile and scuttled under the bed and out of sight. Then a second mouse. Then a third.

Olivia. In a rage with my mother and me, Olivia had come to ransack and besmirch my room and then gone off to commit suicide. It horrified me to think that, crazed with rage as she was, she could have finished off this lunatic fiasco by slicing open her wrists right there on my bed.

There was a stink of rotting food, and another smell, equally strong, but one that I couldn't identify right off, so stunned was I by what I saw and surmised. Directly at my feet was a single sock turned inside out. I picked up the sock and held it to my nose. The sock, congealed into a crumpled mass, smelled not of feet but of dried sperm. Everything I then picked up and held to my nose smelled the same. Everything had been steeped in sperm. The hundred dollars' worth of clothing that I'd bought at the College Shop had been spared only because they'd been on my back when I went off to the infirmary with appendicitis.

While I was away in the hospital somebody camping in my room had been masturbating day and night into almost every item I owned. And it wasn't, of course, Olivia. It was Flusser. It had to be Flusser. *I'll be revenged on the whole pack of you.* And this one-man bacchanalia was the revenge on me.

Suddenly I began to gag—as much from the shock as from the smells—and I stepped out the door to ask aloud of the empty corridor what harm I had done Bertram Flusser that he should perpetrate the grossest vandalism on my piddling possessions. In vain I tried to understand the enjoyment he had taken in defiling everything that was mine. Caudwell at one end and Flusser at the other; my mother at one end and my father at the other; playful, lovely Olivia at one end and broken-down Olivia at the other. And betwixt them all, I importunately defending myself with my fatuous fuck yous.

Sonny Cottler explained everything when he came for me in his car and I took him upstairs to show him the room. Standing in the doorway with me Sonny said, "He loves you, Marcus. These are tokens of his love." "The garbage too?" "The garbage especially," Sonny said. "The John Barrymore of Winesburg has been swept off his feet." "Is that true? Flusser's queer?" "Mad as a fucking hatter, queer as a three-dollar bill. You should have seen him in satin knee breeches in *School for Scandal.* Onstage, Flusser's hilarious—perfect mimic, brilliant farceur. Offstage, he's completely cracked. Offstage, Flusser's a gargoyle. There are such gargoyle people, Marcus, and you have now run into one." "But this isn't love—that's absurd."

"Lots about love is absurd," Cottler told me. "He's proving to you how potent he is." "No," I said, "if it's anything, it's hatred. It's antagonism. Flusser's turned my room into a garbage dump because he hates my guts. And what did I do? I broke the goddamn record that he kept me up with all night long! Only that was weeks ago, that was back when I'd just got here. And I bought a new one—I went out the next day and replaced it! But for him to do a thing so huge and destructive and disgusting as this, that I should stick in his craw so much for so long—it makes no sense. You would think he was miles above caring about anybody like me—and instead, this clash, this quarrel, this loathing! What now? What next? How can I possibly live here anymore?" "You can't for now. We'll set you up tonight with a cot at the house. And I can loan you some clothes." "But look at this place, *smell* this place! He wants me to *wallow* in this shit! Christ, now I have to talk to the dean, don't I? I have to report this vendetta, don't I?" "To the dean? To Caudwell? I wouldn't advise it. Flusser won't go quietly, Marcus, if you're the one who fingers him. Talk to the dean and he'll tell Caudwell you're the man in his life. Talk to the dean and he'll tell Caudwell that you had a lover's spat. Flusser is our abominable bohemian. Yes, even Winesburg has one. Nobody can curb Bertram Flusser. If they throw Flusser out because of this, he'll take you down with him—that I guarantee. The *last* thing to do is to go to the dean. Look, first you're felled by an appendectomy, then all your worldly goods are bespattered by Flusser—of course you can't think straight." "Sonny, I cannot afford to get thrown out of school!" "But you haven't done anything," he said, closing the door to my stinking room. "Something was done to you."

But I and my animosity had done plenty, of course, upon being charged by Caudwell with impregnating Olivia.

I didn't like Cottler and didn't trust him, and the moment I stepped into the car to take him up on his offer of a cot and some clothes, I knew I was making yet another mistake. He was glib, he was cocky, he considered himself superior not just to Caudwell but probably to me as well. A child of the classiest Cleveland Jewish suburb, with long dark lashes and a cleft in his chin, with two letters in basketball and, despite his being a Jew, the president for the second straight year of the Interfraternity Council—the son of a father who wasn't a butcher but the owner of his own insurance firm and of a mother who wasn't a butcher either but the heiress to a Cleveland department-store fortune—Sonny Cottler was just too smooth for me, too self-certain for me, quick and clever in his way but altogether the perfectly exemplary external young man. The smartest thing for me to do was to get the hell out of Winesburg and get myself back to New Jersey and, though it was already a third of the way into the semester, try, before I got grabbed up by the draft, to rematriculate at Robert Treat. Leave the Flussers and the Cottlers and the Caudwells behind you, leave Olivia behind you, and head home by train tomorrow, home where there is only a befuddled butcher to deal with, and the rest is hard-working, coarse-grained, bribe-ridden, semi-xenophobic Irish-Italian-German-Slavic-Jewish-Negro Newark.

But because I was in a state, I went to the fraternity house instead, and there Sonny introduced me to Marty Ziegler, one of the fraternity members, a soft-spoken boy looking as though he hadn't yet required a shave, a junior from Dayton who idolized Sonny, who would do anything Sonny asked, a born follower to a born leader, who, up in the privacy of Sonny's room, agreed on the spot, for only a buck and a half a session, to be my proxy at chapel—to sign my name on the attendance card, to hand it in at the church door on the way out, and to speak to no one about the arrangement, either while he was doing it or after he'd completed the job. He had the trusting smile of one possessed by the desire to be found inoffensive by all, and seemed as eager to please me as he was to please Sonny.

That Ziegler was a mistake, I was certain—the final mistake. Not malevolent Flusser, the college misanthrope, but kindly Ziegler—he was the destiny that now hung over me. I was amazed by what I was doing. No follower, either born or made, yet I too yielded to the born leader, after a day like this one, too exhausted and flabbergasted not to.

"Now," Sonny said, after my newly hired proxy had left the room, "now we've taken care of chapel. Simple, wasn't it?"

So said self-assured Sonny, though I knew without a doubt, even then, knew like the son of my fear-laden father, that this preternaturally handsome Jewish boy with a privileged paragon's princely bearing, used to inspiring respect and being obeyed and ingratiating himself with everyone and never quarreling with anyone and attracting the admiring attention of everyone, used to taking delight in being the biggest thing in his little interfraternity world, would turn out to be the angel of death.

It was already snowing heavily while Sonny and I were up in my room in Neil Hall, and by the time we'd reached the fraternity house, the wind had kicked up to forty miles an hour and, weeks before Thanksgiving, the blizzard of November '51 had begun blanketing the northern counties of the state, as well as neighboring Michigan and Indiana, then western Pennsylvania and upstate New York, and finally much of New England, before it blew out to sea. By nine in the evening two feet of snow had fallen, and it was still snowing, magically snowing, now without a wind howling through the streets of Winesburg, without the town's old trees swaying and creaking and their weakest limbs, whipped by the wind and under the burden of snow, crashing down into the yards and blocking the roads and driveways—now without a murmur from the wind or the trees, just the raggedy clots swirling steadily downward as though with the intention of laying to rest everything discomposed in the upper reaches of Ohio.

Just after nine we heard the roar. It carried all the way from the campus, which lay about half a mile up Buckeye Street from the Jewish fraternity house where I'd eaten my dinner and been given a cot and a dresser of my own—and some of Sonny's freshly laundered clothes to put in it—and installed as the great Sonny's roommate, for that night and longer if I liked. The roar we heard was like the roar of a crowd at a football game after a touchdown's been scored, except that it was unabating. Like the roar of a crowd after a championship's been won. Like the roar that rises from a victorious nation at the conclusion of a hard-fought war.

It all began on the smallest scale and in the most innocently youthful way: with a snowball fight in the empty quadrangle in front of Jenkins among four freshman boys from small Ohio towns, boyish boys with rural backgrounds, who'd run out of their dormitory room to frolic in the first snowstorm of their first fall semester away at college. At the start, the underclassmen who rushed to join them emptied out of Jenkins only, but when residents in the two dorms perpendicular to Jenkins looked from their windows at what was happening in the quad, they began pouring from Neil, then from Waterford, and soon a high-spirited snowball fight was being waged by dozens of happy, hyperkinetic boys cavorting in dungarees and T-shirts, in sweatsuits, in pajamas, even some in only underwear. Within an hour, they were hurling at one another not just snowballs but beer cans whose contents they'd guzzled down while they fought. There were flecks of red blood in the clean snow from where some of them had been cut by the flying debris, which now included textbooks and wastebaskets and pencils and pencil sharpeners and uncapped ink bottles; the ink, cast wide and far, splotched the snow blue-black in the light of the electrified old gas lamps that gracefully lined the walkways. But their bleeding did nothing to dilute their ardor. The sight of their own blood in the white snow may even have been what provided the jolt to transform them from playful children recklessly delighting in the surprise of an unseasonable snowfall into a whooping army of mutineers urged on by a tiny cadre of seditious underclassmen to turn their rambunctious frivolity into stunning mischief and, with an outburst of everything untamed in them (despite regular attendance at chapel), to tumble and roll and skid down the Hill through the deep snow and commence a stupendous night out that nobody of their generation of Winesburgians would ever forget, one christened the next day by the *Winesburg Eagle*, in an emotionally charged editorial expressing the community's angry disgust, as "the Great White Panty Raid of Winesburg College."

They got inside the three girls' residence halls—Dowland, Koons, and Fleming—by bulling through the unplowed snow of the walkways and then on up the unshoveled stairs to the doorways and through the doors that were already shut tight for the night by breaking the glass to get to the locks or simply battering down the doors with fists, feet, and shoulders and tracking gobs of snow and churned-up slush inside the off-limits dormitories. Easily they overturned the on-duty desks that blocked access to the stairwells and then poured up onto

the floors and into the bedrooms and sorority suites. While
coeds ran in every direction in search of a place to hide, the
invaders proceeded to fling open dresser drawer after dresser
drawer, entering and sacking all the rooms to ferret out every
pair of white panties they could find and to set them sailing
out the windows and plummeting down onto the picturesquely
whitened quadrangle below, where by now several hundred
fraternity boys, who'd made their way out of the off-campus
frat houses and through the deep drifts along Buckeye Street
to the women's quad, had gathered to glory in this most un-
Winesburgian wild spree.

"Panties! Panties! Panties!" The word, still as inflammatory
for them as college students as it had been at the onset of puberty, constituted the whole of the cheer exultantly repeated
from below, while up in the rooms of the female students the
several scores of drunken boys, their garments, their hands,
their crew-cut hair, their faces smeared blue-black with ink and
crimson with blood and dripping with beer and melted snow,
reenacted en masse what an inspired Flusser had done all on
his own in my little room under the eaves at Neil. Not all of
them, by no means anywhere close to all of them, just the most
notable blockheads among them—three altogether, two fresh-
men and one sophomore, all of whom were among the first to
be expelled the next day—masturbated into pairs of stolen
panties, masturbated just about as quickly as you could snap
your fingers, before each hurled the deflowered panties, wet
and fragrant with ejaculate, down into the upraised hands of
the jubilant gathering of red-cheeked, snow-capped upperclassmen breathing steam like dragons and egging them on
from below.

Occasionally a single deep male voice, articulating in behalf
of all those there unable to comply any longer with the prevailing system of moral discipline, baldly bellowed out the truth of
it—"We want girls!"—but in the main it was a mob willing to
settle for panties, panties that any number of them soon took
to drawing down over their hair like caps or to pulling on up
past their overshoes so as to sport the intimate apparel of the
other gender atop their trousers as though they had dressed
inside out. Among the myriad objects seen dropping from the
open windows that night were brassieres, girdles, sanitary

napkins, ointment tubes, lipsticks, slips and half slips, nighties, a few handbags, some U.S. currency, and a collection of prettily ornamented hats. Meanwhile, in the quadrangle yard, a large, breasted snowwoman had been built and bedecked in lingerie, a tampon planted jauntily in her lipsticked mouth like a white cigar, and finished off with a beautiful Easter bonnet arest atop a hairdo contrived from a handful of damp dollar bills.

Probably none of this would have happened had the cops been able to get to the campus before the innocuous snowballing out front of Jenkins had begun to veer out of control. But the Winesburg streets and the college paths wouldn't start to be cleared until the snowfall stopped, so neither the officers in the three squad cars belonging to the town nor the guards in the two campus security cars belonging to the college were able to make headway other than on foot. And by the time they reached the women's quad, the residences were a wreck and the mayhem was well beyond containment.

It took Dean Caudwell to stop some other, more grotesque outrage from occurring—Dean Caudwell standing six feet four inches tall on the front porch of Dowland Hall in his overcoat and muffler and calling through a bullhorn he grasped in his ungloved hand, "Winesburgians, Winesburgians, return to your rooms! Return immediately or risk expulsion!" It took that dire warning from the college's most revered and senior dean (and the fact that the draft was gobbling up eighteen-and-a-half-, nineteen-, and twenty-year-olds without college deferments) to begin to dispel the cheering mob of male students packed together into the women's quad and get them heading as quickly as they could back to wherever they'd come from. As for those inside the women's dorms still foraging through the dresser drawers, only when the town and the campus police entered and began hunting them down room by room did the last of the panties cease to drop from the windows—from windows all still wide open despite a nighttime temperature of twenty degrees—and only then did the invaders themselves begin to leap out the windows of the lower floors of Dowland, Koons, and Fleming into the cushion of deep snow accumulated below and, if they didn't break a limb in attempting their escape—as did two of them—to head for the Hill.

*

Later that night, Elwyn Ayers was killed. Being Elwyn, he'd had nothing to do with the panty raid, but after finishing his homework, he had (according to testimony provided by some half dozen of his fraternity brothers) spent the remainder of the evening back of the fraternity house, camped in his LaSalle, running the engine to keep it warm, and getting out only to sweep off the snow that rapidly settled on the roof, the hood, and the trunk and then to spade it away from the four wheels so he could attach a brand-new set of winter chains to the tires. For the sake of the automotive adventure, to see how well the powerful 1940 four-door Touring Sedan with the lengthened wheelbase and the larger carburetor and the 130 horsepower, the last of the prestigious cars named for the French explorer that GM would ever manufacture, could perform in the high-piled snow of the Winesburg streets, he decided to take it for a test spin. Downtown, where the railroad tracks had been kept clear by the stationmaster and his assistant throughout the storm, Elwyn attempted apparently to outrace the midnight freight train to the level crossing that separated Main Street from Lower Main, and the LaSalle, skidding out of control, spun twice around on the tracks and was struck head-on by the snow-plow of the locomotive bound from points east to Akron. The car in which I had taken Olivia to dinner and then out to the cemetery—a historic vehicle, even a monument of sorts, in the history of fellatio's advent onto the Winesburg campus in the second half of the twentieth century—went careening off to the side and turned end-over-end down Lower Main until it exploded in flames, and Elwyn Ayers Jr. was killed, apparently on impact, and then quickly burned up in the wreckage of the car that he had cared for above all else in life and loved in lieu of men or women.

As it turned out, Elwyn was not the first, or even the second, but the third Winesburg senior who over the years since the introduction of the automobile into American life had failed to graduate because of having lost out in his attempt to outrace that midnight freight train. But he had taken the heavy snow-fall for a challenge worthy of him and the LaSalle, and so, like me, my ex-roommate entered the realm of eternal recollection instead of the tugboat business, and here he will have forever to think about the fun of driving that great car. In my mind's eye I kept imagining the moment of impact, when Elwyn's pumpkin-shaped head crashed against the windshield and splattered very like a pumpkin into a hundred chunky pieces of flesh and bone and brain and blood. We had slept in the same room and studied together—and now he was dead at twenty-one. He had called Olivia a cunt—and now he was dead at twenty-one. My first thought on hearing of Elwyn's fatal accident was that I would never have moved had I known beforehand that he was going to die. Up until then, the only people I knew who had died were my two older cousins who'd been killed in the war. Elwyn was the first person who died that I hated. Must I now stop hating him to begin mourning him? Must I now start pretending that I was sorry to hear that he was dead, and horrified to hear how he had died? Must I put on a long face and go to the memorial service at his fraternity house and express condolences to his fraternity brothers, many of whom I knew as drunks who whistled through their fingers at me and called me something sounding suspiciously like "Jew" when they wanted service at the inn? Or should I try to reclaim residence in the room in Jenkins Hall before it wound up being assigned to somebody else?

"Elwyn!" I shout. "Elwyn, can you hear me? It's Messner! I'm dead too!"

Nothing in response. No, no roommates here. But then he wouldn't have replied anyway, the silent, violent, unsmiling prick. Elwyn Ayers, in death as in life, still opaque to me.

"Ma!" I shout next. "Ma—are you here? Dad, are you here? Ma? Dad? Olivia? Are any of you here? Did you die, Olivia? Answer me! You were the only gift Winesburg gave me. Who impregnated you, Olivia? Or did you finally end your life yourself, you charming, irresistible girl?"

But there is no one to speak to; there is only myself to address about my innocence, my explosions, my candor, and the extreme brevity of bliss in the first true year of my young manhood and the last year of my life. The urge to be heard, and nobody to hear me! I am dead. The unpronounceable sentence pronounced.

"Ma! Dad! Olivia! I am thinking of you!"

No response. To provoke no response no matter how

painstaking the attempt to unravel and to be revealed. All minds gone except my own. No response. Profoundly sad.

The next morning, the *Winesburg Eagle*, in a "double" Saturday edition devoted entirely to all that the blizzard had unleashed at the college, reported that Elwyn Ayers Jr., class of '52, the sole fatality of the night, had in fact been the spark plug of the panty raid and had driven through the blinking red lights at the level crossing in an attempt to flee from discovery by the police—a completely cockeyed story and one retracted the following day, though not before it had been picked up and printed on page one of his hometown daily, the *Cincinnati Enquirer*.

Also that morning, promptly at seven A.M., the reckoning began on campus, with every underclassman who admitted to taking part in the panty raid furnished a snow shovel—the cost of which was tacked on to their semester's residence fees—and dragooned into snow-clearing squads whose task was to clear the campus roads and walkways of the thirty-four inches of snow that had been dumped by the blizzard and that in places had drifted to more than six feet. Each squad was overseen by upperclassmen on the university's athletic teams and the enterprise supervised by faculty members from the physical education department. At the same time, interrogations were conducted throughout the day in Caudwell's office. By nightfall eleven underclassmen, nine freshman and two sophomores, had been identified as ringleaders, and, having been denied the possibility of absolving themselves by doing penance on a snow removal crew (or of being punished with semester-long suspensions, as the families of the offenders were hoping would be the worst their young sons would be made to endure for what they tried to argue was no more than an undergraduate prank), they were permanently expelled from the college. Among them were the two who had broken limbs leaping from the women's residence halls and who had appeared before the dean in their fresh white casts, both, reportedly, with tears in their eyes and profuse apologies pouring from their lips. But they begged in vain for understanding, let alone for mercy. To Caudwell they were the two last rats fleeing the ship, and out they went for good. And anyone called before the dean who denied participating in the panty raid and who was subsequently discovered to be lying was summarily expelled as well, bringing the total expulsions to eighteen before the weekend was out. "You can't deceive me," Dean Caudwell told those called to his office, "and you won't deceive me." And he was right: nobody did. Not a one. Not even me in the end.

On Sunday evening, after supper, all Winesburg's male students were assembled in the lecture auditorium of the Williamson Lit. Building to be addressed by President Albin Lentz. It was from Sonny, as we tramped up to the Lit. Building that evening—all student cars having been banned from the still largely snow-covered town—that I learned about Lentz's political career and the speculation locally about his aspirations. He had been elected to two terms as a tough, strikebreaking governor of neighboring West Virginia before serving as an undersecretary in the War Department during World War Two. After running unsuccessfully in that state for a U.S. Senate seat in '48, he'd been offered the presidency of Winesburg by business cronies on the college's board of trustees and arrived on the campus dedicated to making the pretty little college in north-central Ohio into what, in his inaugural address, he called "a breeding ground for the ethical propriety and the patriotism and the high principles of personal conduct that will be required of every young person in this country if we are to win the global battle for moral supremacy in which we are engaged with godless Soviet Communism." There were those who believed that Lentz had accepted the presidency of Winesburg, for which his qualifications were hardly those of an educator, as a steppingstone to the Ohio governorship in '52. If he succeeded, he would become only the second person in the country's history to have governed two states—both states heavily industrial—and thereby establish himself as a candidate for the Republican presidential nomination in '56 who could set out to break the Democrats' hold on their traditional working-class constituency. Among the students, of course, Lentz was known barely at all for his politics but instead for his distinctively rural twang—he was the self-made son of a Logan County, West Virginia, miner—that penetrated his rotund oratory like a nail that then penetrated you. He was known for not mincing his words and for his ceaseless cigar smoking, a predilection that had earned him the campus epithet "the All-Powerful Stogie."

Standing not back of the lectern like a lecturing professor but solidly in front of it with his short legs set slightly apart, he began in an ominous interrogative mode. There was nothing bland about this man: he *had* to be listened to. He aspired not to cut a high-and-mighty figure like Dean Caudwell but to scare the wits out of the audience by his unbridled bluntness. His vanity was a very different sort of force from the dean's—there was no deficiency of intelligence in it. To be sure, he agreed with the dean that nothing was more serious in life than the rules, but his fundamental feelings of condemnation were delivered wholly undisguised (intermittent rhetorical embellishment notwithstanding). Never before had I witnessed such shock and solemnity—and fixed concentration—emanate from a congregation of the Winesburg student body. One could not imagine anyone present who even to himself dared to cry, "This is unseemly! This is not just!" The president could have come down into the auditorium and laid waste to the student assemblage with a club without inciting flight or stirring resistance. It was as though we already *had* been clubbed—and, for all the offenses committed, accepted the beating with gratification—before the assault had even begun.

Probably the lone student who had neglected to show up at a convocation of males billed as mandatory was that sinister free spirit, spite-filled Bert Flusser.

"Does any one of you here," President Lentz began, "happen to know what happened in Korea on the day all you he-men decided to bring disgrace and disrepute down upon the name of a distinguished institution of higher learning whose origins lie in the Baptist Church? On that day, U.N. and Communist negotiators in Korea reached tentative agreement for a truce line on the eastern front of that war-torn country. I take it you know what 'tentative' means. It means that fighting as barbaric as any we have known in Korea—as barbaric as any American forces have known in any war at any time in our history —that very same fighting can flare up any hour of the day or night and take thousands upon thousands more young American lives. Do any of you know what occurred in Korea a few weeks back, between Saturday, October 13, and Friday, October 19? I know that you know what happened here then. On Saturday the thirteenth our football team routed our traditional rival, Bowling Green, 41 to 14. The following Saturday, the twentieth, we upset my alma mater, the University of West Virginia, in a thriller that left us, the heavy underdogs, on top by a score of 21 to 20. What a game for Winesburg! But do you know what happened in Korea that same week? The U.S. First Cavalry Division, the Third Infantry Division, and my old outfit in the First War, the Twenty-fifth Infantry Division, along with our British allies and our Republic of Korea allies, made a small advance in the Old Baldy area. A small advance at a cost of four thousand casualties. Four thousand young men like yourselves, dead, maimed, and wounded, between the time we beat Bowling Green and the time we upset UWV. Do you have any idea how fortunate, how privileged, and how lucky you are to be here watching football games on Saturdays and not there being shot at on Saturdays, and on Mondays, Tuesdays, Wednesdays, Thursdays, Fridays, and Sundays as well? When measured against the sacrifices being made by young Americans of your age in this brutal war against the aggression of the North Korean and Chinese Communist forces—when measured against that, do you have any idea how juvenile and stupid and idiotic your behavior looks to the people of Winesburg and to the people of Ohio and to the people of the United States of America, who have been made aware by their newspapers and the television of the shameful happenings of Friday night? Tell me, did you think you were being heroic warriors by storming our women's dormitories and scaring the coeds there half to death? Did you think you were being heroic warriors by breaking into the privacy of their rooms and laying your hands on their personal belongings? Did you think you were being heroic warriors by taking and destroying possessions that were not your own? And those of you who cheered them on, who did not raise a finger to stop them, who exulted in their manly courage, what about *your* manly courage? How's it going to serve you when a thousand screaming Chinese soldiers come swarming down on you in your foxhole, should those negotiations in Korea break down? As they will, I can guarantee you, with bugles blaring and bearing their bayonets!

What am I going to do with you boys? Where are the adults among you? Is there not a one of you who thought to *defend* the female residents of Dowland and Koons and Fleming? I would have expected a hundred of you, two hundred of you, three hundred of you, to put down this childish insurrection! Why did you not? Answer me! Where is your courage? Where is your honor? *Not a one of you displayed an ounce of honor! Not a one of you!* I'm going to tell you something now that I never thought I would have to say: I am ashamed today to be president of this college. I am ashamed and I am disgusted and I am enraged. I don't want there to be any doubt about my anger. And I am not going to stop being angry for a long time to come, I can assure you of that. I understand that forty-eight of our women students—which is close to ten percent of them —forty-eight have already left the campus in the company of their deeply shocked and shaken parents, and whether they will return I do not yet know. What I reckon from the calls I have been receiving from other concerned families—and the phones in both my office and my home have not stopped ringing since midnight on Friday—a good many more of our women students are considering either leaving college for the year or permanently transferring out of Winesburg. I can't say that I blame them. I can't say that I would expect any daughter of mine to remain loyal to an educational institution where she has been exposed not merely to belittlement and humiliation and fear but to a genuine threat of physical harm by an army of hoodlums imagining, apparently, that they were emancipating themselves. Because that's all you are, in my estimation, those who participated and those who did nothing to stop them—an ungrateful, irresponsible, infantile band of vile and cowardly hoodlums. A mob of disobedient children. Kiddies in diapers unconstrained. Oh, and one last thing. Do any of you happen to know how many atom bombs the Soviets have set off so far in the year 1951? The answer is two. That makes a total of three atomic bombs altogether that our Communist enemies in the USSR have now successfully tested since they have discovered the secret of producing an atomic explosion. We as a nation are facing the distinct possibility of an unthinkable atomic war with the Soviet Union, all the while the he-men of

Winesburg College are conducting their derring-do raids on the dresser drawers of the innocent young women who are their schoolmates. Beyond your dormitories, a world is on fire and you are kindled by underwear. Beyond your fraternities, history unfolds daily—warfare, bombings, wholesale slaughter, and you are oblivious of it all. Well, you won't be oblivious for long! You can be as stupid as you like, can even give every sign, as you did here on Friday night, of passionately *wanting* to be stupid, but history will catch you in the end. Because history is not the background—history is the stage! And you are *on* the stage! Oh, how sickening is your appalling ignorance of your own times! Most sickening of all is that it is just that ignorance that you are purportedly at Winesburg to expunge. What kind of a time do you think you belong to, anyway? Can you answer? Do you *know*? Do you have any idea that you belong to a time *at all*? I have spent a long professional career in the warfare of politics, a middle-of-the-road Republican fighting off the zealots of the left and the zealots of the right. But to me tonight those zealots are as nothing compared to you in your barbaric pursuit of thoughtless fun. 'Let's go crazy, let's have fun! How about cannibalism next!' Well, not here, gentlemen, not within these ivied walls will the delights of intentional wrongdoing go unheeded by those charged with the responsibility to this institution to maintain the ideals and values that you have travestied. This cannot be allowed to go on, and this *will* not be allowed to go on! Human conduct *can* be regulated, and it *will* be regulated! The insurrection is over. The rebellion is quelled. Beginning tonight, everything and everyone will be put back into its proper place and order restored to Winesburg. And decency restored. And dignity restored. And now you uninhibited he-men may rise and leave my sight. And if any of you decide you want to leave it for good, if any of you decide that the code of human conduct and rules of civilized restraint that this administration intends to strictly enforce to keep Winesburg Winesburg aren't suited to a he-man like yourself—that's fine with me! Leave! Go! The orders have been given! Pack up your rebellious insolence and clear out of Winesburg tonight!"

President Lentz had pronounced the words "thoughtless fun"

as scornfully as if they were a synonym for "premeditated murder." And so conspicuous was his abhorrence of "rebellious insolence" that he might have been enunciating the name of a menace resolved to undermine not just Winesburg, Ohio, but the great republic itself.

Out from Under

HERE MEMORY ceases. Syrette after syrette of morphine squirted into his arm had plunged Private Messner into a protracted state of deepest unconsciousness, though without suppressing his mental processes. Since just after midnight, everything lay in limbo except his mind. Prior to the moment of cessation, to the moment when he was past recall and able to remember no more, the series of morphine doses had, in fact, infused the tank of his brain like so much mnemonic fuel while successfully dulling the pain of the bayonet wounds that had all but severed one leg from his torso and hacked his intestines and genitals to bits. The hilltop holes in which they'd been living for a week back of some barbed wire on a spiny ridge in central Korea had been overrun in the night by the Chinese, and bodies in parts lay everywhere. When their BAR jammed he and Brunson, his partner, were finished—he'd not been encircled by so much blood since his days as a boy at the slaughterhouse, watching the ritual killing of animals in accordance with Jewish law. And the steel blade that sliced him up was as sharp and efficient as any knife they used in the shop to cut and prepare meat for their customers. Attempts by two corpsmen to stanch the bleeding and transfuse Private Messner were finally of no use, and brain, kidneys, lungs, heart—everything —shut down shortly after dawn on March 31, 1952. Now he was well and truly dead, out from under and far beyond morphine-induced recollection, the victim of his final conflict, the most ferocious and gruesome conflict of them all. They pulled his poncho over his face, salvaged the grenades in his web belt that he'd never had the chance to throw, and hurried back to Brunson, the next to expire.

In the struggle for the steep numbered hill on the spiny ridge in central Korea, both sides sustained casualties so massive as to render the battle a fanatical calamity, much like the war itself. The few whipped and wounded who hadn't been stabbed to death or blown apart eventually staggered off before first light, leaving Massacre Mountain—as that particular numbered hill came to be known in the histories of our midcentury war—covered with corpses and as void of human life as it had been for the many thousands of years before there arose a just cause for either side to destroy the other. In Private Messner's company alone, only twelve of two hundred survived, and not a one saved who wasn't crying and crazed, including the twenty-four-year-old captain in command, whose face had been crushed from the butt of a rifle swung like a baseball bat. The Communist attack had been launched by more than a thousand troops. The Chinese dead totaled between eight and nine hundred. They'd just kept coming and dying, advancing with bugles blaring "Arise, ye who refuse to be bondslaves!" and retreating through a landscape of bodies and blasted trees, machine-gunning their wounded and all they could locate of ours. The machine guns were Russian made.

In America the following afternoon, two soldiers came to the door of the Messner Newark flat to tell his parents that their only son had been killed in combat. Mr. Messner was never to recover from the news. In the midst of his sobbing he said to his wife, "I told him to watch out. He would never listen. You begged me not to double-lock the door in order to teach him a lesson. But you couldn't teach him a lesson. Double-locking the door taught him nothing. And now he's gone. Our boy is gone. I was right, Marcus, I saw it coming—and now you're gone forever! I cannot bear it. I will never survive it." And he didn't. When the store reopened after the period of mourning, he never joked lightheartedly with a customer again. Either he was silent while he worked, except for his coughing, or he said in a mumble to whomever he was serving, "Our son is dead." He stopped shaving regularly and no longer combed his hair, and soon, sheepishly, the customers started to drift away to find another kosher butcher in the neighborhood to frequent, and more of them took up shopping for their meat and their poultry at the supermarket. One day Mr. Messner was paying so little attention to what he was doing that his knife slipped on a bone and the tip of it entered his abdomen and there was a gush of blood and stitches were required. In all it took eighteen months for his horrendous loss to torture the wretched man to death; he died probably a decade before the emphysema would have grown acute enough to kill him on its own.

The mother was strong and lived on to be almost a hundred, though her life too was ruined. There was not a single day when she did not look at the high school graduation photograph of her handsome boy in its frame on the dining room sideboard and, aloud, ask in a sobbing voice of her late husband, "Why did you hound him out of the house? A moment's rage, and look what it did! What difference did it make what time he got home? At least he was home when he got here! And now where is he? Where are you, darling? Marcus, please, the door is unlocked—come home!" She went to the door then, the door with the notorious lock, and she opened it, opened it wide, and she stood there, knowing better, awaiting his return.

Yes, if only this and if only that, we'd all be together and alive forever and everything would work out fine. If only his father, if only Flusser, if only Elwyn, if only Caudwell, if only Olivia—! If only Cottler—if only he hadn't befriended the superior Cottler! If only Cottler hadn't befriended him! If only he hadn't let Cottler hire Ziegler to proxy for him at chapel! If only Ziegler hadn't got caught! If only he had gone to chapel himself! If he'd gone there the forty times and signed his name the forty times, he'd be alive today and just retiring from practicing law. But he couldn't! Couldn't believe like a child in some stupid god! Couldn't listen to their ass-kissing hymns! Couldn't sit in their hallowed church! And the prayers, those shut-eyed prayers—putrefied primitive superstition! Our Folly, which art in Heaven! The disgrace of religion, the immaturity and ignorance and shame of it all! Lunatic piety about nothing! And when Caudwell told him he had to, when Caudwell called him back into his office and told him that they would keep him on at Winesburg only if he made a written apology to President Lentz for hiring Marty Ziegler to attend chapel in his stead and if thereafter he himself attended chapel not forty but, as a form of instruction as well as a means of penance, a total of eighty times, attended chapel virtually every single Wednesday for the remainder of his college career, what choice did Marcus have, what else could he do but, like the Messner that he was, like the student of Bertrand Russell's that he was, bang down his fist on the dean's desk and tell him for a second time, "Fuck you"?

Yes, the good old defiant American "Fuck you," and that was it for the butcher's son, dead three months short of his twentieth birthday—Marcus Messner, 1932–1952, the only one of his classmates unfortunate enough to be killed in the Korean War, which ended with the signing of an armistice agreement on July 27, 1953, eleven full months before Marcus, had he been able to stomach chapel and keep his mouth shut, would have received his undergraduate degree from Winesburg College—more than likely as class valedictorian—and thus have postponed learning what his uneducated father had been trying so hard to teach him all along: of the terrible, the incomprehensible way one's most banal, incidental, even comical choices achieve the most disproportionate result.

Historical Note

In 1971 the social upheavals and transformations and protests of the turbulent decade of the 1960s reached even hidebound, apolitical Winesburg, and on the twentieth anniversary of the November blizzard and the White Panty Raid an unforeseen uprising occurred during which the boys occupied the office of the dean of men and the girls the office of the dean of women, all of them demanding "student rights." The uprising succeeded in shutting down the college for a full week, and afterward, when classes resumed, none of the ringleaders of either sex who had negotiated an end to the uprising by proposing liberalizing new alternatives to the college officials were punished by expulsion or suspension. Instead, overnight—and to the horror of no authorities other than those by then retired from administering Winesburg's affairs—the chapel requirement was abolished along with virtually all the strictures and parietal rules regulating student conduct that had been in force there for more than a hundred years and that were implemented so faithfully during the tradition-preserving tenure of President Lentz and Dean Caudwell.

THE HUMBLING

For J. T.

1

Into Thin Air

H E'D LOST his magic. The impulse was spent. He'd never failed in the theater, everything he had done had been strong and successful, and then the terrible thing happened: he couldn't act. Going onstage became agony. Instead of the certainty that he was going to be wonderful, he knew he was going to fail. It happened three times in a row, and by the last time nobody was interested, nobody came. He couldn't get over to the audience. His talent was dead.

Of course, if you've had it, you always have something unlike anyone else's. I'll always be unlike anyone else, Axler told himself, because I am who I am. I carry that with me—that people will always remember. But the aura he'd had, all his mannerisms and eccentricities and personal peculiarities, what had worked for Falstaff and Peer Gynt and Vanya—what had gained Simon Axler his reputation as the last of the best of the classical American stage actors—none of it worked for any role now. All that had worked to make him himself now worked to make him look like a lunatic. He was conscious of every moment he was on the stage in the worst possible way. In the past when he was acting he wasn't thinking about anything. What he did well he did out of instinct. Now he was thinking about everything, and everything spontaneous and vital was killed— he tried to control it with thinking and instead he destroyed it. All right, Axler told himself, he had hit a bad period. Though he was already in his sixties, maybe it would pass while he was still recognizably himself. He wouldn't be the first experienced actor to go through it. A lot of people did. I've done this before, he thought, so I'll find some way. I don't know how I'm going to get it this time, but I'll find it—this will pass.

It didn't pass. He couldn't act. The ways he could once rivet attention on the stage! And now he dreaded every performance, and dreaded it all day long. He spent the entire day thinking thoughts he'd never thought before a performance in his life: I won't make it, I won't be able to do it, I'm playing

the wrong roles, I'm overreaching, I'm faking, I have no idea
even of how to do the first line. And meanwhile he tried to
occupy the hours doing a hundred seemingly necessary things
to prepare: I have to look at this speech again, I have to rest, I
have to exercise, I have to look at that speech again, and by the
time he got to the theater he was exhausted. And dreading going out there. He would hear the cue coming closer and closer
and know that he couldn't do it. He waited for the freedom to
begin and the moment to become real, he waited to forget
who he was and to become the person doing it, but instead he
was standing there, completely empty, doing the kind of acting
you do when you don't know what you are doing. He could
not give and he could not withhold; he had no fluidity and he
had no reserve. Acting became a night-after-night exercise in
trying to get away with something.

It had started with people speaking to him. He couldn't
have been more than three or four when he was already mesmerized by speaking and being spoken to. He had felt he was
in a play from the outset. He could use intensity of listening,
concentration, as lesser actors used fireworks. He had that
power offstage, too, particularly, when younger, with women
who did not realize that they had a story until he revealed to
them that they had a story, a voice, and a style belonging to
no other. They became actresses with Axler, they became the
heroines of their own lives. Few stage actors could speak and
be spoken to the way he could, yet he could do neither anymore. The sound that used to go into his ear felt as though it
were going out, and every word he uttered seemed acted instead of spoken. The initial source in his acting was in what he
heard, his response to what he heard was at the core of it, and
if he couldn't listen, couldn't hear, he had nothing to go on.

He was asked to play Prospero and Macbeth at the Kennedy
Center—it was hard to think of a more ambitious double bill
—and he failed appallingly in both, but especially as Macbeth.
He couldn't do low-intensity Shakespeare and he couldn't do
high-intensity Shakespeare—and he'd been doing Shakespeare
all his life. His Macbeth was ludicrous and everyone who saw it
said as much, and so did many who hadn't seen it. "No, they
don't even have to have been there," he said, "to insult you." A
lot of actors would have turned to drink to help themselves

out; an old joke had it that there was an actor who would always drink before he went onstage, and when he was warned
"You mustn't drink," he replied, "What, and go out there
alone?" But Axler didn't drink, and so he collapsed instead.
His breakdown was colossal.

The worst of it was that he saw through his breakdown the
same way he could see through his acting. The suffering was
excruciating and yet he doubted that it was genuine, which
made it even worse. He did not know how he was going to get
from one minute to the next, his mind felt as though it were
melting, he was terrified to be alone, he could not sleep more
than two or three hours a night, he scarcely ate, he thought
every day of killing himself with the gun in the attic—a Rem-
ington 870 pump-action shotgun that he kept in the isolated
farmhouse for self-defense—and still the whole thing seemed
to be an act, a bad act. When you're playing the role of somebody coming apart, it has organization and order; when you're
observing yourself coming apart, playing the role of your own
demise, that's something else, something awash with terror
and fear.

He could not convince himself he was mad any more than
he'd been able to convince himself or anyone else he was Prospero or Macbeth. He was an artificial madman too. The only
role available to him was the role of someone playing a role. A
sane man playing an insane man. A stable man playing a broken man. A self-controlled man playing a man out of control. A
man of solid achievement, of theatrical renown—a large, burly
actor standing six feet four inches tall, with a big bald head and
the strong, hairy body of a brawler, with a face that could
convey so much, a decisive jaw and stern dark eyes and a sizable mouth he could twist every which way, and a low com-
manding voice emanating from deep down that always had a
little growl in it, a man conscientiously on the grand scale who
looked as if he could stand up to anything and easily fulfill all
of a man's roles, the embodiment of invulnerable resistance
who looked to have absorbed into his being the egoism of a
dependable giant—playing an insignificant mite. He screamed
aloud when he awakened in the night and found himself still
locked inside the role of the man deprived of himself, his talent, and his place in the world, a loathsome man who was

nothing more than the inventory of his defects. In the mornings he hid in bed for hours, but instead of hiding from the role he was merely playing the role. And when finally he got up, all he could think about was suicide, and not its simulation either. A man who wanted to live playing a man who wanted to die.

Meanwhile, Prospero's most famous words wouldn't let him be, perhaps because he'd so recently mangled them. They repeated themselves so regularly in his head that they soon became a hubbub of sounds tortuously empty of meaning and pointing at no reality yet carrying the force of a spell full of personal significance. "Our revels now are ended. These our actors, / As I foretold you, were all spirits and / Are melted into air, into thin air." He could do nothing to blot out "thin air," the two syllables that were chaotically repeated while he lay powerless in his bed in the morning and that had the aura of an obscure indictment even as they came to make less and less sense. His whole intricate personality was entirely at the mercy of "thin air."

Victoria, Axler's wife, could no longer care for him and by now needed tending herself. She would cry whenever she saw him at the kitchen table, his head in his hands, unable to eat the meal she had prepared. "Try something," she begged, but he ate nothing, said nothing, and soon Victoria began to panic. She had never seen him give way like this before, not even eight years earlier when his elderly parents had died in an automobile crash with his father at the wheel. He wept then and he went on. He always went on. He took the losses hard but the performance never faltered. And when Victoria was in turmoil, it was he who kept her tough and got her through. There was always a drug drama with her errant son. There was the permanent hardship of aging and the end of her career. So much disappointment, but he was there and so she could bear it. If only he were here now that the man on whom she had depended was gone!

In the 1950s, Victoria Powers had been Balanchine's youngest favorite. Then she hurt her knee, had an operation, danced again, hurt it again, had another operation, and by the time she was rehabilitated the second time round, someone else was Balanchine's youngest favorite. She never recovered her place. There was a marriage, the son, a divorce, a second marriage, a second divorce, and then she met and fell in love with Simon Axler, who, when he'd first come from college two decades earlier to make a career on the New York stage, used to go to the City Center to see her dance, not because he loved ballet but because of his youthful susceptibility to the capacity she had to stir him to lust through the pathway of the tenderest emotions: she remained in his memory for years afterward as the very incarnation of erotic pathos. When they met as forty-year-olds in the late seventies, it was a long time since anyone had asked her to perform, though pluckily she went off every day to her workout at a local dance studio. She had done all she could to keep herself fit and looking youthful, but by then her pathos exceeded any ability she'd ever had to master it artistically.

After the Kennedy Center debacle and his unexpected collapse, Victoria fell apart and fled to California to be close to her son.

All at once Axler was alone in the house in the country and terrified of killing himself. Now there was nothing stopping him. Now he could go ahead and do what he'd found himself unable to do while she was still there: walk up the stairs to the attic, load the gun, put the barrel in his mouth, and reach down with his long arms to pull the trigger. The gun as the sequel to the wife. But once she'd left, he didn't make it through the first hour alone—didn't even go up the first flight of stairs toward the attic—before he had phoned his doctor and asked him to arrange for his admission to a psychiatric hospital that very day. Within only minutes the doctor had found him a place at Hammerton, a small hospital with a good reputation a few hours to the north.

He was there for twenty-six days. Once interviewed, unpacked, relieved of his "sharps" by a nurse, and his valuables taken to the business office for safekeeping, once alone and in the room assigned him, he sat down on the bed and remembered role after role that he had played with absolute assurance since he'd become a professional in his early twenties—what had destroyed his confidence now? What was he doing in this hospital room? A self-travesty had come into being who did not exist before, a self-travesty grounded in nothing, and he was that self-travesty, and how had it happened? Was it purely the passage of time bringing on decay and collapse? Was it a manifestation of aging? His appearance was still impressive. His aims as an actor had not changed nor had his painstaking manner of preparation for a role. There was no one more thorough and studious and serious, no one who took better care of his talent or who better accommodated himself to the changing conditions of a career in the theater over so many decades. To cease so precipitously being the actor he was—it was inexplicable, as though he'd been disarmed of the weight and substance of his professional existence one night while he slept. The ability to speak and be spoken to on a stage—that's what it came down to, and that's what was gone.

The psychiatrist he saw, Dr. Farr, questioned whether what had befallen him could truly be causeless, and in their twice-weekly sessions asked him to examine the circumstances of his life preceding the sudden onset of what the doctor described as "a universal nightmare." By this he meant that the actor's misfortune in the theater—going out on the stage and finding himself unable to perform, the shock of that loss—was the content of troubling dreams any number of people had about themselves, people who, unlike Simon Axler, were not professional actors. Going out on the stage and being unable to perform was among the stock set of dreams that most every patient reported at one time or another. That and walking naked down a busy city street or being unprepared for a crucial exam or falling off a cliff or finding on the highway that your brakes don't work. Dr. Farr asked Axler to talk about his marriage, about his parents' death, about his relations with his drug-addicted stepson, his boyhood, his adolescence, his beginnings as an actor, an older sister who had died of lupus when he was twenty. The doctor wanted to hear in particular detail about the weeks and months leading up to his appearance at the Kennedy Center and to know if he remembered anything out of the ordinary, large or small, occurring during that period. Axler worked hard to be truthful and thereby to reveal the origins of his condition—and with that to recover his powers—but as far as he could tell, no cause for the "universal nightmare" presented itself in anything he said sitting across from the sympathetic and attentive psychiatrist. And that made it all the more a nightmare. Yet he talked to the doctor anyway, each time he showed up. Why not? At a certain stage of misery, you'll try anything to explain what's going on with you, even if you know it doesn't explain a thing and it's one failed explanation after another.

Some twenty days into his stay at the hospital a night came when, instead of waking at two or three and lying sleepless in the midst of his terror till dawn, he slept right through until eight in the morning, so late by hospital standards that a nurse had to come to his room to awaken him so that he could join the other patients for 7:45 breakfast in the dining hall and then begin the day, which included group therapy, art therapy, a consultation with Dr. Farr, and a session with the physical therapist, who was doing her best to treat his perennial spinal pain. Every waking hour was filled with activities and appointments to prevent the patients from retiring to their rooms to lie depressed and miserable on their beds or to sit around with one another, as a number of them did in the evenings anyway, discussing the ways they had tried to kill themselves.

Several times he sat in the corner of the rec room with the small gang of suicidal patients and listened to them recalling the ardor with which they had planned to die and bemoaning how they had failed. Each of them remained immersed in the magnitude of his or her suicide attempt and the ignominy of having survived it. That people could really do it, that they could control their own death, was a source of fascination to them all—it was their natural subject, like boys talking about sports. Several described feeling something akin to the rush that a psychopath must get when he kills someone else sweeping over them when they attempted to kill themselves. A young woman said, "You seem to yourself and to everyone around you paralyzed and wholly ineffectual and yet you can decide to commit the most difficult act there is. It's exhilarating. It's invigorating. It's euphoric." "Yes," said someone else, "there's a grim euphoria to it. Your life is falling apart, it has no center, and suicide is the one thing you can control." One elderly man, a retired schoolteacher who had tried to hang himself in his garage, gave them a lecture on the ways "outsiders" think about suicide. "The one thing that everyone wants to do with suicide is explain it. Explain it and judge it. It's so appalling for the people that are left behind that there has to be a way of thinking about it. Some people think of it as an act of cowardice. Some people think of it as criminal, as a crime against the survivors. Another school of thought finds it heroic and an act of courage. Then there are the purists. The question for them is: was it justified, was there sufficient cause? The more clinical point of view, which is neither punitive nor idealizing, is the psychologist's, which attempts to describe the state of mind of the suicide, what state of mind he was in when he did it." He went tediously on in this vein more or less every night, as though he were not an anguished patient like the rest of them but a guest lecturer who'd been brought in to elucidate the subject that obsessed them night and day. One evening Axler spoke up—to perform, he realized, before his largest audience since he'd given up acting. "Suicide is the role you write for yourself," he told them. "You inhabit it and you enact it. All carefully staged—where they will find you and how they will find you." Then he added, "But one performance only."

In their conversation, everything private was revealed easily and shamelessly; suicide seemed like a very huge aim and living a hateful condition. Among the patients he met, there were some who knew him right off because of his handful of movies, but they were too immersed in their own struggles to take much more notice of him than they did of anyone other than themselves. And the staff was too busy to be distracted for long by his theatrical renown. He was all but unrecognizable in the hospital, not only to others but to himself.

From the moment that he had rediscovered the miracle of a night's sleep and had to be awakened for breakfast by the nurse, he began to feel the dread subside. They had given him one medication for depression that didn't agree with him, then a second, and finally a third that caused no intolerable side effects, but whether it did him any good, he could not tell. He could not believe that his improvement had anything to do with pills or with psychiatric consultations or group therapy or art therapy, all of which felt like empty exercises. What continued to frighten him, as the day of his discharge approached, was that nothing that was happening to him seemed to have to do with anything else. As he'd told Dr. Farr—and further convinced himself by having tried to the best of his ability to search for a cause during their sessions—he had lost his magic as an actor for no good reason and it was just as arbitrarily that the desire to end his life began to ebb, at least for the time being. "*Nothing* has a good reason for happening," he said to the doctor later that day. "You lose, you gain—it's all caprice. The omnipotence of caprice. The likelihood of reversal. Yes, the unpredictable reversal and its power."

Near the end of his stay he made a friend, and each night they had dinner together she repeated her story to him. He had met her first in art therapy, and after that they would sit across from each other at a table for two in the dining hall, chatting like a couple on a date, or—given the thirty-year age difference—like a father and daughter, albeit about her suicide attempt. The day they met—a couple of days after her arrival—there had been only the two of them in the art room along with the therapist, who, as though they were kindergarteners, had handed each sheets of white paper and a box of crayons to play with and told them to draw whatever they wanted. All that was missing from the room, he thought, were the little tables and chairs. To satisfy the therapist, they worked in silence for fifteen minutes and then, again for the sake of the therapist, listened attentively to the response each offered to the other's drawing. She had drawn a house and a garden, and he a picture of himself drawing a picture, "a picture," he told the therapist when she asked him what he'd done, "of a man who has broken down and who commits himself to a psychiatric hospital and goes to art therapy and is asked there by the therapist to draw a picture." "And suppose you were to give your picture a title, Simon. What would it be?" "That's easy. 'What the Hell Am I Doing Here?'"

The five other patients scheduled to be at art therapy either were back on their beds, unable to do anything except lie there and weep, or, as though an emergency had befallen them, had rushed off without an appointment to their doctors' offices and were sitting in the waiting room preparing to lament over the wife, the husband, the child, the boss, the mother, the father, the boyfriend, the girlfriend—whomever it was they never wanted to see again, or whom they would be willing to see again so long as the doctor was present and there was no shouting or violence or threats of violence, or whom they missed horribly and couldn't live without and whom they would do anything to get back. Each of them sat waiting a turn to denounce a parent, to vilify a sibling, to belittle a mate, to vindicate or excoriate or pity themselves. One or two of them who could still concentrate—or pretend to concentrate, or strain to concentrate—on something other than the misery of their grievance would, while waiting for the doctor, leaf through a copy of *Time* or *Sports Illustrated* or pick up the local paper and try to do the crossword puzzle. Everybody else would be sitting there gloomily silent, inwardly intense and rehearsing to themselves—in the lexicon of pop psychology or gutter obscenity or Christian suffering or paranoid pathology—the ancient themes of dramatic literature: incest, betrayal, injustice, cruelty, vengeance, jealousy, rivalry, desire, loss, dishonor, and grief.

She was an elfin, pale-skinned brunette with the bony frailty of a sickly girl of about a quarter her age. Her name was Sybil Van Buren. In the eyes of the actor hers was a thirty-five-year-old body that not only refused to be strong but dreaded even the appearance of strength. And yet, for all her delicacy, she'd said to him, on the way up the path to the main residence hall from art therapy, "Will you eat dinner with me, Simon?" Amazing. Still some kind of wish in her not to be swallowed up. Or maybe she'd asked to stay on at his side in the hope that with a little luck something would ignite between them that would complete the doing in of her. He was big enough for the job, more than whale enough for a tiny bundle of flotsam like her. Even here—where, without assistance from the pharmacopoeia, any show of stability, let alone bravado, was unlikely to quell for long the maelstrom of terror swirling back of the gullet—he had not lost the loose, swaggering gait of the ominous man that had once gone toward making him such an original Othello. And so, yes, if there was still any hope for her of going completely under, perhaps it lay in cozying up to him. That's what he thought at the outset anyway.

"I had lived for so long in the constraints of caution," Sybil told him at dinner that first night. "The efficient housewife who gardens and sews and can repair everything and throws glorious dinner parties as well. The quiet, steady, loyal sidekick of the rich and powerful man, with her unambiguous, whole-hearted, old-fashioned devotion to the rearing of children. The ordinary existence of an insignificant mortal. Well, I went off to go shopping for groceries—what could be more mundane than that? Why would anyone in the world have to worry about that? I'd left my daughter playing out back in the yard and our little boy upstairs sleeping in his crib and my rich and powerful second husband watching a golf tournament on TV. I turned around and came home because when I got to the supermarket I realized I'd forgotten my wallet. The little one was still sleeping. And in the living room the golf game was still going, but my eight-year-old daughter, my little Alison, was sitting up on the sofa without her underpants and my rich and powerful second husband was kneeling on the floor, his head between her plump little legs."

"What was he doing there?"

"What men do there."

Axler watched her cry and said nothing.

"You've seen my artwork," she finally told him. "The sun shining down on a pretty house and the garden all in bloom. You know me. *Everybody* knows me. I think the best of everything. I prefer it that way and so does everyone around me. He got up off his knees, completely unruffled, and told me that she had been complaining about an itch and she wouldn't stop scratching herself, and so, before she did herself any harm, he had taken a look to be sure she was all right. And she was, he assured me. He could see nothing, not a blemish, not a sore, not a rash . . . She was fine. 'Good,' I said. 'I came back for my wallet.' And instead of getting his hunting rifle from the basement and pumping him full of bullets, I found my wallet in the kitchen, said 'Bye again, everyone,' and went off to the store as if what I had witnessed was a commonplace occurrence. In a daze, dumbfounded, I filled two shopping carts. I would have filled two more, four more, six more if the store manager hadn't seen me blubbering away and come over to ask if I was all right. He drove me home in his car. I left our car in the lot there and was driven home. I couldn't negotiate the stairs. I had to be carried up to bed. There I lay for four days, unable to speak or eat, barely able to drag myself to the bathroom. The story was that I'd come down with a fever and been ordered to bed. My rich and powerful second husband could not have been more solicitous. My little darling Alison sweetly brought me a vase of cut flowers from my garden. I could not ask her, I could not bring myself to say, 'Who removed your underpants? What do you want to tell me? If you really had some kind of itch, you would have waited, wouldn't you, until I came home from shopping to show me? But, dear, if you didn't have an itch . . . dear, if there's something you're not telling me because you're afraid to . . . ?' But I was the one who was afraid. I could not do it. By the fourth day I had convinced myself that I had imagined everything, and two weeks later, when Alison was at school and he was at work and the little one was taking his nap, I got out the wine and the Valium and the plastic garbage bag. But I couldn't stand suffocating. I panicked. I took the pills and the wine but then I remember not getting any air and hurrying to rip the bag off. And I don't know what I regret more horribly—having tried to do it or having failed to do it. All I want to do is shoot him. Only now he's alone with them and I'm here. He's all alone with my sweet little girl! It can't be! I called my sister and asked her to stay at the house with them, but he wouldn't let her sleep there. He said there was no need. And so she left. And what can I do? I'm here and Alison's there! I was paralyzed! I did nothing that I should have done! Nothing that anyone would have done! I should have rushed the child to the doctor! I should have called the police! It was a criminal act! There are laws against such things! Instead I did nothing! But he said nothing had happened, you see. He says that I'm hysterical, that I'm deluded, that I'm mad—but I'm not. I swear to you, Simon, I'm not mad. *I saw him doing it.*"

"That's horrible. A horrible transgression," Axler said. "I see why it's done what it did to you."

"It's *evil*. I need someone," she confided in a murmur, "to kill this evil man."

"I'm sure you could find a willing party."

"You?" asked Sybil in a tiny voice. "I'd pay."

"If I was a killer I would do it pro bono," he said, taking the hand she extended to him. "People become infected with the rage when an innocent child is violated. But I'm an out-of-work actor. I'd botch the job and we'd both go to jail."

"Oh, what should I do?" she asked him. "What would you do?"

"Get strong. Cooperate with the doctor and try to get strong as fast as you can so you can go home to your children."

"You believe me, don't you?"

"I'm sure you saw what you saw."

"Can we have dinner together?"

"For as long as I'm here," he said.

"I knew in art therapy that you'd understand. There's so much suffering in your eyes."

Within months of his leaving the hospital, his wife's son died of an overdose and the marriage of the occupationless dancer to the occupationless actor ended in divorce, completing yet one more of the many millions of stories of unhappily entwined men and women.

One day around noon a black town car pulled into the driveway and parked beside the barn. It was a chauffeur-driven Mercedes and the small white-haired man who stepped out of the back seat was Jerry Oppenheim, his agent. After the hospital internment, Jerry had phoned him every week from New York to see how he was doing, but many months had gone by without their speaking—the actor having chosen at one point to stop taking the agent's calls along with most everyone else's—and the visit was unexpected. He watched Jerry, who was over eighty and walked cautiously, negotiate the stone path to the front door, a package in one hand and flowers in the other.

He opened the door before Jerry even had a chance to knock.

"Suppose I hadn't been home?" he said, helping Jerry over the sill.

"I took my chances," Jerry said, smiling gently. He had a gentle face altogether and a courteous demeanor that did not, however, compromise his tenacity in behalf of his clients. "Well, you seem all right physically, at least. Except for that hopeless look on your face, Simon, you don't look bad at all."

"And you—neat as a pin," Axler said, having himself neither changed his clothes nor shaved for days.

"I brought you flowers. I brought us a box lunch from Dean and DeLuca. Have you had lunch?"

He hadn't even had breakfast, so he merely shrugged and took the gifts and helped Jerry out of his coat.

"You drove up from New York," he said.

"Yes. To see how you're doing and talk to you face-to-face. I have news for you. The Guthrie is doing *Long Day's Journey*. They called to ask about you."

"Why me? I can't act, Jerry, and everyone knows it."

"Nobody knows any such thing. Perhaps people know that you had an emotional setback, but that doesn't set you apart from the human race. They're doing the play next winter. It gets awfully cold out there, but you'd be a wonderful James Tyrone."

"James Tyrone is a lot of lines that you have to say, and I can't say them. James Tyrone is a character that you have to be, and I can't be him. There's no way I can play James Tyrone. I can't play anyone."

"Look, you took a tumble in Washington. That happens to practically everyone sooner or later. There's no ironclad security in any art. People run into an obstacle for reasons no one knows. But the obstacle is a temporary impediment. The obstacle disappears and you go on. There isn't a first-rate actor who hasn't felt discouraged and that his career was over and that he was unable to come out of the bad period he was in. There isn't an actor who hasn't gone up in the middle of a speech and not known where he was. But every time you go out on the stage there's a new chance. Actors can recover their talent. You don't lose the skills if you've been out there for forty years. You still know how to enter and sit down in a chair. John Gielgud used to say that there were times he wished he were like a painter or a writer. Then he could retrieve the bad performance he gave that evening and take it out at midnight and redo it. But he couldn't. He had to do it there. Gielgud went through a very bad time when he could do nothing right. So did Olivier. Olivier went through a terrible period. He had a terrible problem. He couldn't look any of the other actors in the eye. He told the other actors, 'Please don't look at me, because it'll throw me.' For a while he couldn't be alone on the stage. He said to the other actors, 'Don't leave me alone out there.'"

"I know the stories, Jerry. I've heard them all. They don't have to do with me. In the past I never had more than two or three bad nights when I couldn't recover. For two or three nights I would think, 'I know I'm good, I'm just not doing it.' Maybe nobody in the audience knew it, but I knew it—it wasn't there. And on those nights when it isn't there for you it's a labor, I know that, and yet somehow you get by. You can get very good at getting by on what you get by on when you don't have anything else. But that's something different entirely. When I had a truly wretched performance, I would lie awake all night afterward thinking, 'I've lost it, I have no talent, I can't do anything.' Hours would go by, but then all of a sudden, at five or six in the morning, I'd understand what went wrong and I couldn't wait to get to the theater that evening and go on. And I'd go on and I couldn't make a mistake. A beautiful feeling. There are days when you can't wait to get there, when the marriage between you and the role is perfect and there's never a time when you're not happy to sail out onto the stage. Those are important days. And for years I had them one after the other. Well, that's over. Now if I were to go out on the stage, I wouldn't know what I was out there for. Wouldn't know where to begin. In the old days I'd do three hours of preparation in the theater for an eight o'clock curtain. By eight I was deeply inside that role—it was like a trance, like a useful trance. In *The Family Reunion* I was in the theater two and a half hours before the first entrance, working up to how to enter when you are pursued by the Furies. That was hard for me, but I did it."

"You can do it again," Jerry said. "You're forgetting who you are and what you've achieved. Your life has hardly come to nothing. Endlessly you would do things on the stage in a way I never expected, and over the years that was thrilling thousands of times for the audience and always thrilling for me. You went as far away as possible from the obvious thing that any other actor would do. You couldn't be routine. You wanted to go everywhere. Out, out, out, as far out as you could go. And the audience believed in you in every moment, wherever you took them. Sure, nothing is permanently established, but so is nothing permanently lost. Your talent's been mislaid, that's all."

"No, it's gone, Jerry. I can't do any of it again. You're either free or you aren't. You're either free and it's genuine, it's real, it's alive, or it's nothing. I'm not free anymore."

"Okay, let's have some lunch then. And put the flowers in some water. The house looks fine. *You* look fine. A little too slimmed down, I would say, but you still look like yourself. You're eating, I hope."

"I eat."

But when they sat down to lunch in the kitchen, with the flowers in a vase between them, Axler was unable to eat. He saw himself stepping out on the stage to play James Tyrone and the audience bursting into laughter. The anxiety and fear were as naked as that. People would laugh at him because it *was* him.

"What do you do with the days?" Jerry asked.

"Walk. Sleep. Stare into space. Try to read. Try to forget myself for at least one minute of each hour. I watch the news. I'm up to date on the news."

"Who do you see?"

"You."

"This is no way for someone of your accomplishment to live."

"You were kind to come all the way out here, Jerry, but I can't do the play at the Guthrie. I'm finished with all that."

"You're not. You're scared of failing. But that's behind you. You don't realize how one-sided and monomaniacal your perspective has become."

"Did I write the reviews? Did this monomaniac write those reviews? Did I write what they wrote about my Macbeth? I was ludicrous and they said as much. I would just think, 'I got through that line, thank God I got through that line.' I would try to think, 'That wasn't as bad as last night,' when in fact it was worse. Everything I did was false, raucous. I heard this horrible tone in my voice and yet nothing could stop me from fucking up. Hideous. Hideous. I never gave a good performance, not one."

"So you couldn't do Macbeth to your satisfaction. Well,

you're not the first. He's a horrible person for an actor to live with. I defy anyone to play him and not be warped by the effort. He's a murderer, he's a killer. Everything is magnified in that play. Frankly, I never understood all that evil. Forget *Macbeth*. Forget those reviews," Jerry said. "It's time to move on. You should come down to New York and begin to work in his studio with Vincent Daniels. You won't be the first whose confidence he's restored. Look, you've done all that tough stuff, Shakespeare, the classics—there's no way this can happen to you with your biography. It's a momentary loss of confidence."

"It isn't a matter of confidence," replied Axler. "I always had a sneaking suspicion that I have no talent whatsoever."

"Well, that's nonsense. That's the depression talking. You hear actors saying it a lot when they're down the way you are. 'I don't have any real talent. I can memorize the lines. That's about it.' I've heard it a thousand times."

"No, listen to me. When I was fully honest with myself I'd think, 'Okay, all right, I have a modicum of talent or I can at least imitate a talented person.' But it was all a fluke, Jerry, a fluke that a talent was given to me, a fluke that it was taken away. This life's a fluke from start to finish."

"Oh, stop this, Simon. You can still hold attention the way a big star actor does on the stage. You are a titan, for God's sake."

"No, it's a matter of falseness, sheer falseness so pervasive that all I can do is stand on the stage and tell the audience, 'I am a liar. And I can't even lie well. I am a fraud.'"

"And that is more nonsense. Think for a moment of all the bad actors—there are lots of them and they somehow get by. So to tell me that Simon Axler," Jerry said, "with his talent, can't get by is absurd. I've seen you in the past, times when you were not so happy, times when you were in psychic torment in every other way, but put a script in front of you, allow you to access this thing that you do so wonderfully, allow you to become another person, and always it's been liberating for you. Well, that's happened before and it can happen again. The love of what you do well—it can return and it will return. Look, Vincent Daniels is an ace at dealing with problems like yours, a tough, canny, intuitive teacher, highly intelligent, and a scrapper himself."

"I know his name," he told Jerry. "But I've never met him. I never had to meet him."

"He's a maverick, he's a scrapper, and he'll get you back to contending. He'll put the fight back in you. He'll start from scratch if he has to. He'll get you to give up everything you've done before if he must. It'll be a struggle, but in the end he'll get you back to where you should be. I've been to his studio and watched Vincent work. He says, 'Do one moment. We're only dealing with the single moment. Play the moment, play whatever plays for you in that moment, and then go on to the next moment. It doesn't matter where you're going. Don't worry about that. Just take it moment, moment, moment, moment. The job is to be in that moment, with no concern about the rest and no idea where you're going next. Because if you can make one moment work, you can go anywhere.' Now it sounds, I know, like the simplest notion, and that's why it's hard—it's so simple that it's the thing that everybody misses. I believe that Vincent Daniels is the perfect man for you right now. I have complete faith in him for you in your predicament. Here's his card. I came up here to give you this."

Jerry handed him the business card, and so he took it at the same time that he said, "Can't do it."

"What will you do instead? What will you do about all the roles you're ripe to play? It breaks my heart when I think of all those parts you were made for. If you accepted the role of James Tyrone, then you could work with Vincent and find your way through it with him. This is the work he does with actors every day. I can't count the number of times at the Tonys or the Oscars that I heard the winning actor say, 'I want to thank Vincent Daniels.' He is the best."

In response Axler simply shook his head.

"Look," Jerry said, "everyone knows the feeling 'I can't do it,' everyone knows the feeling that they will be revealed to be false—it's every actor's terror. 'They've found me out. I've been found out.' Let's face it, there's a panic that comes with age. I'm that much older than you, and I've been dealing with it for years. One, you get slower. In everything. Even in reading you get slower. If I go fast in reading now, too much of it goes away. My speech is slower, my memory is slower. All these things start to happen. In the process, you start to distrust yourself. You're not as quick as you used to be. And especially if you are an actor. You were a young actor and you memorized scripts one after the other after the other, and you never even thought about it. It was just easy to do. And then all of a sudden it's not as easy, and things don't happen so fast anymore. Memorizing becomes a big anxiety for stage actors going into their sixties and seventies. Once you could memorize a script in a day—now you're lucky to memorize a page in a day. So you start to feel afraid, to feel soft, to feel that you don't have that raw live power anymore. It scares you. With the result, as you say, that you're not free anymore. There's nothing happening—and that's terrifying."

"Jerry, I can't go on with this conversation. We could talk all day, and to no avail. You're good to come and see me and bring me lunch and flowers and to try to help me and encourage me and comfort me and make me feel better. It was tremendously thoughtful. I'm pleased to see you looking well. But the momentum of a life is the momentum of a life. I am now incapable of acting. Something fundamental has vanished. Maybe it had to. Things go. Don't think that my career's been cut short. Think of how long I lasted. When I started out in college I was just fooling around, you know. Acting was a chance to meet girls. Then I took my first theatrical breath. Suddenly I was alive on the stage and breathing like an actor. I started young. I was twenty-two and came to New York for an audition. And I got the part. I began to take classes. Sense-memory exercises. Practice making things real. Before your performance create a reality for yourself to step into. I remember that when I began taking class we'd have a pretend teacup and pretend to drink from it. How hot is it, how full is it, is there a saucer, is there a spoon, are you going to put sugar in it, how many lumps. And then you sip it, and others were transported by this stuff, but I never found any of it helpful. What's more, I couldn't do it. I was no good at the exercises, no good at all. I'd try to do this stuff and it never would work. Everything I did well was coming out of instinct, and doing those exercises and knowing those things were making me look like an actor. I would look ridiculous as I held my pretend teacup and pretended to drink from it. There was always a sly voice inside me saying, 'There is no teacup.' Well, that sly voice has now taken over. No matter how I prepare and what I attempt to do, once I am on the stage there is that sly voice all the time—'There is no teacup.' Jerry, it's over: I can no longer make a play real for people. I can no longer make a role real for myself."

After Jerry had left, Axler went into his study and found his copy of *Long Day's Journey into Night*. He tried to read it but the effort was unbearable. He didn't get beyond page 4—he put Vincent Daniels's card there as a bookmark. At the Kennedy Center it was as though he'd never acted before and now it was as though he'd never read a play before—as though he'd never read *this* play before. The sentences unfolded without meaning. He could not keep straight who was speaking the lines. Sitting there amid his books, he tried to remember plays in which there is a character who commits suicide. Hedda in *Hedda Gabler*, Julie in *Miss Julie*, Phaedra in *Hippolytus*, Jocasta in *Oedipus the King*, almost everyone in *Antigone*, Willy Loman in *Death of a Salesman*, Joe Keller in *All My Sons*, Don Parritt in *The Iceman Cometh*, Simon Stimson in *Our Town*, Ophelia in *Hamlet*, Othello in *Othello*, Cassius and Brutus in *Julius Caesar*, Goneril in *King Lear*, Antony, Cleopatra, Enobarbus, and Charmian in *Antony and Cleopatra*, the grandfather in *Awake and Sing!*, Ivanov in *Ivanov*, Konstantin in *The Seagull*. And this astonishing list was only of plays in which he had at one time performed. There were more, many more. What was remarkable was the frequency with which suicide enters into drama, as though it were a formula fundamental to the drama, not necessarily supported by the action as dictated by the workings of the genre itself. Deirdre in *Deirdre of the Sorrows*, Hedvig in *The Wild Duck*, Rebecca West in *Rosmersholm*, Christine and Orin in *Mourning Becomes Electra*, both Romeo and Juliet, Sophocles' Ajax. Suicide is a subject dramatists have been contemplating with awe since the fifth century B.C., beguiled by the human beings who are capable of generating emotions that can inspire this most extraordinary act. He should set himself the task of rereading these plays. Yes, everything gruesome must be squarely faced. Nobody should be able to say that he did not think it through.

Jerry had brought a manila envelope containing a handful of mail addressed to him in care of the Oppenheim Agency.

There was a time when a dozen letters from fans would come to him that way every couple of weeks. Now these few were all that had arrived at Jerry's during the past half year. He sat in the living room idly tearing the envelopes open, reading each letter's first few lines and then balling the page up and throwing it onto the floor. They were all requests for autographed photos—all but one, which took him by surprise and which he read in its entirety.

"I don't know if you'll remember me," the letter began. "I was a patient at Hammerton. I had dinner with you several times. We were in art therapy together. Maybe you won't remember me. I have just finished watching a late-night movie on TV and to my amazement you were in it. You were playing a hardened criminal. It was so startling to see you on the screen, especially in such a menacing role. How different from the man I met! I remember telling you my story. I remember how you listened to me meal after meal. I couldn't stop talking. I was in agony. I thought my life was over. I wanted it to be over. You may not know it but your listening to my story the way you did contributed to my getting through back then. Not that it's been easy. Not that it is now. Not that it ever will be. The monster I was married to has done ineradicable damage to my family. The disaster was worse than I knew when I was hospitalized. Terrible things had been going on for a long time without my knowing anything about them. Tragic things involving my little girl. I remember asking you if you would kill for me. I told you I would pay. I thought because you were so big you could do it. Mercifully you didn't tell me that I was crazy when I said that but sat there listening to my madness as though I were sane. I thank you for that. But a part of me will never be sane again. It can't be. It couldn't be. It shouldn't be. Stupidly I sentenced the wrong person to death."

The letter went on, a single handwritten paragraph stretching loosely over three more big sheets of paper, and it was signed "Sybil Van Buren." He remembered listening to her story—summoning up his concentration and listening like that to someone other than himself was as close as he had come to acting in a long time and may even have helped *him* to recover. Yes, he remembered her and her story and her asking him to kill her husband, as though he *were* a gangster in a movie rather than another patient in a psychiatric hospital who, big as he was, was as incapable as she of violently ending his own suffering with a gun. People go around killing people in movies all the time, but the reason they make all those movies is that for 99.9 percent of the audience it's impossible to do. And if it's that hard to kill someone else, someone you have every reason to want to destroy, imagine how hard it is to succeed in killing yourself.

2

The Transformation

H E'D KNOWN Pegeen's parents as good friends before
Pegeen was born and had seen her first in the hospital as
a tiny infant nursing at her mother's breast. They'd met when
Axler and the newly married Staplefords—he from Michigan,
she from Kansas—appeared together in a Greenwich Village
church basement production of *Playboy of the Western World*.
Axler had played the wonderfully wild lead role of Christy
Mahon, the would-be parricide, while the female lead, Pegeen
Mike Flaherty, the strong-minded barmaid in her father's pub
on the west coast of County Mayo, had been played by Carol
Stapleford, then two months pregnant with a first child; Asa
Stapleford had played Shawn Keogh, Pegeen's betrothed. When
the play's run ended, Axler had been at the closing-night party
to cast his vote for Christy as the name for a son and Pegeen
Mike as the name for a daughter when the Staplefords' baby
arrived.

It was not likely—particularly as Pegeen Mike Stapleford had
lived as a lesbian since she was twenty-three—that when she
was forty years old and Axler was sixty-five they would become
lovers who would speak on the phone every morning upon
awakening and would eagerly spend their free time together at
his house, where, to his delight, she appropriated two rooms for
her own, one of the three bedrooms on the second floor for
her things and the downstairs study off the living room for her
laptop. There were fireplaces in all the downstairs rooms, even
one in the kitchen, and when Pegeen was working in the study,
she had a fire going all the time. She lived a little over an hour
away, journeying along winding hilly roads that carried her
across farm country to his fifty acres of open fields and the
large old black-shuttered white farmhouse enclosed by ancient
maples and big ashes and long, uneven stone walls. There
was nobody but the two of them anywhere nearby. During the
first few months they rarely got out of bed before noon. They
couldn't leave each other alone.

Yet before her arrival he'd been sure he was finished: finished with acting, with women, with people, finished forever with happiness. He had been in serious physical distress for over a year, barely able to walk any distance or to stand or sit for very long because of the spinal pain that he'd put up with all his adult life but whose debilitating progress had accelerated with age—and so he was sure he was finished with everything. One of his legs would intermittently go dead so that he couldn't raise it properly while walking, and he would miss a step or a curb and fall, opening cuts on his hands and even landing on his face, bloodying his lip or his nose. Only a few months earlier his best and only local friend, an eighty-year-old judge who'd retired some years back, had died of cancer; as a result, though Axler had been based two hours from the city, amid the trees and fields, for thirty years—living there when he wasn't out somewhere in the world performing—he didn't have anyone with whom to talk or to eat a meal, let alone share a bed. And he was thinking again about killing himself as often as he had been before being hospitalized a year earlier. Every morning when he awoke to his emptiness, he determined he couldn't go another day shorn of his skills, alone, workless, and in persistent pain. Once again, the focus was down to suicide; at the center of the dispossession there was only that.

On a frigid gray morning after a week of heavy snowstorms, Axler left the house for the carport to drive the four miles into town and stock up on groceries. Pathways around the house had been kept clear every day by a farmer who did his snow-plowing for him, but he walked carefully nonetheless, wearing snow boots with thick treads and carrying a cane and taking tiny steps to prevent himself from slipping and falling. Under his layers of clothes his midsection was enveloped, for safety's sake, in a stiff back brace. As he started out of the house and headed for the carport he spotted a small long-tailed whitish animal standing in the snow between the carport and the barn. It looked at first like a very large rat, and then he realized, from the shape and color of the furless tail and from the snout, that it was a possum about ten inches long. Possums are ordinarily nocturnal, but this one, whose coat looked discolored and scruffy, was down on the snow-covered ground in broad day-light. As Axler approached, the possum waddled feebly off in the direction of the barn and then disappeared into a mound of snow up against the barn's stone foundation. He followed the animal—which was probably sick and nearing its end—and when he got to the mound of snow saw that there was an entry hole cleared at the front. Supporting himself with both hands on his cane, he kneeled down in the snow to peer inside. The possum had retreated too far back into the hole to be seen, but strewn about the front of the cave-like interior was a collection of sticks. He counted them. Six sticks. So that's how it's done, Axler thought. I've got too much. All you need are six.

The following morning while he was making his coffee, he saw the possum through the kitchen window. The animal was standing on its hind legs by the barn, eating snow from a drift, pushing gobs of it into its mouth with its front paws. Hurriedly he put on his boots and his coat, picked up his cane, went out the front door, and came around to the cleared path by the side of the house facing the barn. From some twenty feet away, he called across to the possum in full voice, "How would you like to play James Tyrone? At the Guthrie." The possum just kept eating snow. "You'd be a wonderful James Tyrone!"

After that day, nature's little caricature of him came to an end. He never saw the possum again—either it disappeared or perished—though the snow cave with the six sticks remained intact until the next thaw.

Then Pegeen stopped by. She phoned from the little house she'd rented a few miles from Prescott, a small, progressive women's college in western Vermont, where she'd recently taken a teaching job. He lived an hour west, across the state line in rural New York. It was twenty years or more since he'd seen her as a cheerful undergraduate traveling during her vacation with her mother and father. They'd be in his vicinity and stop off for a couple of hours to say hello. Every few years they all got together like that. Asa ran a regional theater in Lansing, Michigan, the town where he'd been born and raised, and Carol acted in the repertory company and taught an acting class at the state university. He'd seen Pegeen on another visit once before, a smiling, shy, sweet-faced kid of ten who'd climbed his trees and swum rapid laps in his pool, a skinny, athletic tomboy who laughed helplessly at all her father's jokes. And before that he'd seen her suckling on the maternity floor of St. Vincent's Hospital in New York.

Now he saw a lithe, full-breasted woman of forty, though with something of the child still in her smile—a smile in which she automatically raised her upper lip to reveal her prominent front teeth—and a lot of the tomboy still in her rocking gait. She was dressed for the countryside, in well-worn work boots and a red zippered jacket, and her hair, which he had incorrectly remembered as blond, like her mother's, was a deep brown and cut close to her skull, so short at the back as to appear clipped by a barber's trimmer. She had the invulnerable air of a happy person, and though her prototype was Rough Gamine, she spoke in an appealingly modulated voice, as if imitating her actress mother's diction.

As he would eventually learn, it had been some time since she'd had what she wanted rather than its grotesque inversion. She'd spent the last two years of a six-year affair suffering in a painfully lonely household in Bozeman, Montana. "The first four years," she told him one night after they'd become lovers, "Priscilla and I had this wonderfully cozy companionship. We used to go camping and hiking all the time, even when it snowed. In the summers we'd go off to places like Alaska and hike and camp up there. It was exciting. We went to New Zealand, we went to Malaysia. There was something childlike about us adventurously roaming around the world together that I loved. We were like two runaways. Then, starting around year five, she slowly drifted away into the computer, and I was left with no one to talk to except the cats. Until then we had done everything side by side. We'd be tucked up in bed, reading— reading to ourselves, reading passages aloud to each other; for such a long time there was the rapturous rapport. Priscilla would never tell people, 'I liked that book,' but rather, 'We liked that book,' or about some place, 'We liked going there,' or about our plans, 'That's what we're going to do this summer.' We. We. We. And then 'we' weren't we—we was over. We was she and her Mac. We was she and her festering secret that blotted out everything else—that she was going to mutilate the body I loved."

The two of them taught at the university in Bozeman, and

during their final two years as a couple, when Priscilla got home from work, she sat in front of her computer until it was time for bed. She spent her weekends in front of the computer. She ate and drank in front of the computer. There was no more talk, no more sex; even hiking and camping in the mountains Pegeen had to undertake on her own or with people other than Priscilla whom she rounded up for companionship. Then one day, six years after they'd met in Montana and pooled their resources and set themselves up as a couple, Priscilla announced that she had begun taking hormonal injections to promote facial hair growth and deepen her voice. Her plan was to have her breasts surgically removed and become a man. Alone, Priscilla admitted, she had been dreaming this up for a long time, and she would not turn back however much Pegeen pleaded. The very next morning Pegeen moved out of the house they jointly owned, taking with her one of the two cats —"Not so great for the cats," said Pegeen, "but that was the least of it"—and she settled into a room at a local motel. She could barely gather enough composure to meet with her classes. Lonely as it had become living with Priscilla, the wound of the betrayal, the nature of the betrayal, was far worse. She cried all the time and began to write letters to colleges hundreds of miles from Montana looking for a new job. She went to a conference where colleges were interviewing people in environmental science and found a position in the East after sleeping with the dean, who became smitten by her and subsequently hired her. The dean was still Pegeen's devoted protector and paramour when Pegeen drove over to pay Axler a visit and determined that after seventeen years as a lesbian she wanted a man—this man, this actor twenty-five years her senior and her family's friend from decades back. If Priscilla could become a heterosexual male, Pegeen could become a heterosexual female.

That first afternoon, Axler tripped and fell hard on the wide stone step as he led Pegeen into the house, gashing the meaty side of the hand with which he broke the fall. "Where's your first-aid stuff?" she asked. He told her and she went inside to get it and came back out and cleaned his wound with cotton and peroxide and covered it with a couple of Band-Aids. She'd also brought him a glass of water to drink. Nobody had brought him a glass of water for a long time.

He invited her to stay for dinner. She wound up making it. Nobody had made him dinner for a long time either. She finished off a bottle of beer while he sat at the kitchen table and watched her prepare the meal. There was a chunk of Parmesan cheese in the refrigerator, there were eggs, there was some bacon, there was half a container of cream, and with that and a pound of pasta she made them spaghetti carbonara. He was remembering the sight of her as an infant at her mother's breast while observing her as she worked in his kitchen, behaving as though the place were hers. She was a vibrant presence, solid, fit, brimming with energy, and soon enough he was no longer feeling that he was alone on earth without his talent. He was happy—an unexpected feeling. Usually at the dinner hour he had the worst blues of the day. While she cooked he went into the living room and put on Brendel playing Schubert. He couldn't remember the last time he'd bothered listening to music, and back in the best days of his marriage, it was playing all the time.

"What happened to your wife?" she asked, after they'd eaten the spaghetti and shared a bottle of wine.

"Doesn't matter. Too tedious to discuss."

"How long have you been out here without anyone else?"

"Long enough to be lonelier than I ever thought I could be. It's sometimes astonishing, sitting here month after month, season after season, to think that it's all going on without you. Just as it will when you die."

"What happened to acting?" she asked.

"I don't act anymore."

"That can't be," she said. "What happened?"

"Also too tedious to go into."

"Have you retired or did something happen?"

He stood up and came around the table and she stood and he kissed her.

She smiled with surprise. Laughing, she said, "I'm a sexual anomaly. I sleep with women."

"That wasn't hard to figure out."

Here he kissed her a second time.

"So what are you doing?" she asked.

He shrugged. "I can't say that I know. You've never been with a man?" he asked her.

"When I was in college."

"Are you with a woman now?"

"More or less," she replied. "Are you?"

"No."

He felt the strength in her well-muscled arms, he fumbled with her heavy breasts, he cupped her hard behind in his hands and drew her toward him so that they kissed again. Then he led her to the sofa in the living room, where, blushing furiously as he watched her, she undid her jeans and was with a man for the first time since college. He was with a lesbian for the first time in his life.

Months later he'd say to her, "How come you drove over that afternoon?" "I wanted to see if anybody was with you." "And when you saw?" "I thought, Why not me?" "You calculate like that all the time?" "It isn't calculation. It's pursuing what you want. And," she added, "not pursuing what you no longer want."

The dean who'd hired her and brought her to Prescott was furious when Pegeen told her their affair was over. She was eight years older than Pegeen, earned more than twice as much as Pegeen, had been an important dean for over a decade, and so she refused to believe it or to allow it. She phoned Pegeen to scold her first thing every morning and called her numerous times during the night to shout at her and insult her and demand an explanation. Once she phoned from a local cemetery, where, she announced, she was "stomping around in a fury" because of the way Pegeen had treated her. She accused Pegeen of exploiting her to get the job and then opportunistically dropping her within only weeks of taking it. When Pegeen went to the pool to work out with the swim team twice a week in the late afternoon, the dean turned up to swim at that hour and arranged to take the locker next to Pegeen's. The dean called to invite her to a movie, to a lecture, to a concert and dinner. She called every other day to tell Pegeen that she wanted to see her that coming weekend. Pegeen had already made it clear that she was busy on weekends and didn't want to resume seeing her again. The dean pleaded, she shouted—sometimes she cried.

Pegeen was the person she could not live without. A strong, successful, competent woman of forty-eight, a dynamic woman touted to be Prescott's next president, and how easily she could be derailed!

One Sunday afternoon she called his house and asked to speak to Pegeen Stapleford. Axler put down the phone and went into the living room to tell Pegeen the call was for her. "Who is it?" he asked her. Without hesitation, she replied, "Who else could it be? Louise. How does she know where I am? How did she get your number?" He returned to the phone and said, "There's no Pegeen Stapleford here." "Thank you," the caller said and hung up. The next week Pegeen ran into Louise on the campus. Louise told her that she was going away for ten days and that when she came back, Pegeen had "better do something for her" like "make her dinner." Afterward Pegeen was frightened, first because Louise wouldn't leave her alone even after she once again clarified that the affair was over, and second because of the threat Louise's anger embodied. "What's threatened?" he asked. "What? My job. There's no limit to the harm she can do me if she sets her mind to it." "Well, you have me, don't you?" he said. "What does that mean?" "You have me to fall back on. I'm right here."

He was here. She was here. Everyone's possibilities had changed dramatically.

The first article of clothing he bought her was a tan close-fitting waist-length leather jacket with a shearling lining that he saw in the window of a shop in the upscale village that lay ten miles through the woods from his house. He went in and purchased what he guessed correctly to be her size. The jacket cost a thousand dollars. She'd never owned anything that expensive before, and she'd never looked so good in anything before. He told her it was for her birthday, whenever that fell. For the next few days, she didn't take it off her back. Then they drove to New York, ostensibly to have some good meals and go to the movies and get away for the weekend together, and he bought her more clothes—by the time the weekend was over, more than five thousand dollars' worth of skirts, blouses, belts, jackets, shoes, and sweaters, outfits in which she looked very different from the way she looked in the clothes she'd brought east with her from Montana. When she'd first showed up at his house, she owned little that couldn't be worn by a sixteen-year-old boy—only now had she begun to give up walking like a sixteen-year-old boy. In the New York stores, after trying on something new in the dressing room, she'd come out to where he was waiting for her to show him how it looked and to hear what he thought. She was paralyzingly self-conscious for only the first few hours; after that she let it happen, eventually emerging coquettishly from the dressing room smiling with delight.

He bought her necklaces, bracelets, and earrings. He bought her luxurious lingerie to replace the sport bras and the gray briefs. He bought her little satin babydolls to replace her flannel pajamas. He bought her calf-high boots, a brown pair and a black pair. The only coat she owned she'd inherited from Priscilla's late mother. It was way too large for her and shaped like a box, and so over the next few months he bought her flattering new coats—five of them. He could have bought her a hundred. He couldn't stop. Living as he did, he rarely spent anything on himself, and nothing made him happier than making her look like she'd never looked before. And in time nothing seemed to make her happier. It was an orgy of spoiling and spending that suited them both just fine.

Still, she didn't want her parents to learn about the affair. It would cause them too much pain. He thought, More pain than when you told them you were a lesbian? She'd explained to him what had happened on that day back when she was twenty-three. Her mother had cried and said, "I can't imagine anything worse," and her father feigned acceptance but didn't smile again for months. There was a lot of trauma in that home for a long time after Pegeen told them what she was. "Why would learning about me cause them so much pain?" he asked her. "Because they've known you so long. Because you're all the same age." "As you wish," he said. But he couldn't stop pondering her motive. Perhaps she was acting out of the habit of keeping her life in different compartments, the sexual life strictly separated from her life as a daughter; maybe she didn't want the sex contaminated or domesticated by filial concerns. Maybe there was some embarrassment about her turning from sleeping with women to sleeping with a man, and an uncertainty as to whether the switch was going to be permanent. But regardless of what was prompting her, he felt he had made a mistake in allowing her to keep their connection a secret from her family. He was too old not to feel compromised by having to be kept a secret. Nor did he see why a forty-year-old woman should be so concerned about what her parents thought, especially a forty-year-old woman who'd done all sorts of things that her parents disapproved of and whose opposition she weathered. He did not like that she was showing herself to be less than her age, but he didn't push it, not for now, and so her family continued to think she was going along leading her regular life while, with the passing months, she seemed to him, slowly but naturally, to shed the last visible signs of what she now referred to as "my seventeen-year mistake."

Nonetheless, one morning at breakfast, as much to his own surprise as hers, Axler said, "Is this something you really want, Pegeen? Though we've enjoyed each other so far, and the novelty has been strong, and the feeling has been strong, and the pleasure has been strong, I wonder if you know what you're doing."

"Yes, I do. I love this," she said, "and I don't want it to stop."

"But you understand what I'm referring to?"

"Yes. Matters of age. Matters of sexual history. Your old connection to my parents. Probably twenty things besides. And none of them bother me. Do any of them bother you?"

"Would it perhaps be a good idea," he replied, "before hearts get broken, for us to back off?"

"Aren't you happy?" she asked.

"My life has been very precarious over the past few years. I don't feel the strength that it would take having my hopes dashed. I've had my share of marital misery, and before that my share of breakups with women. It's always painful, it's always harsh, and I don't want to court it at this stage of life."

"Simon, we both have been dropped," she said. "You were at the bottom of a breakdown and your wife picked up and left you to fend for yourself. I was betrayed by Priscilla. Not only did she leave me, she left the body that I'd once loved to become a man with a mustache named Jack. If we do fail let it be because of us, not because of them, not because of your past or mine. I don't want to encourage you in a risk, and I know it is a risk. For both of us, by the way. I feel the risk too. It's of a different sort than yours, of course. But the worst outcome possible is for you to take yourself away from me. I could not bear to lose you now. I will if I have to, but as for the risk—the risk has been taken. We've already done it. It's too late for protection by withdrawing."

"You're saying you don't want to get out of this thing while the getting is good?"

"Absolutely. I want you, you see. I've come to trust that I have you. Don't pull away from me. I love this, and I don't want it to stop. There's nothing else I can say. All I can say is that I'll try if you will. This is no longer just a fling."

"We took the risk," he said, echoing her.

"We took the risk," she replied.

Four words meaning that it would be the worst possible time for her to be dropped by him. She will say whatever she needs to say, he thought, even if the dialogue verges on soap opera, to keep it going because she's still aching, all these months later, from the Priscilla shock and the Louise ultimatums. It's not deception her taking this line—it's the way we are instinctively strategic. But eventually a day will come, Axler thought, when circumstances render her in a much stronger position for it to end, whereas I will have wound up in a weaker position merely from having been too indecisive to cut it off now. And when she is strong and I am weak, the blow that's dealt will be unbearable.

He believed he was seeing clearly into their future, yet he could do nothing to alter the prospect. He was too happy to alter it.

Over the months she had let her hair grow nearly to her shoulders, thick brown hair with a natural sheen that she began to think about having cut in a style unlike the cropped mannish one she'd favored throughout her adult life. One weekend she arrived with a couple of magazines full of photos of different hairstyles, magazines of a kind he'd never seen before. "Where'd you get these?" he asked her. "One of my students," she said. They sat side by side on the sofa in the living room while she turned pages and bent back corners where there was a style pictured that might suit her. Finally they narrowed their preferences down to two, and she tore out those pages and he phoned an actress friend in Manhattan to ask her where Pegeen should go to get her hair cut, the same friend who'd told him where to take Pegeen shopping for clothes and where to go to buy her jewelry. "Wish I had a sugar daddy," the friend said. But he hadn't understood it that way. All he was doing was helping Pegeen to be a woman he would want instead of a woman another woman would want. Together they were absorbed in making this happen.

He went with her to an expensive hairdresser's in the East Sixties. A young Japanese woman cut Pegeen's hair after looking at the two photos they'd brought. He had never seen Pegeen look as disarmed as she did sitting in the chair in front of the mirror after her hair had been washed. He'd never before seen her look so weakened or so at a loss as to how to behave. The sight of her, silent, sheepish, sitting there at the edge of humiliation, unable even to look at her reflection, gave the haircut an entirely transformed meaning, igniting all his self-mistrust and causing him to wonder, as he had more than once, if he wasn't being blinded by a stupendous and desperate illusion. What is the draw of a woman like this to a man who is losing so much? Wasn't he making her pretend to be someone other than who she was? Wasn't he dressing her up in costume as though a costly skirt could dispose of nearly two decades of lived experience? Wasn't he distorting her while telling himself a lie—and a lie that in the end might be anything but harmless? What if he proved to be no more than a brief male intrusion into a lesbian life?

But then Pegeen's thick brown shiny hair was cut—cut to below the base of her neck in a choppy way so none of the layers were even, a look that gave her precisely the right cared-for devil-may-care air of slight dishevelment—and she seemed so transformed that all these unanswered questions ceased to trouble him; they did not even require serious thought. It took her a little longer than it took him to be convinced that the two of them had chosen correctly, but in only a few days the haircut and all it signified about her allowing him to shape her, to determine what she should look like and advance an idea of what her true life was, appeared to have become more than just acceptable. Perhaps because she looked so great in his eyes she did not bridle at continuing to submit to his ministrations, alien though that might have been to a lifelong sense of herself. If indeed hers was the will that was submitting—if indeed it wasn't she who had taken him over completely, taken him up and taken him over.

Late one Friday afternoon Pegeen arrived at his house in distress —out in Lansing her family had received a midnight phone call from Louise to tell them how she had been opportunistically exploited and deceived by their daughter.

"What else?" he said.

His question brought Pegeen close to tears. "She told them about you. She said I was living with you."

"And what did they say to that?"

"My mother was the one who answered. He was asleep."

"And how did she take it?"

"She asked me if it was true. I told her I wasn't living with you. I told her we had become close friends."

"What did your father say?"

"He never came to the phone."

"Why didn't he?"

"I don't know. That miserable bitch! Why won't she stop!" she cried. "That obsessive, possessive, jealous, rancorous bitch!"

"Does it really matter to you that she told your parents?"

"Doesn't it matter to you?" Pegeen asked him.

"Only inasmuch as it troubles you. Otherwise not at all. I think it's all to the good."

"What do I say when I talk to my father?" she asked.

"Pegeen Mike—say whatever you like."

"Suppose he decides not to talk to me at all."

"I doubt that will happen."

"Suppose he wants to talk to you."

"Then he and I will talk," Axler said.

"How angry is he?"

"Your father is a reasonable and sensible man. Why would he be angry?"

"Oh, that bitch—she is completely whacked. She's out of control."

"Yes," he said, "the thought of you tortures her. But you're not out of control, I'm not, and neither are your mother and father."

"Then why didn't my father speak to me?"

"If you're so worried, call and ask him. Perhaps you'd like me to speak to him."

"No, I'll do it—I'll do it myself."

She waited until after they'd eaten before phoning Lansing, and then doing it from her study, behind the closed door. After fifteen minutes she came out carrying the phone and pointed with it toward him.

Axler took the phone. "Asa? Hello."

"Hi there. I hear you seduced my daughter."

"I'm having an affair with her, that is true."

"Well, I can't say I'm not a little astonished."

"Well," Axler replied with a laugh, "I can't say that I'm not either."

"When she told me she was going to visit you, I really never figured that this was in the cards," Asa said.

"Well, I'm glad you're all right with it," Axler replied.

There was a pause before Asa answered, "Pegeen's a free agent. She left her childhood long ago. Look, Carol wants to say hello," Asa said and then passed the phone to his wife.

"Well, well," Carol said, "who ever could have imagined this when we were all kiddies in New York?"

"No one," Axler replied. "I couldn't have imagined it the day she showed up here."

"Is my daughter doing the right thing?" Carol asked him.

"I think so."

"What is your plan?" Carol asked.

"I have no plan."

"Pegeen has always surprised us."

"She surprised me too," Axler said. "I think she's no less surprised."

"Well, she surprised her friend Louise."

He did not bother to reply that Louise was something of a surprise herself. Carol's intention, clearly, was to be mild and friendly, but he was sure from the brittleness of her tone that the call was an ordeal and that she and Asa were simply doing the right thing, which was their way, doing the sensible thing that would make Pegeen happiest. They did not want to alienate her at forty as they had at twenty-three when she'd told them she was a lesbian.

In fact, Carol flew in from Michigan the following Saturday to meet Pegeen in New York for lunch. Pegeen drove down to the city that morning and got back about eight that night. He had made dinner for them, and only when dinner was over did he ask her how it had gone.

"Well, what did she say?" Axler asked.

"Do you want me to be entirely honest?" Pegeen replied.

"Please," he said.

"All right," she said, "I'll try to remember as exactly as I can. It was kind of the benign third degree. There was nothing vulgar or self-serving about her. Just Mother's flat-out Kansas candor."

"Go ahead."

"You want to know everything," Pegeen said.

"Yes," he replied.

"Well, first off, at the restaurant, she breezed right by my table—she failed to recognize me. I said, 'Mother,' and then she turned back and she said, 'Oh, my goodness, it's my daughter. Don't you look pretty.' And I said, 'Pretty? Didn't you think I was pretty before?' And she said, 'A new hairdo, clothes of a kind I never saw you wear before.' And I said, 'More feminine, you mean.' 'Decidedly,' she said, 'yes. It's very flattering, dear. How long has this been going on?' I told her, and she said, 'That's a very nice haircut. It couldn't have been inexpensive.' And I said to her, 'I'm just trying something new.' And she said, 'I guess you are trying something new, in many ways. I came out because I want to be sure that you have thought through all the implications of your affair.' I told her that I wasn't sure anyone ever thinks through being with someone romantically. I told her that it made me very happy right now. And so she said, 'News reached us that he was in a psychiatric hospital. Some people say he was there six months, some say a year—I don't really know the facts.' I told her that you were there for twenty-six days a full twelve months ago and that it had to do with performance problems on the stage. I said that you temporarily lost your power to act, and separated from your acting, you came apart. I said that whatever

emotional or mental problems you had then, they didn't mani-
fest themselves in our life together now. I said you were as sane
or saner than anyone I've ever been with, and that when we're
together you seem stable and quite happy. And she asked, 'Is
he still in the same bind with his acting?' And I said yes and
no—you were, but I thought that as a result of meeting me
and being with me, it was no longer the same tragedy it had
been. It was now more like an athlete who's been injured and
sidelined and is waiting to heal. And she said, 'You don't feel
you have to rescue him, do you?' I assured her that I did not,
and she asked how you filled your time, and I said, 'He sees
me. I think he plans to continue seeing me. He reads. He buys
me clothes.' Well, she leaped on that—'So these are clothes he
bought for you. Well, I would think there might be a certain
rescue fantasy working there.' I told her that she was making
too much of it and that it was just fun for both of us, and why
couldn't we leave it at that? I said, 'He's not trying to influence
me in any way I don't want to be influenced.' She asked, 'Do
you go with him when he buys you clothes?' And I said, 'Usually. But again, I think it makes him happy. And I can see that
in him. Since it happens to be an experiment I want to conduct
as well,' I told her, 'I don't see why anyone should be concerned.' And that's when the tenor of the conversation
changed. She said, 'Well, I have to tell you that I am concerned. You're new to the world of men, and it strikes me as
strange—or maybe not so strange—that the man you should
choose to initiate this new life with is a man twenty-five years
older than you are who has been through a breakdown that
led to his being institutionalized. And who now is essentially
unemployed. All those things don't bode well to me.' I told
her that it didn't seem any worse than the situation I was in
before, with someone whom I once loved very much and who
told me one morning, 'I can't go on in this body,' and decided
she wanted to be a man. And then I made my speech, the
speech I'd prepared and recited aloud driving down. I said, 'As
for his age, Mother, I don't see it as a problem. If I'm going to
try to be attractive to men and also learn whether I am attracted to men, this seems to be the best measure of it. This
person is the test. The twenty-five years register with me as
twenty-five years more experience than someone would have if

I were trying this with a man my own age. We're not talking about getting married. I told you—we're just enjoying each other. I'm enjoying him, in part, because he is twenty-five years older.' And she said, 'And he's enjoying you because you're twenty-five years younger.' I said, 'Don't be offended, Mother, but are you at all jealous?' And she laughed and said, 'Dear, I'm sixty-three and happily married to your father for over forty years. It's true,' she said, 'and you may get a kick out of knowing this, but when I played Pegeen Mike and Simon played Christy in the Synge play, I had a crush on him. Who didn't? He was wildly attractive, energetic, exuberant, playful, he was a big forceful actor, a wonderful actor, already his talent obviously a huge cut above everyone else's. So, yes, I had a crush, but I was already married and pregnant with you. The crush was something I passed through. I think I've seen him no more than ten times in the intervening years. I respect him enormously as an actor. But I continue to be concerned by that hospital stay. It's no small thing for someone to commit himself to a psychiatric hospital and to be there for however long or short a period it was. Look,' she said, 'for me the important thing is that you're not going into this blind. You don't want to be doing something that, for lack of experience, a twenty-year-old might do. I don't want you to act out of innocence.' And I said, 'I'm hardly innocent, Mother.' I asked her what she was afraid might happen that couldn't happen with anyone. And she said, 'What am I afraid of? I'm afraid of the fact that he is growing older by the day. That's the way it works. You're sixty-five and then you're sixty-six and then you're sixty-seven, and so on. In a few years he'll be seventy. You'll be with a seventy-year-old man. And it won't stop there,' she told me. 'After that he'll become a seventy-five-year-old man. It never stops. It goes on. He'll begin to have health problems such as the elderly have, and maybe things even worse, and you're going to be the person responsible for his care. Are you in love with him?' she said. I said I thought that I was. And she asked, 'Is he in love with you?' And I said I thought that you were. I said, 'I think it'll be fine, Mother. It has occurred to me that he has to worry more than I do. That this is a more precarious situation for him than it is for me.' She asked, 'How so?' I said, 'Well, as you say, I'm trying this for the first time. Although it's a novelty for him as well, it's not nearly as much of one as it is for me. I've been very surprised by how much I've enjoyed it. But I couldn't yet declare that it's definitely the permutation I will always want.' And she said, 'Well, all right, I don't want to go on and on and give this an urgency it doesn't have and may never have. I just thought it was important for me to see you, and I must say, once again, I'm very impressed by your appearance.' And I asked her, 'Does it make you think you would still have preferred a daughter who was straight?' She said, 'It makes me think that you would prefer not to be a lesbian any longer. You can, of course, do whatever you like. In your independent youth you educated *us* about that. But I can't fail to notice the physical change. You've taken great care that everybody *should* notice that. You even do your eyes. It's an impressive transformation.' That's when I said, 'What do you think Dad would think?' And she said, 'He couldn't be here because a new play opens in a few days and he can't leave it. But he wanted to come to see you, and as soon as the play is on, he will come, if that's all right with you. And then you can ask him directly what he thinks. So there we are. Want to go shopping?' she said to me. 'I'm admiring your shoes. Where'd you get them?' I told her, and she said, 'Would you object if I bought a pair like that? Want to go with me to get them?' And so we took a taxi to Madison Avenue and she bought a pair of two-toned pink-and-beige patent leather pumps with a pointy toe and a kitten heel in her size. Now she's walking around Michigan in my Prada shoes. She also admired my skirt, so we went shopping for a skirt for her cut like mine down in SoHo. Good ending, isn't it? But late in the afternoon, you know what she said, before leaving for the airport with her bags from the shopping? This, and not the shoes, is the true ending. She said, 'What you were trying to do with me at lunch, Pegeen, was make it sound like the sanest and most rea-sonable arrangement on the planet, when of course it isn't. But people on the outside are only going to frustrate you if they try to talk you out of what you wake up every day wanting and what is buoying you above everybody's humdrum sameness. I have to tell you that when I first learned of this I thought it was wacky and ill advised. And now that I've spoken with you and spent the day with you and been shopping with you for the first time, really, since you went off to college, now that I've seen that you're completely calm, rational, and thoughtful about it, I still think it's wacky and ill advised.'"

Here Pegeen stopped. It had taken her close to half an hour to repeat the conversation to him, and in that time he had not spoken or moved from his chair, nor had he told her to stop on any of those several occasions when he thought he'd heard enough. But it was not in his interest to tell her to stop—it was in his interest to find out everything, to hear everything, even, if he had to, to hear her say, "I couldn't yet declare that it's definitely the permutation I will always want."

"That's it. That's all," Pegeen said. "That's pretty close to what was said."

"Was it better or worse than you expected?" he asked.

"Much better. I was very anxious driving down there."

"Well, it sounds as though you had no need to be. You handled yourself very well."

"Then I was very anxious coming back, about telling you all this and knowing that, if I was truthful, you weren't going to like everything you heard."

"Well, there was no need for that either."

"Really? I hope my telling you everything hasn't turned you against my mother."

"Your mother said what a mother would say. I understand." He laughed and said, "I can't say that I disagree with her."

Softly, and flushing as she spoke, Pegeen said, "I hope it hasn't turned you against me."

"It's made me admire you," he said. "You didn't flinch from anything, either in talking with her or now in talking with me."

"Truly? You're not hurt?"

"No." But of course he was—hurt and angry. He had sat there listening quietly—intently listening as he'd been listening all his life, offstage and on—but he was particularly stung by Carol's clarification of the aging process and the jeopardy in which it placed her daughter. Nor, however softly he now spoke, was he unperturbed by "wacky and ill advised." The whole thing disgusted him, really. It might be all right if Pegeen were twenty-two and there were forty years' difference between them, but why this peculiar proprietary relationship with an adventurous forty-year-old? And what the hell did a woman of forty care what her parents wanted? A part of them, he thought, should be happy that she was with him, if only from a venal point of view. Here is this eminent man with a lot of money who's going to take care of her. After all, she's not getting any younger herself. She settles down with someone who's achieved something in life—what's so wrong with that? Instead the message is: Don't set yourself up to be caretaker of a crazy old guy.

However, since Pegeen had seemingly rejected Carol's account of him, he thought it best to stay silent about that as well as everything else that he didn't like. What would be the good of attacking her mother for butting in? Better to appear to laugh it off. If she should come to see him through her mother's eyes, there was nothing he could say or do to stop her anyway.

"You're wonderful to me," Pegeen said to him. "You're what the doctor ordered."

"And you to me," he said, and he left it at that. He didn't go on from there to add, "As for your parents, I'd just as soon spare them, but I can't arrange my life according to their feelings. Their feelings don't matter that much to me, frankly, and at this stage of the game they really shouldn't matter that much to you either." No, he would not take off in that direction. Instead he would sit tight and be patient and hope the family would fade away.

The next day Pegeen devoted to stripping the wallpaper in her study. The wallpaper had been chosen by Victoria many years before, and though Axler didn't care about it one way or another, Pegeen couldn't stand the look of it and asked if she could take it down. He told her the room was hers to do with as she liked, as was the upstairs back bedroom and the bathroom beside it, as indeed was every room in the house. He told her he could easily get a painter in to do the job, but she insisted on stripping the walls and painting them herself, thereby making the study officially hers. She had all the necessary tools for stripping wallpaper at her house, and she had brought them with her to begin the job that Sunday, the very day after her mother, down in New York, had questioned the wisdom of her being there at all. He must have gone in to watch her removing the wallpaper ten times during the course of the day, and each time came away with the same reassuring thought: she wouldn't be working away like that if Carol had succeeded in persuading her to leave him. She wouldn't be doing what she was doing if she weren't planning to stay.

That evening Pegeen drove back to the college, where she had a class to teach early the following morning. When the phone rang around ten on Sunday night he thought it was she who was calling to say that she was safely home. It wasn't. It was the jilted dean. "Be forewarned, Mr. Famous: she's desirable, she's audacious, and she's utterly ruthless, utterly cold-hearted, incomparably selfish, and completely amoral." And with that, the dean hung up.

The next morning Axler dropped off his car to be serviced, and the mechanic gave him a ride back home in his tow truck. He would return the car to Axler at the end of the day when the job was done. Around noon, when Axler went into the kitchen to make a sandwich for himself, he happened to look out the window and saw something dart across the field adjacent to the barn and then disappear behind it. It was a person this time, not a possum. He stood back from the kitchen window and waited to see if perhaps there was a second, third, or fourth person lurking anywhere else. There had been a worrisome series of break-ins throughout the county in recent months, mainly into unoccupied houses owned by weekenders, and he wondered if the absence of a car in his carport had caught the attention of the robbers and made him a target for a daytime theft. Quickly, he headed for the attic to get his shotgun and load it with shells. Then he went back downstairs to survey his property from the kitchen window. A hundred yards to the north, on the road that ran perpendicular to his, he could see a parked car, but it was too far for him to make out whether there was anyone inside it. It was unusual to see a car parked there at any time of the day or night—there was a thickly wooded hill on the far side of the road, and on his side, open fields leading up to his barn, carport, and house. Suddenly the person hiding back of the barn came sneaking along the side of the barn and made a rush for the front of the house. From the kitchen he saw that the intruder was a tall, thin, redheaded woman dressed in jeans and a navy blue ski jacket.

She was peering into the living room through a front window. As he was still uncertain whether or not she was alone, for the moment he froze, the gun in his hands. Soon she began to move from one window to the next, stopping each time to get a good look at the room inside. He slipped out of the house through the back door and, without her seeing him, came to within ten feet of where she was staring into one of the living room windows on the south side of the house.

Aiming the rifle at her, he spoke. "What can I do for you, lady?"

"Oh!" she cried when she turned and saw him. "Oh, I'm sorry."

"Are you alone?"

"Yes. I'm alone. I'm Louise Renner."

"You're the dean."

"Yes."

She did not look much older than Pegeen, but she was a good deal taller, only inches shorter than he was, and what with her erect carriage and the red hair pulled away from her high forehead and knotted severely at the back of her neck, there was a heroically statuesque aura to this woman. "What do you think you're doing?" he asked her.

"I'm trespassing, I know. I intended no harm. I thought no one was home."

"Have you been here before?"

"Only to drive by."

"Why?"

"Could you lower that gun? It's making me very nervous."

"Well, you made me nervous, peeking into my windows."

"I'm sorry. I apologize. I've been stupid. This is shameful. I'll go."

"What were you up to?"

"You know what I was up to," she said.

"You tell me."

"I only wanted to see where she goes every weekend."

"You're in a bad way. You drove from Vermont to find that out."

"She promised we'd be together forever, and three weeks later she left. I apologize again. This has never happened to me before. I should never have come here."

"And it probably doesn't help much, your meeting me."

"It doesn't."

"It makes you boil with jealousy," he said.

"With hatred, if you want the truth."

"It's you who phoned last night."

"I'm not completely in charge of myself," she replied.

"You're obsessed, so you phone, you're obsessed, so you stalk. You're a very attractive woman nonetheless."

"I've never been told that before by a man with a gun."

"I don't know why she left you for me," he said.

"Oh, don't you?"

"You're a red-haired Valkyrie and I'm an old man."

"An old man who's a star, Mr. Axler. Don't pretend to be no one."

"Would you like to come inside?" he asked.

"Why? Do you want to seduce me too? Is that your specialty, retooling lesbians?"

"Madam, it isn't I who was the Peeping Tom. It isn't I who phoned her parents in Michigan at midnight. It isn't I who anonymously phoned 'Mr. Famous' last night. No need to take the accusatory tone so quickly."

"I'm not myself."

"Do you think she's worth it?"

"No. Of course not," she said. "She's not at all beautiful. She's not that intelligent. And she's not that grown up. She's an unusually childish person for her age. She's a kid, really. She turned her Montana lover into a man. She's turned me into a beggar. Who knows what she's turning you into. She leaves a trail of disaster. Where does the power come from?"

"Take a guess," he said.

"Is it that that makes for disaster?" the dean asked.

"Something about her sexually is very potent," he said, and saw her cringe at the words. But then it could not be easy for the loser to stand there and confront the person who had won.

"There's plenty that's potent," the dean said. "She's a girl-boy. She's a child-adult. There's an adolescent in her that's not grown up. She's a cunning naif. But it's not her sexuality on its own that does it—it's us. It's we who endow her with the power to wreck. Pegeen's nobody, you know."

"You wouldn't be suffering so if she were nobody. She

wouldn't be here if she were nobody. Look, you might as well step inside. Then you can see everything up close." And he could hear more about Pegeen, seared though her observations would be by Pegeen's having "exploited" her. Yes, he wanted to hear her speak out of the depths of her wound about the closest person on earth to him.

"This has been more than enough," the dean said.

"Come inside," he said.

"No."

"Are you afraid of me?" he asked.

"I've done something foolish for which I apologize. I've trespassed and I'm sorry. And now I'd like you to let me go."

"I'm not holding you. You have a way of trying to turn the moral tables on me. But I didn't invite you here in the first place."

"Then why do you want me to come inside? Because of the triumph it would be to sleep with the woman that Pegeen used to sleep with?"

"I have no such ambition. I'm satisfied with things as they are. I was being polite. I could offer you a cup of coffee."

"No," the dean said coldly. "No, you want to fuck me."

"Is that what you want me to want?"

"That is what you want."

"Is that what you came here to try to get me to do? So as to pay Pegeen back in kind?"

All at once she could conceal her misery no longer and burst into tears. "Too late, too late," she sobbed.

He did not understand what she was referring to, but he didn't ask. She cried with her face buried in her hands while he turned and, with the gun at his side, went back into the house through the rear door, trying to believe that nothing Louise had said about Pegeen, either there outside the house or the night before on the phone, could possibly be taken seriously.

When he called Pegeen that night he made no reference to what had happened that afternoon nor did he tell Pegeen about Louise's visit when she came for the weekend, nor, while they were having sex, was he able to keep the red-haired Valkyrie out of his mind and the fantasy of what hadn't happened.

3

The Last Act

THE PAIN from the spinal condition made it impossible for him to fuck her from above or even from the side, and so he lay on his back and she mounted him, supporting herself on her knees and her hands so as not to lower her weight onto his pelvis. At first she lost all her know-how up there and he had to guide her with his two hands to give her the idea. "I don't know what to do," Pegeen said shyly. "You're on a horse," Axler told her. "Ride it." When he worked his thumb into her ass she sighed with pleasure and whispered, "Nobody's ever put anything in there before"—"Unlikely," he whispered back —and when later he put his cock in there, she took as much as she could of it until she couldn't take any more. "Did it hurt?" he asked her. "It hurt, but it's you." Often she would hold his cock in her palm afterward and stare as the erection subsided. "What are you contemplating?" he asked. "It fills you up," she said, "the way dildos and fingers don't. It's alive. It's a living thing." She quickly mastered riding the horse, and soon while she worked slowly up and down she began to say, "Hit me," and when he hit her, she said mockingly, "Is that as hard as you can do it?" "Your face is already red." "Harder," she said. "Okay, but why?" "Because I've given you permission to do it. Because it hurts. Because it makes me feel like a little girl and it makes me feel like a whore. Go ahead. Harder."

She had a small plastic bag of sex toys that she brought with her one weekend, and she spilled them out on the sheets when they were getting ready for bed. He'd seen his share of dildos, but never, other than in pictures, the strap-on leather harness that held the dildo secure and enabled one woman to mount and penetrate another. He'd asked her to bring her toys with her, and now he watched as she pulled the harness over her thighs and on up to her hips, where she tightened it like a belt. She looked like a gunslinger getting dressed, a gunslinger with a swagger. Then she inserted a green rubber dildo into a slot in the harness that was just about level with her clitoris. She stood alongside the bed wearing only that. "Let me see yours," she said. He removed his pants and threw them over the side of the bed while she grabbed the green cock and, having lubricated it first with baby oil, pretended to masturbate like a man. Admiringly he said, "It looks authentic." "You want me to fuck you with it." "No, thanks," he said. "I wouldn't hurt you," she said cajolingly, kittenishly lowering her voice. "I promise to be very gentle with you," she said. "Funny, but you don't look like you'll be gentle." "You mustn't be deceived by appearances. Oh, let me," she said, laughing, "you'll *like* it. It's a new frontier." "*You'll* like it. No, I'd prefer you to suck me off," he said. "While I wear my cock," she said. "Yes." "While I wear my big thick green cock." "That's what I want." "While I wear my big green cock and you play with my tits." "That sounds right." "And after I suck you off," she said, "you'll suck me off. You'll go down on my big green cock." "I could do that," he said. "So—that you could do. You draw strange boundaries. In any event, you should know you're still a very twisted man to be turned on by a girl like me." "I may well be a twisted man, but I don't believe you qualify as a girl like you any longer." "Oh, don't you now?" "Not with that two-hundred-dollar haircut. Not with those clothes. Not with your own mother following your fashion in footwear." Her hand continued slowly pumping the dildo. "You really think you've fucked the lesbian out of me in ten months?" "Are you telling me that you're still sleeping with women?" he asked. She just kept pumping the dildo. "Are you, Pegeen?" With her free hand she held up two fingers. "What does that mean?" he asked. "Twice." "With Louise?" "Don't be crazy." "With whom, then?" She flushed. "Two teams of girls were playing softball on the field I drive by on the way to school. I parked the car and I got out and went over and stood by the bench." After a pause, she confessed, "When the game was over the pitcher with the blond ponytail came to the house with me." "And the second time?" "The other pitcher with the blond ponytail." "That leaves quite a few players waiting their turn," he said. "I didn't intend to do it," she said, still stroking the green cock. "Perhaps, Pegeen Mike," he said, falling into the Irish accent he hadn't used since acting in *Playboy*, "you should tell me if you have plans to do it again. I'd rather you wouldn't," he said, knowing himself helpless to hold on to her and keep her his alone, knowing that his ardor had been laughable—and trying to hide his feelings behind the brogue. "I told you, I wasn't planning to do it at all," and then, either because desire had overpowered her or because she wanted to shut him up, she lowered her lips down the length of his cock while his gaze remained hypnotically fastened to hers, and the helplessness in him, the knowledge that the affair was a futile folly and that Pegeen's history was unmalleable and Pegeen unattainable and that he was bringing a new misfortune down on his head, began to abate. The oddity of this combination would have put off many people. Only the oddity was what was so exciting. But the terror remained too, the terror of going back to being completely finished. The terror of becoming the next Louise, the reproachful, crazed, avenging ex.

Pegeen's father hadn't helped things any when he had come to see her in New York on the Saturday following her mother's visit. Asa picked up where Carol had left off in citing the dangers of their liaison, moving from her lover's perilous age to his perilous psychiatric condition. Axler's strategy remained the same, however: tolerate whatever you hear; don't rush to challenge the parents so long as Pegeen doesn't yield.

"Your mother was right—that's a wonderful haircut," she'd reported her father's telling her. "And she was right about your clothes too," he'd said. "Yes? Do you think I look nice?" "You look terrific," he'd said. "Better than I used to?" "Different. Quite different." "Do I look more like the daughter you would have liked to have had?" "You certainly have an air you never had before. Now tell me about Simon." "After the hard time he had at the Kennedy Center," she'd said, "he wound up at a psychiatric hospital. Is that what you want to talk about?" she'd asked. "Yes, it is," he'd said. "We all have serious problems, Dad." "We all have serious problems but we don't all wind up in psychiatric hospitals." "While we're at it," she'd said, "what about the difference in age? Don't you want to ask about that?" "Let me ask you something else: are you starstruck, Pegeen? You know how certain kinds of characters carry around their force field, an encircling electric force field? It comes, in his case, with being a star. Are you starstruck?" She'd laughed.

"At the beginning, probably. By this time, I assure you, he's just himself." "May I ask how committed you are to each other?" he'd said. "We don't really talk about it." "Maybe you ought to talk about it with me then. Are you going to marry him, Pegeen?" "I don't think he's interested in marrying anyone." "Are you?" "Why are you treating me as though I'm twelve?" she'd said. "Because it may be that where men are concerned you are more twelve than forty. Look, Simon Axler's an intriguing actor, and probably to a woman an intriguing man. But he is the age he is, and you are the age you are. He has had the life he's had, with its triumphant ups and its cataclysmic downs, and you have had the life you have had. And because those downs of his worry me greatly, I'm not going to talk about them as glibly as you do. I'm not going to tell you that I'm not going to try to bring any pressure to bear on you. I am going to do just that."

And that he did—unlike the mother, he didn't end the day shopping with his daughter but instead he phoned her at her house every night around dinnertime to continue, in much the same strong vein, the conversation that had begun at lunch in New York. Rarely did father and daughter speak for less than an hour.

In bed, the evening after she'd seen her father in New York, Axler had said to her, "I want you to know, Pegeen, that I'm flabbergasted by all this stuff with your parents. I don't understand the place they are coming to play in our lives. It seems entirely too large and, all things considered, a little absurd. On the other hand, I recognize that at any stage of life there are mysteries about people and their attachments to their parents that can be surprising. This being so, let me make a proposal: if you want me to fly out to Michigan and talk to your father, I'll fly out to Michigan, and I'll sit and listen to every word he wants to say, and when he tells me why he's against this, I won't even argue—I'll side with him. I'll tell him that everything he's concerned about makes perfect sense and that I agree—it is an unlikely arrangement on the face of it, and there are, to be sure, risks involved. But the fact remains that his daughter and I feel as we do about each other. And the fact that he and Carol and I were friends as youngsters back in

New York is of no relevance whatsoever. That's the only defense I will make, Pegeen, if you want me to go and see him. It's up to you. I'll do it this week if you want me to. I'll do it tomorrow if that's what you want."

"His seeing me was quite enough," she replied. "There's no need for this to be carried further. Especially as you have made it clear that you think it's already been carried too far."

"I'm not so sure you're right," he said. "Better to take on the raging father—"

"But my father isn't raging, it isn't in his nature to rage, and I don't think there's any need to provoke a scene when there isn't a scene in the offing."

He thought, Oh, there's a scene in the offing all right—the two upstanding squares you have for parents are not through. But he only said to her, "Okay. I simply wanted to make the offer. It's finally up to you."

But was that so? Wasn't it up to him to neutralize them by opposing them rather than by simply leaving things to turn out opportunely on their own? He should, in fact, have accompanied her to New York—he should have insisted on being there and facing Asa down. Despite what Pegeen had said to assure him, he was reluctant to give up the idea that Asa was a father in a rage whom he should confront rather than flee. *Are you starstruck?* Of course that's what he would believe, he who never got the big roles. Yes, thought Axler, that my fame stole away his only daughter, the fame that Asa himself could never garner.

It was in the middle of the next week that he got around to reading the previous Friday's county newspaper and the front-page story about a murder that had taken place in a well-to-do suburban town some twenty-five miles away. A man in his forties, a successful plastic surgeon, had been shot dead by his estranged wife. The wife was Sybil Van Buren.

The two were apparently living apart by then. She had driven to his house across town from hers, and as soon as he opened the door had shot him twice in the chest, killing him instantly. She had dropped the murder weapon on the doorstep, then gone back and sat in her parked car until the police came and took her to the station to be booked. When she had left home that morning, she had already arranged for the baby-sitter to spend the day with the two children.

Axler phoned Pegeen and told her what had happened.

"Did you think she could have done this?" Pegeen asked.

"Such a helpless person? No. Never. She had the motive—the molestation—but homicide? She asked if I would murder him for her. She said, 'I need someone to kill this evil man.'"

"What a shocking story," Pegeen said.

"This fragile-looking woman built on the frailest, childlike scale. The least menacing person one could encounter."

"They'll never convict her," Pegeen said.

"Maybe they will, maybe they won't. Maybe she'll plead temporary insanity and get off. But what will become of her then? What will become of the child? If the little girl wasn't already doomed because of what the stepfather did, now she's doomed because of what her mother's done. Not to mention their little boy."

"Would you like me to come tonight? You sound shaky."

"No, no," he said. "I'm all right. I've just never known anyone who's killed somebody off the stage."

"I'm going to come over later," Pegeen said.

And when she did, they sat in the living room after dinner and he repeated to her in detail everything he remembered Sybil Van Buren saying to him at the hospital. He found her letter—the letter that had been mailed to him in care of Jerry's office—and gave it to Pegeen to read.

"The husband claimed to be innocent," Axler explained. "He claimed she was seeing things."

"Was she?"

"I didn't think so. I saw her suffering. I believed her story."

During the day, he had read the article again and again and repeatedly looked at the photograph of Sybil that the paper had published, a studio portrait in which she looked less like a married woman in her thirties, let alone a Clytemnestra, than like a high school cheerleader, someone who as yet had been through nothing in life.

The following day he phoned Information and, easy as that, got the Van Burens' phone number. When he called, a woman answered who identified herself as Sybil's sister. He told her who he was and told her about Sybil's letter. He read it to her over the phone. They agreed she would pass it on to Sybil's lawyer.

"Are you able to see her?" he asked.

"Only with the lawyer. She gets teary about not seeing the children. Otherwise she's unnervingly calm."

"Does she talk about the murder?"

"She says, 'It had to be done.' You'd think it was her fiftieth, not her first. She's in a very strange state. The gravity seems to escape her. It's as though the gravity is all behind her."

"For the moment," he said.

"I've been thinking the same. There's a great crash going to occur. She won't be living behind this placid mask for long. There must be a suicide watch on her cell. I'm frightened of what's coming next."

"Of course. What she did in no way jibes with the woman I knew. Why did she do this after all this time?"

"Because even when John moved out, he continued to deny everything and to tell her that she was delusional, and that put her into a mad frenzy. On the morning that she was going to see him, she told me that by whatever means it took she was going to extract a confession from him. I said, 'Don't see him. It will only drive you over the edge.' And I was right. I was the one who had wanted her to go to the district attorney and bring charges. I was the one who told her that she should have him put behind bars. But she refused: he wasn't a nobody and the case would wind up in the papers and on TV and Alison would get dragged into a courtroom nightmare to be exposed to yet more horror. Her saying this is why I never dreamed that extracting a confession 'by any means' would involve the use of his hunting rifle—using his hunting rifle might wind up in the papers too, you see. But when she got to John's that Saturday morning she didn't wait for him to let her into the house. She didn't wait to hear him speak a single word. It isn't that they had an argument and it escalated and she shot him. Seeing his face was all it took—right there in the front doorway, she pulled the trigger twice and he was dead. She told me, 'He wanted mayhem, so I gave him mayhem.'"

"Does the little girl know anything?"

"She hasn't been told yet. That's not going to be easy.

Nothing about this is going to be easy. The late Dr. Van Buren made sure of that. The suffering that's going to be Alison's is unimaginable to me."

Axler repeated to himself for days afterward, *The suffering that's going to be Alison's.* It was probably the very thought that had driven Sybil to murder her husband—thereby enlarging Alison's suffering forever.

One night in bed Pegeen said to him, "I've found a girl for you. She's on the Prescott swim team. I swim with her in the afternoon. Lara. How would you like me to bring you Lara?"

She was slowly rising and falling above him and all the lights were out, though the room was dimly lit by the full moon shining through the branches of the tall trees out back of the house.

"Tell me about Lara," he said.

"Oh, you'd like her all right."

"Obviously you do already."

"I watch her in the pool. I watch her in the locker room. A rich kid. A privileged kid. She's never known a minute's hardship. She's perfect. Blond. Crystal blue eyes. Long legs. Strong legs. Perfect breasts."

"How perfect?"

"It makes you awfully hard to hear about Lara," she said.

"The breasts," he said.

"She's nineteen. They're solid and they're just up there. Her cunt is shaved and there's just a fringe of blond hair to either side."

"Who's fucking her? The boys or the girls?"

"I don't know yet. But somebody's been having some fun down there."

From then on Lara was with them whenever they wanted her.

"You're fucking her," Pegeen would say. "That's Lara's perfect little pussy."

"You fucking her too?"

"No. Just you. Close your eyes. You want her to make you come? You want Lara to make you come? All right, you blond little bitch—make him come!" Pegeen cried, and no longer did he have to tell her how to ride the horse. "Squirt it all over her. Now! Now! Yes, that's it—squirt in her face!"

They went to a local inn one night for dinner. From the rustic dining room you could see out over the road to a big lake emblazoned by the sunset. She wore her newest clothes; they'd gone shopping for them on an impulsive visit to New York the week before: a little clinging black jersey skirt, a red cashmere sleeveless shell with a red cashmere cardigan knotted over her shoulders, sheer black stockings, a soft leather shoulder bag trimmed with small leather streamers, and on her feet a pair of pointy black slingbacks cut to show the cleavage of the foot. She looked soft and curvaceous and enticing, red above and everything black from the waist down, and she carried herself with such casual comfort that she might have been dressing like that all her life. She wore the shoulder bag, as the saleswoman had suggested, with the strap slung across her body like a bandolier and the bag riding her hip.

To try to prevent his back from locking and his leg from going dead, it was his habit to get up and walk around two or three times during a meal, and so after the main course and before dessert Axler stood and for the second time strolled through the restaurant and across the inn's public sitting room and into the bar. There he saw an attractive young woman drinking by herself. She must have been in her twenties, and from the way she was talking to the bartender he could tell she was a little drunk. He smiled when she looked his way and, so as to prolong his stay, he asked the bartender if he knew the ball score. Then he asked her if she was local or staying at the inn. She said she had just taken a job at the antique shop down the road and had stopped in after work for a drink. He asked if she knew anything about antiques, and she said her parents owned an antique shop farther upstate. She had been working at a shop in Greenwich Village for three years and had decided to get away from the city and try her luck in Washington County. He asked how long she'd been out here, and she said she'd arrived only the month before. He asked what she was drinking, and when she told him he said, "Next one's on me," and indicated to the bartender that he should put the drink on his tab.

When dessert arrived he said to Pegeen, "There's a girl at the bar getting drunk."

"What does she look like?"

"Like she can take care of herself."

"You want to?"

"If you do," he said.

"How old is she?" she said.

"I'd say twenty-eight. You'd be in charge. You and the green cock."

"You'd be in charge," she said to him. "You and the real cock."

"We'd be in charge together," he said.

"I want to see her," she said.

He paid the bill and they left the restaurant and went to stand in the doorway of the bar. He stood behind Pegeen with his arms encircling her. He could feel her trembling with excitement as she watched the girl drinking at the bar. Her trembling thrilled him. It was as though they had merged into one maniacally tempted being.

"You like her?" he whispered.

"She looks as if she could be quite indecent, given half a chance. She looks like she's ready for a life of crime."

"You want to take her home."

"She's not Lara but she'd do."

"What if she vomits in the car?"

"You think she's about to?"

"She's been at it a long time. When she passes out at the house, how do we get rid of her?"

"Murder her," Pegeen said.

While still closely holding Pegeen in front of him, he called across the bar, "Do you need a ride, young lady?"

"Tracy."

"Do you need a ride, Tracy?"

"I've got my car," Tracy replied.

"Are you in any shape to drive it? I can drop you off at home." Pegeen was still quivering in his arms. She's a cat, he thought, before the cat pounces, the falcon before it soars from the falconer's wrist. The animal you can control—until you let it loose. He thought, I am providing her Tracy the way I give her the clothes. Everyone felt emboldened with Lara because there was no Lara there and so no consequences. This he knew to be different. It dawned on him that he was ceding all the power to Pegeen.

"I can get my husband to pick me up," Tracy said.

He'd noticed earlier that she wore no wedding ring. "No, let us drive you. Where do you want to go?"

Tracy mentioned a town twelve miles to the west.

The bartender, who knew Axler lived in the opposite direction, went about his job as if he were a deaf-mute. Because of Axler's movies, practically everyone in the rural town of nine hundred knew who he was, though few had any idea that his reputation rested on his lifetime's achievement on the stage. The drunken young woman paid her bill and climbed off the stool and grabbed her jacket to leave. She was taller than he'd imagined and larger, too—a stray perhaps, but no waif— a buxom blond with an extensive body and a kind of ready-made Nordic prettiness. In all, a coarser, commonplace version of stately Louise.

He put Tracy in the back seat with Pegeen and drove them along the dark country roads, empty of traffic, to his house. It was as though they were abducting her. The swiftness with which Pegeen moved did not take him by surprise. She was not constrained by inhibition or fear as she had been when she'd gotten her haircut, and he was already enthralled merely by what he could hear from the back of the car. In the bedroom at home Pegeen emptied onto the bed her plastic bag of implements, among them the toy-like cat-o'-nine-tails with its very soft, thin wisps of black unknotted leather.

Axler wondered what was going on in Tracy's mind. She gets into a car with two people she's never seen before, they drive her to a house on a dirt road deep in the country, and then she steps out of the car into a three-ring circus. She may be drunk but she's also young. How oblivious to risk can she be? Or do Pegeen and I inspire trust? Or is risk what Tracy's looking for? Or is she too drunk to care? He wondered if she had ever done anything like this before. He wondered again why she was doing it now. It didn't make sense that this Tracy should fall into their laps to do all of the Lara-like stuff they'd been dreaming excitedly about in bed. Though what did make sense? His being unable to go out and act on a stage? His having been a psychiatric inpatient? His conducting a love affair with a lesbian whom he'd first seen nursing at her mother's breast?

When a man gets two women together, it is not unusual for one of the women, rightly or wrongly feeling neglected, to wind up crying in a corner of the room. From how this was going so far, it looked as though the one who'd wind up crying in the corner would be him. Yet as he watched from the far side of the bed, he did not feel painfully overlooked. He had let Pegeen appoint herself ringmaster and would not participate until summoned. He would watch without interfering. First Pegeen stepped into the contraption, adjusted and secured the leather straps, and affixed the dildo so that it jutted straight out. Then she crouched above Tracy, brushing Tracy's lips and nipples with her mouth and fondling her breasts, and then she slid down a ways and gently penetrated Tracy with the dildo. Pegeen did not have to force her open. She did not have to say a word—he imagined that if either one of them did begin to speak, it would be in a language unrecognizable to him. The green cock plunged in and out of the abundant naked body sprawled beneath it, slow at first, then faster and harder, then harder still, and all of Tracy's curves and hollows moved in unison with it. This was not soft porn. This was no longer two unclothed women caressing and kissing on a bed. There was something primitive about it now, this woman-on-woman violence, as though, in the room filled with shadows, Pegeen were a magical composite of shaman, acrobat, and animal. It was as if she were wearing a mask on her genitals, a weird totem mask, that made her into what she was not and was not supposed to be. She could as well have been a crow or a coyote, while simultaneously Pegeen Mike. There was something dangerous about it. His heart thumped with excitement —the god Pan looking on from a distance with his spying, lascivious gaze.

It was English that Pegeen spoke when she looked over from where she was, now resting on her back beside Tracy, combing the little black cat-o'-nine-tails through Tracy's long hair, and, with that kidlike smile that showed her two front teeth, said to him softly, "Your turn. Defile her." She took Tracy by one shoulder, whispered "Time to change masters," and gently rolled the stranger's large, warm body toward his. "Three children got together," he said, "and decided to put on a play," whereupon his performance began.

*

Around midnight they drove Tracy back to the lot beside the inn where she'd left her car.

"You two do this often?" Tracy asked from the back seat, where she lay encircled by Pegeen's arms.

"No," Pegeen said. "Do you?"

"Never in my life."

"So what do you think?" asked Pegeen.

"I can't think. My head's too crammed with everything to think. I feel tripped out. I feel like I've taken drugs."

"Where did you get the bravado for this?" Pegeen asked her. "The booze?"

"Your clothes. The way you looked. I thought, I have nothing to fear. Tell me, is he that actor?" Tracy asked Pegeen, as though he weren't in the car.

"He is," Pegeen said.

"That's what the bartender said. Are you an actress?" she asked Pegeen.

"Off and on," Pegeen said.

"It was crazy," Tracy said.

"It was," Pegeen replied, the wielder of the cat-o'-nine-tails and connoisseur of the dildo, who was herself no dabbler, who had indeed carried things to the limit.

Tracy kissed Pegeen passionately when they said goodnight. Passionately Pegeen returned the kiss and stroked her hair and clutched her breasts, and in the parking lot beside the inn where they'd all met, the two momentarily clung together. Then Tracy got into her car, and before she drove off, he heard Pegeen tell her, "See you soon."

They drove home with Pegeen's hand down in his pants. "The smell," she said, "it's on us," while Axler thought, I miscalculated—I didn't think it through. He was the god Pan no longer. Far from it.

While Pegeen showered, he sat downstairs in the kitchen and had a cup of tea as if nothing had happened, as if another ordinary night had been passed at home. The tea, the cup, the saucer, the sugar, the cream—all answered a need for the matter-of-fact.

"I want to have a child." He imagined Pegeen speaking

those words. He imagined her telling him when she came into the kitchen after the shower, "I want to have a child." He was imagining the least likely thing that might happen, which was why he was imagining it; he was out to force his foolhardiness back into a domestic container.

"With whom?" he imagined himself asking her.

"With you. You are the choice of my life."

"As your family has duly warned you, I'm closing in on seventy. When the child is ten I'll be seventy-five, seventy-six. By then I may not be your choice. I'll be in a wheelchair with this spine of mine, if not already dead."

"Forget about my family," he imagined her saying. "I want you to be the father of my child."

"Are you going to keep this a secret from Asa and Carol?"

"No. All that's over. You were right. Louise did me a favor with that phone call. No more secrecy. They'll have to live with things as they are."

"And where did this desire come from to mother a child?"

"From becoming what I've become for you."

He imagined himself saying, "Who could have foreseen this evening taking this turn?"

"Not at all," he imagined Pegeen replying. "It's the next step. If we're to continue, I want three things. I want you to have back surgery. I want you to resume your career. I want you to impregnate me."

"You want a lot."

"Who taught me to want a lot?" he imagined her saying. "That's my proposal for a real life. What more can I offer?"

"Back surgery is very tricky. The doctors I've seen say it would do no good in my case."

"You can't go on locked up with that pain. You can't go on hobbling around forever."

"And my career is trickier still."

"No," he imagined her saying, "it's a matter of adopting a plan to end the uncertainty. A bold long-term plan."

"That's all that's required," he imagined himself answering.

"Yes. It's time to be bold with yourself."

"If anything, it sounds like it's time to be cautious."

But because in her company he had begun to be rejuvenated, because he had done everything in his power to get himself to believe that she who'd begun by offering him a glass of water—only to go from there to pulling off the feat of feats, the sex-change act—could indeed make contentment real with him, he thought the most hopeful thoughts he could. In this kitchen reverie of the rectified life he imagined himself seeing an orthopedist who sent him for an MRI and after that for a presurgical myelogram and after that for surgery. Meanwhile he would have contacted Jerry Oppenheim and told him that if anyone wanted to offer him a role, he was available to work again. Then, still at the kitchen table exciting himself by elaborating these thoughts while Pegeen finished showering upstairs, he imagined Pegeen having a healthy baby the very month that he opened at the Guthrie Theater in the role of James Tyrone. He would have found Vincent Daniels's card where he had left it as a bookmark in the copy of *Long Day's Journey*. He would have gone to see Vincent Daniels with the script and they would have worked together every day until they found the way to get him to stop distrusting himself, so that when he went onstage at the Guthrie on opening night, the lost magic returned, and he knew while the words were flying so naturally, so effortlessly out of his mouth that he was in the midst of a performance as good as any he had ever given and that maybe being incapacitated for so long, however painful, hadn't been the worst thing that could have happened. Now the audience believed him anew in every moment. Where, previously, confronting the scariest part of acting—the line, saying something, saying something spontaneously with freedom and ease—he had felt himself naked, without the protection of any approach, now everything was once again emanating from instinct and he needed no other means of approach. The stretch of bad luck was over. The self-inflicted torment was over. He had recovered his confidence, the grief was displaced, the abominable fear was dispelled, and everything that had fled him was back where it belonged. The reconstruction of a life had to begin somewhere, and for him it had started with falling for Pegeen Stapleford, amazingly just the woman to have recruited for the job.

It seemed to him now that the kitchen scenario was no longer the aery tale with which he'd begun but that he was imagining a new possibility, a reclamation of exuberance that it was his intention to fight for and to implement and to enjoy. Axler felt the determination that was originally his when he came to New York to audition at the age of twenty-two.

The next morning, as soon as Pegeen had left to drive back to Vermont, he called a hospital in New York and asked for a doctor with whom he could consult about the genetic hazards of fathering a child at sixty-five. He was referred to the office of a specialist and given an appointment for the following week. He said nothing about any of this to Pegeen.

The hospital was far uptown, and after parking the car in a garage, he made his way with mounting excitement to the doctor's office. He was given the usual medical forms to fill out and then greeted by a Filipino man of about thirty-five who said he was Dr. Wan's assistant. There was a windowed room off the waiting area, and the assistant led him there so that they could be alone. It seemed a room designed to be used by children, with low tables and small chairs scattered about and children's drawings pinned to one wall. The two of them sat at one of the tables and the assistant began to ask him about himself and his family and the diseases they had suffered from and the diseases they had died of. The doctor's assistant recorded the answers on a sheet of paper printed with the skeleton of a family tree. Axler told him as much as he knew from as far back as his knowledge of the family extended. Then the assistant took a second sheet and asked about the family of the prospective mother. Axler could tell him only that Pegeen's parents were both living; he knew nothing about their medical histories or those of Pegeen's aunts, uncles, grandparents, and great-grandparents. The assistant asked for her family's country of origin, as he had asked for Axler's, and, having recorded the information, told Axler that he would give all the data to Dr. Wan and that after he and the doctor had conferred, she would come out to talk to Axler.

Alone in the room, Axler felt ecstatic with the return of his force and his naturalness and the abandonment of his humiliation and the end of his disappearance from the world. This wasn't reverie any longer; the revitalization of Simon Axler was truly under way. And under way in this room full of children's furniture, of all places. The scale of the furniture reminded him of the art therapy session at Hammerton, when he and Sybil Van Buren had been given crayons and paper in order to draw pictures for their therapist. He remembered how he had obediently set to coloring with the crayons like the child he'd once been in kindergarten class. He remembered the mortifying consequences of having ended up in Hammerton, how every trace of assuredness had vanished; he remembered how all he found to deliver him from a pervasive sense of defeat and dread was the conversation that he listened to in the rec room after dinner, the stories of those among the hospitalized infatuated still with how they had tried to kill themselves. Now, however, a huge man sitting awkwardly amid these little tables and chairs, he was at one with the actor, conscious of the achievement behind him and convinced that life could begin again.

Dr. Wan was a small, slender young woman who said that she would, of course, need Pegeen's history too, but that she could begin at least to address his fears about birth defects in the offspring of aging fathers. She told him that although the ideal age for men to father children is their twenties, and although the risk of passing on genetic vulnerability or developmental disorders like autism is significantly increased after forty, and although older men had more sperm with damaged DNA than younger men, the odds of fathering normal offspring without birth defects were not necessarily dire for a man of his age and health, especially as some, though not all, birth defects could be detected during pregnancy. "The testicular cells that give rise to sperm divide every sixteen days," Dr. Wan explained to him while they sat across from each other at the little table. "This means that the cells have split about eight hundred times by age fifty. And with each cell division, the chance increases for errors in the sperm's DNA." Once Pegeen had provided her with the other half of the story, she could more fully evaluate their situation and work with them together should they wish to proceed further. She gave him her card along with a pamphlet that spelled out in detail the nature and risk of birth defects. She also explained that there might be decreased fertility at his age, and so, at his request, she provided him with a referral to a laboratory to have a sperm analysis. That way they could determine if there was likely to be any difficulty with conception. "There can be a problem," she told him, "of sperm count, of motility, or morphology." "I understand," he said and, to express an uncontrollable sense of gratitude, reached out to clutch her hand. The doctor smiled at him as if she were the older of the two and said, "Call me if you have questions."

Back at home, he had an enormous urge to phone Pegeen and tell her of the great idea that had taken hold of him and what he had done about it. But that conversation would have to wait until they were together the following weekend and had hours and hours to talk. Alone in bed that night, he read the pamphlet Dr. Wan had given him. "It takes healthy sperm to make a healthy baby . . . About 2 to 3 percent of all babies are born with a major birth defect . . . More than 20 rare but devastating genetic disorders have been linked to aging fathers . . . The older a man is when he conceives a child, the more likely his partner is to miscarry . . . Older fathers are more likely to have children with autism, schizophrenia, and Down syndrome . . ." He went through the pamphlet once and then again, and sobering as he found the information, mindful as he now was of the risks, he would not be dissuaded from his plans by what he read. Instead, too excited to sleep, thinking something wonderful was happening, he found himself down in the living room, further enlivened by listening to music, and, along with feelings of fearlessness such as he had not known for years, experiencing the deep biological longing for a child that is more commonly associated with a woman than with a man. Nothing about their being together seemed improbable any longer. She had to go with him to see Dr. Wan. Once everyone had the whole story, the two of them would soberly assess what should come next.

He had planned to begin the conversation after dinner on Friday evening. But when Pegeen arrived for the weekend late Friday afternoon, she went off to her study with a slew of student exams to mark and left it to him to make dinner. And after dinner she withdrew again to the study to grade more exams. He thought, Let her get everything done now. Then we'll have the weekend to talk.

In bed in the dark—two weeks to the day after the tryst with Tracy—when he began to kiss and to fondle Pegeen, she pulled away and said, "My heart's not in it tonight." "All right," he said and, unable to arouse her, rolled over to his side but without relinquishing her hand, which he held on to with his own hand—the hand that still wanted to touch everything—until she'd fallen asleep. When he awakened in the middle of the night, he wondered, What did it mean that her heart wasn't in it, why had she been so unwilling to be near him from the moment she'd arrived?

He found out first thing the next morning, before he even had a chance to begin to tell her about his meeting with Dr. Wan and all that lay behind that meeting and all that potentially lay ahead of them; he found out that in going to see Dr. Wan he hadn't so much educated himself in order to avoid doing something rash as to dig himself deeper into an unreal world.

"This is the end," she said to Axler at the breakfast table. Each was seated across from the other in the very chairs as when she had told him in months gone by that they had already taken the risk.

"End of what?" he asked.

"Of this."

"But *why*?"

"It's not what I want. I made a mistake."

So began the end, as abruptly as that, and it concluded some thirty minutes later with Pegeen at the front door clutching her full duffle bag and Axler in tears. This was the very antithesis of his expectations that night in the kitchen two weeks back. The very antithesis of his expectations when he'd gone to see Dr. Wan. Everything he wanted, she was preventing him from having!

And she was crying now as well; it was not as easy to pull off as it had seemed in the first moment at the kitchen table. But still she would not be budged, and however much he wept, she remained silent. The picture she made at the front door, back in her boy's zippered red jacket and holding her duffle bag, expressed it all: this form of hardship she could endure. She was not about to sit down over a cup of coffee and have a heart-to-heart talk that would lead to a rapprochement. She wanted only to be free of him and to satisfy the common enough human wish to move on and try something else.

"You cannot nullify everything!" he shouted angrily, and with that Pegeen, the mightier of the two, opened the door.

At last she spoke, sobbing. "I tried to be perfect for you."

"What the hell does that mean? Was it ever a matter of being perfect? 'Don't pull away from me. I love this, and I don't want it to stop.' I was idiot enough to believe what you said. I was idiot enough to think you were doing what you wanted to do."

"It was what I wanted to do. I wanted so much to see if I could do it."

"So it was an experiment, right down to the end. Another adventure for Pegeen Mike—like picking up a pitcher on a softball team."

"I can't be a substitute for your acting anymore."

"Oh, don't pull that! That's disgusting!"

"But it's true! I'm what you have instead of that! I'm supposed to make up for that!"

"That's the most ludicrous bullshit I've ever heard. And you know it. Go, Pegeen! If that's your vindication, go! 'We took the risk.' *I* took the risk! You just said whatever you thought I wanted to hear so that you could get what you wanted as long as you wanted it."

"I did no such thing!" she cried.

"It's Tracy, isn't it?"

"What is?"

"You're dumping me for Tracy!"

"I'm not, Simon! No!"

"You're not leaving me because I don't have a job! You're leaving me for that girl! You're going to that girl!"

"Where I go is my business. Oh, just *let* me go!"

"Who's holding you back? Not me! Never!" He pointed at the duffle bag into which she had crammed all the new clothes of hers that had been hanging in his closets and folded in his bureau drawers. "Pack your sex toys?" he asked. "Remember your harness?"

She did not answer, but the emotion flashing through her was hatred, or so he understood the look in her eyes.

"Yes," he said, "take the tools of your trade and go. Now

your parents can sleep at night—you're no longer with an old man. Now there's no interloper between you and your father. You're unburdened of your impediment. No more admonitions from home. Safely returned to your original position. Good. Go on to the next one. I never had the strength for you anyway."

A man's way is laid with a multitude of traps, and Pegeen had been the last. He'd stepped hungrily into it and taken the bait like the most craven captive on earth. There was no other way for it to wind up, and yet he was the last to find out. Improbable? No, predictable. Abandoned after so long? Clearly not so long for her as for him. Everything enchanting about her was gone, and in the time it had taken her to say "This is the end," he was condemned to his hole with the six sticks, alone and emptied of the desire to live.

She left in her car, and the process of collapse took less than five minutes, a collapse from a fall brought on himself and from which there was now no recovery.

He went up to the attic and sat there for a whole day and well into the night, preparing to pull the trigger of his shotgun and intermittently ready to rush down the stairs and wake Jerry Oppenheim at home, ready to call Hammerton and speak to his doctor, ready to dial 911.

And at a dozen different moments throughout the day, ready to call Lansing and tell Asa what a treacherous son of a bitch he was to have turned Pegeen against him. That was how it had happened, he was sure. Pegeen had been right all along to want to keep the news of their affair from her family. "Because they've known you so long," she'd explained to him when he'd asked why she preferred to keep him a secret. "Because you're all the same age." Had he made the trip to Michigan when he first suggested to Pegeen his going out there to talk to Asa, he might perhaps have had a chance to win. But to phone Asa now would accomplish nothing. Pegeen was gone. Gone to Tracy. Gone to Lara. Gone to the pitcher with the ponytail. Wherever she was, he no longer had to worry about the genetic hazards of being an aging father with testicular cells that had already divided well over eight hundred times.

By dinnertime he could restrain himself no longer and,

carrying the gun with him, he came down from the attic to the phone.

Carol answered.

"It's Simon Axler."

"Why, yes. Hello, Simon."

"Let me speak to Asa." His voice was trembling and his heartbeat had quickened. He had to sit in a kitchen chair to continue. It was very like the way he'd felt in Washington the last time he had tried to go out on a stage to perform. And yet none of this might be happening if only Louise Renner hadn't made that vengeful midnight phone call telling the Staplefords about their daughter and him.

"Are you all right?" Carol asked.

"Not really. Pegeen has walked out on me. Let me speak to Asa."

"Asa is still at the theater. You could try his office there."

"Put him on, Carol!"

"I just told you, he's not home yet."

"Isn't it wonderful news? Isn't it a great relief? You no longer have to worry about your daughter tending to the needs of a feeble old man. You no longer have to worry that she'll have to be keeper to a madman and nursemaid to an invalid. But then I'm not telling you anything you don't know—I'm not telling you anything you didn't help to cook up."

"You're telling me that Pegeen has left you?"

"Let me speak to Asa."

There was a pause, and then, unlike him, with perfect composure, she said, "You can try to reach Asa at his office. I'll give you the number and you can call him there."

He did not know now, any more than when he decided to call, whether he was doing the right thing, the wrong thing, the weak thing, or the strong thing. He set the gun on the kitchen table and took down the number Carol gave him and hung up without saying anything further. If he were given this role to act in a play, how would he do it? How would he do the phone call? In a voice that was trembling or a voice that was firm? With wit or with savagery, renunciation or rage? He could no more figure out how to play the elderly lover abandoned by the mistress twenty-five years his junior than he'd been able to figure out how to play Macbeth. Shouldn't he just have blown his brains out while Carol was at the other end listening? Wouldn't *that* have been the best way to play it?

He could stop, of course. He could stop the madness right here. He wasn't going to win Pegeen back by going on to dial Asa's number, yet he dialed it. He wasn't trying to win her back. There was no winning her back. No, he simply would not be outmaneuvered and outwitted by a second-rate actor who held sway, with the second-rate actress who was his wife, over a regional theater in the middle of nowhere. The Staplefords couldn't make it on the stage in New York, they couldn't make it in film in California, so they're making great dramatic art, he thought, out beyond the corruptions of the commercial world. No, he would not be defeated by these two mediocrities. He would not be a boy overcome by her parents!

The phone rang only once before Asa answered and said hello.

"Just how did it benefit you," Axler began, seething, shouting resentfully, "to turn her against me? You couldn't stand that she was a lesbian in the first place. That's what she said—neither you nor Carol could bear it. You were appalled when she told you. Well, with me she had relinquished all that, with me she had opened herself to a new way of life—and was happy! You never saw the two of us together. Pegeen and I were *happy*! But instead of being grateful to me, you persuade her to pick up and leave! Even her going back to being a lesbian was preferable to her being with me! Why? Why? Explain this to me, please."

"First, Simon, you must calm down. I won't listen to a tirade."

"Do you have some special dislike of me dating back to the beginning? Is there envy here, Asa, or revenge perhaps, or jealousy? What harm have I done her? I'm sixty-six, I haven't been working, my spine's a problem—where is the horror in that? Where is the threat to your daughter in that? Did it prevent me from offering her anything she wanted? I gave Pegeen everything I possibly could! I tried to satisfy her in every conceivable way!"

"I'm sure you did. She said as much to Carol and me. No one could fault you for your generosity and no one has."

"You know she's left me."

"I do now."

"You didn't before?"

"No."

"I don't believe you, Asa."

"Pegeen does what she wants to do. She's done that all her life."

"Pegeen did what you wanted her to do!"

"I am well within my rights as a father to be concerned about a daughter and give counsel to her. I would be remiss if I didn't."

"But how could you 'give counsel' when you knew nothing about what was going on between us? All you had in your head was a vision of me, with all my renown, with all my success, stealing away what was rightfully yours! It wasn't fair, Asa, was it, that I should have Pegeen too!"

Shouldn't he have played that line for a laugh instead of delivering it in a fit of anger? Shouldn't he have been quietly sardonic, as though it were a deliberately needling overstatement rather than his sounding out of his mind? Oh, play it however you like, Axler told himself. Probably you're playing it for laughs anyway without your even knowing it.

He detested his tears but he was all at once crying again, crying from the shame and the loss and the rage all tangled together, and so he hung up on the call to Asa that he never should have made in the first place. Because it was he, finally, who was responsible for what had happened. Yes, he had tried to satisfy her in every imaginable way, and so, idiotically, he'd introduced Tracy into their life and undone everything. But then how could he have foreseen that? Tracy was party to a game, a beguiling sex game of the kind that any number of couples play for diversion and excitement. How could he foresee a pickup at the bar would end with his losing Pegeen for good? Would someone smarter have known better? Or was this a continuation of the turn his luck had taken playing Prospero and Macbeth? Was all of this owing to stupidity, or was it just his way of digging himself one layer deeper down into the final demise?

And who was this Tracy? The new salesgirl at a rural antique shop. A lonesome drunk at a country inn. Who was she compared with him? This was impossible! How could he be overthrown for Tracy? How could he be defeated by Asa? Was Pegeen leaving him for Tracy because subterraneanly it hurled his little girl back into Papa's arms? And suppose she wasn't leaving him for Tracy. Or leaving him because of her family's objections. Then what had made him repugnant to her? Why was he suddenly taboo?

He carried the gun into Pegeen's study and stood there looking at the room that she had stripped of Victoria's wallpaper and then painted a shade of peach, the room that she had made into hers just as he, holding nothing back, had invited her to make him into hers. He suppressed an urge to fire a shot into the back of her desk chair and sat in it instead. He saw for the first time that all the books she'd brought from home had been removed from the bookcase beside the desk. When did she empty those shelves? How far back did the decision to leave him go? Had it been there all along, even while she was stripping these walls?

Now he suppressed the urge to fire the gun into the bookcase. Instead he ran his hand over the empty shelves that had housed her books, and tried in vain to think of what he could have done differently over all these months that would have made her want to stay.

After what must have been at least an hour, he decided not to be found dead in Pegeen's room, in Pegeen's chair. The culprit wasn't Pegeen. The failures were his, as was the bewildering biography on which he was impaled.

When, long after calling Asa, sometime around midnight—having retreated back to the attic several hours before—he could not pull the trigger even after he had gone so far as to place the barrel of the gun inside his mouth, he challenged himself to remember tiny Sybil Van Buren, that conventional suburban housewife weighing less than a hundred pounds who finished what she set out to do, who took on the gruesome role of a murderer, and succeeded at it. Yes, he thought, if she could summon up the force to do something so terrible to the husband who was her demon, then I can at least do this to myself. He imagined the steeliness that went into her carrying her plan to the brutal end: the ruthless madness that she'd mobilized in leaving the two small children at home, her driving single-mindedly to the estranged husband's house, her mounting the stairs, ringing the bell, raising the rifle, and, when he opened the door, without hesitation her firing twice at point-blank range—if she could do that, I can do this!

Sybil Van Buren became the benchmark of courage. He repeated to himself the inspiring formula to action, as though a simple word or two could get him to accomplish the most unreal of all things: *if she could do that, I can do this, if she could do that* . . . until finally it occurred to him to pretend that he was committing suicide in a play. In a play by Chekhov. What could be more fitting? It would constitute his return to acting, and, preposterous, disgraced, feeble little being that he was, a lesbian's thirteen-month mistake, it would take everything in him to get the job done. To succeed one last time to make the imagined real he would have to pretend that the attic was a theater and that he was Konstantin Gavrilovich Treplev in the concluding scene of *The Seagull*. In his mid-twenties, when, as a theatrical prodigy, he accomplished everything he tried and achieved everything he wanted, he had played the part of Chekhov's aspiring young writer who feels a failure at everything, desperate with defeat at work and love. It was in an Actors Studio Broadway production of *The Seagull*, and it marked his first big New York success, making him the most promising young actor of the season, full of certainty and a sense of singularity, and leading to every unforeseeable contingency.

If she could do that, I can do this.

There was a note of eight words found alongside him when his body was discovered on the floor of the attic by the cleaning woman later that week. "The fact is, Konstantin Gavrilovich has shot himself." It was the final line spoken in *The Seagull*. He had brought it off, the well-established stage star, once so widely heralded for his force as an actor, whom in his heyday people would flock to the theater to see.

NEMESIS

For H. L.

ACKNOWLEDGMENTS

Sources from which I've drawn information include *The Throws Manual*, by George D. Dunn, Jr., and Kevin McGill; *The Encyclopedia of Religion*, edited by Mircea Eliade; *Teaching Springboard Diving*, by Anne Ross Fairbanks; *Camp Management* and *Recreational Programs for Summer Camps*, by H. W. Gibson; *Dirt and Disease*, by Naomi Rogers; *Polio's Legacy*, by Edmund J. Sass; *A Paralyzing Fear*, by Nina Gilden Seavey, Jane S. Smith, and Paul Wagner; *Polio Voices*, by Julie Silver and Daniel Wilson; and *A Manufactured Wilderness*, by Abigail Van Slyck. Particularly useful was *The Book of Woodcraft*, by Ernest Thompson Seton, from which I have liberally drawn on pages 409–412, and *Manual of the Woodcraft Indians*, also by Seton, from which I have quoted on page 377.

1

Equatorial Newark

THE FIRST case of polio that summer came early in June, right after Memorial Day, in a poor Italian neighborhood crosstown from where we lived. Over in the city's southwestern corner, in the Jewish Weequahic section, we heard nothing about it, nor did we hear anything about the next dozen cases scattered singly throughout Newark in nearly every neighborhood but ours. Only by the Fourth of July, when there were already forty cases reported in the city, did an article appear on the front page of the evening paper, titled "Health Chief Puts Parents on Polio Alert," in which Dr. William Kittell, superintendent of the Board of Health, was quoted as cautioning parents to monitor their children closely and to contact a physician if a child exhibited symptoms such as headache, sore throat, nausea, stiff neck, joint pain, or fever. Though Dr. Kittell acknowledged that forty polio cases was more than twice as many as normally reported this early in the polio season, he wanted it clearly understood that the city of 429,000 was by no means suffering from what could be characterized as an epidemic of poliomyelitis. This summer as every summer, there was reason for concern and for the proper hygienic precautions to be taken, but there was as yet no cause for the sort of alarm that had been displayed by parents, "justifiably enough," twenty-eight years earlier, during the largest outbreak of the disease ever reported—the 1916 polio epidemic in the northeastern United States, when there had been more than 27,000 cases, with 6,000 deaths. In Newark there had been 1,360 cases and 363 deaths.

Now even in a year with an average number of cases, when the chances of contracting polio were much reduced from what they'd been back in 1916, a paralytic disease that left a youngster permanently disabled and deformed or unable to breathe outside a cylindrical metal respirator tank known as an iron lung—or that could lead from paralysis of the respiratory muscles to death—caused the parents in our neighborhood considerable apprehension and marred the peace of mind of children who were free of school for the summer months and able to play outdoors all day and into the long twilit evenings. Concern for the dire consequences of falling seriously ill from polio was compounded by the fact that no medicine existed to treat the disease and no vaccine to produce immunity. Polio—or infantile paralysis, as it was called when the disease was thought to infect mainly toddlers—could befall anyone, for no apparent reason. Though children up to sixteen were usually the sufferers, adults too could become severely infected, as had the current president of the United States.

Franklin Delano Roosevelt, polio's most renowned victim, had contracted the disease as a vigorous man of thirty-nine and subsequently had to be supported when he walked and, even then, had to wear heavy steel-and-leather braces from his hips to his feet to enable him to stand. The charitable institution that FDR founded while he was in the White House, the March of Dimes, raised money for research and for financial assistance to the families of the stricken; though partial or even full recovery was possible, it was often only after months or years of expensive hospital therapy and rehabilitation. During the annual fund drive, America's young donated their dimes at school to help in the fight against the disease, they dropped their dimes into collection cans passed around by ushers in movie theaters, and posters announcing "You Can Help, Too!" and "Help Fight Polio!" appeared on the walls of stores and offices and in the corridors of schools across the country, posters of children in wheelchairs—a pretty little girl wearing leg braces shyly sucking her thumb, a clean-cut little boy with leg braces heroically smiling with hope—posters that made the possibility of getting the disease seem all the more frighteningly real to otherwise healthy children.

Summers were steamy in low-lying Newark, and because the city was partially ringed by extensive wetlands—a major source of malaria back when that, too, was an unstoppable disease—there were swarms of mosquitoes to be swatted and slapped away whenever we sat on beach chairs in the alleys and driveways at night, seeking refuge out of doors from our sweltering flats, where there was nothing but a cold shower and ice water to mitigate the hellish heat. This was before the advent of home air conditioning, when a small black electric fan, set on a table to stir up a breeze indoors, offered little relief once the temperature reached the high nineties, as it did repeatedly that summer for stretches of a week or ten days. Outdoors, people lit citronella candles and sprayed with cans of the insecticide Flit to keep at bay the mosquitoes and flies that were known to have carried malaria, yellow fever, and typhoid fever and were believed by many, beginning with Newark's Mayor Drummond, who launched a citywide "Swat the Fly" campaign, to carry polio. When a fly or a mosquito managed to penetrate the screens of a family's flat or fly in through an open door, the insect would be doggedly hunted down with fly swatter and Flit out of fear that by alighting with its germ-laden legs on one of the household's sleeping children it would infect the youngster with polio. Since nobody then knew the source of the contagion, it was possible to grow suspicious of almost anything, including the bony alley cats that invaded our backyard garbage cans and the haggard stray dogs that slinked hungrily around the houses and defecated all over the sidewalk and street and the pigeons that cooed in the gables of the houses and dirtied front stoops with their chalky droppings. In the first month of the outbreak—before it was acknowledged as an epidemic by the Board of Health—the sanitation department set about systematically to exterminate the city's huge population of alley cats, even though no one knew whether they had any more to do with polio than domesticated house cats.

What people did know was that the disease was highly contagious and might be passed to the healthy by mere physical proximity to those already infected. For this reason, as the number of cases steadily mounted in the city—and communal fear with it—many children in our neighborhood found themselves prohibited by their parents from using the big public pool at Olympic Park in nearby Irvington, forbidden to go to the local "air-cooled" movie theaters, and forbidden to take the bus downtown or to travel Down Neck to Wilson Avenue to see our minor league team, the Newark Bears, play baseball at Ruppert Stadium. We were warned not to use public toilets or public drinking fountains or to swig a drink out of someone else's soda-pop bottle or to get a chill or to play with strangers or to borrow books from the public library or to talk on a public pay phone or to buy food from a street vendor or to eat until we had cleaned our hands thoroughly with soap and water. We were to wash all fruit and vegetables before we ate them, and we were to keep our distance from anyone who looked sick or complained of any of polio's telltale symptoms.

Escaping the city's heat entirely and being sent off to a summer camp in the mountains or the countryside was considered a child's best protection against catching polio. So too was spending the summer some sixty miles away at the Jersey Shore. A family who could afford it rented a bedroom with kitchen privileges in a rooming house in Bradley Beach, a strip of sand, boardwalk, and cottages a mile long that had already been popular for several decades among North Jersey Jews. There the mother and the children would go to the beach to breathe in the fresh, fortifying ocean air all week long and be joined on weekends and vacations by the father. Of course, cases of polio were known to crop up in summer camps as they did in the shore's seaside towns, but because they were nothing like as numerous as those reported back in Newark, it was widely believed that, whereas city surroundings, with their unclean pavements and stagnant air, facilitated contagion, settling within sight or sound of the sea or off in the country or up in the mountains afforded as good a guarantee as there was of evading the disease.

So the privileged lucky ones disappeared from the city for the summer while the rest of us remained behind to do exactly what we shouldn't, given that "overexertion" was suspected of being yet another possible cause of polio: we played inning after inning and game after game of softball on the baking asphalt of the school playground, running around all day in the extreme heat, drinking thirstily from the forbidden water fountain, between innings seated on a bench crushed up against one another, clutching in our laps the well-worn, grimy mitts we used out in the field to mop the sweat off our foreheads and to keep it from running into our eyes—clowning and carrying on in our soaking polo shirts and our smelly sneakers, unmindful of how our imprudence might be dooming any one of us to lifelong incarceration in an iron lung and the realization of the body's most dreadful fears.

Only a dozen or so girls ever appeared at the playground, mainly kids of eight or nine who could usually be seen jumping rope where far center field dropped off into a narrow school street closed to traffic. When the girls weren't jumping rope they used the street for hopscotch and running-bases and playing jacks or for happily bouncing a pink rubber ball at their feet all day long. Sometimes when the girls jumping rope played double dutch, twirling two ropes in opposite directions, one of the boys would rush up unbidden and, elbowing aside the girl who was about to jump, leap in and mockingly start bellowing the girls' favorite jumping song while deliberately entangling himself in their flying ropes. "H, my name is Hippopotamus—!" The girls would holler at him "Stop it! Stop it!" and call out for help from the playground director, who had only to shout from wherever he was on the playground to the troublemaker (most days it was the same boy), "Cut it out, Myron! Leave the girls alone or you're going home!" With that, the uproar subsided. Soon the jump ropes were once again snappily turning in the air and the chanting taken up anew by one jumper after another:

> A, my name is Agnes
> And my husband's name is Alphonse,
> We come from Alabama
> And we bring back apples!
>
> B, my name is Bev
> And my husband's name is Bill,
> We come from Bermuda
> And we bring back beets!
> C, my name is . . .

With their childish voices, the girls encamped at the far edge of the playground improvised their way from A to Z and back again, alliterating the nouns at the end of the line, sometimes preposterously, each time around. Leaping and darting about with excitement—except when Myron Kopferman and his like would apishly interfere—they exhibited astounding energy; unless they were summoned by the playground director to retreat to the shade of the school because of the heat, they didn't vacate that street from the Friday in June when the spring term ended to the Tuesday after Labor Day when the fall term began and they could jump rope only after school and at recess.

The playground director that year was Bucky Cantor, who, because of poor vision that necessitated his wearing thick eyeglasses, was one of the few young men around who wasn't off fighting in the war. During the previous school year, Mr. Cantor had become the new phys ed teacher at Chancellor Avenue School and so already knew many of us who habituated the playground from the gym classes he taught. He was twenty-three that summer, a graduate of South Side, Newark's mixed-race, mixed-religion high school, and Panzer College of Physical Education and Hygiene in East Orange. He stood slightly under five feet five inches tall, and though he was a superior athlete and strong competitor, his height, combined with his poor vision, had prevented him from playing college-level football, baseball, or basketball and restricted his intercollegiate sports activity to throwing the javelin and lifting weights. Atop his compact body was a good-sized head formed of emphatically slanting and sloping components: wide pronounced cheekbones, a steep forehead, an angular jaw, and a long straight nose with a prominent bridge that lent his profile the sharpness of a silhouette engraved on a coin. His full lips were as well defined as his muscles, and his complexion was tawny year-round. Since adolescence he had worn his hair in a military-style crewcut. You particularly noticed his ears with that haircut, not because they were unduly large, which they were not, not necessarily because they were joined so closely to his head, but because, seen from the side, they were shaped much like the ace of spades in a pack of cards, or the wings on the winged feet of mythology, with topmost tips that weren't rounded off, as most ears are, but came nearly to a point. Before his grandfather dubbed him Bucky, he was known briefly as Ace to his childhood street pals, a nickname inspired not merely by his precocious excellence at sports but by the uncommon configuration of those ears.

Altogether the oblique planes of his face gave the smoky gray eyes back of his glasses—eyes long and narrow like an Asian's—a deeply pocketed look, as though they were not so much set as cratered in the skull. The voice emerging from this precisely delineated face was, unexpectedly, rather high-pitched, but that did not diminish the force of his appearance. His was the cast-iron, wear-resistant, strikingly bold face of a sturdy young man you could rely on.

One afternoon early in July, two cars full of Italians from East Side High, boys anywhere from fifteen to eighteen, drove in and parked at the top of the residential street back of the school, where the playground was situated. East Side was in the Ironbound section, the industrial slum that had reported the most cases of polio in the city so far. As soon as Mr. Cantor saw them pull up, he dropped his mitt on the field—he was playing third base in one of our pickup games—and trotted over to where the ten strangers had emptied out of the two cars. His athletic, pigeon-toed trot was already being imitated by the playground kids, as was his purposeful way of lightly lifting himself as he moved on the balls of his feet, and the slight sway, when he walked, of his substantial shoulders. For some of the boys his entire bearing had become theirs both on and off the playing field.

"What do you fellows want here?" Mr. Cantor said.

"We're spreadin' polio," one of the Italians replied. He was the one who'd come swaggering out of the cars first. "Ain't that right?" he said, turning to preen for the cohorts backing him up, who appeared right off to Mr. Cantor to be only too eager to begin a brawl.

"You look more like you're spreadin' trouble," Mr. Cantor told him. "Why don't you head out of here?"

"No, no," the Italian guy insisted, "not till we spread some polio. We got it and you don't, so we thought we'd drive up and spread a little around." All the while he talked, he rocked back and forth on his heels to indicate how tough he was. The brazen ease of his thumbs tucked into the front two loops of his trousers served no less than his gaze to register his contempt.

"I'm playground director here," Mr. Cantor said, pointing back over his shoulder toward us kids. "I'm asking you to leave the vicinity of the playground. You've got no business here and I'm asking you politely to go. What do you say?"

"Since when is there a law against spreadin' polio, Mr. Playground Director?"

"Look, polio is not a joke. And there's a law against being a public nuisance. I don't want to have to call the police. How about leaving on your own, before I get the cops to escort you out of here?"

With this, the leader of the pack, who was easily half a foot taller than Mr. Cantor, took a step forward and spat on the pavement. He left a gob of viscous sputum splattered there, only inches from the tip of Mr. Cantor's sneakers.

"What's that mean?" Mr. Cantor asked him. His voice was still calm and, with his arms crossed tightly over his chest, he was the embodiment of immovability. No Ironbound rough-necks were going to get the better of him or come anywhere near his kids.

"I told you what it means. We're spreadin' polio. We don't want to leave you people out."

"Look, cut the 'you people' crap," Mr. Cantor said and took one quick, angry step forward, placing him only inches from the Italian's face. "I'll give you ten seconds to turn around and move everybody out of here."

The Italian smiled. He really hadn't stopped smiling since he'd gotten out of the car. "Then what?" he asked.

"I told you. I'm going to get the cops to get you out and keep you out."

Here the Italian guy spat again, this time just to the side of Mr. Cantor's sneakers, and Mr. Cantor called over to the boy who had been waiting to bat next in the game and who, like the rest of us, was silently watching Mr. Cantor face down the ten Italians. "Jerry," Mr. Cantor said, "run to my office. Telephone the police. Say you're calling for me. Tell them I need them."

"What are they going to do, lock me up?" the chief Italian guy asked. "They gonna put me in the slammer for spitting on your precious Weequahic sidewalk? You own the sidewalk too, four eyes?"

Mr. Cantor didn't answer and just remained planted between the kids who'd been playing ball on the asphalt field behind him and the two carloads of Italian guys, still standing on the street at the edge of the playground as though each were about to drop the cigarette he was smoking and suddenly brandish a weapon. But by the time Jerry returned from Mr. Cantor's basement office—where, as instructed, he had telephoned the police—the two cars and their ominous occupants were gone. When the patrol car pulled up only minutes later, Mr. Cantor was able to give the cops the license plate numbers of both cars, which he'd memorized during the standoff. Only after the police had driven away did the kids back of the fence begin to ridicule the Italians.

It turned out that there was sputum spread over the wide area of pavement where the Italian guys had congregated, some twenty square feet of a wet, slimy, disgusting mess that certainly appeared to be an ideal breeding ground for disease. Mr. Cantor had two of the boys go down in the school basement to find a couple of buckets and fill them with hot water and ammonia in the janitor's room and then slosh the water across the pavement until every inch of it was washed clean. The kids sloshing away the slime reminded Mr. Cantor of how he'd had to clean up after killing a rat at the back of his grandfather's grocery store when he was ten years old.

"Nothing to worry about," Mr. Cantor told the boys. "They won't be back. That's just life," he said, quoting a line favored by his grandfather, "there's always something funny going on," and he rejoined the game and play was resumed. The boys observing from the other side of the two-story-high chainlink fence that enclosed the playground were mightily impressed by Mr. Cantor's taking on the Italians as he did. His confident, decisive manner, his weightlifter's strength, his joining in every day to enthusiastically play ball right alongside the rest of us —all this had made him a favorite of the playground regulars from the day he'd arrived as director; but after the incident with the Italians he became an outright hero, an idolized, protective, heroic older brother, particularly to those whose own older brothers were off in the war.

It was later in the week that two of the boys who'd been at the playground when the Italians had come around didn't show up for a few days to play ball. On the first morning, both had awakened with high fevers and stiff necks, and by the second evening—having begun to grow helplessly weak in their arms and legs and to have difficulty breathing—had to be rushed to the hospital by ambulance. One of the boys, Herbie Steinmark, was a chubby, clumsy, amiable eighth grader who, because of his athletic ineptness, was usually assigned to play right field and bat last, and the other, Alan Michaels, also an eighth grader, was among the two or three best athletes on the playground and the boy who'd grown closest to Mr. Cantor. Herbie's and Alan's constituted the first cases of polio in the neighborhood. Within forty-eight hours there were eleven additional cases, and though none were kids who'd been at the playground that day, word spread through the neighborhood that the disease had been carried to the Weequahic section by the Italians. Since so far their neighborhood had reported the most cases of polio in the city and ours had reported none, it was believed that, true to their word, the Italians had driven across town that afternoon intending to infect the Jews with polio and that they had succeeded.

Bucky Cantor's mother had died in childbirth, and he had been raised by his maternal grandparents in a tenement housing twelve families on Barclay Street off lower Avon Avenue, in one of the poorer sections of the city. His father, from whom he'd inherited his bad eyesight, was a bookkeeper for a big downtown department store who had an inordinate fondness for betting on horses. Shortly after his wife's death and his son's birth he was convicted of larceny for stealing from his employer to cover his gambling debts—it turned out he'd been lining his pockets from the day he'd taken the job. He served two years in jail and, after his release, never returned to Newark. Instead of having a father, the boy, whose given name was Eugene, took his instruction in life from the big, bear-like, hard-working grandfather in whose Avon Avenue grocery store he worked after school and on Saturdays. He was five when his father married for a second time and hired a lawyer to get the boy to come to live with him and his new wife down in Perth Amboy where he had a job in the shipyards. The grandfather, rather than going out to hire his own lawyer, drove straight to Perth Amboy, where there was a confrontation in which he was said to have threatened to break his one-time son-in-law's neck should he dare to try in any way to interfere in Eugene's life. After that, Eugene's father was never heard from again.

It was from heaving crates of produce around the store with his grandfather that he began to develop his chest and arms, and from running up and down the three flights to their flat innumerable times a day that he began to develop his legs. And it was from his grandfather's intrepidness that he learned how to pit himself against any obstacle, including having been born the son of a man his grandfather would describe for as long as he lived as "a very shady character." He wanted as a boy to be physically strong, just like his grandfather, and not to have to wear thick glasses. But his eyes were so bad that when he put the glasses away at night to get ready for bed, he could barely make out the shape of the few pieces of furniture in his room. His grandfather, who had never given a second thought to his own disadvantages, instructed the unhappy child—when he'd first donned glasses at the age of eight—that his eyes were now as good as anyone else's. After that, there was nothing further to be said on the subject.

His grandmother was a warm, tenderhearted little woman, a good, sound parental counterweight to his grandfather. She bore hardship bravely, though teared up whenever mention was made of the twenty-year-old daughter who had died in child-birth. She was much loved by the customers in the store, and at home, where her hands were never still, she followed with half an ear *Life Can Be Beautiful* and the other soap operas she liked where the listener is always shuddering, always nervous, at the prospect of the next misfortune. In the few hours a day when she was not assisting in the grocery, she devoted herself wholeheartedly to Eugene's welfare, nursing him through mea-sles, mumps, and chickenpox, seeing that his clothes were al-ways clean and mended, that his homework was done, that his report cards were signed, that he was taken to the dentist regu-larly (as few poor children were in those days), that the food she cooked for him was hearty and plentiful, and that his fees were paid at the synagogue where he went after school for Hebrew classes to prepare for his bar mitzvah. But for the trio of common infectious childhood diseases, the boy had unwav-ering good health, strong even teeth, an overall sense of physi-cal well-being that must have had something to do with the way she had mothered him, trying to do everything that was thought, in those days, to be good for a growing child. Be-tween her and her husband there was rarely squabbling—each knew the job to do and how best to do it, and each carried it off with an avidity whose example was not lost on young Eugene.

The grandfather saw to the boy's masculine development, always on the alert to eradicate any weakness that might have been bequeathed—along with the poor eyesight—by his natural father and to teach the boy that a man's every endeavor was imbued with responsibility. His grandfather's dominance wasn't always easy to abide, but when Eugene met his expectations, the praise was never grudging. There was the time, when he was just ten, that the boy came upon a large gray rat in the dim stockroom back of the store. It was already dark outside when he saw the rat scuttling in and out of a stack of empty grocery cartons that he had helped his grandfather to unpack. His impulse was, of course, to run. Instead, knowing his grandfather was out front with a customer, he reached noiselessly into a corner for the deep, heavy coal shovel with which he was learning how to tend the furnace that heated the store.

Holding his breath, he advanced on tiptoe until he had stalked the panicked rat into a corner. When the boy lifted the shovel into the air, the rat rose on its hind legs and gnashed its frightening teeth, deploying itself to spring. But before it could leave the floor, he brought the underside of the shovel swiftly downward and, catching the rodent squarely on the skull, smashed its head open. Blood intermingled with bits of bone and brain drained into the cracks of the stockroom floorboards as—having failed to suppress completely a sudden impulse to vomit—he used the shovel blade to scoop up the dead animal. It was heavy, heavier than he could have imagined, and looked larger and longer resting in the shovel than it had up on its hind legs. Strangely, nothing—not even the lifeless strand of tail and the four motionless feet—looked quite as dead as the pairs of needle-thin, bloodstained whiskers. With his weapon raised over his head, he had not registered the whiskers; he had not registered anything other than the words "Kill it!" as if they were being formulated in his brain by his grandfather. He waited until the customer had left with her grocery bag and then, holding the shovel straight out in front of him—and poker-faced to reveal how unfazed he was—he carried the dead rat through to the front of the store to display to his grandfather before continuing out the door. At the corner, jiggling the carcass free of the shovel, he poked it through the iron grate into the flowing sewer. He returned to the store and, with a scrub brush, brown soap, rags, and a bucket of water, cleaned the floor of his vomit and the traces of the rat and rinsed off the shovel.

It was following this triumph that his grandfather—because of the nickname's connotation of obstinacy and gutsy, spirited, strong-willed fortitude—took to calling the bespectacled ten-year-old Bucky.

The grandfather, Sam Cantor, had come alone to America in the 1880s as an immigrant child from a Jewish village in Polish Galicia. His fearlessness had been learned in the Newark streets, where his nose had been broken more than once in fights with anti-Semitic gangs. The violent aggression against Jews that was commonplace in the city during his slum boyhood did much to form his view of life and his grandson's view in turn. He encouraged the grandson to stand up for himself as a man and to stand up for himself as a Jew, and to understand that one's battles were never over and that, in the relentless skirmish that living is, "when you have to pay the price, you pay it." The broken nose in the middle of his grandfather's face had always testified to the boy that though the world had tried, it could not crush him. The old man was dead of a heart attack by July 1944, when the ten Italians drove up to the playground and single-handedly Mr. Cantor turned them back, but that didn't mean he wasn't there throughout the confrontation.

A boy who'd lost a mother at birth and a father to jail, a boy whose parents figured not at all in his earliest recollections, couldn't have been more fortunate in the surrogates he'd inherited to make him strong in every way—he'd only rarely allow the thought of his missing parents to torment him, even if his biography had been determined by their absence.

Mr. Cantor had been twenty and a college junior when the U.S. Pacific Fleet was bombed and nearly destroyed in the surprise Japanese attack at Pearl Harbor on Sunday, December 7, 1941. On Monday the eighth he went off to the recruiting station outside City Hall to join the fight. But because of his eyes nobody would have him, not the army, the navy, the coast guard, or the marines. He was classified 4-F and sent back to Panzer College to continue preparing to be a phys ed teacher. His grandfather had only recently died, and however irrational the thought, Mr. Cantor felt as though he had let him down and failed to meet the expectations of his undeflectable mentor. What good were his muscular build and his athletic prowess if he couldn't exploit them as a soldier? He hadn't been lifting weights since early adolescence merely to be strong enough to hurl the javelin—he had made himself strong enough to be a marine.

After America entered the war, he was still walking the streets while all the able-bodied men his age were off training to fight the Japs and the Germans, among them his two closest friends from Panzer, who'd lined up outside the recruiting station with him on the morning of December 8. His grandmother, with whom he still lived while commuting to Panzer, heard him weeping in his bedroom the night his buddies Dave and Jake went off to Fort Dix to begin basic training without him, heard him weeping as she'd never known Eugene to weep before. He was ashamed to be seen in civilian clothes, ashamed when he watched the newsreels of the war at the movies, ashamed when he took the bus home to Newark from East Orange at the end of the school day and sat beside someone reading in the evening paper the day's biggest story: "Bataan Falls," "Corregidor Falls," "Wake Island Falls." He felt the shame of someone who might by himself have made a difference as the U.S. forces in the Pacific suffered one colossal defeat after another.

Because of the war and the draft, jobs in the school system for male gym teachers were so numerous that even before he graduated from Panzer in June of 1943, he had nailed down a position at ten-year-old Chancellor Avenue School and signed on as the summertime playground director. His goal was to teach phys ed and coach at Weequahic, the high school that had opened next door to Chancellor. It was because both schools had overwhelmingly Jewish student bodies and excellent scholastic credentials that Mr. Cantor was drawn to them. He wanted to teach these kids to excel in sports as well as in their studies and to value sportsmanship and what could be learned through competition on a playing field. He wanted to teach them what his grandfather had taught him: toughness and determination, to be physically brave and physically fit and never to allow themselves to be pushed around or, just because they knew how to use their brains, to be defamed as Jewish weaklings and sissies.

The news that swept the playground after Herbie Steinmark and Alan Michaels were transported by ambulance to the isolation ward at Beth Israel Hospital was that they were both completely paralyzed and, no longer able to breathe on their own, were being kept alive in iron lungs. Though not everybody had shown up at the playground that morning, there were still enough kids for four teams to be organized for their daylong round robin of five-inning games. Mr. Cantor estimated that altogether, in addition to Herbie and Alan, some fifteen or twenty of the ninety or so playground regulars were missing—kept home, he assumed, by their parents because of the polio scare. Knowing as he did the protectiveness of the Jewish parents in the neighborhood and the maternal concern of the watchful mothers, he was in fact surprised that a good many more hadn't wound up staying away. Probably he had done some good by speaking to them as he had the day before.

"Boys," he had said, gathering them together on the field before they disbanded for dinner, "I don't want you to begin to panic. Polio is a disease that we have to live with every summer. It's a serious disease that's been around all my life. The best way to deal with the threat of polio is to stay healthy and strong. Try to wash yourself thoroughly every day and to eat right and to get eight hours of sleep and to drink eight glasses of water a day and not to give in to your worries and fears. We all want Herbie and Alan to get better as soon as possible. We all wish this hadn't happened to them. They're two terrific boys, and many of you are their close friends. Nevertheless, while they are recovering in the hospital, the rest of us have to go on living our lives. That means coming here to the playground every day and participating in sports as you always do. If any of you feel ill, of course you must tell your parents and stay at home and look after yourself until you've seen a doctor and are well. But if you're feeling fine, there's no reason in the world why you can't be as active as you like all summer long."

From the kitchen phone that evening he tried several times to call the Steinmark and Michaels families to express his concern and the concern of the boys at the playground and to find out more about the condition of the two sick boys. But there was no answer at either house. Not a good sign. The families must still have been at the hospital at nine-fifteen at night.

Then the phone rang. It was Marcia, calling from the Poconos. She had heard about the two kids at his playground. "I spoke to my folks. They told me. Are you all right?"

"I'm fine," he said, extending the cord of the phone so he could stand where it was a touch cooler, closer to the screen of the open window. "All the other boys are fine. I've been trying to reach the families of the boys in the hospital to find out how they're doing."

"I miss you," Marcia said, "and I worry about you."

"I miss you too," he said, "but there's nothing to worry about."

"Now I'm sorry I came up here." She was working for the second summer as a head counselor at Indian Hill, a camp for Jewish boys and girls in Pennsylvania's Pocono Mountains seventy miles from the city; during the year she was a first-grade teacher at Chancellor—they'd met as new faculty members the previous fall. "It sounds awful," she said.

"It's awful for the two boys and their families," he said, "but the situation is far from out of hand. You shouldn't think it is."

"My mother said something about the Italians coming up to the playground to spread it."

"The Italians didn't spread anything. I was there. I know what happened. They were a bunch of wiseguys, that's all. They spit all over the street, and we washed it away. Polio is polio—nobody knows how it spreads. Summer comes and there it is, and there's nothing much you can do."

"I love you, Bucky. I think of you constantly."

Discreetly, so none of the neighbors could hear him through the open window, he lowered his voice and replied, "I love you too." It was difficult to tell her that because he had disciplined himself—sensibly, he thought—not to pine for her too much while she was away. It was also difficult because he'd never declared himself that openly to another girl and still found the words awkward to say.

"I have to get off the phone," Marcia said. "There's somebody waiting behind me. Please take care of yourself."

"I do. I will. But don't worry. Don't be frightened. There's nothing to be frightened about."

The next day, news raced through the community that within the Weequahic school district there were eleven new cases of polio—as many as had been reported there in the previous three years combined, and it was still only July, with a good two months to go before the polio season was over. Eleven new cases, and during the night Alan Michaels, Mr. Cantor's favorite, had died. The disease had finished him off in seventy-two hours.

The day following was Saturday, and the playground was open to organized activities only until noon, when the rising and falling whine of the air-raid sirens sounded in their weekly test from utility poles across the city. Instead of going back to Barclay Street after closing up, to help his grandmother with the week's grocery shopping—the stock of their own grocery store had been sold for a pittance after his grandfather's death —he showered in the boys' locker room and put on a clean shirt and trousers and a pair of polished shoes that he'd brought with him in a paper bag. Then he walked the length of Chancellor Avenue, all the way down the hill to Fabyan Place, where Alan Michaels's family lived. Despite polio's striking in the neighborhood, the store-lined main street was full of people out doing their Saturday grocery shopping and picking up their dry-cleaning and their drug prescriptions and whatever they needed from the electrical shop and the ladies' wear shop and the optical shop and the hardware store. In Frenchy's barber shop every seat was occupied by one of the neighborhood men waiting to get a haircut or a shave; in the shoe repair shop next door, the Italian shopkeeper—the street's only non-Jewish shop owner, not excluding Frenchy—was busy finding people's finished shoes in a pile of them on his cluttered counter while the Italian radio station blared through his open doorway. Already the stores had their front awnings rolled down to keep the sun from beaming hotly through the plate-glass window looking onto the street.

It was a bright, cloudless day and the temperature was rising by the hour. Boys from his gym classes and from the playground became excited when they spotted him out on Chancellor Avenue—since he lived not in the neighborhood but down in the South Side school district, they were used to seeing him only in his official capacities as gym teacher and playground director. He waved when they called "Mr. Cantor!" and he smiled and nodded at their parents, some of whom he recognized from PTA meetings. One of the fathers stopped to talk to him. "I want to shake your hand, young man," he said to Mr. Cantor. "You told those dagos where to get off. Those dirty dogs. One against ten. You're a brave young man." "Thank you, sir." "I'm Murray Rosenfield. I'm Joey's father." "Thank you, Mr. Rosenfield." Next, a woman who was out shopping stopped to speak to him. She smiled politely and said, "I'm Mrs. Lewy. I'm Bernie's mother. My son worships you, Mr. Cantor. But I have one thing to ask you. With what's going on in the city, do you think the boys should be running around in heat like this? Bernie comes home soaked to the skin. Is that a good idea? Look at what's happened to Alan. How does a family recover from something like this? His two brothers away in the war, and now this." "I don't let the boys overexert themselves, Mrs. Lewy. I watch out for them." "Bernie," she said, "doesn't know when to quit. He can run all day and all night if somebody doesn't stop him." "I'll be sure to stop him if he gets too hot. I'll keep my eye on him." "Oh, thank you, thank you. Everybody is very happy that it's you who's looking after the boys." "I hope I'm helping," Mr. Cantor replied. A small crowd had gathered while he'd been talking to Bernie's mother, and now a second woman approached and reached for his sleeve to get his attention. "And where's the Board of Health in all this?" "Are you asking me?" Mr. Cantor said. "Yes, you. Eleven new cases in the Weequahic section overnight! One child dead! I want to know what the Board of Health is doing to protect our children." "I don't work for the Board of Health," he replied. "I'm playground director at Chancellor." "Somebody said you were with the Board of Health," she charged him. "No, I'm not. I wish I could help you but I'm attached to the schools." "You dial the Board of Health," she said, "and you get a busy signal. I think they purposely leave the phone off the hook." "The Board of Health was here," another woman put in. "I saw them. They put a quarantine sign up on a house on my street." Her voice full of distress, she said, "There's a case of polio on my street!" "And the Board of Health does nothing!" someone else said angrily. "What is the city doing to stop this? Nothing!" "There's got to be something to do—but they're not doing it!" "They should inspect the milk that kids drink—polio comes from dirty cows and their infected milk." "No," said someone else, "it isn't the cows—it's the bottles. They don't sterilize those milk bottles right." "Why don't they fumigate?" another voice said. "Why don't they use disinfectant? Disinfect *everything*." "Why don't they do like they did when I was a child? They tied camphor balls around our necks. They had something that stunk bad they used to call asafetida—maybe that would work now." "Why don't they spread some kind of chemical on the streets and kill it that way?" "Forget about chemicals," someone else said. "The most important thing is for the children to wash their hands. Constantly wash their hands. Cleanliness! Cleanliness is the only cure!" "And another important thing," Mr. Cantor put in, "is for all of you to calm down and not lose your self-control and panic. And not communicate panic to the children. The important thing is to keep everything in their lives as normal as possible and for you all, in what you say to them, to try to stay reasonable and calm." "Wouldn't it be better if they stayed home till this passes over?" another woman said to him. "Isn't home the safest place in a crisis like this? I'm Richie Tulin's mother. Richie is crazy about you, Mr. Cantor. All the boys are. But wouldn't Richie be better off, wouldn't all the boys be better off, if you closed down the playground and they stayed at home?" "Shutting down the playground isn't up to me, Mrs. Tulin. That would be up to the superintendent of schools." "Don't think I'm blaming you for what's happening," she said. "No, no, I know you're not. You're a mother. You're concerned. I understand everyone's concern." "Our Jewish children are our riches," someone said. "Why is it attacking our beautiful Jewish children?" "I'm not a doctor. I'm not a scientist. I don't know why it attacks who it attacks. I don't believe that anyone does. That's why everybody tries to find who or what is guilty. They try to figure out what's responsible so they can eliminate it." "But what about the Italians? It had to be the

Italians!" "No, no, I don't think so. I was there when the Italians came. They had no contact with the children. It was not the Italians. Look, you mustn't be eaten up with worry and you mustn't be eaten up with fear. What's important is not to infect the children with the germ of fear. We'll come through this, believe me. We'll all do our bit and stay calm and do everything we can to protect the children, and we'll all come through this together," he said. "Oh, thank you, young man. You're a splendid young man." "I have to be going, you'll have to excuse me," he told them all, looking one last time into their anxious eyes, beseeching him as though he were something far more powerful than a playground director twenty-three years old.

Fabyan Place was the last street in Newark before the railroad tracks and the lumberyards and the border with Irvington. Like the other residential streets that branched off Chancellor, it was lined with two-and-a-half-story frame houses fronted by red-brick stoops and hedged-in tiny yards and separated from one another by narrow cement driveways and small garages. At the curb in front of each stoop was a young shade tree planted in the last decade by the city and looking parched now after weeks of torrid temperatures and no rain. Nothing about the clean and quiet street gave evidence of unhealthiness or infection. In every house on every floor either the shades were pulled or the drapes drawn to keep out the ferocious heat. There was no one to be seen anywhere, and Mr. Cantor wondered if it was because of the heat or because the neighbors were keeping their children indoors out of respect for the Michaels family—or perhaps out of terror of the Michaels family.

Then a figure emerged from around the Lyons Avenue corner, making its solitary way through the brilliant light burning down on Fabyan Place and already softening the asphalt street. Mr. Cantor recognized who it was, even from afar, by the peculiar walk. It was Horace. Every man, woman, and child in the Weequahic section recognized Horace, largely because it was always so disquieting to find him heading one's way. When the smaller children saw him they ran to the other side of the street; when adults saw him they lowered their eyes. Horace was the neighborhood's "moron," a skinny man in his thirties or forties—no one knew his age for sure—whose mental development had stopped at around six and whom a psychologist would likely have categorized as an imbecile, or even an idiot, rather than the moron he'd been unclinically dubbed years before by the neighborhood youngsters. He dragged his feet beneath him, and his head, jutting forward from his neck like a turtle's, bobbed loosely with each step, so that altogether he appeared to be not so much walking as staggering forward. Spittle gathered at the corners of his mouth on the rare occasions when he spoke, and when he was silent he would sometimes drool. He had a thin, irregular face that looked as if it had been crushed and twisted in the vise of the birth canal, except for his nose, which was big and, given the narrowness of his face, oddly and grotesquely bulbous, and which inspired some of the kids to taunt him by shouting "Hey, bugle nose!" when he shuffled by the stoop or the driveway where they were congregated. His clothing gave off a sour smell regardless of the season, and his face was dotted with blood spots, tiny nicks in his skin certifying that though Horace might have the mind of a baby, he also had the beard of a man and, however hazardously, shaved himself, or was shaved by one of his parents, before he went out every day. Minutes earlier he must have left the little apartment back of the tailor shop around the corner where he lived with his parents, an aged couple who spoke Yiddish to each other and heavily accented English to the customers in the shop and were said to have other, normal children who were grown and lived elsewhere—amazingly enough, one of Horace's two brothers was said to be a doctor and the other a successful businessman. Horace was the family's youngest, and he was out walking the neighborhood streets every day of the year, in the worst of summer as in the worst of winter, when he wore an oversized mackinaw with its hood pulled up over his earmuffs and black galoshes with the toggles undone and mittens for his large hands that were attached to the cuffs of his sleeves with safety pins and that dangled there unused no matter what the temperature. It was an outfit in which, trudging along, he looked even more outlandish than he did ordinarily making the rounds of the neighborhood alone.

Mr. Cantor found the Michaels house on the far side of the street, climbed the stoop steps, and, in the small hallway with the mailboxes, pushed the bell to their second-floor flat and heard it ringing upstairs. Slowly someone descended the interior stairs and opened the frosted glass door at the foot of the stairwell. The man who stood there was large and heavyset, and the buttons on his short-sleeved shirt pulled tightly across his belly. He had grainy dark patches under his eyes, and when he saw Mr. Cantor he was silent, as though grief had left him too stupefied to speak.

"I'm Bucky Cantor. I'm the playground director at Chancellor and a phys ed teacher there. Alan was in one of my gym classes. He was one of the boys who played ball up at the playground. I heard what happened and came to offer my condolences."

The man was a long time answering. "Alan talked about you," he finally said.

"Alan was a natural athlete. Alan was a very thoughtful boy. This is terrible, shocking news. It's incomprehensible. I came to tell you how upset I am for all of you."

It was very hot in the hallway, and both the men were perspiring heavily.

"Come upstairs," Mr. Michaels said. "We'll give you something cold."

"I don't want to bother you," Mr. Cantor replied. "I wanted to express my condolences and tell you what a fine boy you had for a son. He was a grownup in every way."

"There's iced tea. My sister-in-law made some. We had to call the doctor for my wife. She's been in bed since it happened. They had to give her phenobarb. Come and have some iced tea."

"I don't want to intrude."

"Come. Alan told us all about Mr. Cantor and his muscles. He loved the playground." Then, his voice breaking, he said, "He loved life."

Mr. Cantor followed the large, grief-stricken man up the stairs and into the flat. All the shades were lowered and no lights were on. There was a console radio beside the sofa and two big soft club chairs opposite that. Mr. Cantor sat on the sofa while Mr. Michaels went to the kitchen and returned with a glass of iced tea for the guest. He motioned for Mr. Cantor to sit closer to him in one of the club chairs and then, sighing audibly, painfully, he sat in the other chair, which had an ottoman at its foot. Once he was stretched out across the ottoman and the chair, he looked as though he too, like his wife, were in bed, drugged and incapable of moving. Shock had rendered his face expressionless. In the near darkness, the stained skin beneath his eyes looked black, as if it had been imprinted in ink with twin symbols of mourning. Ancient Jewish death rites call for the rending of one's garments on learning of the death of a loved one—Mr. Michaels had affixed two dark patches to his colorless face instead.

"We have sons in the army," he said, speaking softly so no one in another room could hear, and slowly, as if out of great fatigue. "Ever since they've been overseas, not a day has gone by when I haven't expected to hear the worst. So far they have survived the worst fighting, and yet their baby brother wakes up a few mornings back with a stiff neck and a high fever, and three days later he's gone. How are we going to tell his brothers? How are we going to write this to them in combat? A twelve-year-old youngster, the best boy you could want, and he's gone. The first night he was so miserable that in the morning I thought that maybe the worst was over and the crisis had passed. But the worst had only begun. What a day that boy put in! The child was on fire. You read the thermometer and you couldn't believe it—a temperature of a hundred and six! As soon as the doctor came he immediately called the ambulance, and at the hospital they whisked him away from us—and that was it. We never saw our son alive again. He died all alone. No chance to say so much as goodbye. All we have of him is a closet with his clothes and his schoolbooks and his sports things, and there, over there, his fish."

For the first time, Mr. Cantor noticed the large glass aquarium up against the far wall, where not only were the shades drawn but dark drapes were pulled shut across a window that must have faced the driveway and the house next door. A neon light shone down on the tank, and inside he could see the population of tiny, many-hued fish, more than a dozen of them, either vanishing into a miniature grotto, green with miniature shrubbery, or sweeping the sandy bottom for food, or veering upward to suck at the surface, or just suspended stock-still near a silver cylinder bubbling air in one corner of

the tank. Alan's handiwork, Mr. Cantor thought, a neatly out-
fitted habitat fastidiously managed and cared for.

"This morning," Mr. Michaels said, gesturing back over his
shoulder at the tank, "I remembered to feed them. I jumped
up in bed and remembered."

"He was the best boy," Mr. Cantor said, leaning across the
chair so he could be heard while keeping his voice low.

"Always did his schoolwork," Mr. Michaels said. "Always
helped his mother. Not a selfish bone in his body. Was going
to begin in September to prepare for his bar mitzvah. Polite.
Neat. Wrote each of his brothers V-mail letters every single
week, letters full of news that he read to us at the dinner table.
Always cheering his mother up when she would get down in
the dumps about the two older boys. Always making her laugh.
Even when he was a small boy you could have a good time
laughing with Alan. Our house was where all their friends
came to have a good time. The place was always full of boys.
Why did Alan get polio? Why did he have to get sick and die?"

Mr. Cantor clutched the cold glass of iced tea in his hand
without drinking from it, without even realizing he was holding it.

"All his friends are terrified," Mr. Michaels said. "They're
terrified that they caught it from him and now they are going
to get polio too. Their parents are hysterical. Nobody knows
what to do. What is there to do? What should we have done? I
rack my brain. Can there be a cleaner household than this one?
Can there be a woman who keeps a more spotless house than
my wife? Could there be a mother more attentive to her children's welfare? Could there be a boy who looked after his
room and his clothes and himself any better than Alan did?
Everything he did, he did it right the first time. And always
happy. Always with a joke. So why did he die? Where is the
fairness in that?"

"There is none," Mr. Cantor said.

"You do only the right thing, the right thing and the right
thing and the right thing, going back all the way. You try to be
a thoughtful person, a reasonable person, an accommodating
person, and then this happens. Where is the sense in life?"

"It doesn't seem to have any," Mr. Cantor answered.

"Where are the scales of justice?" the poor man asked.

"I don't know, Mr. Michaels."

"Why does tragedy always strike down the people who least deserve it?"

"I don't know the answer," Mr. Cantor replied.

"Why not me instead of him?"

Mr. Cantor had no response at all to such a question. He could only shrug.

"A boy—tragedy strikes a *boy*. The cruelty of it!" Mr. Michaels said, pounding the arm of his chair with his open hand. "The meaninglessness of it! A terrible disease drops from the sky and somebody is dead overnight. A child, no less!"

Mr. Cantor wished that he knew a single word to utter that would alleviate, if only for a moment, the father's anguished suffering. But all he could do was nod his head.

"The other evening we were sitting outside," Mr. Michaels said. "Alan was with us. He had come back from tending his plot in the victory garden. He did that religiously. Last year we actually ate Alan's vegetables that he raised all summer long. A breeze came up. Unexpectedly it got breezy. Do you remember, the other night? Around eight o'clock, how refreshing it seemed?"

"Yes," Mr. Cantor said, but he hadn't been listening. He'd been looking across the room at the tropical fish swimming in the aquarium and thinking that without Alan to tend them, they would starve to death or be given away or, in time, be flushed down the toilet by somebody in tears.

"It seemed like a blessing after the broiling day we'd had. You wait and wait for a breeze. You think a breeze will bring some relief. But you know what I think it did instead?" Mr. Michaels asked. "I think that breeze blew the polio germs around in the air, around and around, the way you see leaves blow around in a flurry. I think Alan was sitting there and breathed in the germs from the breeze . . ." He couldn't continue; he had begun to cry, awkwardly, inexpertly, the way men cry who ordinarily like to think of themselves as a match for anything.

Here a woman came out of a back bedroom; it was the sister-in-law who was looking after Mrs. Michaels. She stepped gently with her shoes on the floor, as though inside the bedroom a restless child had finally fallen asleep.

Quietly she said, "She wants to know who you're talking to."

"This is Mr. Cantor," said Mr. Michaels, wiping his eyes. "He is a teacher from Alan's school. How is she?" he asked his sister-in-law.

"Not good," she reported in a low voice. "It's the same story. 'Not my baby, not my baby.'"

"I'll be right in," he said.

"I should be going," Mr. Cantor said and got up from his chair and set the untouched iced tea down on a side table. "I only wanted to pay my respects. May I ask when the funeral is?"

"Tomorrow at ten. Schley Street Synagogue. Alan was the rabbi's Hebrew school favorite. He was *everybody's* favorite. Rabbi Slavin himself came here and offered the shul as soon as he heard what had happened. As a special honor to Alan. Everybody in the world loved that boy. He was one in a million."

"What did you teach him?" the sister-in-law asked Mr. Cantor.

"Gym."

"Anything with sports in it, Alan loved," she said. "And what a student. The apple of everyone's eye."

"I know that," said Mr. Cantor. "I see that. I can't express to you how very sorry I am."

Downstairs, as he stepped out onto the stoop, a woman rushed out of the first-floor flat and, excitedly taking him by his arm, asked, "Where is the quarantine sign? People have been coming and going from upstairs, in and out, in and out, and why isn't there a quarantine sign? I have small children. Why isn't there a quarantine sign protecting my children? Are you a patrolman from the Sanitary Squad?"

"I don't know anything about the Sanitary Squad. I'm from the playground. I teach at the school."

"Who is in charge then?" A small, dark woman laden with fear, her face contorted with emotion, she looked as if her life had already been wrecked by polio rather than by her children's having to live precariously within its reach. She looked no better than Mr. Michaels did.

"I suppose the Board of Health is in charge," Mr. Michaels said.

"Where are they?" she pleaded. "Where is somebody who is in charge! People on the street won't even walk in front of our house—they walk deliberately on the other side. The child is already dead," she added, incoherent now with desperation, "and still I'm waiting for a quarantine sign!" And here she let out a shriek. Mr. Cantor had never heard a shriek before, other than in a horror movie. It was different from a scream. It could have been generated by an electrical current. It was a high-pitched, protracted sound unlike any human noise he knew, and the eerie shock of it caused his skin to crawl.

He'd had no lunch, so he made his way to Syd's to get a hot dog. He was careful to walk on the shady side of the street, across from where nothing was sheltered from the glare of the sun and where he thought he could see heat waves shimmering above the sidewalk. Most of the shoppers had disappeared. It was one of those overpowering summer days when the thermometer registered an astonishing one hundred degrees and when, if the playground were open, he would have curtailed the softball games and encouraged the kids to use the chess- and checkerboards and the Ping-Pong tables set up in the shadow of the school. A lot of the boys took salt tablets that their mothers had given them for the heat, and wanted to go on playing no matter how high the temperature soared, even when the field's asphalt surface began to feel spongy and to radiate heat under their sneakers and the sun was so hot that you would think that rather than darkening your bare skin it would bleach you of all color before cremating you on the spot. Fresh from hearing Alan's father's lamentation, Mr. Cantor wondered if for the rest of the summer he oughtn't to shut down all sports when the temperature hit ninety. That way, he'd at least be doing something, though whether it was something that would make any difference to the spread of polio, he had no idea.

Syd's was almost empty. Somebody was cursing at the pinball machine in the gloom at the back of the store, and two high school boys he did not know were goofing around by the jukebox, which was playing "I'll Be Seeing You," one of the summer's favorites. It was a song that Marcia liked to hear on the radio and that was as popular as it was because of all the wives and girlfriends left behind when their husbands and boyfriends went off for the duration of the war. He remembered now that he and Marcia had danced to the song on her back porch during the week before she'd left for Indian Hill. Dancing slowly together in a shuffling embrace while listening to "I'll Be Seeing You" had made them start to long for each other even before Marcia was gone.

There was no one sitting in any of the booths and nobody on any of the counter stools when Bucky took a seat adjacent to the screen door and the long serving window that opened onto Chancellor Avenue, in the path of whatever air might drift in from the street. A big fan was going at either end of the counter, but they didn't seem to do much good. The place was hot and the smell pervasive of french fries deep-frying in fat.

He got a hot dog and a frosted root beer and began to eat at the counter by himself. Out the window, across the way, trudging slowly up the hill in the annihilating heat of equatorial Newark, there was Horace again, no doubt headed to the playground, not understanding that today was Saturday and that, in the summer, the playground closed on Saturdays at noon. (It was not clear whether he understood what "summer," "playground," "closed," or "noon" was either, just as his failure to cross to the other side of the street probably meant that he could not perform the rudimentary thinking to conceptualize "shade" or even just seek it out instinctively, as any dog would on a day like this.) When Horace found none of the kids back of the school, what would he do next? Sit for hours on the bleachers waiting for them to turn up, or resume those neighborhood wanderings that made him look like someone out sleepwalking in the middle of the day? Yes, Alan was dead and polio a threat to the lives of all the city's children, and yet Mr. Cantor couldn't but find something dispiriting about watching Horace walk the streets by himself beneath the ferocity of that sun, isolated and brainless in a blazing world.

When the boys were playing ball Horace would either seat himself silently at the end of the bench where the team at bat was sitting or else get up and perambulate the field, stopping a foot or two away from one of the players in the field and remain there without moving. This went on all the time, and everybody knew that the only way a fielder could get rid of Horace—and get back to concentrating on the game—was to shake the moron's lifeless hand and say to him, "How ya doin',

Horace?" Whereupon Horace would appear to be satisfied and head off to stand beside another of the players. All he asked of life was that—to have his hand shaken. None of the playground boys ever laughed at him or teased him—at least not when Mr. Cantor was around—except for the uncontrollably energetic Kopfermans, Myron and Danny. They were strong, burly boys, good at sports, Myron the overexcitable, belligerent one and Danny the mischievous, secretive one. The older one especially, eleven-year-old Myron, had all the makings of a bully and had to be reined in when there was a disagreement among the boys on the field or when he interfered with the girls jumping rope. Mr. Cantor spent no small portion of his time trying to inculcate in untamed Myron the spirit of fair play and also to caution him to refrain from pestering Horace.

"Look," Myron would say, "look, Horace. Look what I'm doing." When Horace saw the tip of Myron's sneaker beating rhythmically up and down on the bleacher step, his fingers would begin to twitch and his face would grow bright red and soon he would be waving his arms in the air as if he were fighting off a swarm of bees. More than once that summer Mr. Cantor had to tell Myron Kopferman to cut it out and not do it again. "Do what? Do what?" Myron asked, managing to mask none of his insolence with a wide grin. "I'm tapping my foot, Mr. Cantor—don't I have a right to tap my foot?" "Knock it off, Myron," Mr. Cantor replied. The ten-year-old Kopferman boy, Danny, had a cap gun made of metal and modeled to look like a real revolver which he carried in his pocket, even when he was in the field playing second base. The cap gun produced a small explosive sound and smoke when the trigger was pressed. Danny liked to come up behind the other boys and try to frighten them with it. Mr. Cantor tolerated these hijinks only because the other boys were never really frightened. But one day Danny took out the toy weapon and waved it at Horace and told him to stick his hands in the air, which Horace did not do, and so Danny gleefully fired off five rounds of caps. The noise and smoke set Horace to howling, and in his clumsy, splayfooted way, he went running from his playground tormentor. Mr. Cantor confiscated the gun, and after that kept it in a drawer in his office, along with the toy "sheriff's" handcuffs that Danny had employed earlier in the summer to scare the playground's younger kids. Not for the first time he sent Danny Kopferman home for the day with a note telling his mother what her younger son had gotten up to. He doubted that she'd ever seen it.

Yushy, the guy in the mustard-smeared apron who'd been working for years behind the counter at Syd's, said to Mr. Cantor, "It's dead around here."

"It's hot," Mr. Cantor answered. "It's summer. It's the weekend. Everybody's down the shore or staying indoors."

"No, nobody's coming in because of that kid."

"Alan Michaels."

"Yeah," Yushy said. "He ate a hot dog here, and he went home and got polio and died, and now everybody's afraid to come in. It's bullshit. You don't get polio from a hot dog. We sell thousands of hot dogs and nobody gets polio. Then one kid gets polio and everybody says, 'It's the hot dogs at Syd's, it's the hot dogs at Syd's!' A boiled hot dog—how do you get polio from a boiled hot dog?"

"People are frightened," Mr. Cantor said. "They're scared to death, so they worry about everything."

"It's the wop bastards that brought it around," Yushy said.

"That's not likely," Mr. Cantor said.

"They did. They spit all over the place."

"I was there. We washed the spit away with ammonia."

"You washed the spit away but you didn't wash the polio away. You can't wash the polio away. You can't see it. It gets in the air and you open your mouth and breathe it in and next thing you got the polio. It's got nothing to do with hot dogs."

Mr. Cantor offered no response and, while listening to the end of the familiar song playing on the jukebox—and suddenly missing Marcia—finished up eating.

> I'll be seeing you,
> In every lovely summer's day,
> In every thing that's light and gay,
> I'll always think of you that way . . .

"Suppose the kid had had an ice cream sundae at Halem's," Yushy said. "Would nobody eat ice cream sundaes at Halem's? Suppose he had chow mein up at the chinks'—would nobody go up to the chinks' for chow mein?"

"Probably," Mr. Cantor said.

"And what about the other kid that died?" Yushy asked.

"What other kid?"

"The kid that died this morning."

"What kid died? Herbie Steinmark died?"

"Yeah. He didn't eat no hot dogs here."

"Are you sure he died? Who told you Herbie Steinmark died?"

"Somebody. Somebody came in just before and told me. A couple of guys told me."

Mr. Cantor paid Yushy for the food and then, despite the tremendous heat—and unafraid of the heat—ran from Syd's across Chancellor and back to the playground, where he raced down the stairs to the basement door, unlocked it, and headed for his office. There he picked up the telephone and dialed the number of Beth Israel Hospital, one of a list of emergency numbers on a card that was thumbtacked to the notice board over his phone. Directly above it was another card, bearing a quotation he had written out in pen from Joseph Lee, the father of the playground movement, whom he'd read about at Panzer; it had been up there since the first day he arrived on the job. "Play for the adult is recreation, the renewal of life; play for the child is growth, the gaining of life." Tacked up beside that was a notice that had arrived in the mail just the day before from the head of the recreation department to all playground directors:

> In view of the danger to Newark children in the present outbreak of polio, please give very strict attention to the following. If you have not sufficient washroom supplies on hand, order them at once. Go over wash bowls, toilet bowls, floors and walls daily with disinfectant, and see that everything is immaculately clean. Toilet facilities must be thoroughly scrubbed throughout the premises under your supervision. Give the above your personal and unremitting attention as long as the present outbreak menaces the community.

When he got through to the hospital, he asked the operator for patient information and then asked for the condition of Herbert Steinmark. He was told that the patient was no longer in the hospital. "But he's in an iron lung," Mr. Cantor protested. "The patient is deceased," said the operator.

Deceased? What could that word have to do with plump, round, smiling Herbie? He was the least coordinated of all the boys at the playground, and the most ingratiating. He was always among the boys who helped him put out the equipment first thing in the morning. In gym class at Chancellor, he was hopeless on the pommel horse and the parallel bars and with the rings and the climbing rope, but because he tried hard and was persistently good-natured, Mr. Cantor had never given him lower than a B. Alan the natural athlete and Herbie the hopeless athlete, completely lacking physical agility—both had been playing on the field the day the Italians tried to invade the playground, and both were dead, polio fatalities at the age of twelve.

Mr. Cantor rushed down the basement hall to the washroom that was used by the playground boys and, at the mercy of his grief, with no idea what to do with his misery, he grabbed the janitor's mop, a bucket of water, and a gallon can of disinfectant and swabbed the entire tile floor, profusely sweating while he worked. Next he went into the girls' washroom, and vigorously, in a mad rage, he cleaned the floor there. Then, with his clothes and his hands reeking of disinfectant, he took the bus home.

The next morning, after shaving, showering, and eating breakfast, he repolished his good shoes, put on his suit, a white shirt, and the darker of his two ties, and took the bus to Schley Street. The synagogue was a low, dismal yellow-brick box of a building across the street from an overgrown lot that had been converted into a neighborhood victory garden, probably the one where Alan had taken diligent care of his own vegetable plot. Mr. Cantor could see a few women, wearing broad-brimmed straw hats for protection from the morning sun, bent over and weeding small patches of land adjacent to an advertising billboard. In front of the synagogue a row of cars was parked, one of them a black hearse, whose driver stood at the curb moving a cloth over the front fender. Inside the hearse Mr. Cantor could see the casket. It was impossible to believe that Alan was lying in that pale, plain pine box merely from having caught a summertime disease. That box from which you cannot force your way out. That box in which a twelve-year-old was twelve years old forever. The rest of us live and grow older by the day, but he remains twelve. Millions of years go by, and he is still twelve.

Mr. Cantor took his folded yarmulke out of his pants pocket, slipped it on his head, and went inside, where he found an empty seat near the back. He followed the prayers in the prayer book and joined the congregation in the recitations. Midway through, a woman's voice was heard to scream, "She fainted! Help!" Rabbi Slavin briefly stopped the service while someone, most likely a doctor, rushed along the aisle and up the stairs to the balcony, to tend to whoever had passed out in the women's section. The synagogue temperature must have been at least ninety by then, and highest probably in the balcony. No wonder somebody had fainted. If the service didn't soon come to an end, people would start fainting everywhere. Even Mr. Cantor felt a little woozy inside his one suit, a woolen suit made to be worn in the winter.

The seat next to him was empty. He kept wanting Alan to walk in and take it. He wanted Alan to walk in with his baseball mitt and sit down beside him and, as he regularly did at noon on the playground bleachers, eat the sandwich out of his lunch bag beside Mr. Cantor.

The eulogy was delivered by Alan's uncle, Isadore Michaels, whose pharmacy had stood for years on the corner of Wainwright and Chancellor and whom all the customers called Doc. He was a jovial-looking man, heavyset and dark-complexioned like Alan's father, with those same grainy patches under his eyes. He alone was speaking because no other family member felt able to control his emotions enough to do it. There were many people sobbing, and not only in the women's section.

"God blessed us with Alan Avram Michaels for twelve years," his uncle Isadore said, smiling bravely. "And He blessed me with a nephew who I loved like my own child from the day he was born. On his way home every day after school, Alan would always stop by the store and sit at the counter and order a chocolate malted. When he was first starting school he was the skinniest kid in the world, and the idea was to fatten him up. If I was free, I'd go over to the soda fountain and make the malted for him myself and add in extra malt to put some pounds on him. Once that ritual began, it went on year after year. How I would enjoy those after-school visits from my extraordinary nephew!"

Here he had to take a moment to collect himself.

"Alan," he resumed, "was an authority on tropical fish. He could talk like an expert about everything you do to take care of all the different kinds of tropical fish. There was nothing more thrilling than to visit the house and sit with Alan alongside his aquarium and have him explain to you everything about each of the fish and how they had babies and so on. You could sit there with him for an hour and he still wouldn't be finished telling you all that he knew. You came away from being with Alan and you had a smile on your face and your spirits were lifted, and you'd learned something besides. How did he do it? How did this child do all that he did for all of us adults? What was Alan's special secret? It was to live every day of life, seeing the wonder in everything and taking delight in everything, whether it was his after-school malted, or his tropical fish, or the sports in which he excelled, or contributing to the war effort in the victory garden, or what he'd studied that day at school. Alan packed more healthy fun into his twelve years than most people get in a lifetime. And Alan gave more pleasure to others than most people give in a lifetime. Alan's life is ended . . ."

Here he had to stop again, and when he continued it was with a husky voice and on the edge of tears.

"Alan's life is ended," he repeated, "and yet, in our sorrow, we should remember that while he lived it, it was an endless life. Every day was endless for Alan because of his curiosity. Every day was endless for Alan because of his geniality. He remained a happy child all of his life, and with everything the child did, he always gave it his all. There are fates far worse than that in this world."

Afterward, Mr. Cantor stood outside on the synagogue steps to pay his respects to Alan's family and to thank Alan's uncle for all he had said. Who would have imagined, watching him in his white coat at the drugstore, measuring out tablets for someone's prescription, how eloquent an orator Doc Michaels could be, especially while the people scattered throughout the congregation, upstairs and down, were openly wailing from the impact of his words? Mr. Cantor saw four boys from the playground exiting together from the service: the Spector boy, the Sobelsohn boy, the Taback boy, and the Finkelstein boy. They all wore ill-fitting suits and white shirts and ties and hard shoes, and perspiration streamed down their faces. It wasn't impossible that their greatest hardship that day was their being strangled in all that heat by a starched collar and a tie rather than their having their initial encounter with death. Still, they had dressed in their best clothes and come to the synagogue despite the weather, and Mr. Cantor walked up to them and took each by the shoulder and then reassuringly patted his back. "Alan would be glad you were here," he told them quietly. "It was very thoughtful of you to do this."

Then someone touched *him* on the back. "Who are you going with?"

"What?"

"There—" The person pointed to a car some way from the hearse. "There, go with the Beckermans," and he was pushed toward a Plymouth sedan parked down the curb.

It hadn't been his plan to go out to the cemetery. After the synagogue service, he intended to return to help his grandmother finish up the weekend chores. But he got into the car whose door was being held open for him and sat in the back seat beside a woman with a black-veiled hat who was fanning herself by waving a handkerchief in front of her face, whose powder was streaky with perspiration. In the driver's seat was a chunky little man in a dark suit whose nose was broken like his grandfather's and maybe for the same reason: anti-Semites. Seated alongside him was a plain, dark-haired girl of fifteen or sixteen, who was introduced as Alan's cousin Meryl. The elder Beckermans were Alan's aunt and uncle on his mother's side. Mr. Cantor introduced himself as one of Alan's teachers.

They had to sit in the hot car some ten minutes, waiting for the funeral cortege to form behind the hearse. Mr. Cantor tried to remember what Isadore Michaels had said in his eulogy about how Alan's life, while Alan lived it, had seemed to the boy to be endless, but invariably he wound up instead imagining Alan roasting like a piece of meat in his box.

They proceeded down Schley Street to Chancellor Avenue, where they made a left and began the slow trek up Chancellor, past Alan's uncle's pharmacy and toward the grade school and

the high school at the top of the hill. There was hardly any
other traffic—most of the stores were closed except for Tabatch-
nick's, catering to the Sunday morning smoked-fish trade, the
corner candy stores that were selling the Sunday papers, and
the bakery, selling coffee cake and bagels for Sunday breakfast.
In his twelve years, Alan would have been out on this street a
thousand times, heading back and forth to school and to the
playground, going out to get something for his mother, meeting his friends at Halem's, walking all the way up and all the
way down the hill to Weequahic Park to go fishing and ice-
skating and rowing on the lake. Now he was riding down
Chancellor Avenue for the last time, at the head of a funeral
cortege and inside that box. If this car is an oven, Mr. Cantor
thought, imagine the inside of that box.

Everyone in the car had been silent until they nearly reached
the crest of the hill and were passing Syd's hot dog joint.

"Why did he have to eat in that filthy hole?" Mrs. Beckerman said. "Why couldn't he wait to get home and take something from the Frigidaire? Why do they allow that place to
remain open across from a school? In summertime, no less."

"Edith," Mr. Beckerman said, "calm down."

"Ma," Alan's cousin Meryl said, "all the kids eat there. It's a
hangout."

"It's a cesspool," Mrs. Beckerman said. "In polio season, for
a boy with Alan's brains to go into a place like that, in this
heat—"

"Enough, Edith. It's hot. We all know it's hot."

"There's his school," Mrs. Beckerman said as they reached
the top of the hill and were passing the pale stone façade of the
grade school where Mr. Cantor taught. "How many children
love school the way Alan did? From the day he started, he
loved it."

Perhaps the observation was being addressed to him, as a
representative of the school. Mr. Cantor said, "He was an
outstanding student."

"And there's Weequahic. He would have been an honor
student at Weequahic. He was already planning to take Latin.
Latin! I had a nickname for him. I called him Brilliant."

"That he was," Mr. Cantor said, thinking of Alan's father at
the house and his uncle at the synagogue and now his aunt in

the car—all of them gushing for the same good reason: because Alan deserved no less. They will lament to their graves losing this marvelous boy.

"In college," Mrs. Beckerman said, "he planned to study science. He wanted to be a scientist and cure disease. He read a book about Louis Pasteur and knew everything about how Louis Pasteur discovered that germs are invisible. He wanted to be another Louis Pasteur," she said, mapping out the whole of a future that was never to be. "Instead," she concluded, "he had to go to eat in a place *crawling* with germs."

"Edith, that's enough," Mr. Beckerman said. "We don't know how he got sick or where. Polio is all over the city. There's an epidemic. It's every place you look. He got a bad case and he died. That's all we know. Everything else is talk that gets you nowhere. We don't know what his future would have been."

"We do!" she said angrily. "That child could have been anything!"

"Okay, you're right. I'm not arguing. Let's just get to the cemetery and give him a proper burial. That's all we can do for him now."

"And the two other boys," Mrs. Beckerman said. "God forbid anything should happen to them."

"They made it this far," Mr. Beckerman said, "they'll make it the rest of the way. The war will soon be over and Larry and Lenny will be safely home."

"And they'll never see their baby brother again. Alan will still be gone," she said. "There's no bringing him back."

"Edith," he said, "we *know* that. Edith, you're talking and you're not saying anything that everybody doesn't know."

"Let her speak, Daddy," Meryl said.

"But what good does it do," Mr. Beckerman asked, "going on and on?"

"It does good," the girl said. "It does her good."

"Thank you, darling," Mrs. Beckerman said.

All the windows were rolled down, but Mr. Cantor felt as though he were wrapped not in a suit but a blanket. The cortege had reached the park and turned right onto Elizabeth Avenue and was passing through Hillside and across the railroad overpass into Elizabeth, and he hoped that it wasn't much more time before they reached the cemetery. He imagined that if Alan lay roasting in that box for much longer, the box would somehow ignite and explode, and as though a hand grenade had gone off inside, the boy's remains would come bursting out all over the hearse and the street.

Why does polio strike only in the summer? At the cemetery, standing there bareheaded but for his yarmulke, he had to wonder if polio couldn't be caused by the summer sun itself. At midday, in its full overhead onslaught, it seemed to have more than sufficient strength to cripple and kill, and to be rather more likely to do so than a microscopic germ in a hot dog.

A grave had been dug for Alan's casket. It was the second open grave Mr. Cantor had ever seen, the first having been his grandfather's, three years earlier, just before the war began. Then he'd been weighed down caring for his grandmother and holding her close to him throughout the cemetery service so that her legs didn't give way. After that, he'd been so busy looking after her and staying in every night with her and eventually getting her out once a week for a movie and an ice cream sundae that it was a while before he could find the time to contemplate all he himself had lost. But as Alan's casket was lowered into the ground—as Mrs. Michaels lunged for the grave, crying "No! Not my baby!"—death revealed itself to him no less powerfully than the incessant beating of the sun on his yarmulke'd head.

They all joined the rabbi in reciting the mourner's prayer, praising God's almightiness, praising extravagantly, unstintingly, the very God who allowed everything, including children, to be destroyed by death. Between the death of Alan Michaels and the communal recitation of the God-glorifying Kaddish, Alan's family had had an interlude of some twenty-four hours to hate and loathe God for what He had inflicted upon them—not, of course, that it would have occurred to them to respond like that to Alan's death, and certainly not without fearing to incur God's wrath, prompting Him to wrest Larry and Lenny Michaels from them next.

But what might not have occurred to the Michaels family had not been lost on Mr. Cantor. To be sure, he himself hadn't dared to turn against God for taking his grandfather when the old man reached a timely age to die. But for killing Alan with polio at twelve? For the very existence of polio? How could there be forgiveness—let alone hallelujahs—in the face of such lunatic cruelty? It would have seemed far less of an affront to Mr. Cantor for the group gathered in mourning to declare themselves the celebrants of solar majesty, the children of an ever-constant solar deity, and, in the fervent way of our hemisphere's ancient heathen civilizations, to abandon themselves in a ritual sun dance around the dead boy's grave—better that, better to sanctify and placate the unrefracted rays of Great Father Sun than to submit to a supreme being for whatever atrocious crime it pleases Him to perpetrate. Yes, better by far to praise the irreplaceable generator that has sustained our existence from its beginning—better by far to honor in prayer one's tangible daily encounter with that ubiquitous eye of gold isolated in the blue body of the sky and its immanent power to incinerate the earth—than to swallow the official lie that God is good and truckle before a cold-blooded murderer of children. Better for one's dignity, for one's humanity, for one's worth altogether, not to mention for one's everyday idea of whatever the hell is going on here.

. . . *Y'hei sh'mei raboh m'vorakh l'olam ul'olmei ol'mayoh.*
May His great Name be blessed forever and ever.
Yis'borakh v'yish'tabach v'yis'po'ar v'yis'romam v'yis'nasei
Blessed, praised, glorified, exalted, extolled,
v'yis'hadar v'yis'aleh v'yis'halal sh'mei d'kud'shoh
mighty, upraised, and lauded be the Name of the Holy One,
B'rikh hu . . .
Blessed is He.

Four times during the prayer, at the grave of this child, the mourners repeated, "*Omein.*"

Only when the funeral cortege had left the sprawl of tombstones behind and was exiting between the gates onto McClellan Street did he suddenly remember the visits he used to make as a boy to the Jewish cemetery on Grove Street where his mother, and now his grandfather, were buried and where his grandmother and he would be buried in turn. As a child he'd been taken by his grandparents to visit his mother's grave every year to commemorate her birthday in May, though from his first childhood visit on, he could not believe that she was interred there. Standing between his tearful grandparents, he always felt that he was going along with a game by pretending that she was—never more than at the cemetery did he feel that his having had a mother was a made-up story to begin with. And yet, despite his knowing that his annual visit was the queerest thing he was called upon to do, he would not ever refuse to go. If this was part of being a good son to a mother woven nowhere into his memories, then he did it, even when it felt like a hollow performance.

Whenever he tried at the graveside to summon up a thought appropriate to the occasion, he would remember the story his grandmother had told him about his mother and the fish. Of all her stories—standard inspirational stories about how clever Doris had been in school and how helpful she'd been around the house and how she'd loved as a child to sit at the cash register in the store ringing up the sales, just the way he did when he was small—this was the one that had lodged in his mind. The unforgotten event occurred on a spring afternoon long before her death and his birth, when, to prepare for Passover, his grandmother would walk up Avon Avenue to the fish store to choose two live carp from the fishmonger's tank and bring them home in a pail and keep them alive in the tin tub that the family used for taking baths. She'd fill the tub with water and leave the fish there until it was time to chop off their heads and tails, scale them, and cook them to make gefilte fish. One day when Mr. Cantor's mother was five years old, she'd come bounding up the stairs from kindergarten, found the fish swimming in the tin tub, and after quickly removing her clothes, got into the tub to play with them. His grandmother found her there when she came up from the store to fix her an after-school snack. They never told his grandfather what the child had done for fear that he might punish her for it. Even when the little boy was told about the fish by his grandmother—he was then himself in kindergarten—he was cautioned to keep the story a secret so as not to upset his grandfather, who, in the first years after his cherished daughter's death, was able to deflect the anguish of losing her only by never speaking of her.

It may have seemed odd for Mr. Cantor to think of this

story at his mother's graveside, but what else that was memorable was there to think about?

By the end of the next week, Weequahic had reported the summer's highest number of polio cases of any school district in the city. The playground itself was geographically ringed with new cases. Across from the playground on Hobson Street a ten-year-old girl, Lillian Sussman, had been stricken; across from the school on Bayview Avenue a six-year-old girl, Barbara Friedman, had been stricken—and neither was among the girls who jumped rope regularly at the playground, though there were now less than half as many of them around since the polio scare had begun. And down from the playground on Vassar Avenue, the two Kopferman brothers, Danny and Myron, had also been stricken. The evening of the day he heard the news about the Kopferman boys, he telephoned their house. He got Mrs. Kopferman. He explained who he was and why he was calling.

"You!" shouted Mrs. Kopferman. "You have the nerve to call?"

"Excuse me," Mr. Cantor said. "I don't understand."

"What don't you understand? You don't understand that in summertime you use your head with children running around in the heat? That you don't let them drink from the public fountain? That you watch when they are pouring sweat? Do you know how to use the eyes that God gave you and watch over children during polio season? No! Not for a minute!"

"Mrs. Kopferman, I assure you, I am careful with all the boys."

"So why do I have two paralyzed children? Both my boys! All that I've got! Explain that to me! You let them run around like animals up there—and you wonder why they get polio! Because of you! Because of a reckless, irresponsible idiot like you!" And she hung up.

He had called the Kopfermans from the kitchen, after he had sent his grandmother downstairs to sit outside with the neighbors and he had finished cleaning up from dinner. The day's heat had not broken, and indoors it was suffocatingly hot. When he hung up from the phone call he was saturated with perspiration, even though before eating he had taken a shower and changed into fresh clothes. How he wished his grandfather were around for him to talk to. He knew that Mrs. Kopferman was hysterical; he knew that she was overcome with grief and crazily lashing out at him; but he would have liked to have his grandfather there to assure him that he was not culpable in the ways she had said. This was his first direct confrontation with vile accusation and intemperate hatred, and it had unstrung him far more than dealing with the ten menacing Italians at the playground.

It was seven o'clock and still bright outdoors when he went three flights down the scuffed steps of the outside wooden staircase to visit for a moment with the neighbors before he took a walk. His grandmother was sitting with them in front of the building, using a citronella candle to keep the mosquitoes away. They sat on fold-up beach chairs and were talking about polio. The older ones, like his grandmother, had lived through the city's 1916 epidemic and were lamenting the fact that in the intervening years science had been unable to find a cure for the disease or come up with an idea of how to prevent it. Look at Weequahic, they said, as clean and sanitary as any section in the city, and it's the worst hit. There was talk, somebody said, of keeping the colored cleaning women from coming to the neighborhood for fear that they carried the polio germs up from the slums. Somebody else said that in his estimation the disease was spread by money, by paper money passing from hand to hand. The important thing, he said, was always to wash your hands after you handled paper money or coins. What about the mail, someone else said, you don't think it could be spread by the mail? What are you going to do, somebody retorted, suspend delivering the mail? The whole city would come to a halt.

Six or seven weeks ago they would have been talking about the war news.

He heard a phone ringing and realized it was from their flat and that it must be Marcia calling from camp. Every school day for the past year they'd see each other at least once or twice in the corridors during school hours and then spend the weekends together, and this was the first extended period since they'd met that they were apart. He missed her, and he missed the Steinberg family, who had been kind and welcoming to him from the start. Her father was a doctor and her mother had formerly been a high school English teacher, and they lived, with Marcia's two younger sisters—twins in the sixth grade at Maple Avenue School—in a large, comfortable house on Goldsmith Avenue, a block up from Dr. Steinberg's Elizabeth Avenue office. After Mrs. Kopferman had accused Mr. Cantor of criminal negligence, he had thought about going to see Dr. Steinberg to talk to him about the epidemic and find out more about the disease. Dr. Steinberg was an educated man (in this way unlike the grandfather, who'd never read a book), and when he spoke Mr. Cantor always felt confident that he knew what he was talking about. He was no replacement for his grandfather—and no replacement, certainly, for a father of his own—but he was now the man he most admired and relied on. On his first date with Marcia, when he asked about her family, she had said of her father that he was not only wonderful with his patients but that he had a gift for keeping everybody in their household content and justly settling all her kid sisters' spats. He was the best judge of character she'd ever known. "My mother," she'd say, "calls him 'the impeccable thermometer of the family's emotional temperature.' There's no doctor I know of," she told him, "who's more humane than my dad."

"It's you!" Mr. Cantor said after racing up the stairs to get the phone. "It's boiling here. It's after seven and it's still as hot as it was at noon. The thermometers look stuck. How are you?"

"I have something to tell you. I have spectacular news," Marcia said. "Irv Schlanger got his draft notice. He's leaving camp. They need a replacement. They desperately need a waterfront director for the rest of the season. I told Mr. Blomback about you, I gave him all your credentials, and he wants to hire you, sight unseen."

Mr. Blomback was the owner-director of Indian Hill and an old friend of the Steinbergs. Before he went into the camp business, he had been a young high school vice principal in Newark and Mrs. Steinberg's boss when she was starting out as a new teacher.

"Marcia," Mr. Cantor said to her, "I've got a job."

"But you could get away from the epidemic. I'm so worried about you, Bucky. In the hot city with all those kids. In such close contact with all those kids—and right at the center of the epidemic. And that heat, day after day of that heat."

"I've got some ninety kids at the playground, and so far, among those kids we've had only four polio cases."

"Yes, and two *deaths*."

"That's still not an epidemic at the playground, Marcia."

"I meant in Weequahic altogether. It's the most affected part of the city. And it's not even August, the worst month of all. By then Weequahic could have *ten* times as many cases. Bucky, please, leave your job. You could be the boys' waterfront director at Indian Hill. The kids are great, the staff is great, Mr. Blomback is great—you'd love it here. You could be waterfront director for years and years to come. We could be working here every summer. We could be together as a couple and you'd be safe."

"I'm safe here, Marcia."

"You're *not*."

"I can't quit my job. This is my first year. How can I walk out on all those kids? I can't leave them. They need me more than ever. This is what I have to be doing."

"Darling, you're a fine and dedicated teacher, but that doesn't mean you're indispensable to a playground's summer program. *I* need you more than ever. I love you so much. I miss you so much. I dread the idea of something happening to you. What possible good are you doing our future by putting yourself in harm's way?"

"Your father deals with sick people all the time. He's in harm's way all the time. Do you worry about him that much?"

"This summer? Yes. Thank God my sisters are here at the camp. Yes, I worry about my father and about my mother and about everybody I love."

"And would you expect your father to pick up and leave his patients because of the polio?"

"My father is a doctor. He chose to be a doctor. Dealing with sick people is his job. It isn't yours. Your job is dealing with *well* people, with children who are healthy and can run around and play games and have fun. You would be a sensational waterfront director. Everybody here would love you. You're an excellent swimmer, you're an excellent diver, you're an excellent teacher. Oh, Bucky, it's a once-in-a-lifetime opportunity. And," she said, lowering her voice, "we could be alone up here. There's an island in the lake. We could canoe over there at night after lights out. We wouldn't have to worry about your grandmother or my parents or about my sisters snooping around the house. We could finally, finally be alone."

He could take all her clothes off, he thought, and see her completely naked. They could be alone on a dark island without their clothes on. And, with no one nearby to worry about, he could caress her as unhurriedly and as hungrily as he liked. And he could be free of the Kopferman family. He would not have any more Mrs. Kopfermans hysterically charging that he had given their children polio. And he could stop hating God, which was confusing his emotions and making him feel very strange. On their island he could be far from everything that was growing harder and harder to bear.

"I can't leave my grandmother," Mr. Cantor said. "How is she going to get the groceries up the three flights? She gets pains in her chest from carrying things up the stairs. I have to be here. I have to do the laundry. I have to do the shopping. I have to take care of her."

"The Einnemans can look after her for the rest of the summer. They'd go to the grocery store for her. They'd do her few pieces of laundry. They'd be more than willing to help out. She babysits for them already. They're crazy about her."

"The Einnemans are great neighbors, but it's not their job. It's mine. I can't leave Newark."

"What shall I tell Mr. Blomback?"

"Tell him thank you but I can't leave Newark, not at a time like this."

"I'm not going to tell him anything," Marcia replied. "I'm going to wait. I'm going to give you a day to think about it. I'm going to call again tomorrow night. Bucky, you most definitely wouldn't be shirking the duties of your job. There's nothing unheroic about leaving Newark at a time like this. I know you. I know what you're thinking. But you're so brave as it is, sweetheart. I get weak in the knees when I think about how brave you are. If you come to Indian Hill, you'd really just be doing another job no less conscientiously. And you'd be fulfilling another duty you have to yourself—to be happy. Bucky, this is simply prudence in the face of danger—it's common sense!"

"I'm not going to change my mind. I want to be with you, I miss you every day, but I can't possibly leave here now."

"But you must think of your own welfare too. Sleep on it, sweetheart, please, please do."

It was the Einnemans and the Fishers whom his grandmother was sitting with outside. The Fishers, an electrician and his wife in their late forties, had an eighteen-year-old son, a marine, waiting to ship out from California to the Pacific, and a daughter who was a salesgirl for the downtown department store from which his father had embezzled, an inescapable fact that would flash through Mr. Cantor's mind whenever they happened to meet leaving for work in the morning. The Einnemans were a young married couple with an infant boy who lived directly downstairs from the Cantors. The baby was outside with them, sleeping in his carriage; since the child had been born, Mr. Cantor's grandmother had been helping to look after him.

They were still talking about polio, now by recalling its frightening precursors. His grandmother was remembering when whooping cough victims were required to wear armbands and how, before a vaccine was developed, the most dreaded disease in the city was diphtheria. She remembered getting one of the first smallpox vaccinations. The site of the injection had become seriously infected, and she had a large, uneven circle of scarred flesh on her upper right arm as a result. She pushed up the half-sleeve of her housedress and extended her arm to show it to everyone.

After a while Mr. Cantor told them he was going to take a walk, and went off first to the drugstore on Avon Avenue and got an ice cream cone at the soda fountain. He chose a stool under one of the revolving fans and sat there to eat his ice cream—and to think. Any demand made upon him he had to fulfill, and the demand now was to take care of his endangered kids at the playground. And he had to fulfill it not for the kids alone but out of respect for the memory of the tenacious grocer who, with all his gruff intensity and despite all his limitations, had fulfilled every demand he ever faced. Marcia had it dead wrong—it would be hard to shun the responsibilities of his job any more execrably than by decamping to join her in the Pocono Mountains.

He could hear a siren in the distance. He heard sirens off and on, day and night now. They were not the air-raid sirens—

those went off only once a week, at noon on Saturdays, and they did not induce fear so much as provide solace by proclaiming the city ready for anything. These were the sirens of ambulances going to get polio victims and transport them to the hospital, sirens stridently screaming, "Out of the way—a life is at stake!" Several city hospitals had recently run out of iron lungs, and patients in need of them were being taken to Belleville, Kearny, and Elizabeth until a new shipment of the respirator tanks reached Newark. He could only hope that the ambulance wasn't headed for the Weequahic section to pick up another of his kids.

He had begun to hear rumors that if the epidemic got any worse, all the city's playgrounds might have to be shut down in order to prevent the children from being in close contact there. Normally such a decision would be up to the Board of Health, but the mayor was opposed to any unnecessary disruption to the summer lives of Newark's boys and girls and would make the final decision himself. He was doing everything he could to calm the city's parents and, according to the paper, had appeared in each of the wards to inform concerned citizens about all the ways the city was ensuring that filth and dirt and garbage were removed regularly from public and private property. He reminded them to keep their trash cans firmly covered and to join the "Swat the Fly" campaign by keeping their screens in good repair and swatting and killing the disease-carrying flies that bred in filth and found their way indoors through open doors and unscreened windows. Garbage pickup was to be increased to every other day, and to abet the anti-fly campaign, fly swatters would be distributed free by "sanitary inspectors" visiting the residential neighborhoods to make certain that all streets were cleared of refuse. In his attempt to assure parents that everything was under control and generally safe, the mayor made a special point of telling them, "The playgrounds will remain open. Our city kids need their playgrounds in the summer. The Prudential Life Insurance Company of Newark and Metropolitan Life of New York both tell us that fresh air and sunshine are the principal weapons with which to eliminate the disease. Give the children plenty of sunshine and fresh air on the playgrounds and no germ can long withstand the impact of either. Above all," he told his audiences, "keep your yards and cellars clean, don't lose your heads, and we'll soon see a decline in the spread of this scourge. And swat the fly unmercifully. You cannot overestimate the evil that flies do."

Mr. Cantor started up Avon to Belmont swaddled by the stifling heat and enveloped by the stifling smell. On days when the wind came from the south, up from the Rahway and Linden refineries, there was the acrid smell of burning in the air, but tonight the currents were from the north, and the air had the distinctively foul stench that issued from the Secaucus pig farms, a few miles up the Hackensack River. Mr. Cantor knew of no street odor more foul. During a heat wave, when Newark seemed drained of every drop of pure air, it could sometimes be so sickeningly fecal-smelling that a strong whiff would make you gag and race indoors. People were already blaming the eruption of polio cases on the city's proximity to Secaucus—contemptuously known as "the Hog Capital of Hudson County"—and on the infectious properties inhering in that all-blanketing miasma that was, to those downwind of it, a toxic compound of God only knew what vile, pestilential, putrid ingredients. If they were right, breathing in the breath of life was a dangerous activity in Newark—take a deep breath and you could die.

Yet in spite of everything uninviting about the night, there was a string of boys on rattly old bicycles coasting full speed down the uneven cobblestones between the trolley tracks on Avon Avenue and screaming "Geronimo!" at the top of their lungs. There were boys cavorting around and grabbing at one another in front of the candy stores. There were boys seated on the tenement stoops, smoking and talking among themselves. There were boys in the middle of the street lazily tossing fly balls to one another under the streetlights. On an empty corner lot a hoop had been raised on the side wall of an abandoned building, and, by the light of the liquor store across the street, where derelicts staggered in and out, a few boys were practicing underhand foul shots. He passed another corner where some boys were gathered around a mail collection box, atop which one of their pals was perched, yodeling for their amusement. There were families camped out on fire escapes, playing radios trailing extension cords that were plugged in a wall socket inside, and more families gathered in the dim alleyways between buildings. Passing by the tenement dwellers on his walk, he saw women fanning themselves with paper fans a local dry cleaner gave free to his customers, and he saw workmen, home from the factory floor, sitting and talking in their sleeveless undershirts, and the word he heard again and again in the snatches of conversation was, of course, "polio." Only the children seemed capable of thinking of anything else. Only the children (the children!) acted as though, outside the Weequahic section at least, summertime was still a carefree adventure.

Neither on the neighborhood streets nor back at the drugstore ice cream counter did he run into any of the boys he'd grown up with and played ball with and gone through school with. By now, but for a few 4-Fs like himself—guys with heart murmurs or fallen arches or eyes as bad as his own who were working in war plants—they had all been drafted.

On Belmont, Mr. Cantor cut through the traffic at Hawthorne Avenue, where a couple of candy stores still had lights on and where he could hear the voices of boys hanging out along the street calling to one another. From there he headed up to Bergen Street and into the residential side streets of the wealthier end of the Weequahic section, on the side of the hill running down to Weequahic Park. Eventually he came to Goldsmith Avenue. Only when he was practically there did he realize that he wasn't out taking an aimless stroll halfway across the city on a hot summer night but heading very specifically for Marcia's. Maybe his intention was simply to look at the big brick house standing amid the other large brick houses flanking it and think of her and turn around and head back where he'd come from. But after circling once around the block, he found himself just paces from the Steinberg door, and with resolve he headed up the flagstone walk to ring the bell. The screened porch with the glider that faced the front lawn was where Marcia and he would sit and neck when they came back from the movies, until her mother called from upstairs to ask nicely if it wasn't time for Bucky to go home.

It was Dr. Steinberg who came to the door. Now he knew why he'd been roaming far from the tenements of Barclay Street, breathing in this stinking air.

"Bucky, my boy," Dr. Steinberg said, opening his arms and smiling. "What a nice surprise. Come in, come in."

"I went to get some ice cream and took a walk over here," Mr. Cantor explained.

"You miss your girl," Dr. Steinberg said, laughing. "So do I. I miss all three of my girls."

They went through the house to the screened porch at the back, which looked out onto Mrs. Steinberg's garden. Mrs. Steinberg was staying at their summer house at the shore, where, the doctor said, he would be joining her for weekends. How would Bucky like a cold drink, Dr. Steinberg asked. There was fresh lemonade in the refrigerator. He'd bring him a glass.

The Steinbergs' house was the kind Mr. Cantor had dreamed about living in when he was a kid growing up with his grandparents in their third-floor three-room flat: a large one-family house with spacious halls and a central staircase and lots of bedrooms and more than one bathroom and two screened-in porches and thick wall-to-wall carpeting in all the rooms and wooden venetian blinds covering the windows instead of Woolworth's blackout shades. And, at the rear of the house, a flower garden. He'd never seen a full-blown flower garden before, except for the renowned rose garden in Weequahic Park, which his grandmother had taken him to visit as a child. That was a public garden kept up by the parks department; as far as he'd known, *all* gardens were public. A private flower garden flourishing in a Newark backyard amazed him. His own cemented-over backyard was riven with cracks, and stretches of it were stripped of crumbling chunks that over the decades the neighborhood kids had pried loose for missiles to fling murderously at the alley cats or larkily at a passing car or in anger at one another. Girls in the building played hopscotch there until the boys drove them out to play aces up; there was the jumble of the building's beat-up metal garbage cans; and crisscrossing overhead were the clotheslines, a drooping web of them, rope strung on pulleys from a rear window in each tenement flat to a weathered telephone pole at the far side of the dilapidated yard. During earliest childhood, whenever his grandmother leaned out of the window to hang the week's wash, he stood nearby passing her the clothespins. Sometimes he would wake up screaming from nightmares of her leaning so far over the sill to hang a bedsheet that she tumbled out of the third-story window. Before his grandparents determined how and when to make intelligible to him that his mother had died in childbirth, he had come to imagine that she had died in just such a fall of her own. That's what having a backyard had meant to him until he was old enough to comprehend and deal with the truth—a place of death, a small rectangular graveyard for the women who loved him.

But now, just the thought of Mrs. Steinberg's garden filled him with pleasure and reminded him of all he valued most about the Steinbergs and how they lived, and of everything that his kindly grandparents couldn't offer him and that he'd always secretly hungered for. So unschooled was he in extravagance that he took the presence in a house of more than one bathroom as the height of luxurious living. He'd always possessed a strong family sense without himself having a traditional family, so sometimes when he was alone in the house with Marcia—which was rare because of the lively presence of her younger sisters—he would imagine that the two of them were married and the house and the garden and the domestic order and the surfeit of bathrooms were theirs. How at ease he felt in their house—yet it seemed a miracle to him that he had ever gotten there.

Dr. Steinberg came back out onto the porch with the lemonade. The porch was dark except for a lamp burning beside the chair where Dr. Steinberg had been reading the evening paper and smoking his pipe. He picked up the pipe and struck a match and, repeatedly drawing and puffing, he fussed with it until it was relit. The rich sweetness of Dr. Steinberg's tobacco served to ameliorate a little the citywide stink of Secaucus.

Dr. Steinberg was slender, agile, on the short side. He wore a substantial mustache and glasses that, though thick, were not as thick as Mr. Cantor's. His nose was his most distinctive feature: curved like a scimitar at the top but bent flat at the tip, and with the bone of the bridge cut like a diamond—in short, a nose out of a folktale, the sort of sizable, convoluted, intricately turned nose that, for many centuries, confronted though they have been by every imaginable hardship, the Jews had never stopped making. The irregularity of the nose was most conspicuous when he laughed, which he did often. He was unfailingly friendly, one of those engaging family physicians who, when they step into the waiting room holding someone's file folder, make the faces of all their patients light up—whenever he came at them with his stethoscope, they'd find themselves acutely happy to be under his care. Marcia liked that her father, a man of natural, unadorned authority, would jokingly but truthfully refer to his patients as his "masters."

"Marcia told me that you've lost some of your boys. I'm sorry to hear that, Bucky. Death is not that common among polio victims."

"So far, four have gotten polio and two have died. Two boys. Grade school boys. Both twelve."

"It's a lot of responsibility for you," Dr. Steinberg said, "looking after all those boys, especially at a time like this. I've been practicing medicine for over twenty-five years, and when I lose a patient, even if it's to old age, I still feel shaken. This epidemic must be a great weight on your shoulders."

"The problem is, I don't know if I'm doing the right thing or not by letting them play ball."

"Did anyone say you're doing the wrong thing?"

"Yes, the mother of two of the boys, brothers, who have gotten polio. I know she was hysterical. I know she was lashing out in frustration, yet knowing it doesn't seem to help."

"A doctor runs into that too. You're right—people in great pain become hysterical and, confronted with the injustice of illness, they lash out. But boys' playing ball doesn't give them polio. A virus does. We may not know much about polio, but we know that. Kids everywhere play hard out of doors all summer long, and even in an epidemic it's a very small percentage who become infected with the disease. And a very small percentage of those who get seriously ill from it. And a very small percentage of those who die—death results from respiratory paralysis, which is relatively rare. Every child who gets a headache doesn't come down with paralytic polio. That's why it's important not to exaggerate the danger and to carry on normally. You have nothing to feel guilty about. That's a natural reaction sometimes, but in your case it's not justified." Pointing at him meaningfully with the stem of his pipe, he warned the young man, "We can be severe judges of ourselves when it is in no way warranted. A misplaced sense of responsibility can be a debilitating thing."

"Dr. Steinberg, do you think it's going to get worse?"

"Epidemics have a way of spontaneously running out of steam. Right now there's a lot going on. Right now we have to keep up with what's happening while we wait and see whether this is fleeting or not. Usually the great majority of the cases are children under five. That's how it was in 1916. The pattern we're seeing with this outbreak, at least here in Newark, is somewhat different. But that doesn't suggest that the disease is going to go unchecked in this city forever. There's still no cause for alarm as far as I can tell."

Mr. Cantor hadn't felt as relieved in weeks as he did while being counseled by Dr. Steinberg. There was no place in all of Newark, including his family's flat—including even the gym floor at Chancellor Avenue School where he taught his phys ed classes—where he felt any more content than he did on the screened-in porch at the rear of the Steinberg home, with Dr. Steinberg seated in his cushioned wicker armchair and pulling on his well-worn pipe.

"Why is the epidemic worst in the Weequahic section?" Mr. Cantor asked. "Why should that be?"

"I don't know," Dr. Steinberg said. "Nobody knows. Polio is still a mysterious disease. It was slow coming this time. At first it was mainly in the Ironbound, then it jumped around the city, and suddenly it settled in Weequahic and took off."

Mr. Cantor told Dr. Steinberg about the incident with the East Side High Italians who'd driven up from the Ironbound and left the pavement at the playground entrance awash with their spit.

"You did the right thing," Dr. Steinberg told him. "You cleaned it up with water and ammonia. That was the best thing to do."

"But did I kill the polio germs, if there were any?"

"We don't know what kills polio germs," Dr. Steinberg said. "We don't know who or what carries polio, and there's still some debate about how it enters the body. But what's important is that you cleaned up an unhygienic mess and reassured the boys by the way you took charge. You demonstrated your competence, you demonstrated your equanimity—that's what the kids have to see. Bucky, you're shaken by what's happening now, but strong men get the shakes too. You must understand that a lot of us who are much older and more experienced with illness than you are are also shaken by it. To stand by as a doctor unable to stop the spread of this dreadful disease is painful for all of us. A crippling disease that attacks mainly children and leaves some of them dead—that's difficult for any adult to accept. You have a conscience, and a conscience is a valuable attribute, but not if it begins to make you think you're to blame for what is far beyond the scope of your responsibility."

He thought to ask: Doesn't God have a conscience? Where's His responsibility? Or does He know no limits? But instead he asked, "Should the playground be shut down?"

"You're the director. Should it?" Dr. Steinberg asked.

"I don't know what to think."

"What would the boys do if they couldn't come to the playground? Stay at home? No, they'd play ball somewhere else—in the streets, in the empty lots, they'd go down to the park to play ball. You can't get them to stop congregating together just by expelling them from the playground. They won't stay home—they'll hang around the corner candy store together, banging the pinball machine and pushing and shoving one another for fun. They'll drink out of each other's soda bottles no matter how much you tell them not to. Some of them will be so restless and bored they'll go too far and get into trouble. They're not angels—they're boys. Bucky, there's nothing you're doing that's making things worse. To the contrary, you're making things better. You're doing something useful. You're contributing to the welfare of the community. It's important that neighborhood life goes on as usual—otherwise, it's not only the stricken and their families who are victims, but Weequahic itself becomes a victim. At the playground you help keep panic at bay by overseeing those kids of yours playing the games they love. The alternative isn't to send them someplace else where they won't have your supervision. The alternative isn't to lock them up in their houses and fill them with dread. I'm against the frightening of Jewish kids. I'm against the frightening of Jews, period. That was Europe, that's why Jews fled.

This is America. The less fear the better. Fear unmans us. Fear degrades us. Fostering less fear—that's your job and mine."

There were sirens in the distance, off to the west where the hospital was. In the garden there were only shrill crickets and pulsating lightning bugs and the many varieties of fragrant flowers, their petals massed on the other side of the porch screens and, with Mrs. Steinberg away at the shore, more than likely watered by Dr. Steinberg after he'd eaten his dinner. A bowl of fruit lay on the glass top of the wicker coffee table in front of the wicker sofa where Mr. Cantor was sitting. Dr. Steinberg reached for a piece of fruit and told Mr. Cantor to help himself.

He bit into a delicious peach, a big and beautiful peach like the one Dr. Steinberg had taken from the bowl, and in the company of this thoroughly reasonable man and the soothing sense of security he exuded, he took his time eating it, savoring every sweet mouthful right down to the pit. Then, wholly unprepared for the moment but unable to contain himself, he placed the pit into an ashtray, leaned forward, and compressing his sticky hands tightly together between his knees, he said, "I would like your permission, sir, to ask Marcia to become engaged."

Dr. Steinberg burst out laughing and, raising his pipe in the air as though it were a trophy, he stood and did a little jig. "You have it!" he said. "I couldn't be more thrilled. And Mrs. Steinberg will be just as thrilled. I'm going to call her right now. And you're going to get on and tell her the news yourself. Oh, Bucky, this is just swell! Of course you have our permission. Marcia couldn't have hooked herself a better fellow. What a lucky family we are!"

Startled to hear Dr. Steinberg characterize *his* family as the lucky ones, Mr. Cantor felt himself flush with excitement, and he jumped to his feet too and heartily shook Dr. Steinberg's hand. Until that moment he hadn't planned to mention engagement to anyone until the new year, when he would be a bit more secure financially. He was still saving to buy a gas stove for his grandmother, to replace the coal stove she cooked on in the kitchen, and had figured that he'd have enough by December, if he didn't have to buy an engagement ring before then. But it was all the comfort he had derived from her kindly father, concluding with their enjoying those perfect peaches together on the back porch, that had roused him to seek permission there and then. What had done it was his knowing that Dr. Steinberg, merely by his presence, seemed able to answer the questions that nobody else could: what the hell is going on, and how do we get out of this? And something else had galvanized him as well: the sound of the ambulance sirens crisscrossing Newark in the night.

The next morning was the worst so far. Three more boys had come down with polio—Leo Feinswog, Paul Lippman, and me, Arnie Mesnikoff. The playground had jumped from four to seven cases overnight. The sirens that he and Dr. Steinberg had heard the evening before could well have been from the ambulances speeding them to the hospital. He learned about the three new cases from the kids who came with their mitts that morning ready to spend the day playing ball. On an ordinary weekday he'd have two games going, one at each of the diamonds at either corner of the playground, but on this morning there weren't nearly enough boys on hand to field four teams. Aside from those who had taken ill, some sixty had apparently been kept away by apprehensive parents. The remainder he gathered together to talk to on the section of wooden bleachers that backed on to the rear wall of the school.

"Boys, I'm glad to see you here. Today's going to be another scorcher—you can tell that already. But that doesn't mean we're not going to go out on the field and play. It does mean we're going to take some precautions so none of you overdo it. Every two and a half innings we're taking a break in the shade, right here on the bleachers, for fifteen minutes. No running around during that time. That means everybody. Between noon and two, when it's hottest, there's going to be no softball at all. The ball fields are going to be empty. You want to play checkers, chess, Ping-Pong, you want to sit and talk on the bleachers, you want to bring a book or a magazine with you to read during the time-out . . . that's all fine. That's our new daily schedule. We're going to have as good a summer as we can, but we're going to do everything in moderation on days like this. Nobody here is going to get sunstroke out in that savage heat." He inserted "sunstroke" at the last moment, instead of saying "polio."

There were no complaints. There were no comments at all. They listened solemnly and nodded in agreement. It was the first time since the epidemic had begun that he could sense their fear. They each knew more than casually one or another of those who'd come down with the disease the day before, and in a way that they hadn't previously grasped the nature of the threat, they at last understood the chance they stood of catching polio themselves.

Mr. Cantor picked two teams of ten to start the first game. There were ten kids left over, and he told them they would go on to substitute, five to a side, after the first fifteen-minute break. That's the way they'd proceed throughout the day.

"All right?" Mr. Cantor said, clapping his hands enthusiastically. "It's a summer day like any other, and I want you to go out and play ball."

Instead of playing himself, he decided to start off the morning by sitting with the ten boys who were waiting their turn to join the game and who seemed unusually subdued. Back of center field, where the girls regularly gathered in the school street, Mr. Cantor noted that of the original dozen or so who had begun meeting there every weekday morning earlier in the summer, only three were present today—only three whose parents would apparently allow them to leave the vicinity of their homes for fear of their making contact with the other playground kids. The missing girls may have been among the neighborhood children he'd heard about who had been sent to take refuge with relatives a safe distance from the city, and some among those whisked from the menace to be immersed in, immunized by, the hygienic ocean air of the Jersey Shore.

Now two of the girls were turning the rope while one was jumping—and with nobody any longer quivering on her skinny legs, ready to rush in after her. The jumper's high tweeting voice could be heard that morning as far away as the bleachers, where boys normally full of jokes and wisecracks who had no trouble blabbering away all day long found themselves now with nothing to say.

K, my name is Kay
And my husband's name is Karl,
We come from Kansas
And we bring back kangaroos!

Mr. Cantor finally broke the long silence. "Any of you have friends who got sick?" he asked them.

They either nodded or quietly said yes.

"That's tough for you, I know. Very tough. We have to hope they get better and that they're soon back on the playground."

"You can wind up in an iron lung forever," said Bobby Finkelstein, a shy boy who was among the quietest of them, one of the boys he'd seen wearing a suit on the steps of the synagogue after Alan Michaels's funeral service.

"You can," said Mr. Cantor. "But that's from respiratory paralysis, and that's very rare. You're far more likely to recover. It's a serious disease, it can do great harm, but there are recoveries. Sometimes they're partial, but many times they're total. Most cases are relatively light." He spoke with authority, the source of his knowledge being Dr. Steinberg.

"You can die," Bobby said, pursuing this subject in a way that in the past he'd pursued few others. Mostly he seemed to enjoy letting the extroverts do the talking, yet about what had happened to his friends he could not keep himself from going on. "Alan and Herbie died."

"You can die," Mr. Cantor allowed, "but the chances are slight."

"They weren't slight for Alan and Herbie," Bobby replied.

"I meant the chances are slight overall in the community, in the city."

"That doesn't help Alan and Herbie," Bobby insisted, his voice quavering.

"You're right, Bobby. You're right. It doesn't. What happened to them was terrible. What's happened to all the boys is terrible."

Now another of the boys on the bleachers spoke up, Kenny Blumenfeld, though what he was saying was unintelligible because of the state he was in. He was a tall, strong boy, intelligent, articulate, already at fourteen in his second year at Weequahic High and, unlike most of the other boys, mature in his ability to put emotion aside in matters of winning and losing. He, along with Alan, had been a leader on the playground, the boy who was always chosen captain of a team, the boy who had the longest arms and legs and hit the longest ball—and yet it was Kenny, the oldest and biggest and most grown-up of them all, as sturdy emotionally as he was physically, who was drumming his clenched fists on his thighs as tears coursed down his face.

Mr. Cantor went over to where he was seated and sat next to him.

Through his tears, speaking hoarsely, Kenny said, "All my friends are getting polio! All my friends are going to be cripples or going to be dead!"

In response Mr. Cantor placed his hand on Kenny's shoulder but said nothing. He looked out onto the field where the two teams were deep in the game, oblivious of what was happening on the sidelines. He remembered Dr. Steinberg cautioning him not to exaggerate the danger, and yet he thought: Kenny's right. Every one of them. Those on the field and those on the bleachers. The girls jumping rope. They're all kids, and polio is going after kids, and it will sweep through this place and destroy them all. Each morning that I show up there'll be another few gone. There's nothing to stop it unless they shut down the playground. And even shutting it down won't help—in the end it's going to get every last child. The neighborhood is doomed. Not a one of the children will survive intact, if they survive at all.

And then, out of nowhere, he thought of that peach he'd eaten on the Steinbergs' back porch the night before. He could all but feel its juice trickling onto his hand, and for the first time he was frightened for himself. What was amazing was how long he had kept the fear in check.

He watched Kenny Blumenfeld weeping over his friends beset by polio, and suddenly he wanted to flee from working in the midst of these kids—to flee from the unceasing awareness of the persistent peril. To flee, as Marcia wanted him to.

Instead he sat quietly beside Kenny until the crying had subsided. Then he told him, "I'll be back—I'm going to play for a while." He stepped down off the bleachers and walked onto the field, where he said to Barry Mittelman, the third baseman, "Get out of the sun now, get in the shade, get some water," and taking Barry's mitt, he installed himself at third, vigorously working the pocket with his knuckles.

By the end of the day, Mr. Cantor had played at every position on the field, giving the boys on either side a chance to sit out an inning in the shade so as not to get overheated. He did not know what else to do to prevent the polio from spreading. Playing in the outfield, he'd had to hold his glove up to the peak of his baseball cap in order not to be blinded by the sun, a four o'clock sun no less punishing than the twelve o'clock sledgehammer. To his surprise, just beyond him on the school street he could hear the three sun-baked girls, still feverishly at it, still thrilling to the cadences of a thumping heart.

> S, my name is Sally
> And my husband's name is Sam . . .

At about five, when the boys were into the final inning of the last game of the day—the fielders with their sopping polo shirts cast aside on the nearby asphalt and the boys in the batter's box shirtless too—Mr. Cantor heard loud hollering from deep center field. It was Kenny Blumenfeld, enraged with, of all people, Horace. Mr. Cantor had noticed Horace down at the end of the bench earlier in the afternoon but soon lost track of him and couldn't remember seeing him again. Probably he'd gone off to meander around the neighborhood and had only just returned to the playground and, disposed as he was to go out onto the field and stand silent and motionless beside one of the players, had chosen to approach Kenny and be near the biggest boy on either team. Earlier in the day it was Kenny who, uncharacteristically, had been racked with sobs about the ravaging of his friends, and now, again uncharacteristically, it was Kenny who was shouting at Horace and threateningly waving him off with his mitt. Not only was Kenny the biggest boy, but without his shirt on it was apparent that he was the strongest one too. By contrast, Horace, wearing his usual summer outfit of an oversized half-sleeve shirt and ballooning cotton trousers with an elasticized waistband and long-outmoded brown-and-white perforated shoes, seemed undernourished to the point of emaciation. His chest was sunken, his legs were spindly, and his scrawny marionette arms, dangling weakly at his sides, looked as if you could snap them in two as easily as you break a stick over your knee. He looked as though a good fright could kill him, let alone a blow from a boy built like Kenny.

Instantly, Mr. Cantor sprang off the bench where he was seated and ran at full speed to the outfield while all the boys in the game and on the bleachers ran along with him and the three girls on the street stopped jumping rope, seemingly for the first time all summer.

"Get him away from me!" Kenny—the boy who was the model of maturity for the others, whom Mr. Cantor never had reason to admonish for failing to exercise self-control—that same Kenny was now howling, "Get him away from me or I'll kill him!"

"What is it? What's going on?" Mr. Cantor asked. Horace stood there with his head hanging and tears rolling down his face and keening, emitting a kind of radio signal from high in the back of his throat—a thin, oscillating sound of distress.

"Smell him!" Kenny screamed. "He has shit all over him! Get him the hell away from me! It's him! He's the one who's carrying the polio!"

"Calm down, Ken," Mr. Cantor said, trying to take hold of the boy, who wildly fought his way free. They were surrounded by the players on both teams now, and when several of the boys rushed forward to grab Kenny by the arms and pull him back from where he was excoriating Horace, he turned to strike out at them with his fists, and all of them jumped away.

"I'm not calming down!" Kenny cried. "He's got shit all over his underwear! He's got shit all over his hands! He doesn't wash and he isn't clean, and then he wants us to take his hand, and shake his hand, and that's how he's spreading polio! He's the one who's crippling people! He's the one who's killing people! Get out of here, you! Get! Go!" And again he waved his mitt violently in the air as though warding off the attack of a rabid dog.

Meanwhile, managing to keep clear of Kenny's flailing arms, Mr. Cantor was able to interpose himself between the hysterical boy and the terrified creature onto whom he was pouring out his rage.

"You have to go home, Horace," Mr. Cantor quietly told

him. "Go home to your parents. It's time for your supper. It's time to eat."

Horace did smell—he smelled horribly. And though Mr. Cantor repeated his words a second time, Horace kept on crying and keening and saying nothing.

"Here, Horace," Mr. Cantor said and extended his hand to him. Without looking up, Horace took the hand limply in his and Mr. Cantor shook Horace's hand as heartily as he had shaken Dr. Steinberg's after receiving his permission to become engaged to Marcia the night before.

"How ya doin', Horace?" Mr. Cantor whispered, pumping Horace's hand up and down. "How ya doin', boy?" It took a little longer than usual, but then, just as it always had in the past when Horace moseyed out to stand beside a player on the field, the handshake ritual did the trick, and Horace, assuaged, turned toward the playground exit to leave, whether for home or elsewhere nobody knew, probably not even Horace. All the boys who had heard Kenny's raving hung way back from Horace as they watched him lurch off alone into the wall of heat, while the girls, shrilly screaming "He's after us! The moron is chasing us!" ran with their jump ropes toward the late-afternoon Chancellor Avenue traffic, ran as fast as they could from the sight of how deep the human blight can go.

To quiet Kenny down, Mr. Cantor asked him to stay behind when the rest of the boys headed off and to help him put the playground equipment away in the basement storage room. Then, quietly talking to Kenny as they walked, Mr. Cantor accompanied him to his house, down the hill on Hansbury Avenue.

"It's piling up on everyone, Ken. You're not the only one in the neighborhood," he told him, "who's feeling the pressure of the polio. Between the polio and the weather, there isn't anybody who isn't at the end of his rope."

"But he's spreading it, Mr. Cantor. I'm sure of it. I shouldn't have gone nuts, I know he's a moron, but he's not clean and he's spreading it. He walks all over the place and drools over everything and shakes everyone's hand and that's how he spreads the germs everywhere."

"First off, Ken, we don't know what spreads it."

"But we *do*. Filth, dirt, and shit," Kenny said, his outrage revving up again. "And he's filthy, dirty, and shitty, and he's spreading it. I know it."

On the pavement in front of Kenny's house, Mr. Cantor took him firmly by his shoulders, and Kenny, shuddering with revulsion, instantly shook free of his hands and cried, "Don't touch me! You just touched him!"

"Go inside," Mr. Cantor said, still composed but retreating a step. "Take a cold shower. Get a cold drink. Cool off, Ken, and I'll see you tomorrow up at the playground."

"But you're only being blind to who's spreading it because he's so helpless! Only he's not just helpless—he's dangerous! Don't you understand, Mr. Cantor? He doesn't know how to wipe his ass, so he gets it all over everyone else!"

That evening, watching his grandmother while she served him his dinner, he found himself wondering if this was how his mother would have come to look if she had been lucky enough to live another fifty years—frail, stooped, brittle-boned, with hair that decades earlier had lost its darkness and thinned to a white fluff, with stringy skin in the crooks of her arms and a fleshy lobe hanging from her chin and joints that ached in the morning and ankles that swelled and throbbed by nightfall and translucent papery skin on her mottled hands and cataracts that had shrouded and discolored her vision. As for the face above the ruin of her neck, it was now a tightly drawn mesh of finely patterned wrinkles, grooves so minute they appeared to be the work of an implement far less crude than the truncheon of old age—an etching needle perhaps, or a lacemaker's tool, manipulated by a master craftsman to render her as ancient-looking a grandmother as any on earth.

There had been a strong resemblance between his mother and his grandmother when his mother was growing up. He had seen it in photographs, where, of course, he had first noticed his own strong resemblance to his mother, particularly in the framed studio portrait of her that rested on the bureau in his grandparents' bedroom. The picture, taken for her high school graduation when she was eighteen, was in the 1919 South Side yearbook that Bucky leafed through often as a young schoolboy beginning to discover that the other boys in his class were not grandsons living with grandparents but sons

living with a mother and father in what he came to think of as
"real families." He best understood how precarious his footing
in the world was when adults bestowed upon him the look
that he despised, the pitying look that he knew so well, since
he sometimes got it from teachers too. The look made only
too clear that the intervention of his mother's aging parents
was all that had stood between him and the bleak four-story
red-brick building on nearby Clinton Avenue with its black
iron fence and its windows of pebbled glass covered with iron
grates and its heavy wooden doorway adorned with a white
Jewish star and the broad lintel above it carved with the three
most forlorn words he'd ever read: HEBREW ORPHAN ASYLUM.

Even though the graduation picture on the bedroom bureau
was said by his grandmother to catch perfectly the kindly spirit
that animated his mother, it was not his favorite photograph of
her, because of the dark academic robe she wore over her
dress, the sight of which never failed to sadden him, as if the
robe in the picture were a portent, the harbinger of her shroud.
Nonetheless, alone at home when his grandparents were working around the corner in the store, he would sometimes drift
into his grandparents' room to run the tip of one finger over
the glass that protected the picture, tracing the contours of his
mother's face as though the glass had been removed and the
face there was flesh. He did this despite its causing him to feel
keenly not the presence he was seeking but rather the absence
of one he'd never seen anywhere other than in photos, whose
voice he'd never heard speaking his name, whose maternal
warmth he'd never luxuriated in, a mother who had never got
to care for him or feed him or put him to bed or help him with
his schoolwork or watch him grow up to be the first of the
family slated to go to college. Yet could he truthfully say he
hadn't been sufficiently cherished as a child? Why was the genuine tenderness of a loving grandmother any less satisfying than
the tenderness of a mother? It shouldn't have been, and yet
secretly he felt that it was—and secretly felt ashamed for har-
boring such a thought.

After all this time, it had suddenly occurred to Mr. Cantor
that God wasn't simply letting polio rampage through the
Weequahic section but that twenty-three years back, God had
also allowed his mother, only two years out of high school and

younger than he was now, to die in childbirth. He'd never thought about her death that way before. Previously, because of the loving care that he received from his grandparents, it had always seemed to him that losing his mother at birth was something that was meant to happen to him and that his grandparents' raising him was a natural consequence of her death. So too was his father's being a gambler and a thief something that was meant to happen and that couldn't have been otherwise. But now that he was no longer a child he was capable of understanding that why things couldn't be otherwise was because of God. If not for God, if not for the *nature* of God, they *would* be otherwise.

He couldn't repeat such an idea to his grandmother, who was no more reflective than his grandfather had been, and he did not feel inclined to talk about it with Dr. Steinberg. Though very much a thinking man, Dr. Steinberg was also an observant Jew and might take offense at the turn of mind that the polio epidemic was inspiring in Mr. Cantor. He wouldn't want to affront any of the Steinbergs, least of all Marcia, for whom the High Holidays were a source of reverence and a time of prayer when she dutifully attended synagogue services with her family on all three days. He wanted to show respect for everything that the Steinbergs held dear, including, of course, the religion that he shared with them, even if, like his grandfather—for whom duty was a religion, rather than the other way around— he was an indifferent practitioner of it. And to be wholly respectful had always been easy enough until the moment he found his anger provoked because of all the kids he was losing to polio, including the incorrigible Kopferman boys. His anger provoked not against the Italians or the houseflies or the mail or the milk or the money or malodorous Secaucus or the merciless heat or Horace, not against whatever cause, however unlikely, people, in their fear and confusion, might advance to explain the epidemic, not even against the polio virus, but against the source, the creator—against God, who made the virus.

"You're not wearing yourself down, are you, Eugene?" Dinner was over and he was cleaning up while she sat at the table sipping a glass of water from the icebox. "You rush to the playground," she said, "you rush to visit the families of your boys, you rush on Sunday to the funeral, you rush home in the evening to help me—maybe this weekend you should stop rushing around in this heat and take the train and find a bed for the weekend down the shore. Take a break from everything. Get away from the heat. Get away from the playground. Go swimming. It'll do you a world of good."

"That's a thought, Grandma. That's not a bad idea."

"The Einnemans can look in on me, and Sunday night you'll come home refreshed. This polio is wearing you out. That's no good for anyone."

Over dinner he had told her about the three new cases at the playground and said that he was going to telephone the families later, when they got home from the hospital.

Meanwhile, the sirens were sounding again, and very close to the house, which was unusual, since as far as he knew there'd been no more than three or four cases in the entire residential triangle formed by Springfield, Clinton, and Belmont avenues. Theirs were the lowest numbers for any neighborhood in the city. At the southern end of the triangle, where he lived with his grandmother and where the rents were half what they were in Weequahic, there had been but a single case of polio—the victim an adult, a man of thirty, a stevedore who worked at the port—while in the Weequahic section, with its five elementary schools, there had been more than a hundred and forty cases, all in children under fourteen, in the first weeks of July alone.

Yes, of course—the shore, where some of his playground kids had already escaped with their mothers for the remainder of the summer. He knew a rooming house back from the beach in Bradley where he could get one of the cots in the cellar for a buck. He could do his diving off the high board of the boardwalk's big saltwater pool, dive all day long and then at night stroll along the boards to Asbury Park and pick up a mess of fried clams and a root beer at the arcade and sit on one of the benches facing the ocean and happily feast away while watching the surf come crashing in. What could be more removed from the Newark polio epidemic, what could be more of a tonic for him, than the booming black nighttime Atlantic? This was the first summer since the war began when the danger of German U-boats in nearby waters or of waterborne German saboteurs coming ashore after dark was considered to be over, when the blackout had been lifted, and—though the coast guard still patrolled the beaches and maintained pillboxes along the coast—when the lights were on again all along the Jersey Shore. That meant that both the Germans and the Japanese were suffering crippling defeats and that, nearly three years after it had begun, America's war was beginning to come to an end. It meant that his two best college buddies, Big Jake Garonzik and Dave Jacobs, would be returning home unscathed, if only they could make it through the remaining months of combat in Europe. He thought of the song Marcia liked so much: "I'll be seeing you in all the old familiar places." That will be the day, he thought, when he could see Jake and Dave in the old familiar places!

He had never gotten over the shame of not being with them, for all that there was nothing he could do about it. They had wound up together in an airborne unit, jumping from planes into battle—what he would have wanted to do, exactly what he was *constructed* to do. Some six weeks earlier, at dawn on D-Day, they had been members of a huge paratroop force that had landed behind the German lines on the Normandy peninsula. Mr. Cantor knew from staying in touch with their families that despite the many casualties taken during the invasion, the two of them had survived. From following the maps in the paper plotting the Allies' progress, he figured that they had probably been in the heavy fighting to capture Cherbourg late in June. The first thing Mr. Cantor looked for in the *Newark News* that his grandmother got from the Einnemans every night after they'd finished reading it was whatever he could find about the U.S. army's campaign in France. After that, he read the box on the front page of the *News* that was called "The Daily Polio Bulletin" and that appeared just below a reproduction of a quarantine sign. "Board of Health of Newark, New Jersey," the sign read. "Keep out. This house contains a case of polio. Any person violating the isolation and quarantine rules and regulations of the board or who willfully removes, defaces, or obstructs this card without authority is liable to a fine of $50." The polio bulletin, which was also broadcast every day on the local radio station, kept Newarkers up to date on the number and location of every new case in the city. So far this summer, what people heard or read there was never what they hoped to find there—that the epidemic was on the wane —but rather that the tally of new cases had increased yet again from the day before. The impact of the numbers was, of course, disheartening and frightening and wearying. For these weren't the impersonal numbers one was accustomed to hearing on the radio or reading in the paper, the numbers that served to locate a house or record a person's age or establish the price of a pair of shoes. These were the terrifying numbers charting the progress of a horrible disease and, in the sixteen wards of Newark, corresponding in their impact to the numbers of the dead, wounded, and missing in the real war. Because this was real war too, a war of slaughter, ruin, waste, and damnation, war with the ravages of war—war upon the children of Newark.

Yes, he could certainly use a few days on his own down the shore. That, in fact, was what he'd been planning on doing when the summer began—with Marcia gone, to head to the shore every weekend to dive the day away and then walk the boards to Asbury at night to eat his favorite seashore meal. The cellar was dank where he rented a cot and the water was rarely hot in the shower everyone used and there was sand in the sheets and towels, but, second only to throwing the javelin, diving was his favorite sport. Two days of diving would help him to shake loose, at least temporarily, from the preoccupation with his stricken boys and quiet his agitation over Kenny Blumenfeld's hysterical outbursts and maybe clear his head of the malice he felt toward God.

Then, when his grandmother was outside with the neighbors and he was about finished with cleaning up and had just sat down at the table in his sleeveless undershirt and briefs to drink yet another glass of ice water, Marcia called. Dr. Steinberg had agreed to wait for Mr. Cantor to talk with Marcia before he or Mrs. Steinberg said anything to her about the engagement, so she was calling without any knowledge of the conversation on the back porch the evening before. She was calling to tell him she loved him and she missed him and to learn what he had decided about coming to the camp to take over from Irv Schlanger as waterfront director.

"What should I tell Mr. Blomback?" she asked.

"Tell him yes," Mr. Cantor said, and he startled himself no less by what he'd just agreed to than he had done asking permission of Dr. Steinberg to become engaged to his daughter. "Tell him I will," he said.

Yet he'd had every intention of taking his grandmother's suggestion and going to the shore for the weekend and marshaling his forces so as to return to his job rejuvenated. If Jake and Dave could parachute into Nazi-occupied France on D-Day and help to anchor the Allied beachhead by fighting their way into Cherbourg against the stiffest German opposition, then surely he could face the dangers of running the playground at Chancellor Avenue School in the midst of a polio epidemic.

"Oh, Bucky," cried Marcia, "that's swell! Knowing you, I was so frightened you were going to say no. Oh, you're coming, you're coming to Indian Hill!"

"I'll have to call O'Gara and tell him, and he'll have to get somebody to take my place. O'Gara's the guy in charge of playgrounds at the superintendent's office. That could take a couple of days."

"Oh, do it as fast as you can!"

"I'll have to speak to Mr. Blomback myself. About the salary. I've got the rent and my grandmother to think about."

"I'm sure the salary's going to be no problem."

"And I have to talk to you about getting engaged," he said.

"What? You what?"

"We're getting engaged, Marcia. That's why I'm taking the job. I asked your father's permission last night over at the house. I'm coming to camp and we're getting engaged."

"We are?" she said, laughing. "Isn't it customary for the girl to be asked, even a girl as pliant as me?"

"Is it? I've never done it before. Will you be my fiancée?"

"Of course! Oh my goodness, Bucky, I'm so happy!"

"So am I," he said, "tremendously happy," and for the moment, because of this happiness, he was almost able to forget the betrayal of his playground kids; he was almost able to forget his outrage with God for the murderous persecution of Weequahic's innocent children. Talking to Marcia about their engagement, he was almost able to look the other way and to rush to embrace the security and predictability and contentment of a normal life lived in normal times. But when he hung up, there confronting him were his ideals—ideals of truthfulness and strength fostered in him by his grandfather, ideals of courage and sacrifice that he shared with Jake and Dave, ideals nurtured by him in boyhood to place himself beyond the reach of a crooked father's penchant for deceit—his ideals as a man demanding of him that he immediately reverse course and return for the rest of the summer to the work he had contracted to perform.

How could he have done what he'd just done?

In the morning he carried the equipment up from the storage room and organized two teams and got a softball game under way for the fewer than twenty kids who'd shown up to play. Then he returned to the basement to call O'Gara from his office and tell him that he was leaving his job at the end of the week to take over as waterfront director at a summer camp in the Poconos. That morning before he'd left for the playground, he'd gotten news over the radio that there were twenty-nine new polio cases in the city, sixteen of them in Weequahic.

"That's the second guy this morning," O'Gara said. "I got a Jewish guy over at Peshine Avenue playground who's quitting on me too." O'Gara was a tired old man with a big gut and an antagonistic manner who'd been running the city playgrounds for years and whose prowess as a Central High football player at the time of the First World War still constituted the culmination of his life. His brusqueness wasn't necessarily killing, yet it unsettled Mr. Cantor and left him feeling shifty and childishly grubbing about for the words to justify his decision. O'Gara's brusqueness wasn't unlike his grandfather's, perhaps because it was acquired on the same tough streets of the Third Ward. His grandfather was, of course, the last person he wanted to be thinking about while doing something so out of keeping with who he really was. He wanted to be thinking about Marcia and the Steinbergs and the future, but instead there was his grandfather to deliver the verdict with just a bit of an Irish intonation.

"The fellow I'm taking over for at the camp has been drafted," Mr. Cantor responded. "I've got to leave on Friday for the camp."

"This is what I get for giving you a plum job just a year out of college. You realize that you haven't exactly won my confidence by pulling a stunt like this. You realize that leaving me in the lurch in July like this isn't likely to make me disposed to ever hire you again, Cancer."

"Cantor," Mr. Cantor corrected him, as he always had to when they spoke.

"I don't care how many guys are away in the army," O'Gara said. "I don't like people quitting on me right in the midst of everything." And then he added, "Especially people who *aren't* in the army."

"I'm sorry to be leaving, Mr. O'Gara. And," he said, speaking in a shriller tone than he'd intended, "I'm sorry I'm not in the army—sorrier than you know." To make matters worse, he added, "I have to go. I have no choice."

"What?" O'Gara snapped back. "You have no choice, do you? Sure you got a choice. What you're doing is called making a choice. You're making your escape from the polio. You sign up for a job, and then there's the polio, and the hell with the job, the hell with the commitment, you run like hell as fast as you can. All you're doing is running away, Cancer, a world-champion muscleman like you. You're an opportunist, Cancer. I could say worse, but that will do." And then, with revulsion, he repeated, "An opportunist," as though the word stood for every degrading instinct that could possibly stigmatize a man.

"I have a fiancée at the camp," Mr. Cantor replied lamely.

"You had a fiancée at the camp when you signed on at Chancellor."

"No, no, I didn't," he rushed to say, as if to O'Gara that would make a difference. "We only became engaged this week."

"All right, you got an answer for everything. Like the guy from Peshine. You Jewish boys got all the answers. No, you're not stupid—*but neither is O'Gara, Cancer.* All right, all right, I'll get somebody up there to take your place, if there is anyone in this town who can fill your shoes. In the meantime, you have a rollicking time roasting marshmallows with your girlfriend at your kiddie camp."

It was no less humiliating than he'd thought it would be, but he'd done it and it was over. He just had to get through three more days at the playground without contracting polio.

2

Indian Hill

HE'D NEVER been to the Pocono Mountains before, or up through the rural northwestern counties of New Jersey to Pennsylvania. The train ride, traversing hills and woods and open farmland, made him think of himself as on a far greater excursion than just traveling to the next state over. There was an epic dimension to gliding past a landscape wholly unfamiliar to him, a sense he'd had the few previous times he'd been aboard a train—including the Jersey line that carried him to the shore—that a future new and unknown to him was about to unfold. Sighting the Delaware Water Gap, where the river separating New Jersey and Pennsylvania cut dramatically through the mountain range just fifteen minutes from his stop at Stroudsburg, only heightened the intensity of the trip and assured him—admittedly without reason—that no destroyer could possibly overleap so grand a natural barrier in order to catch him.

This marked the first time since his grandfather's death, three years earlier, that he would be leaving his grandmother in the care of anyone else for more than a weekend, and the first time he'd be out of the city for more than a night or two. And it was the first time in weeks that thoughts of polio weren't swamping him. He still mourned the two boys who had died, he was still oppressed by thinking of all of his other boys stricken with the crippling disease, yet he did not feel that he had faltered under the exigencies of the calamity or that someone else could have performed his job any more zealously. With all his energy and ingenuity, he had wholeheartedly confronted a devastating challenge—until he had chosen to abandon the challenge and flee the torrid city trembling under its epidemic and resounding with the sirens of ambulances constantly on the move.

At the Stroudsburg station, Carl, the Indian Hill driver, a large baby-faced man with a bald head and a shy manner, was waiting for him in the camp's old station wagon. Carl had

come to town to pick up supplies and to meet Bucky's train.
On shaking Carl's hand, Bucky had a single overriding thought:
He's not carrying polio. And it's cool here, he realized. Even
in the sun, it's cool!

Leaving town with his duffel bag stashed in the rear of the
wagon, they passed along the pleasant main street of two- and
three-story brick buildings—housing a row of street-level stores
with business offices on the upper floors—and then turned
north and began a slow ascent along zigzagging roads into the
hills. They passed farms, and he saw horses and cows in the
fields, and occasionally he caught sight of a farmer on a tractor.
There were silos and barns and low wire fences and rural mailboxes atop wooden posts and no polio anywhere. At the top of
a long climb they made a sharp turn off the blacktop onto a
narrow unpaved road that was marked with a sign with the
words CAMP INDIAN HILL burned into the wood and a picture
below it of a teepee in a circle of flames—the same emblem
that was on the side of the station wagon. After bouncing a
couple of miles through the woods over the hard ridges of the
dirt road—a twisting pitted track that was deliberately left that
way, Carl told him, to discourage access to Indian Hill by
anything other than bona fide camp traffic—they emerged into
an open green oval that was the entrance to the camp grounds.
Its impact was very like what he experienced upon entering
Ruppert Stadium with Jake and Dave to see the Newark Bears
play the first Sunday doubleheader of the season and—after
stepping out from the dim stadium recesses onto the bright
walkway that led to the seats—surveying the spacious sweep of
mown grass secreted in one of the ugliest parts of the city. But
that was a walled-in ballpark. This was the wide-open spaces.
Here the vista was limitless and the refuge even more beautiful
than the home field of the Bears.

A metal pole stood at the center of the oval flying an American flag and, below it, a flag bearing the camp emblem. There
was also a teepee nearby, some twelve or fifteen feet high, with
the long supporting poles jutting through the hole at the apex.
The gray canvas was decorated at the top with two rows of a
zigzag lightning-like design and near the bottom with a wavy
line that must have been meant to represent a range of mountains. To either side of the teepee was a weathered totem pole.

Down the slope from the green oval was the bright metallic sheen of a vast lake. A wooden dock ran along the shoreline, and, about fifty feet from one another, three narrow wooden piers jutted out some hundred feet into the lake; at the end of two of the piers were the diving platforms. This must be the boys' waterfront that was to be his domain. Marcia had told him that the lake was fed by natural springs. The words sounded like the name of an earthly wonder: natural springs— yet another way of saying "no polio." He was wearing a white short-sleeved shirt with his tie, and stepping from the wagon, he could feel on his arms and face that, though the sun was still strong, the air here was cooler even than in Stroudsburg. As he hefted his duffel bag strap over his shoulder, he was overtaken with the joy of beginning again, the rapturous in-toxication of renewal—the bursting feeling of "I live! I live!"

He followed a dirt path to a small log building overlooking the lake, where Mr. Blomback had his office. Carl had insisted on relieving Bucky of his heavy bag and driving it up to the cabin called Comanche, where he'd be living with the oldest boys in camp, the fifteen-year-olds, and their counselor. Each of the cabins in the boys' and the girls' camps was named for an Indian tribe.

He knocked on the screen door and was welcomed warmly by the owner, a tall, gangly man with a long neck and a large Adam's apple and some wisps of gray hair crisscrossing his sunburned skull. He had to have been in his late fifties, and yet, in khaki shorts and a camp polo shirt, he looked sinewy and fit. Bucky knew from Marcia that when Mr. Blomback had become a young widower in 1926, he gave up a promising scholastic career as a vice principal at Newark's West Side High and bought the camp with his wife's family money to have a place to teach his two little boys the Indian lore that he had come to love as a summer outdoorsman. The boys were grown now and off in the army, and running the camp and directing the staff and visiting Jewish families in New Jersey and Penn-sylvania to recruit youngsters for the camp season was Mr. Blomback's year-round job. His rustic office—constructed of raw logs like the building's exterior—had five full Indian head-dresses, arranged on pegs, decorating the wall back of the desk; group photos of campers crowded the other walls, except

where there were several shelves filled with books, all, said Mr.
Blomback, concerned with Indian life and lore.

"This is the bible," he told Bucky, and handed him a thick
volume called *The Book of Woodcraft*. "This book was my inspiration. This too," and he handed him a second and thinner
book, *Manual of the Woodcraft Indians*. Obediently Bucky
thumbed through the pages of *Manual of the Woodcraft Indians*, where he saw printed pen-and-ink drawings of mushrooms
and birds and the leaves of a great number of trees, none of
which were identifiable to him. He saw a chapter title, "Forty
Birds That Every Boy Should Know," and had to accept the fact
that he, already a man, didn't know more than a couple of them.

"These two books have been every camp owner's inspiration," Mr. Blomback told him. "Ernest Thompson Seton single-
handedly began the Indian movement in camping. A great and
influential teacher. 'Manhood,' Seton says, 'is the first aim of
education. We follow out of doors those pursuits that, in a
word, make for manhood.' Indispensable books. They hold up
always a heroic human ideal. They accept the red man as the
great prophet of outdoor life and woodcraft and use his meth-
ods whenever they are helpful. They propose initiation tests of
fortitude, following the example of the red man. They propose
that the foundation of all power is self-control. 'Above all,' says
Seton, 'heroism.' "

Bucky nodded, agreeing that these were weighty matters,
even if he'd never heard of Seton before.

"Every August fourteenth the camp commemorates Seton's
birthday with an Indian Pageant. It's Ernest Thompson Seton
who has made twentieth-century camping one of our country's
greatest achievements."

Again Bucky nodded. "I'd like to read these books," he said,
handing them back to Mr. Blomback. "They sound like important books, especially for educating young boys."

"At Indian Hill, educating boys *and* girls. I'd like you to
read them. As soon as you get settled in, you can come and
borrow my copies. Peerless books, published when the century
was young and the whole nation, led by Teddy Roosevelt, was
turning to the outdoor life. You are a godsend, young fellow,"
he said. "I've known Doc Steinberg and the Steinberg family
all my life. If the Steinbergs vouch for you, that's good enough

for me. I'm going to get one of the counselors to give you a tour of the camp, and I'm going to take you myself on a tour of the waterfront and introduce you to everyone there. They've all been anticipating your arrival. We have two goals at the waterfront: to teach our youngsters water skills and to teach our youngsters water safety."

"I learned the principles of both at Panzer, Mr. Blomback. I run the phys ed classes at Chancellor Avenue School with safety as my first concern."

"The parents have put their children in our care for the summer months," said Mr. Blomback. "Our job is not to fail them. We haven't had a single waterfront accident here since I bought the camp eighteen years ago. Not one."

"You can trust me, sir, to make safety foremost."

"Not a single accident," Mr. Blomback repeated sternly. "Waterfront director is one of the most responsible positions in the camp. Maybe the most responsible. A camp can be ruined by one careless accident in the water. Needless to say, every camper has a water buddy in his own grade. They must enter and leave the water together. A checkup for buddies is made before each swim and after each swim and at intervals during the swim. Lone swimming can result in fatalities."

"I think of myself as a responsible person, sir. You can rely on me to ensure the safety of every camper. Rest assured, I know about the importance of the buddy system."

"Okay, they're still serving lunch," Mr. Blomback said. "Today it's macaroni and cheese. Dinner is roast beef. Friday night is roast beef night at Indian Hill, rationing or no rationing. Come with me to the dining lodge and we'll get you something to eat. And here—here's a camp polo shirt. Take off your tie, slip it over your shirt for now, and we'll go to lunch. Irv Schlanger left his sheets, blankets, and towels. You can use them. Laundry pickup is Mondays."

The shirt was the same as the one Mr. Blomback was wearing: on the front was the name of the camp and beneath it the teepee in a circle of flames.

The dining lodge, a large timbered pavilion with open sides only steps along a wooden walkway from Mr. Blomback's lakeside office, was swarming with campers, the girls and their counselors seated at round tables on one side of the main aisle and the boys and their counselors on the other. Outside was the mild warmth of the sun—a sun that seemed benign and welcoming rather than malevolent, a nurturing Father Sun, the good god of brightness to a fecund Mother Earth—and the flickering luster of the lake and the lush green mesh of July's growing things, about which he knew barely any more than he knew about the birds. Inside was the noisy clamor of children's voices reverberating in the spacious lodge, the racket that reminded him of how much he enjoyed being around kids and why it was he loved his work. He'd nearly forgotten what that pleasure was like during the hard weeks of watching out for a menace against which he could offer no protection. These were happy, energetic kids who were not imperiled by a cruel and invisible enemy—they could actually be shielded from mishap by an adult's vigilant attention. Mercifully he was finished with impotently witnessing terror and death and was back in the midst of unworried children brimming with health. Here was work within his power to accomplish.

Mr. Blomback had left him alone with his lunch, saying they'd meet up again when Bucky had finished. In the dining lodge, nobody as yet knew or cared who he was—kids and counselors alike were engaged in a happy frenzy of socializing while they ate, cabinmates talking and laughing, at some tables bursting into song, as though it weren't the hours since breakfast but many years since they'd been together like this. He was searching the tables for Marcia, who herself probably wasn't yet on the lookout for him. On the phone the night before, both had assumed that by the time he was settled into his cabin and got under way at the waterfront, lunch would be long over and that he'd only arrive in the dining lodge at dinnertime.

When he found her table, he was so overjoyed that he had to restrain himself from standing and shouting her name. The truth of it was that during those last three days on the playground he thought he would never see her again. From the moment he'd agreed to the Indian Hill job, he was sure he'd come down with polio and lose everything. But here she was, a strikingly dark-eyed girl with thick, curly, black-black hair that she'd had cut for the summer—there are few true blacks in nature, and Marcia's hair was one of them. Her hair had reached glamorously down to her shoulders when they first

met at a faculty get-together to introduce new staff the previous fall. She appealed to him so on that first afternoon that it
was a while before, face-to-face, he could look straight into her
eyes or could stop himself from ogling her from afar. Then
he'd seen her walking assuredly at the head of her silent class,
leading her pupils through the corridors to the auditorium,
and he fell for her all over again. That the kids called her Miss
Steinberg mesmerized him.

Now she was deeply tanned and wearing a white camp polo
shirt like his, which only enhanced the darkness of her good
looks, and specifically of those eyes, whose irises struck him as
not only darker but rounder than anyone else's, two dream
targets, their concentric circles colored brownish black. He'd
never seen her any prettier, even if she looked less like one of
the counselors than like one of the campers, barely resembling
the tastefully dressed first-grade teacher who already, at twenty-
two, carried herself with the outward composure of an experienced professional. He noticed that her girlish little nose was
dabbed with a white ointment and wondered which she was
treating, sunburn or poison ivy. And then he had the most
cheering thought: *That's* what you worried about up here, that's
what you warned the children about—poison ivy!

There was no way to get Marcia's attention in the midst of
the dining lodge hubbub. Several times he raised an arm in the
air, but she did not see him, even though he held his hand
aloft and waved it about. Then he saw Marcia's sisters, the
Steinberg twins, Sheila and Phyllis, sitting side by side several
tables away from Marcia. They were eleven now and looked
entirely unlike their older sister, freckled youngsters with frizzy
reddish hair and long, painfully skinny legs and noses already
evolving like their father's, and both already nearly as tall as
Marcia. He waved in their direction, but they were talking ani-
matedly with the girls at their table and they didn't see him
either. From the moment he'd met them he'd been completely
won over by Sheila and Phyllis, their vivacity, their intelligence,
their intensity, even by the ungainliness that had begun to
overtake them. I am going to know these two for the rest of
my life, he thought, and the prospect filled him with enormous
pleasure. We will all be part of the same family. And then, all at
once, he was thinking of Herbie and Alan, who had died be-

cause they'd spent the summer in Newark, and of Sheila and Phyllis, kids almost the same age who were flourishing because they were spending the summer at Indian Hill. And then there were Jake and Dave, fighting the Germans somewhere in France while he was ensconced in this noisy funhouse of a summer camp with all these exuberant kids. He was struck by how lives diverge and by how powerless each of us is up against the force of circumstance. And where does God figure in this? Why does He set one person down in Nazi-occupied Europe with a rifle in his hands and the other in the Indian Hill dining lodge in front of a plate of macaroni and cheese? Why does He place one Weequahic child in polio-ridden Newark for the summer and another in the splendid sanctuary of the Poconos? For someone who had previously found in diligence and hard work the solution to all his problems, there was now much that was inexplicable to him about why what happens, happens as it does.

"Bucky!" The twins had spotted him and, above the din, were calling across to him. They were standing by their table and waving their arms. "Bucky! You made it! Hurray!"

He waved back and the twins began pointing excitedly toward where their sister was sitting.

He smiled and mouthed "I see, I see" while the twins called to Marcia, "Bucky's here!"

Marcia stood to look around, so he stood too, and now at last she saw him, and with both of her hands she threw him a kiss. He was saved. Polio hadn't beaten him.

He spent the afternoon at the waterfront, watching as the counselors there—high school boys of seventeen, who hadn't yet reached draft age—put the campers through their swimming drills and exercises. There was nothing that wasn't familiar to him from the Teaching Swimming and Diving course he'd taken at Panzer. He looked to have inherited a beautifully run program and a perfect environment to work in—not an inch of the waterfront looked neglected, the docks, piers, platforms, and diving boards were all in superb condition, and the water was dazzlingly clear. Wooded hills thick with trees rose steeply all along the edge of the lake. The campers' cabins were tucked into low hills on the near side of the lake, the girls' camp beginning at the end of one wing of the dining lodge and the boys' at the other. About a hundred yards out there was a small wooded island covered with slanting trees whose bark appeared to be white. This must be the island where Marcia had said they could go to be safely alone.

She had managed to leave a note for him with the secretary at Mr. Blomback's office: "I couldn't believe my eyes, seeing my future husband here. I can get off at 9:30. Meet you outside the dining lodge. As the kids like to say, 'You send me.' M."

When the last of the swimming classes was over and the campers returned to their cabins to get ready for Friday night dinner and the movie that would follow, Bucky remained alone at the waterfront, delighted by how his first hours on the job had gone and elated by the company of all these unworried, wonderfully active children. He'd been in the water getting to know the counselors and how they worked and helping the kids with their strokes and their breathing, so he hadn't a chance to step out on the high board and dive. But all afternoon he'd been thinking about it, as if when he took that first dive he would be truly here.

He walked out along the narrow wooden pier that led to the high board, removed his glasses, and set them at the foot of the ladder. Then, half blind, he climbed to the board. Looking out, he could see his way to the edge of the board but distinguish little beyond that. The hills, the woods, the white island, even the lake had disappeared. He was alone on the board above the lake and could barely see a thing. The air was warm, his body was warm, and all he could hear was the pock of tennis balls being hit and the occasional clank of metal on metal where some campers off in the distance were pitching horseshoes and striking the stake. And when he breathed in, there was nothing to smell of Secaucus, New Jersey. He filled his lungs with the harmless clean air of the Pocono Mountains, then bounded three steps forward, took off, and, in control of every inch of his body throughout the blind flight, did a simple swan dive into water he could see only the instant before his arms broke neatly through and he plumbed the cold purity of the lake to its depths.

*

At five forty-five, he was nearing the entrance to the dining lodge with the boys from his cabin when two campers broke away from a crowd of girls drifting in with their counselors and began calling his name. They were the Steinberg girls, twins so alike that, even up close, he had trouble telling them apart. "It's Sheila! It's Phyllis!" he cried as they hurled themselves into his arms. "You two look terrific," he said. "Look how dark you are. And you've grown again. Darn it, you're as tall as I am." "Taller!" they shouted, squirming all over him. "Oh, don't say that," Bucky said, laughing, "please, not taller already!" "Are you going to put on a diving exhibition?" one of them said. "Nobody's asked me to so far," he replied. "We're asking you to! A diving exhibition for the whole camp! All those twisting and backward things that you do in the air."

The girls had seen him dive a couple of months back, when he'd been invited down the shore to the Steinbergs' summer home in Deal for the Memorial Day weekend, and they'd all gone together to the swim club at the beach where the Steinbergs were members. It was the first time he'd been an overnight guest of the family's, and once he'd put aside his jitters about what someone of his background might talk about with such educated people, he found that Marcia's mother and father couldn't have been more kind and companionable. He remembered the pleasure he had taken in giving the twins basic instruction, at the low board of the swimming pool, on balancing themselves and taking off. They were timid to begin with, but by the end of the afternoon he had them doing straight dives off the board. By then he was their matinee idol, and they would wrest him from their older sister at every opportunity. And he was taken with them, the girls Dr. Steinberg appreciatively referred to as his "identically sparkling duo."

"I missed you two," he said to the twins. "Are you staying for the rest of the summer?" they asked. "I sure am." "Because Mr. Schlanger went into the army?" "That's right." "That's what Marcia said, but at first we thought she was dreaming." "I think I'm dreaming, being here," Bucky replied. "I'll see you girls later," he said, and, showing off for their cabinmates, they each lifted their faces to kiss him demonstratively on the lips. And, as they ran for the dining lodge entrance, no less demonstratively, they called, "We love you, Bucky!"

He ate next to the Comanche cabin counselor, Donald Kaplow, a seventeen-year-old who was a track-and-field enthusiast and threw the discus for his high school. When Bucky told him that he threw the javelin, Donald said that he had brought his equipment with him to camp, and whenever he had time off he practiced his throws in an open hayfield back of the girls' camp, where they held the big Indian Pageant in August. He wondered if Bucky would come along sometime to watch and give him some pointers. "Sure, sure," said Bucky.

"I watched you this afternoon," Donald said. "From the porch of our cabin you can see the lake. I watched you dive. Are you a competitive diver?"

"I can do the elementary competitive dives, but, no, I'm not a competitor."

"I never got my dives down. I repeat all kinds of ridiculous mistakes."

"Maybe I can help," Bucky said.

"Would you?"

"If there's time, sure."

"Oh, that's great. Thanks."

"We'll take them one by one. All you probably need are a few faults corrected and you'll be fine."

"And I'm not hogging your time?"

"Nope. If and when I have the time, it's yours."

"Thanks again, Mr. Cantor."

When he looked over to the girls' side of the dining lodge to see if he could find Marcia, he caught the eye of one of the Steinberg twins, who frantically waved her arm at him. He smiled and waved back and realized that in less than a day he had rid himself of his polio thoughts, except for a few minutes earlier, when he was reminded by Donald of Alan Michaels. Though Donald was five years older and already six feet tall, they were both nice-looking boys with broad shoulders and lean frames and long, strong legs, both avid to latch on to an instructor who could help them improve themselves at sports. Boys like Alan and Donald, seeming to sense right off the depth of his devotion to teaching and his capacity to give them assurance where they needed it, were quickly drawn into his mentoring orbit. Had Alan lived, he more than likely would have grown into an adolescent much like Donald Kaplow. Had Alan lived, had Herbie Steinmark lived, Bucky more than likely wouldn't be here and the unimaginable wouldn't be happening at home.

He and Marcia canoed across the lake—he'd never been in a canoe before, but Marcia showed him how to handle the paddle, and watching her, he picked it up after only a few strokes. They moved slowly into the dark, and when they reached the narrow island, which was far longer than he'd realized at the boys' waterfront, they steered around to the far side, where they dragged the canoe ashore and pulled it back into a small grove of trees. They had hardly spoken from the time they touched hands outside the dining lodge and hurried over to the girls' waterfront to silently lift a canoe from the rack there.

There was no moon, no stars, no light except from a few of the cabins on the hillside back on shore. There had been the roast beef dinner in the dining lodge—where Donald Kaplow, with a boy's voracious appetite, had downed slice after slice of juicy red meat—and now there was a movie playing in the rec hall for the older kids, so the only sound that carried from the camp was the distant noise of the movie track. Close by they could hear the orchestral thrumming of frogs, and from far away a long rumble of thunder was audible every few minutes. The drama of the thunder didn't make their being alone together on the wooded island in their khaki shorts and camp polo shirts any less momentous or diminish the stimulus of their scanty clothes. Their arms and legs bare, they stood in a little cleared patch in among the trees, the two so close to each other that he could plainly see her despite the dark. Marcia, on her own, had gone out in the canoe and prepared the clearing a few nights earlier, readying the spot for their rendezvous by using her hands to rake away the leaves that had piled up the previous fall.

All around them the island was thickly packed with clusters of trees, which weren't entirely white, as they had looked to him from the waterfront, but bore black slashes encircling their bark as though they'd been scarred by a whip. The trunks of a number of them were bent or broken, some growing almost doubled over, some jaggedly torn apart halfway to the ground, some completely sheared off, ravaged by the weather or disease. The trees still intact were so elegantly slender that he could have wrapped his fingers around any one of them with as little difficulty as when he playfully clasped one of Marcia's thighs in the ring of his ten strong fingers. The upper branches and drooping branchlets of the undamaged trees spanned the clearing, creating a latticed dome of saw-toothed leaves and delicately thin, overarching limbs. It was a perfect hideaway, sequestration such as they could only dream about while, necking heavily on the Steinbergs' front porch, they attempted to muffle those readily identifiable noises that signal arousal, intense pleasure, and climax.

"What do you call these trees?" he asked, putting his hand out to touch one. All at once, he had become inexplicably shy, just as when they had been introduced at that first faculty get-together and he found himself moving woodenly and with a ridiculously unnatural expression on his face. She had surprised him by extending her little hand to shake, and he was so befuddled that he wasn't sure what to do with it—the allure of her petite figure left him unable even to think of how to address her. The encounter had been colossally embarrassing for someone whose grandfather had raised him to believe that he must consider nothing beyond his strength to undertake, least of all saying hello to a girl who probably didn't weigh a hundred pounds.

"Birches," she answered. "They're white birches—silver birches."

"Some of the bark is peeling away." He easily stripped a swatch of thin silvery bark from the tree trunk under his hand and showed it to her, there in the dark, as though they were children on a nature hike.

"The Indians used birch bark for canoes," she told him.

"Of course," he said. "Birch bark canoes. I never thought it was the name of a tree."

There was silence between them while they listened to the mumble of the movie voices floating over the water and the thunder far away and the frogs nearby and the thud of something across the lake knocking against the swimming dock or the piers. His heartbeat quickened when he realized it could be Mr. Blomback, coming after them in another canoe.

"Why are there no birds out here?" he asked finally.

"There are. Birds don't sing at night."

"Don't or do?"

"Oh, Bucky," she whispered beseechingly, "must we really go on like this? Undress me, please. Undress me now."

After their weeks of separation, he had needed her to tell him that. He needed this intelligent girl to tell him everything, really, about life beyond the playground and the athletic field and the gym. He needed her entire family to tell him how to live a grown man's life in all the ways that nobody, including his grandfather, had yet done.

Instantly he undid the belt and the buttons on her shorts and slid them down over her legs to the ground. Meanwhile, she raised her arms like a child, and first he took the flashlight she was carrying out of her hand and then he gently pulled the polo shirt off over her head. She reached around to unhook her bra while he knelt and, with the bizarre, somewhat shaming sensation that he had lived for this moment, pulled her underpants down her legs and off over her feet.

"My socks," she said, having already kicked off her sneakers. He pulled off her socks and stuffed them into the sneakers. The socks were spotless and white and, along with the rest of what she was wearing, faintly fragrant of bleach from the camp laundry.

Without her clothes, she was small and slim, with beautifully formed, lightly muscled legs and thin arms and fragile wrists and tiny breasts, affixed high on her chest, and nipples that were soft, pale, and unprotuberant. The slender elfin female body looked as vulnerable as a child's. She certainly didn't look like someone familiar with copulation, nor was that far from the truth. One late-fall weekend when the rest of her family was away in Deal and when, at about four on a Saturday afternoon, with the shades pulled down in her bedroom on Goldsmith Avenue, he had taken her virginity—and lost his own —she had whispered to him afterward, "Bucky, teach me about sex," as if of the two of them she were the less experienced. They lay together on the bed for hours after that—*her* bed, he had thought, the very four-poster with carved posts and a flowered chintz canopy and a ruffled skirt in which she had been sleeping since childhood—while she, in a soft confiding voice, as though there were indeed others in the empty house, spoke of her unbelievable good luck in having not just her wonderful family but Bucky to love too. He then told her more than he ever had before about his boyhood, expressing himself more easily with her than he had with any girl he'd ever known, with *anyone* he'd ever known, revealing all he normally kept to himself about what made him happy and what made him sad. "I was the son of a thief," he admitted and found himself able to speak these words to her without a trace of shame. "He went to jail for stealing money. He's an ex-convict. I've never seen him. I don't know where he lives, or even if he's alive or dead. If he had raised me, who's to know if I wouldn't have turned out to be a thief myself? On my own, without grandparents like mine, in a neighborhood like mine," he told her, "it wouldn't have been hard to end up a bum."

Lying face-to-face in the four-poster, they went on with their stories until it was dusk, then dark, until both had said just about everything and revealed themselves to each other as fully as they knew how. And then, as if he weren't sufficiently captivated by her, Marcia whispered into his ear something she had just then learned. "This is the only way to talk, isn't it?"

"You," Marcia whispered after he'd undressed her. "Now you."

Quickly he pulled off his things and set them down next to hers at the edge of their clearing.

"Let me look at you. Oh, thank God," she said and burst into tears. He quickly gathered her into his arms, but it did not help. She sobbed without restraint.

"What is it?" he asked her. "What's the matter?"

"I thought you were going to die!" she exclaimed. "I thought you were going to become paralyzed and die! I couldn't sleep, I was so frightened. I'd come out here whenever I could to be alone and pray to God to keep you healthy. I never prayed so hard for anyone in my life. 'Please protect Bucky!' I'm crying like this out of happiness, darling! Such great, great happiness! You're here! You didn't get it! Oh, Bucky, hold me tight, hold me as close as you can! You're safe!"

*

When they were dressed and ready to return to camp, he could not help himself and instead of chalking up her words to how relieved she was and forgetting them, he said what he shouldn't have said about her praying to the god whom he had repudiated. He knew there was no good reason to conclude this momentous day by returning to a subject so inflammatory, especially as he'd never heard her speak like that before and probably wouldn't ever again. It was a subject entirely too grave for the moment, and irrelevant, really, now that he was here. Yet he could not restrain himself. He'd been through too much back in Newark to squelch his feelings—and he'd left Newark and its pestilence a mere twelve hours ago.

"Do you really think God answered your prayers?" he asked her.

"I can't really know, can I? But you're here, aren't you? You're healthy, aren't you?"

"That doesn't prove anything," he said. "Why didn't God answer the prayers of Alan Michaels's parents? They must have prayed. Herbie Steinmark's parents must have prayed. They're good people. They're good Jews. Why didn't God intervene for them? Why didn't He save their boys?"

"I honestly don't know," Marcia helplessly answered.

"I don't either. I don't know why God created polio in the first place. What was He trying to prove? That we need people on earth who are crippled?"

"God didn't create polio," she said.

"You think not?"

"Yes," she said sharply, "I think not."

"But didn't God create everything?"

"That isn't the same thing."

"Why isn't it?"

"Why are you arguing with me, Bucky? What are we arguing *for*? All I said was that I prayed to God because I was frightened for you. And now you're here and I'm overwhelmingly happy. And out of that you've made an argument. Why do you want to fight with me when we haven't seen each other for weeks?"

"I don't want to fight," he said.

"Then don't," she said, more bewildered than angry.

All this while the thunder had been rolling in regularly and the lightning flickering nearby.

"We should go," she said. "We should get back while the storm is still a way off."

"But how can a Jew pray to a god who has put a curse like this on a neighborhood of thousands and thousands of Jews?"

"I don't know! What exactly are you driving at?"

He was suddenly afraid to tell her—afraid that if he persisted in pressing her to understand what he did, he would lose her and the family with her. They had never before argued or clashed over anything. Never once had he sensed in his loving Marcia a speck of opposition—or she in him, for that matter —and so, just in time, before he began to ruin things, Bucky reined himself in.

Together they dragged the canoe down to the edge of the lake, and within moments, without speaking, they were vigorously paddling toward camp and arrived well before the downpour began.

Donald Kaplow and the other boys were asleep when Bucky entered the Comanche cabin and made his way down the narrow aisle between the footlockers. Quietly as he could, he got into his pajamas, stowed away his clothes, and slid between the fresh sheets that formerly belonged to Irv Schlanger and that he'd made the bed with earlier in the day. He and Marcia had not parted pleasantly, and he continued to feel the distress from when they'd hurriedly kissed good night at the landing and, each fearing that something other than God might lie at the root of their first quarrel, had run off in opposite directions for their cabins.

The rain began pounding on the cabin roof while Bucky lay awake thinking about Dave and Jake fighting in France in a war from which he'd been excluded. He thought of Irv Schlanger, the draftee who'd gone off to war after having slept only the night before in this very bed. Time and again it seemed as if everybody had gone off to war except him. To have been preserved from the fighting, to have escaped the bloodshed—all that someone else might have considered a boon, he saw as an affliction. He was raised to be a fearless battler by his grandfather, trained to think he must be a hugely responsible man, ready and fit to defend what was right, and instead, confronted with the struggle of the century, a worldwide conflict between good and evil, he could not take even the smallest part.

Yet he *had* been given a war to fight, the war being waged on the battlefield of his playground, the war whose troops he had deserted for Marcia and the safety of Indian Hill. If he could not fight in Europe or the Pacific, he could at least have remained in Newark, fighting their fear of polio alongside his endangered boys. Instead he was here in this haven devoid of danger; instead he had chosen to leave Newark for a summer camp atop a secluded mountain, concealed from the world at the far end of a narrow unpaved road and camouflaged from the air by a forest of trees—and doing what there? Playing with children. And happy at it! And the happier he felt, the more humiliating it was.

Despite the heavy rain drilling on the cabin roof and turning the grassy playing fields and the worn dirt trails into an enormous soggy puddle, despite the boom of thunder reverberating through the range of mountains and lightning jaggedly branching downward all around the camp, none of the boys in the two rows of bunks so much as stirred in their sleep. This simple, cozy log cabin—with its colorful school pennants and its decorated canoe paddles and its sticker-laden footlockers and its narrow camp beds with shoes, sneakers, and sandals lined up beneath them, with its securely sleeping crew of robust, healthy teenage boys—seemed as far from war, from *his* war, as he could have gotten. Here he had the innocent love of his two future sisters-in-law and the passionate love of his future wife; here he already had a boy like Donald Kaplow eagerly seeking instruction from him; here he had a marvelous waterfront to preside over and dozens of energetic youngsters to teach and encourage; here, at the end of the day, he had the high board to dive from in peace and tranquillity. Here he was shielded by as secure a refuge as you could find from the killer on the rampage at home. Here he had everything that Dave and Jake were without and that the kids on the Chancellor playground were without and that everyone in Newark was without. But what he no longer had was a conscience he could live with.

He would have to go back. Tomorrow he would have to

take a train from Stroudsburg and, once back in Newark, make contact with O'Gara and tell him he wanted to resume work at the playground on Monday. Since the recreation department was short-handed because of the draft, there should be no problem recovering his job. In all, he would have been gone from the playground for a day and a half—and no one could say that a day and a half off in the Poconos constituted negligence or desertion.

But wouldn't Marcia take his returning to Newark as a blow, as somehow castigating her, especially since their evening on the island had ended unhappily? If he picked up and left tomorrow, what repercussions would that have for their plans? He already intended to go into town as soon as he had an hour free and, with the fifty dollars he'd drawn out of the savings account for his grandmother's stove, buy Marcia an engagement ring at the local jewelry store . . . But he could not worry—not about Marcia's ring, not about Marcia's misunderstanding why he was going, not about leaving Mr. Blomback in the lurch, not about disappointing Donald Kaplow or the Steinberg twins. He had made a profound mistake. Rashly, he had yielded to fear, and under the spell of fear he had betrayed his boys and betrayed himself, when all he'd had to do was stay where he was and do his job. Marcia's lovingly trying to rescue him from Newark had led to his foolishly undermining himself. The kids here would do fine without him. This was no war zone. Indian Hill was where he *wasn't* needed.

Outside, just when it seemed it could not come down any harder, the rain reached a startling crescendo and began gushing like floodwater down the cabin's pitched roof and over the brimming gutters and sweeping past the closed windows in plummeting sheets. Suppose it were to rain like this in Newark, suppose it were to rain there for days on end, millions and millions of water drops slashing the houses and alleyways and streets of the city—would that wash the polio away? But why speculate about what was not and could not be? He had to head home! His impulse was to get up and pack his belongings in his duffel bag so as to be ready to catch the first morning train. But he didn't want to wake the boys or make it look as if he were rushing off in a panic. It was his rushing here that had been undertaken in a panic. He was leaving after having recovered his courage for an ordeal whose reality was undeniable, yet an ordeal whose hazards couldn't compare to those that threatened Dave and Jake as they battled to extend the Allied foothold in France.

As for God, it was easy to think kindly of Him in a paradise like Indian Hill. It was something else in Newark—or Europe or the Pacific—in the summer of 1944.

By the next morning the wet world of the storm had vanished, and the sun was too brilliant, the weather too invigorating, the high excitement of the boys beginning their new day unfettered by fear too inspiring for him to imagine never awakening again within these cabin walls plastered with pennants from a dozen schools. And jeopardizing their future by precipitously abandoning Marcia was too horrifying to contemplate. The view from the cabin porch of the ripple-free gloss of the lake into which he had dived so deeply at the end of his first day and, in the distance, of the island where they had canoed to make love beneath the canopy of birch leaves—to divest himself of this after just one day was impossible. He was even fortified by the sight of the soaked floorboards at the entrance to the cabin, where the wind had whipped the raindrops across the porch and through the screen door—even that ordinary marker of a torrential downpour somehow sustained him in his decision to stay. Under a sky scoured to an eggshell smoothness by that driving storm, with birds calling and flying about overhead, and in the company of all these exhilarated kids, how could he do otherwise? He wasn't a doctor. He wasn't a nurse. He could not return to a tragedy whose conditions he was impotent to change.

Forget about God, he told himself. Since when is God your business anyway? And, enacting the role that was his business, he headed off for breakfast with the boys, filling his lungs with fresh mountain air purified of all contaminants. While they trooped across the grassy slope of the hill, a rich moist green smell, brand new to him, rose from the rain-soaked earth and seemed to certify that he was indisputably in tune with life. He had always lived in a city flat with his grandparents and had never before felt on his skin that commingling of warmth and coolness that is a July mountain morning, or known the fullness of emotion it could excite. There was something so enlivening about spending one's workday in this unbounded space, something so beguiling about stripping Marcia of her clothes in the dark of an empty island apart from everyone, something so thrilling about going to sleep beneath a blitz-krieg of thunder and lightning and awakening to what looked like the first morning ever that the sun had shone down on human activity. I'm here, he thought, and I'm happy—and so he was, cheered even by the squishing sound made by tramp-ing on the sodden grass cushioning his every step. It's all here! Peace! Love! Health! Beauty! Children! Work! What else was there to do but stay? Yes, everything he saw and smelled and heard was a telling premonition of that phantom, future hap-piness.

Later in the day there was an unusual incident, one said never to have occurred at the camp before. A huge swarm of butterflies settled over Indian Hill, and for about an hour in the middle of the afternoon they could be seen erratically dip-ping and darting over the playing fields and thickly perched on the tape of the tennis nets and alighting on the clusters of milkweed growing plentifully at the fringe of the camp grounds. Had they been blown in overnight on the strong storm winds? Had they lost their way while migrating south? But why would they be migrating so early in the summer? Nobody, not even the nature counselor, knew the answer. They appeared en masse as if to scrutinize every blade of grass, every shrub, every tree, every vine stem, fern frond, weed, and flower petal in the mountaintop camp before reorienting them-selves to resume their flight to wherever it was they were headed.

While he stood in the hot sun at the dock, watching the faces full of sunlight bobbing about in the water, one of the butterflies landed on Bucky and began to sip on his bare shoulder. Miraculous! Imbibing the minerals of his perspira-tion! Fantastic! Bucky remained motionless, observing the butterfly out of the corner of his eye until the thing levitated and was suddenly gone. Later, recounting the episode to the boys in the cabin, he told them that his butterfly looked as though it had been designed and painted by the Indians, with its veined wings patterned in orange and black and the black edging minutely dotted with tiny white spots—what he did not tell them was that he was so astonished by the gorgeous butterfly's feeding on his flesh that when it flew off he allowed himself to half believe that this too must be an omen of bounteous days to come.

Nobody at Indian Hill was afraid of the butterflies blanketing the camp and brightly clouding the air. Rather, everyone smiled with delight at all that silent, spirited flitting about, campers and counselors alike thrilled to feel themselves engulfed by the weightless fragility of those innumerable, colorful fluttering wings. Some campers came racing out of their cabins wielding butterfly nets that they'd made in crafts, and the youngest children ran madly after the rising, plunging butterflies, trying to catch them with their outstretched hands. Everybody was happy, because everybody knew that butterflies didn't bite or spread disease but disseminated the pollen that made seed plants grow. What could be more salutary than that?

Yes, the playground in Newark was behind him. He would not leave Indian Hill. There he was prey to polio; here he was food for butterflies. Vacillation—a painful weakness previously unknown to him—would no longer subvert his assurance of what needed to be done.

By this point in the summer, the beginners in the boys' camp had progressed beyond blowing bubbles in the water and practicing the face-down float and were at least swimming the dog paddle; many were beyond that, well into the elementary backstroke and crawl, and a few of the beginners were already jumping into the deep water and swimming twenty feet to the shallow edge of the lake. He had five counselors on his staff, and though they seemed adept at handling boys of all ages and at conducting the swimming program under his supervision, Bucky found himself, from the first day, drawn into the water to work with what the counselors privately called the "sinkers," the young ones who were least sure of themselves and making the slowest progress and who seemed lacking in natural buoyancy. He would walk out along the pier to the deep-water platform where a counselor was instructing the older boys in diving; he would spend time with kids who were working hard to improve their butterfly stroke; but invariably he would return to the young ones and get down into the water with them and work on their flutter kick and their scissors kick and their frog kick, reassuring them with the support of his hands and just a few words that he was right there and they were in no danger of choking on a mouthful of water, let alone of drowning. By the end of a day at the waterfront he thought, exactly as he had when he began at Panzer, that there could be no more satisfying job for a man than giving a boy learning a sport, along with the basic instruction, the security and confidence that all will be well and getting him over the fear of a new experience, whether it was in swimming or boxing or baseball.

A matchless day, with dozens to come. Before dinner he'd get his wettish welcome on the lips from the twins, who'd be waiting for him at the dining lodge steps and who sent up a cry of "Kiss! Kiss!" the moment he came into sight, and after dinner he had promised Donald Kaplow he would work with him on his dives. Then, at nine-thirty, off to the dark island with his wife-to-be. She'd left another note in an envelope at Mr. Blomback's office. "More. Meet me. M." He had already arranged with Carl to drive him into Stroudsburg during the week so he could buy Marcia's engagement ring.

About half an hour after dinner, while the boys from their cabin played in a pickup softball game on the diamond by the flagpole, he and Donald went down to the dock for Bucky to watch Donald's springboard dives. Donald started off with a front dive, a back dive, and a front jackknife.

"Good!" Bucky said to him. "I don't understand what you think is wrong with them."

Donald smiled at the compliment but asked anyway, "Is my approach right? Is my hurdle right?"

"You bet they are," Bucky said. "You know what you want to do and you do it. You do a model jackknife. First the upper part of the body bends over and the legs do nothing. Then the lower part of the body comes up behind while the head and arms are stable. Right in every detail. Do you do a back somersault? Let's see it. Watch out for the board."

Donald was a natural diver and didn't exhibit a single one of the faults that Bucky might have expected to see in the back somersault. When Donald came up from the dive and was still in the water pushing the hair out of his eyes, Bucky called to him, "Good forceful spin. You keep the tuck nice and tight. Timing, balance—great job all around."

Donald climbed out of the water onto the dock, and when Bucky tossed him a towel, he rubbed himself dry. "Is it too chilly out here for you?" Bucky asked. "Are you cold?"

"No, not at all," Donald answered.

The sun was still radiant and the big sky still blue but the temperature had dropped close to ten degrees since dinner. Hard to believe that only days earlier he and his playground boys had been suffering the very heat that incubated the pestilence that was ravaging his city and making people crazy with fear. And dizzying to realize that up here every last thing had changed for the better. If only the temperature in Newark could drop like this and stay like this for the rest of July and August!

"You're shivering," Bucky said. "Let's pick up again same time tomorrow. How about it?"

"But just the forward somersault, please? I'll do it first from the end of the board," Donald said, and he took up his position with his arms in front, his elbows flexed, and his knees slightly bent. "This isn't my best dive," he said.

"Concentrate," Bucky said. "Upward arm lift and then tuck."

Donald readied himself and then dived forward and up, rolled into the tuck, and came down feet-first, making a classic vertical entry into the lake.

"Did I screw up?" Donald asked when he surfaced. He had to shade his eyes from the western sun and the sparkling glare it threw across the water in order to see Bucky clearly.

"Nope," Bucky told him. "Momentarily your hands lost contact with your legs, but that didn't matter much."

"Didn't it? Let me do it again," he said, breaststroking up to the ladder. "Let me get it right."

"Okay, Ace," Bucky said, laughing, and pinning on Donald the nickname he'd been dubbed with on the street as a little kid with pointy ears, back before his grandfather had stepped in to rename him for good. "One last forward somersault and we go inside."

This time, starting from the foot of the board, Donald began with his regular approach and takeoff and expertly completed the dive. His hands moved faultlessly from his shins to the sides of his knees and then to the sides of his thighs in the break.

"Great!" Bucky called to him as he emerged at the surface. "Great height, great spin. Nice and forceful from beginning to end. Where are all those mistakes you told me you make? You don't make any."

"Mr. Cantor," he said excitedly as he climbed back onto the dock, "let me show you my half twist and my back jackknife and then we'll go in. Let me finish the sequence. I'm not cold, really."

"But I am," Bucky said, laughing, "and I'm dry and have a shirt on."

"Well," replied Donald, "that's the difference between seventeen and twenty-four."

"Twenty-three," said Bucky, laughing again and as pleased as he could be—pleased by Donald and his perseverance and filled with contentment knowing that Marcia and the twins were only steps away. It was almost as if they were a family already. As if Donald, only six years his junior, were Marcia's and his own son and, incongruously, the twins' nephew. "Look," he said, "the temperature is going down by the minute. We've got the whole rest of the summer to practice out here." And he tossed Donald his sweatshirt to put on and, for good measure, had him wrap the towel around the waist of his wet trunks.

On the trudge up the slope to the cabin, Donald said, "I want to join the naval air corps when I'm eighteen. My best friend went in a year ago. We write all the time. He told me about the training. It's tough. But I want to get into the war before it ends. I want to fly against the Japs. I've wanted to since Pearl Harbor. I was fourteen when the war began, old enough to know what was happening and to want to do something about it. I want to be in on it when the Japs surrender. What a day that's going to be."

"I hope you get the chance," Bucky told him.

"What kept you out, Mr. Cantor?"

"My eyesight. These things." He tapped his glasses with a fingernail. "I've got my closest buddies fighting in France. They jumped into Normandy on D-Day. I wish I could have been with them."

"I follow the war in the Pacific," Donald said. "In Europe

it's going to be quick now. This is the beginning of the end for Germany. But in the Pacific there's still plenty of fighting to be done. Last month, in the Marianas, we destroyed one hundred forty Jap planes in two days. Imagine being in on that."

"There's plenty of fighting left on both fronts," Bucky told him. "You won't miss out."

As they mounted the Comanche cabin steps, Donald asked, "Can you watch the rest of the dives after dinner tomorrow night?"

"Sure I can."

"And thanks, Mr. Cantor, for giving me all that time."

And there on the cabin porch, Donald reached out a bit stiffly to shake his hand—a surprising formality with its own ingratiating appeal. One session at the diving board and already they were like old friends, though while standing there with Donald at the end of a beautiful summer day, Bucky was unexpectedly stung by the thought of all the boys he'd abandoned on the playground. Try as he would to take delight in everything here, he couldn't yet succeed entirely in shutting out the inexcusable act and the place where he was no longer esteemed.

Between the time that he left Donald and had arranged to meet Marcia, he went to the phone booth back of the camp office to call his grandmother. Probably he wasn't going to catch her in, because she would be sitting outside on a beach chair with the Einnemans and the Fishers, but as it happened, though the heat was supposed to return again the next day, the city had cooled off for twenty-four hours and she was able to sit in their flat with the windows open and the fan on and to listen to her programs on the radio. She asked how he was and how Marcia and the twins were, and when he told her that he and Marcia were getting engaged, she said, "I don't know whether to laugh or cry. My Eugene."

"Laugh," he said, laughing.

"Yes, I'm happy for you, darling," she said, "but I wish your mother had lived to see this. I only wish she had lived to see the man her son turned out to be. I wish Grandpa could be here. He would be excited for his boy. So proud. Dr. Steinberg's daughter."

"I wish he could be here too, Grandma. I think about him up here," Bucky said. "I thought about him yesterday when I went off the high board. I remembered how he taught me to swim at the Y. I was about six. He threw me into the pool and that was it. How are you, Grandma? Are the Einnemans looking after you all right?"

"Of course they are. Don't you worry about me. The Einnemans are very helpful, and I can take care of myself anyway. Eugene, I have to tell you something. There have been thirty new cases of polio in the Weequahic section. Seventy-nine in the city in just the last day. Nineteen dead. All records. And there have been more cases of polio at the Chancellor playground. Selma Shankman called me. She told me the boys' names and I wrote them down."

"Who are they, Grandma?"

"Let me get my glasses. Let me get the piece of paper," she said.

Several counselors were now standing in line outside the booth waiting to use the phone, and he signaled to them through the glass that he would be only another few minutes. Meanwhile, he waited in dread to hear the names. Why cripple children, he thought. Why a disease that cripples children? Why destroy our irreplaceable children? They're the best kids in the world.

"Eugene?"

"I'm here."

"All right. These are the names. These are the boys who are hospitalized. Billy Schizer and Erwin Frankel. And one death."

"Who died?"

"A boy named Ronald Graubard. He got sick and died overnight. Did you know him?"

"I know him, Grandma, yes. I know him from the playground and from school. I know them all. Ronnie is dead. I can't believe it."

"I'm sorry to have to tell you," his grandmother said, "but I thought, because you were so close to all those boys, you would want to know."

"You were right. Of course I want to know."

"There are people in the city who are calling for a quarantine of the Weequahic section. There's talk from the mayor's office about a quarantine," she told him.

"A quarantine of all of Weequahic?"

"Yes. Barricading it off so nobody can go in or out. They would close it off at the Irvington line and the Hillside line and then at Hawthorne Avenue and at Elizabeth Avenue. That's what it said in tonight's paper. They even printed a map."

"But there are tens of thousands of people there, people who have jobs and have to go to work. They can't just pen people in like that, can they?"

"Things are bad, Eugene. People are up in arms. People are terrified. Everybody is frightened for their children. Thank God you're away. The bus drivers on the eight and fourteen lines say they won't drive into the Weequahic section unless they have protective masks. Some say they won't drive in there at all. The mailmen don't want to deliver mail there. The truck drivers who transport supplies to the stores, to the groceries, to the gas stations, and so on don't want to go in either. Strangers drive through with their windows rolled up no matter how hot it is outside. The anti-Semites are saying that it's because they're Jews that polio spreads there. Because of all the Jews—that's why Weequahic is the center of the paralysis and why the Jews should be isolated. Some of them sound as if they think the best way to get rid of the polio epidemic would be to burn down Weequahic with all the Jews in it. There is a lot of bad feeling because of the crazy things people are saying out of their fear. Out of their fear and out of their hatred. I was born in the city, and I've never known anything like this in my life. It's as if everything everywhere is collapsing."

"Yes, it sounds very bad," he said, dropping the last of his coins into the phone.

"And, Eugene, of course—I almost forgot. They're shutting down the playgrounds. As of tomorrow. Not just Chancellor but all over the city."

"They are? But the mayor was set on keeping them open."

"It's in tonight's paper. All the places where children congregate are being shut down. I have the article in front of me. Movie theaters are shutting down for children under sixteen.

The city pool is shutting down. The public library with all its branches is shutting down. Pastors are shutting down Sunday schools. It's all in the paper. Schools might not open on schedule if things continue like this. I'll read you the opening line. 'There is a possibility that the public schools—'"

"But what does it say specifically about the playgrounds?"

"Nothing. It's just in a list of things that the mayor is now closing."

So if he'd remained in Newark a few days longer, he would never have had to quit. Instead he would have been released, free to do whatever he wanted and to go wherever he liked. If only he'd stayed, he would never have had to phone O'Gara and take what he took from O'Gara. If only he'd stayed, he would never have had to walk out on his kids and look back for a lifetime at his inexcusable act.

"Here. Here's the headline," she said. "'Day's Record in City Polio Cases. Mayor Closes Facilities.' Should I send you the article, darling? Should I tear it out?"

"No, no. Grandma, there are counselors waiting to use the phone and I don't have more change anyway. I have to go. Goodbye for now."

Marcia was waiting by the entrance to the dining lodge, and together, wearing heavy sweaters against the unseasonable cold, they slipped down to the waterfront, where they found the canoe and started off across the lake through a rising mist, the silence broken only by the slurp of the paddle blades dipping into the water. At the island they paddled around to the far side and dragged the canoe ashore. Marcia had brought a blanket. He helped her to shake it open and spread it in the clearing.

"What's happened?" she asked. "What's the matter?"

"News from my grandmother. Seventy-nine new cases in Newark overnight. Thirty new cases at Weequahic. Three new cases at the playground. Two hospitalized and one dead. Ronnie Graubard. A quick, bright little fellow, full of spark, and he's dead."

Marcia took his hand. "I don't know what to say, Bucky. It's dreadful."

He sat down on the blanket and she sat beside him. "I don't know what to say either," he told her.

"Isn't it time for them to close the playground?" she asked.

"They have. They've closed it. They've closed all the playgrounds."

"When?"

"As of tomorrow. The mayor's shutting them down, my grandmother said."

"Well, wasn't that the best thing to do? He should have done it a long time ago."

"I should have stayed, Marcia. For as long as the playground was open, I should never have left."

"But it was only the other day that you got here."

"I left. There's nothing more to say. A fact is a fact. I left."

He drew her close to him on the blanket. "Here," he said. "Lie here with me," and he pressed her body to his. They held each other without speaking. There was nothing more that he knew of to say or to think. He had left while all the boys had stayed, and now two more of them were sick and one was dead.

"Is this what you've been thinking about since you got here? That you left?"

"If I were in Newark I would go to Ronnie's funeral. If I were in Newark I would visit the families. Instead I'm here."

"You can still do that when you get back."

"That's not the same thing."

"But even if you had stayed, what could you have done?"

"It isn't a matter of *doing*—it's a matter of being there! I should be there now, Marcia! Instead I'm at the top of a mountain in the middle of a lake!"

They held each other without speaking. Fifteen minutes must have passed. All Bucky could think of were their names, and all he could see were their faces: Billy Schizer. Ronald Graubard. Danny Kopferman. Myron Kopferman. Alan Michaels. Erwin Frankel. Herbie Steinmark. Leo Feinswog. Paul Lippman. Arnie Mesnikoff. All he could think of was the war in Newark and the boys that he had fled.

Another fifteen minutes must have passed before Marcia spoke again. In a hushed voice she said to him, "The stars are breathtaking. You never see stars like this at home. I'll bet this is the first time you've ever seen a night sky so full of stars."

He said nothing.

"Look," she said, "how when the leaves move they let the starlight through. And the sun," she said a moment later, "did you see the sun this evening just as it was beginning to go down? It seemed so close to camp. Like a gong you could reach out and strike. All that's up there is so vast," she said, still vainly, naively trying to stop him from feeling unworthy, "and we are infinitesimal."

Yes, he thought, and there's something more infinitesimal than us. The virus destroying everything.

"Listen," Marcia said. "Shhh. Hear that?" There had been a social at the rec hall earlier in the evening, and the campers who had stayed behind to clean up must have put a record on the record player to keep them company while they gathered up soda bottles and swept the floor and the rest of the kids went off with their counselors to get ready for lights out. Over the silence of the dark lake came Marcia's favorite song of the summer. It was the song that was playing on the jukebox at Syd's the day Bucky had gone to extend his condolences to Alan's family, the same day he'd learned from Yushy the counterman that Herbie had died too.

" 'I'll be seeing you,' " Marcia sang to him softly, " 'in all the old familiar places—' " And here she stood, pulled him after her, and, determined not to let his spirits drop any further—and not knowing what else to do—she got him to begin to dance.

" 'That this heart of mine embraces,' " she sang, her cheek pressed to his chest, " 'all day through . . .' " And her voice rose appealingly on the elongated "through."

He did as she wanted and obligingly held her to him and, shuffling her slowly around the middle of the clearing that they had made their own, remembered the night before she'd left for Indian Hill at the end of June, when they'd danced together just like this to the radio music on her family's porch. It was a night when all they'd had to be concerned about was Marcia's going away for the summer.

" 'In that small café,' " she sang, her voice thin and whispery, " 'the park across the way . . .' "

Amid the island's little forest of leaning birches, their soft wood bent, as Marcia had explained, from the pounding they took in the hard Pocono winters, the two clung to each other with their unparalyzed arms, swaying together to the music on their unparalyzed legs, pressing together their unparalyzed trunks, and able now to hear the words only intermittently —". . . everything that's light and gay . . . think of you . . . when night is new . . . seeing you"—before the song stopped. Someone across the lake had lifted the arm of the record player and switched it off, and the lights in the rec hall went out one at a time, and they could hear kids calling to one another, "Night! Good night!" Then the flashlights came on, and from the dance floor of the island ballroom, he and Marcia could see points of light flickering here and there as each of the kids— safe, healthy, unafraid, unharmed—traced a path back to the cabins.

"We have each other," Marcia whispered, removing his glasses and hungrily kissing his face. "No matter what happens in the world, we have each other's love. Bucky, I promise, you'll always have me singing to you and loving you and, whatever happens, I'll always be standing at your side."

"We do," he said to her, "we have each other's love." Yet what difference does that make, he thought, to Billy and Erwin and Ronnie? What difference does that make to their families? Hugging and kissing and dancing like lovesick teenagers ignorant of everything—what could that do for anyone?

When he got back to the cabin—everyone there in the deep sleep induced by a day full of hiking and swimming and playing ball—he found a note on his bed from Donald. "Call your grandmother," it said. Call her? But he'd spoken to her only a couple of hours earlier. He sped out the door and raced down to the phone booth wondering what had happened to her and thinking he should never have left her alone to come to camp. Of course she couldn't manage by herself, not when she had those pains in her chest every time she tried to carry anything up the stairs. He'd left her alone and now something had happened.

"Grandma, it's Eugene. What's wrong? Are you all right?"

"I'm all right. I have some news. That's why I called the camp. I didn't want to alarm you, but I thought you would want to know right away. It's not good news, Eugene. I wouldn't have called long distance otherwise. It's more tragedy. Mrs. Garonzik phoned from Elizabeth a few minutes ago. To speak to you."

"Jake," Bucky said.

"Yes," she said. "Jake is dead."

"How? How?"

"In action in France."

"I don't believe it. He was indestructible. He was a brick wall. He was six feet three inches tall and two hundred and fifteen pounds. He was a powerhouse. He can't be dead!"

"I'm afraid it's true, darling. His mother said he was killed in action. In a town whose name I can't remember now. I should have written it down. Eileen is there with the family."

The mention of Eileen shocked him anew. Jake had met Eileen McCurdy in high school, and she'd been Jake's girl throughout his years at Panzer. The two were to marry and set up house in Elizabeth as soon as he returned from the war.

"He was so big and with such good manners," his grandmother was saying. "Jake was one of the nicest boys you ever brought around. I can see him now, eating right in the kitchen here that first night he came home with you for dinner. Dave came too. Jake wanted 'Jewish food.' He ate sixteen latkes."

"He did. Yes, I remember. And we laughed, all of us laughed." Tears were coursing down Bucky's face now. "Dave's alive, though. Dave Jacobs is alive."

"I can't say that I know, darling. There's no way I would know. I assume so. I hope so. I haven't heard anything. But according to tonight's news, the war in France is not going well. They said on the radio that there are many dead. Terrible battles with the Germans. Many dead and many wounded."

"I can't lose both my friends," Bucky replied weakly, and when he hung up he headed not back to the cabin but down to the waterfront. There, despite the new rush of cold air pushing in, he sat on the diving dock and stared into the darkness, repeating to himself the lionizing epithets by which Jake was known on the sports page of the campus paper—Bruiser Jake, Big Jake, Man Mountain Jake . . . He could no more imagine Jake dead than he could imagine himself dead, which didn't serve, however, to stop his tears.

At about midnight, he walked back to the pier, but instead of going up the hill to the cabin, he turned and went out again along the wooden walkway to the diving dock. He proceeded to pace the length of the walkway until a dim light began to illuminate the lake, and he remembered that in just such a light another of the dearly beloved dead, his grandfather, would drink hot tea out of a glass—tea spiked in winter with a shot of schnapps—before heading off to buy his day's produce at the Mulberry Street market. When school was out Bucky sometimes went with him.

He was still struggling to bring himself under control so as to return to the cabin before anyone awoke, when the birds in the woods started singing. It was dawn at Camp Indian Hill. Soon there'd be the murmur of young voices from the cabins and then the happy shouting would begin.

Once a week, Indian Night was celebrated separately in the boys' and girls' camps. At eight, all the boys came together at the campfire circle in a wide clearing high above the lake. At the center of the circle was a pit lined with flat stones. The logs there were stacked horizontally and laid crisscross in log-cabin style, tapering upward some three feet from the two large, heavy logs at the base. The fire logs were ringed by a stone barrier of small, picturesquely irregular boulders. Some eight or ten feet back from the stone barrier the circle of benches began. The seats were made of split logs and the bases of stone, and they extended concentrically outward until there were four rows in all, divided into three sections. The woods began some twenty feet back of the last row of benches. Mr. Blomback called the structure the Council Ring and the weekly gathering there the Grand Council.

At the edge of the Council Ring there was a teepee, larger and more elaborately embellished than the teepee at the camp entrance. That was the Council Tent, decorated at the top with bands of red, green, yellow, blue, and black, and with a border at the bottom of red and black. There was also a totem pole, whose crest was carved with the head of an eagle, and below that with a large unfurled wing jutting stiffly out to either side. The dominant colors of the totem pole were black, white, and red, the last two being the colors for the camp's color war.

The totem pole stood about fifteen feet high and could be seen by anyone looking up from a boat on the lake. To the west, across the lake, where the girls were holding their own Indian Night, the sun was beginning to set, and full darkness would come by the time the Grand Council was over. Only faintly could you hear the post-dinner kitchen clatter from the dining lodge, while beyond the lake a striated sky drama, a long lava flow of burnt orange and bright pink and bloody crimson, registered the lingering end of the day. An iridescent, slow-moving summer twilight was creeping over Indian Hill, a splashy gift from the god of the horizon, if there was such a deity in the Indian pantheon.

The boys and their counselors—each designated a "brave" for the evening—arrived at Grand Council dressed in outfits that in large part came out of the crafts shop. All wore beaded headbands, fringed tunics that were originally ordinary shirts, and leggings that were trousers stitched with fringe at the outside seam. On their feet they wore moccasins, some cut from leather in the crafts shop and a good many of which were high-top sneakers that had been wrapped like moccasins at the ankle with bead and fringe. A number of the boys had feathers in their headbands—dropped bird plumage that they'd found in the woods—some wore beaded armbands tied inches above the elbow, and many carried canoe paddles that were painted with symbols colored, like the totem pole, in red, black, and white. Others had bows borrowed from the archery shack slung over their shoulders—bows without the arrows—and a few carried simulated tom-toms of tightly drawn calfskin and drum beaters with beaded handles that they made in crafts. Several held in their hands rattles that were decorated baking-powder cans filled with pebbles. The youngest campers used their own bed blankets wrapped around them as Indian robes, which also served to keep them warm as the evening temperature dropped.

Bucky's Indian outfit had been gathered together for him by the crafts counselor. Like the faces of the others, his had been darkened with cocoa powder to simulate an Indian's skin tone, and he had two diagonal stripes—"war paint"—applied to either cheek, one of black drawn with charcoal and the other of red drawn with lipstick. He sat next to Donald Kaplow and with the rest of the Comanche boys, who were seated farther down along the bench. Everywhere the boys loudly talked and joked until two campers carrying calfskin drums got up from the benches and walked to the stone surround of the campfire logs and, facing each other, began to solemnly bang on the drums while those carrying rattles shook them, no two in the same rhythm.

Then everyone turned to look toward the teepee. Mr. Blomback emerged from the oval doorway in a feather headdress, white feathers with brown tips all around his head and trailing behind in a tail down to below his waist. His tunic, his leggings, even his moccasins were elaborately decorated with leather fringe and bands of beadwork and long tufts of what looked like human hair but was probably a woman's hairpiece from the five-and-ten. In one hand he carried a club—"Great Chief Blomback's war club," Donald whispered—that was replete with feathers, and in the other hand a peace pipe, consisting of a long wooden stem ending in a clay bowl and strung along the stem with still more feathers.

All the campers stood until Mr. Blomback stolidly made his way from the teepee to the center of the Council Ring. The drumming and the rattling stopped, and the campers took their seats.

Mr. Blomback handed his war club and peace pipe to the two drummers and, dramatically folding his arms over his chest, looked around at all the campers on the encircling benches. His heavy application of cocoa powder did not altogether cover his prominent Adam's apple, but otherwise he looked astonishingly like a real chief. In years gone by he had saluted the braves Indian fashion—using an upraised right arm with the palm forward—and they would collectively return the salute, simultaneously grunting "Ugh!" But this greeting had to be abandoned with the arrival on the world scene of the Nazis, who employed that salute to signify "Heil Hitler!"

"When first the brutal anthropoid stood up and walked erect," Mr. Blomback began, "—there was man! The great event was symbolized and marked by the lighting of the first campfire."

Donald turned to Bucky and whispered, "We get this every week. The little kids don't understand a word. No worse, I guess, than what happens in shul."

"For millions of years," Mr. Blomback continued, "our race has seen in this blessed fire the means and emblem of light, warmth, protection, friendly gathering, council."

He paused as the roar of an airplane engine passed over the camp. This happened now round the clock. An army air corps base had opened at the beginning of the war some seventy miles to the north, and Indian Hill was on its flyway.

"All the hallow of the ancient thoughts," Mr. Blomback said, "of hearth, fireside, home, is centered on its glow, and the home tie itself is weakened with the waning of the home fire. Only the ancient sacred fire of wood has power to touch and thrill the chords of primitive remembrance. Your campfire partner wins your love, and having camped in peace together— having marveled together at the morning sun, the evening light, the stars, the moon, the storms, the sunset, the dark of night—yours is a lasting bond of union, however wide your worlds may be apart."

Unfolding his two fringed arms, he extended them toward the assembly, and in unison the campers retorted to the stream of grandiloquence: "The campfire is the focal center of all primitive brotherhood. We shall not fail to use its magic."

The drummers now took up their tom-tom beat, and Donald whispered to Bucky, "An Indian historian. Somebody Seton. That's his god. Those are his words. Mr. Blomback uses the same Indian name as Seton: Black Wolf. He doesn't think any of this is nonsense."

Next a figure wearing the mask of a big-beaked bird stood in the front row and approached the ready-laid fire. He bowed his head to Mr. Blomback and then addressed the campers.

"Meetah Kola nayhoon-po omnicheeyay neechopi."

"It's our medicine man," whispered Donald. "It's Barry Feinberg."

"Hear me, my friends," the medicine man continued, translating his Indian sentence into English. "We are about to hold a council."

A boy stepped forward from the first row carrying several pieces of wood in his hand, one shaped like a bow, another a stick about a foot long with a sharpened end, and several smaller pieces. He set them on the ground near the medicine man.

"Now light we the council fire," the medicine man said, "after the manner of the forest children, not in the way of the white man, but—even as Wakonda himself doth light his fire—by the rubbing together of two trees in the storm, so cometh forth the sacred fire from the wood of the forest."

The medicine man knelt, and many of the campers stood to watch as he used the bow and the long, pointed drill and the other odd bits of wood to attempt to ignite a fire.

Donald whispered to Bucky, "This can take a while."

"Can it even be done?" Bucky whispered back.

"Chief Black Wolf can do it in thirty-one seconds. For the campers it's harder. They sometimes have to give in and do it in the way of the helpless white man, by striking a match."

Some of the campers were standing on their benches to get a better look. After a few minutes, Mr. Blomback sidled over to the medicine man and, gesturing as he spoke, quietly gave him some tips.

Everyone waited several minutes more before a whoop went up from the campers, as first there was smoke and then a spark, which when blown upon, ignited a small flame in the tinder of dry pine needles and birch bark shavings. The tinder in turn ignited the kindling at the base of the logs, and the campers chanted in unison, "Fire, fire, fire, burn! Flames, flames, flames, turn! Smoke, smoke, smoke, rise!"

Then, with the mournful loud-soft-soft-soft beat of the two tom-toms, the dancing began: the Mohawks did the snake dance, the Senecas the caribou dance, the Oneidas the dog dance, the Hopis the corn dance, the Sioux the grass dance. In one dance the braves jumped strenuously about with their heads high in the air, in another they did a skipping step on the balls of their feet with a double hop on each foot, in a third they carried deer antlers before them, made of crooked tree limbs bound together. Sometimes they howled like wolves and sometimes they yapped like dogs, and in the end, when it was fully dark and the burning fire alone lit the Council Ring, twenty of the campers, each armed with a war club and wearing necklaces of beads and claws, set out by the light of the fire to hunt Mishi-Mokwa, the Big Bear. Mishi-Mokwa was impersonated by the largest boy in camp, Jerome Hochberger, who slept across the aisle from Bucky. Jerome was wrapped in somebody's mother's old fur coat that he'd pulled up over his head.

"I am fearless Mishi-Mokwa," Jerome growled from within the coat. "I, the mighty mountain grizzly, king of all the western prairies."

The hunters had a leader who was also from Bucky's cabin, Shelly Schreiber. With the drums beating loudly behind him and light from the fire flashing on his painted face, Shelly said, "These are all my chosen warriors. We go hunting Mishi-Mokwa, he the Big Bear of the mountains, he that ravages our borders. We will surely seek and slay him."

Here a lot of the little kids began to call, "Slay him! Slay him! Slay Mishi-Mokwa!"

The hunters gave a war whoop, dancing as though they were bears on their hind legs. Then they set out looking for the trail of the Big Bear by conspicuously smelling the ground. When they reached him, he rose with a loud snarl, eliciting screams of fright from the small boys on the nearby benches.

"Ho, Mishi-Mokwa," said the leader of the hunters, "we have found you. If you do not come before I count to a hundred, I will brand you a coward wherever I go."

Suddenly, the bear sprang up at them, and as the campers cheered, the hunters proceeded to club him senseless with war clubs of straw wrapped in burlap. When he was stretched across the ground in the fur coat, the hunters danced around Mishi-Mokwa, each in turn grasping his lifeless paw and shouting, "How! How! How!" The campers' cheering continued, the delight enormous at finding themselves encompassed by murder and death.

Next, two counselors, a small one and a tall one, identified as Short Feather and Long Feather, told a series of animal tales that made the younger children scream with feigned horror, and then Mr. Blomback, having removed his feather headdress and set it down alongside his peace pipe and war club, led the boys in singing familiar camp songs for some twenty minutes, thus bringing them down to earth from the excitement of playing Indian. This was followed by his saying, "And here's the important war news from last week. Here's what's been happening beyond Indian Hill. In Italy, the British army broke across the Arno River into Florence. In the Pacific, United States assault forces invaded Guam, and Tojo—"

"Boo! Boo, Tojo!" a group of older boys called out.

"Tojo, the premier of Japan," Mr. Blomback resumed, "was ousted as chief of the Japanese army staff. In England, Prime Minister Churchill—"

"Yay, Churchill!"

"—predicted that the war against Germany could come to end earlier than expected. And right here in Chicago, Illinois, as many of you know by now, President Roosevelt was nominated for a fourth term by the Democratic National Convention."

Here a good half of the campers came to their feet, shouting, "Hurray! Hurray, President Roosevelt!" while somebody beat wildly on one of the tom-toms and somebody else shook a rattle.

"And now," said Mr. Blomback when it was quiet again, "bearing in mind the American troops fighting in Europe and the Pacific, and bearing in mind all of you boys who, like me, have relatives in the service, the next-to-last song to end the campfire will be 'God Bless America.' We dedicate it to all of those who are overseas tonight, fighting for our country."

After they had stood to sing "God Bless America," the boys raised their arms in their fringed sleeves, draped them around one another's shoulders, and, with one row of campers swaying in one direction and the rows of campers in front and behind swaying in the other, they sang "Till We Meet Again," the anthem of comradery that calmly brought to a close every Indian Night. When it was sung for the last Indian Night of the season, many of the homebound campers would wind up in tears.

Meanwhile, Bucky alone had been brought to tears by the singing of "God Bless America" and the memory of the great college friend who had not been out of his thoughts since he'd learned of his death fighting in France. Bucky had done his best throughout the ceremonies to attend to what was going on around the fire as well as to listen to Donald quietly kibitzing beside him, but all he could really think about was Jake's death and Jake's life, about all that might have become of him had he lived. While the boys were hunting down the Big Bear, Bucky had been remembering the statewide college meet in the spring of '41 when Jake had set not just a Panzer College record but a U.S. collegiate record by throwing the shot fifty-six feet three inches. How did he do it, a reporter from the *Newark Star-Ledger* had asked him. Grinning widely—and flashing at Bucky his trophy with the tiny bronze shot-putter perched atop it, frozen at the point of the shot's release—Jake told him. "Easy," he said with a wink. "The left shoulder is high, the right shoulder is higher, the right elbow is even higher, and the right hand is the highest. There's the scheme. Follow that, and the shot takes care of itself." Easy. Everything for Jake was easy. He would surely have gone on to throw in the Olympics, would have gone on to marry Eileen as soon as he got home, would have garnered a job in college coaching . . . With all that talent, what could have stopped him?

> Round the campfire
> 'Neath the stars so bright,
> We have met in comradeship tonight.
> Round about the whispering trees
> Guard our golden memories.
> And so, before we close our eyes in sleep
> Let us pledge each other that we'll keep
> Indian Hill's friendships deep,
> Till we meet again.

After the singing of the farewell song, the campers buddied up in pairs and followed their counselors down from the benches around the dying campfire, which a couple of junior counselors stayed behind to extinguish. As they headed back to their cabins with their twinkling flashlights disappearing into the dark woods, an occasional war whoop went up from the departing boys, and some of the blanketed little ones, still under the spell of the blazing fire, could be heard gleefully shouting "How! How! How!" A few, by shining their flashlights upward from their chins while grimacing and widening their eyes, made monster faces to scare each other one last time before Indian Night was over. For close to an hour the voices of laughing and giggling children could be heard reverberating from cabin to cabin, and, even after everyone was asleep, the smell of wood smoke permeated the camp.

It was six untroubled days later—the best days at the camp so far, lavish July light thickly spread everywhere, six masterpiece mountain midsummer days, one replicating the other—that someone stumbled jerkily, as if his ankles were in chains, to the Comanche cabin's bathroom at three A.M. Bucky's bed was at the end of a row just the other side of the bathroom wall, and when he awakened he heard the person in there being sick. He reached under his bed for his glasses and looked down the aisle to see who it was. The empty bed was Donald's. He got up and, with his lips close to the bathroom door, quietly said, "It's Bucky. You need help?"

Donald replied weakly, "Something I ate. I'll be okay." But soon he was retching again, and Bucky, in his pajamas, waited on the edge of his bed for Donald to come out of the bathroom.

Gary Weisberg, whose bed was next to Bucky's, had awakened and, seeing Bucky sitting up, rose on his elbows and whispered, "What's the matter?"

"Donald. Upset stomach. Go back to sleep."

Donald finally emerged from the bathroom and Bucky held his elbow with one hand and slipped an arm around his waist to help him back to bed. He got him under the covers and took his pulse.

"Normal," Bucky whispered. "How do you feel?"

Donald replied with his eyes shut. "Washed out. Chills."

When Bucky put his hand to Donald's forehead it felt warmer than it should. "You want me to take you to the infirmary? Fever and chills. Maybe you should see the nurse."

"I'll be okay," Donald said in a faint voice. "Just need sleep."

But in the morning, with Donald so feeble he couldn't get up from the bed to brush his teeth, Bucky again put his hand to the boy's forehead and said, "I'm taking you to the infirmary."

"It's the flu," Donald said. "Diving in the cold." He tried to smile. "Can't say I wasn't warned."

"Probably the cold did do it. But you're still running a

temperature and you should be in the infirmary. Are you in pain? Does anything hurt?"

"My head."

"Severe?"

"Kind of."

The boys in the cabin had all gone off to breakfast without Donald and Bucky. Rather than waste time having Donald change into his clothes, Bucky slipped Donald's bathrobe over his pajamas in order to walk him in his slippers down to the small infirmary that stood close to the camp entrance. One of Indian Hill's two nurses would be on duty there.

"Let me help you up," Bucky said.

"I can do it," Donald said. But when he went to stand, he was unable to, and, startled, he fell backward onto the bed.

"My leg," he said.

"Which leg? Both legs?"

"My right leg. It's like it's dead."

"We're going to get you to the hospital."

"Why can't I walk?" Donald's voice was suddenly quavering with fear. "Why can't I use my leg?"

"I don't know," Bucky told him. "But the doctors will find out and get you back on your feet. You wait. Try to be calm. I'm calling an ambulance."

He ran as fast as he could down the hill to Mr. Blomback's office, thinking, Alan, Herbie, Ronnie, Jake—wasn't that enough? Now Donald too?

The camp director was in the dining lodge having breakfast with the campers and counselors. Bucky slowed to a walk as he entered the lodge and saw Mr. Blomback in his usual seat at the center table. It was one of the mornings especially loved by the campers, when the cook served pancakes and you could smell the rivers of maple syrup flooding the campers' plates. "Mr. Blomback," he said quietly, "can you step outside a moment? Something urgent."

Mr. Blomback got up and the two of them went out the door and walked a few steps from the dining lodge before Bucky said, "I think Donald Kaplow has polio. I left him in his bed. One leg is paralyzed. His head hurts him. He has a fever and he was up during the night being sick. We better call an ambulance."

"No, an ambulance will alarm everybody. I'll take him to the hospital in my car. You're sure it's polio?"

"His right leg is paralyzed," Bucky replied. "He can't stand on it. His head aches. He's completely done in. Doesn't that sound like polio?"

Bucky ran up the hill while Mr. Blomback got his car and drove after him and parked outside the cabin. Bucky wrapped Donald in a blanket, and he and Mr. Blomback helped him off the bed and out onto the porch that looked down to the lake, the two of them holding him up on either side. In the time Bucky had been gone, Donald's unparalyzed left leg had weakened, so his two feet dragged limply behind him as they carried him down the stairs and into the car.

"Don't speak to anyone yet," Mr. Blomback said to Bucky. "We don't want the kids to panic. We don't want the counselors to panic. I'm taking him to the hospital now. I'll call his family from there."

When Bucky looked at the boy lying in the back seat of the car with his eyes closed and beginning now to struggle to breathe, he remembered how on the second night at the lake Donald had done his dives even more confidently, with greater smoothness and balance, than he had on the first; he remembered how robust he'd been, how after Donald's finishing his repertoire, Bucky had worked with him for half an hour more on a swan dive. And he remembered how with each dive Donald had gotten better and better.

Bucky rapped on the window and Donald opened his eyes. "You're going to be all right," Bucky told him, and Mr. Blomback started away. Bucky ran alongside the car, calling in to Donald, "We're going to be diving again in a matter of days," even though the boy's deterioration was plainly discernible and the look in his eyes was gruesome—two feverish eyes scanning Bucky's face, frantically seeking a panacea that no one could provide.

Fortunately the campers were still at breakfast, and Bucky ran up the cabin steps to make up Donald's bed as best he could without the blanket in which he'd wrapped him. Then he went out onto the porch to look down at the lake, where his staff would be assembling in a little while, and to ask himself the obvious question: Who brought polio here if not me?

The boys in the cabin were told that Donald had been taken to the hospital with stomach flu and was to be kept there until he recovered. In fact, a spinal tap at the hospital confirmed that Donald Kaplow had polio, and his parents were notified by Mr. Blomback, and they set out from their home in Hazleton for Stroudsburg. Bucky put in his day at the waterfront, working with the counselors, spending time in the water with the young kids and at the diving board correcting the dives of the older kids, who were crazy about diving and who would do nothing else all day long if they were allowed. Then, when his workday was over and the campers were back in their cabins, changing out of their dirtied clothes for dinner, he took off his glasses and went up on the high board and for half an hour concentrated on doing every difficult dive he knew. When he was finished and came out of the water and put on his glasses, he still hadn't gotten what had happened out of his mind—the speed with which it had happened or the idea that he had made it happen. Or the idea that the outbreak of polio at the Chancellor playground had originated with him as well. All at once he heard a loud shriek. It was the shriek of the woman downstairs from the Michaels family, terrified that her child would catch polio and die. Only he didn't just hear the shriek —he was the shriek.

They took the canoe to the island again that night. Marcia as yet knew nothing about Donald Kaplow's illness. Mr. Blomback intended to notify the entire camp at breakfast the following morning, in the company of Dr. Huntley, the camp physician from Stroudsburg, who visited the camp regularly and, along with the camp nurses, was usually called upon to treat little more than ringworm, impetigo, pinkeye, ivy poisoning, and, at worst, a broken bone. Though Mr. Blomback expected there would be some parents who would immediately remove their children from the camp, he was hoping that with Dr. Huntley's help in minimizing fear and curtailing any panic, he could carry on operating normally to the end of the season. He had confided this to Bucky when he returned from the hospital and reminded him to say nothing and to leave the announcement to him. Donald's condition had worsened. He now had excruciating muscle and joint pain and would proba-

bly need an iron lung to help him breathe. His parents had
arrived, but by then Donald had been placed in isolation, and
because of the danger of contagion, they hadn't been allowed
to see him. The doctors had commented to Mr. Blomback on
the rapidity with which Donald's flu-like symptoms had evolved
into the most life-threatening strain of the disease.

All of this Bucky recounted to Marcia once they reached the
island.

She gasped at his words. She was seated on the blanket and
put her face in her hands. Bucky was pacing around the clearing, unable as yet to tell her the rest. It had been hard enough
for her to hear about Donald without her having to hear in the
next breath about him.

"I have to talk to my father" were the first words she spoke.
"I have to phone him."

"Why not let Mr. Blomback tell the camp first?"

"He should have told the camp already. You cannot wait
around with a thing like this."

"You think he should disband the camp?"

"That's what I want to ask my father. This is terrible. What
about the rest of the boys in your cabin?"

"They seem to be all right so far."

"What about you?" she asked.

"I feel fine," he said. "I have to tell you, I spent two sessions
at the lake with Donald a few days back. I was helping him
with his dives. He couldn't have been healthier."

"When was that?"

"About a week ago. After dinner. I let him dive in the cold.
That was probably an error. A bad error."

"Oh, Bucky, this isn't your fault. It's just so frightening. I'm
frightened for you. I'm frightened for my sisters. I'm frightened for every kid in the camp. I'm frightened for myself. One
case isn't one case in a summer camp full of kids living side by
side. It's like a lit match in the dry woods. One case here is a
hundred times more dangerous than it is in a city."

She remained seated and he resumed pacing. He was afraid
to approach her because he was afraid to infect her, if he hadn't
infected her already. If he hadn't infected everyone! The little
ones at the lake! His waterfront staff! The twins, whom he
kissed every night at the dining lodge! When, in his agitation,

he removed his glasses to rub nervously at his eyes, the birch trees encircling them looked in the moonlight like a myriad of deformed silhouettes—their lovers' island haunted suddenly with the ghosts of polio victims.

"We have to go back," Marcia said. "I have to phone my father."

"I told Mr. Blomback I wouldn't tell anyone."

"I don't care. I am responsible for my sisters, if nothing else. I have to tell my father what has happened and ask him what to do. I'm scared, Bucky. I'm very scared. It was always as if polio would never notice that there were kids in these woods— that it couldn't find them here. I thought if they just stayed in camp and didn't go anywhere they'd be okay. How could it possibly hunt them down *here*?"

He couldn't tell her. She was too aghast to be told. And he was too confused by the magnitude of it all to do the telling. The magnitude of what had been done. The magnitude of what *he* had done.

Marcia got up from the blanket and folded it, and they pulled the canoe into the water and started back to camp. It was close to ten when they got to the landing. The counselors were up in the cabins getting their campers into bed. The lights were on in Mr. Blomback's office, but otherwise the camp seemed deserted. There was no line waiting to use the pay phone, though there'd be one tomorrow, once word was out about Donald and the turn that camp life had taken.

Marcia closed the folding door of the phone booth so there was no chance of her being overheard by anyone who might be about, and Bucky stood beside the booth, trying to tell from her reactions what Dr. Steinberg was saying. Marcia's voice was muffled, so all Bucky heard standing outside the booth were the insects droning and humming, sending his mind back to that chokingly close evening in Newark when he had sat out on the rear porch with Dr. Steinberg, eating that wonderful peach.

Her distress seemed to lessen once she heard her father's voice at the other end of the phone, and after only a few minutes she lowered herself onto the booth's little seat and talked to him from there. Bucky was supposed to have gone into Strouds-burg with Carl at noon that day to buy her engagement ring.

Now the engagement was forgotten. It was polio only that was on Marcia's mind, as it had been on his all summer. There was no escape from polio, and not because it had followed him to the Poconos but because he had carried it to the Poconos with him. How, Marcia asked, had polio hunted us down here? Through the contagion of the newcomer, her boyfriend! Remembering all the boys who'd gotten polio while he was working earlier in the summer at Chancellor, remembering the scene that had erupted on the field the afternoon Kenny Blumenfeld had to be restrained from assaulting Horace, Bucky thought that it wasn't the moron that Kenny should have wanted to kill for spreading polio—it was the playground director.

Marcia opened the door and stepped out of the booth. Whatever her father told her had calmed her down, and with her arms around Bucky, she said, "I got so frightened for my sisters. I know you'll be all right, you're strong and fit, but I got so worried for those two girls."

"What did your father say?" he asked, speaking with his head turned so that he was not breathing into her face.

"He said that he's going to call Bill Blomback but that it sounds as if he's doing everything there is to do. He says you don't evacuate two hundred and fifty kids because of one case of polio. He says the kids should go on with their regular activities. He says he thinks a lot of parents are going to panic and pull their kids out. But that I shouldn't panic or panic the girls. He asked about you. I said you've been a rock. Oh, Bucky, I feel better. He and my mother are going to drive up this weekend instead of going down the shore. They want to reassure the girls themselves."

"Good," he said, and though he held her tightly, he was mindful to kiss her hair and not her lips when they separated for the night, as if by this time that could alter anything.

The next morning, at the close of breakfast, Mr. Blomback swung the cowbell whose ringing always preceded his announcements to the camp. The campers quieted down as he rose to his feet. "Good morning, boys and girls. I have a serious message to deliver to you this morning," he said, speaking evenly, with nothing in his voice to indicate alarm. "It concerns the health of one of our counselors. He is Donald Kaplow of the Comanche cabin. Donald became ill here two nights ago and yesterday morning awakened with a high fever. Mr. Cantor quickly notified me of Donald's condition, and it was decided that he should be taken to Stroudsburg Hospital. There, tests were performed and it was determined that Donald has contracted polio. His parents have arrived at the hospital to be with him. He is being treated and cared for by the hospital staff. I have Dr. Huntley, the camp physician, here with me, and he wants to say a few words to you."

The counselors and campers were, of course, startled to learn that everything in camp had suddenly changed—that everything in *life* had changed—and they waited in silence to hear what the doctor had to tell them. He was a middle-aged man with an unruffled manner who had been the camp's physician since its inception. He had a bland, reassuring way about him that was enhanced by his rimless spectacles and his thinning white hair and his pale plain face. He was dressed like no one else in camp, in a suit, white shirt, tie, and dark shoes.

"Good morning. For those of you who don't already know me, I'm Dr. Huntley. I know that if and when any of you ever feel ill, you tell your counselor and your counselor arranges for you to see Miss Rudko or Miss Southworth, the camp nurses, and if necessary, you see me. Well, I want to encourage you to continue with this same procedure during the days and weeks ahead. Any sign of illness, promptly notify your counselor, as you always would. If you have a sore throat, if you have a stiff neck, if you have an upset stomach, notify your counselor. If you have a headache, if you think you have a fever, notify your counselor. If you don't feel well generally, notify your counselor. Your counselor will get you to the nurse, who will look after you and who will be in touch with me. Because I want you all to be well so as to enjoy the remaining weeks of the summer."

Having spoken no more than those few calming words, Dr. Huntley sat down and Mr. Blomback stood again. "I want all you campers to know that before the morning is over I am going to phone each of your families to tell them about this development. In the meantime, I'd like to see the head counselors in my office right after breakfast. Everyone else," he said, "that's it for now. Today's program is unchanged. Regular activities. Go out into the sunshine and have a good time—it's another beautiful day."

Marcia rushed off to Mr. Blomback's office with the three other head counselors, and Bucky, instead of going down to the waterfront, which he'd had every intention of doing upon leaving the dining lodge, found himself running to catch up to Dr. Huntley before he stepped into his car, parked by the flagpole, and drove back to town.

Behind him he heard his name called. "Bucky! Wait a minute! Wait for us!" It was the Steinberg twins, racing to catch him. "Wait up!"

"Girls, I have to see Dr. Huntley."

"Bucky," said one of the twins, grabbing his hand, "what are we supposed to *do*?"

"You heard Mr. Blomback. Just go on with your activities."

"But polio—!" When they tried to reach out to hold him around the waist and nuzzle for reassurance against his broad chest, he instantly backed away for fear of breathing into the two identical panic-stricken faces.

"Don't you worry about polio," he said. "There's nothing to worry about. Sheila, Phyllis, I have to run—it's very important," and he left them there unconsoled, cringing up against each other.

"But we need you!" one of them called after him. "Marcia's with Mr. Blomback!"

"This afternoon!" he called back. "I promise! I'll see you soon!"

Dr. Huntley had opened the door to his car and was just getting in when Bucky reached him. "Dr. Huntley, I have to talk to you. I'm the waterfront director in the boys' camp. Bucky Cantor."

"Yes, Bill Blomback mentioned you."

"Dr. Huntley, I have to tell you something. I came up from Newark a week ago Friday. I'd been working there in a playground in the Weequahic neighborhood, where there's an epidemic of polio. Donald Kaplow and I were working out at the waterfront together after dinner for two nights. We've had lunch side by side every day. We pass each other in the cabin. I sat next to him at Indian Night. Now he's come down with polio. Doctor, am I the one who gave it to him? Am I going to give it to others? Is that possible?"

By now Dr. Huntley had stepped out of the car, the better to catch the overwrought words being spoken to him by this perfectly vigorous-looking young man. "How do you feel?" he asked Bucky.

"I feel fine."

"Well, the chances are slight that you are a healthy infected carrier. Though it could happen, it would be a very uncommon abnormality. Most usually, the carrier stage coincides with the clinical stage. But to ease your mind," the doctor said, "to be a hundred percent sure, we should take you in for a spinal tap and draw off some spinal fluid for analysis. Certain changes to spinal fluid are indicative of polio. We should do that right away, this morning, to put your mind at rest. You can drive with me to the hospital, and then we'll call Carl to drive you back here."

Bucky raced down to the waterfront to tell the staff he'd be gone for the morning and to put one of the senior counselors in charge till he returned, and then he met Dr. Huntley, who was waiting for him in his car for the ride into Stroudsburg. If only the test revealed that he was not the person responsible! If only he were about to be proved blameless! Then, when the examination at the hospital was over and everything certified to be okay, he could stop off at the Stroudsburg jewelry store on the way back to camp to buy the engagement ring for Marcia. He hoped to be able to afford something set with a genuine jewel.

Later that day, the cars began to arrive to take campers home. They continued arriving into the late evening and on into the next day, so that within forty-eight hours after Mr. Blomback had announced to the camp at breakfast that one of the counselors had come down with polio, more than a hundred of the two hundred and fifty campers had been removed by their parents. The next day, two more boys in Bucky's cabin—one of them Jerome Hochberger, the big boy in the fur coat who had played the bear on Indian Night—were diagnosed with polio and the entire camp was immediately shut down. Another nine of the Indian Hill campers fell ill and had to be hospitalized with polio when they got home, among them Marcia's sister Sheila.

3

Reunion

WE NEVER saw Mr. Cantor in the neighborhood again. The result of the spinal tap administered at Stroudsburg Hospital came back positive, and though he displayed no symptoms for almost forty-eight hours more, he was rushed onto the contagion ward, where he could have no visitors. And finally the cataclysm began—the monstrous headache, the enfeebling exhaustion, the severe nausea, the raging fever, the unbearable muscle ache, followed in another forty-eight hours by the paralysis. He was there for three weeks before he no longer needed catheterization and enemas, and they moved him upstairs and began treatment with steamed woolen hot packs wrapped around his arms and legs, all of which were initially stricken. He underwent four torturous sessions of the hot packs a day, together lasting as long as four to six hours. Fortunately his respiratory muscles hadn't been affected, so he never had to be moved inside an iron lung to assist with his breathing, a prospect that he dreaded more than any other. And his learning that Donald Kaplow was still in the same hospital, barely being kept alive in an iron lung, filled him with terror and tears. Donald the diver, Donald the discus thrower, Donald the naval-air-pilot-to-be, no longer powered by his lungs and his limbs!

Eventually Mr. Cantor was moved by ambulance to a Sister Kenny Institute in Philadelphia, where, by this point in the summer, the epidemic was nearly as bad as it was in Newark and the hospital's wards were so crowded that he was fortunate to get a bed. There the hot pack treatment continued, along with painful stretching of the contracted muscles of his arms and legs and of his back—which the paralysis had twisted—in order to "reeducate" them. He spent the next fourteen months in rehabilitation at the Kenny Institute, gradually recovering the full use of his right arm and partial use of his legs, though he was left with a twisted lower spine that had to be corrected several years later by a surgical fusion and a bone graft and the insertion of metal rods attached to the spine. The recuperation from the surgery put him on his back in a body cast for six months, tended day and night by his grandmother. He was at the Kenny Institute when President Roosevelt unexpectedly died, in April 1945, and the country went into mourning. He was there when defeated Germany surrendered in May, when the atomic bombs were dropped on Hiroshima and Nagasaki in August, and when Japan asked to surrender to the Allies a few days later. World War II was over, his buddy Dave would be coming home unscathed from fighting in Europe, America was jubilant, and he was still in the hospital, disfigured and maimed.

At the Kenny Institute he was one of the few who weren't bedridden. After a few weeks, he got into a wheelchair and was using it when he returned to Newark. There he continued treatment as an outpatient and, in time, recovered all the muscle function in his right leg. His bills had been astronomical, thousands and thousands of dollars, but they were paid by the Sister Kenny Institute and the March of Dimes.

He never returned to teaching phys ed at Chancellor or supervising the playground, nor did he realize his dream of coaching track and field at Weequahic. He left education entirely, and after a couple of unfortunate starts—employed first as a clerk in the Avon Avenue grocery store that had once been his grandfather's and then, when as a result of his disability he could find no other job, as a service station attendant on Springfield Avenue, where he was utterly unlike the crude guys working there and where customers sometimes called him Gimp—he took the civil service exam. Because he scored high and was a college graduate, he found a desk job with the post office downtown and so was able to support himself and his grandmother on his government salary.

I ran into him in 1971, years after I had graduated from architecture school and had set up my office in a building diagonally across the street from the main Newark post office. We could have passed each other on Broad Street a hundred times before the day I finally recognized him.

I was one of the Chancellor Avenue playground boys who, in the summer of '44, contracted polio and was then confined to a wheelchair for a year before protracted rehabilitation made it possible for me to locomote myself on a crutch and a cane, and with my two legs braced, as I do to this day. Some ten years back, after serving an apprenticeship with an architectural firm in the city, I started a company with a mechanical engineer who, like me, had had polio as a kid. We opened a consulting and contracting firm specializing in architectural modification for wheelchair accessibility, our options ranging from building additional rooms onto existing houses down to installing grab bars, lowering closet rods, and relocating light switches. We design and install ramps and wheelchair lifts, we widen doorways, we make bathroom, bedroom, and kitchen modifications —everything to improve life for wheelchair-bound people like my partner. The wheelchair-bound may require household structural changes that can be costly, but we do our best to keep to our estimates and to hold prices down. Along with the quality of our work, this is what largely accounts for our success. The rest was the luck of location and timing, of being the only such outfit in populous northern New Jersey at a moment when serious attention was beginning to be paid to the singular needs of the disabled.

Sometimes you're lucky and sometimes you're not. Any biography is chance, and, beginning at conception, chance—the tyranny of contingency—is everything. Chance is what I believed Mr. Cantor meant when he was decrying what he called God.

Mr. Cantor still had a withered left arm and useless left hand, and the damage to the muscles in his left calf caused a dip in his gait. The leg had begun getting much weaker in recent years, both the lower and the upper leg, and the limb had also begun to be severely painful for the first time since his rehabilitation nearly thirty years before. As a result, following a doctor's examination and a couple of visits to his hospital's brace shop, he had taken to wearing a full leg brace beneath his trousers to support his left leg. It didn't ease the pain much, but along with a cane it helped with balance and steadiness on his feet. However, if things continued to deteriorate—as they often do in later years for many polio survivors who come to suffer what is known as post-polio syndrome—it might not be long, he said, before he wound up back in a chair.

We came upon each other at noon one spring day in 1971 on

busy Broad Street, midway between where the two of us
worked. It was I who spotted him, even though he wore a
protective mustache now and, at the age of fifty, his once black
hair was no longer cut in a military crewcut but rose atop his
head like a white thicket—the mustache was white as well. And
he no longer, of course, had that athletic, pigeon-toed stride.
The sharp planes of his face were padded by the weight he'd
gained, so he was nowhere as striking as when the head beneath the tawny skin looked to be machined to the most rigor-
ous rectilinear specifications—when it was a young man's head
unabashedly asserting itself. That original face was now interred in another, fleshier face, a concealment people often see
when looking with resignation at their aging selves in the
mirror. No trace of the compact muscleman remained, the
muscles having melted away while the compactness had bur-
geoned. Now he was simply stout.

I was by then thirty-nine, a short, heavy man myself, bearded
and bearing little if any resemblance to the frail kid I'd been
growing up. When I realized on the street who he was, I got
so excited I shouted after him, "Mr. Cantor! Mr. Cantor! It's
Arnold Mesnikoff. From the Chancellor playground. Alan
Michaels was my closest friend. He sat next to me all through
school." Though I'd never forgotten Alan, I hadn't uttered his
name aloud in the many years since he'd died, back in that decade when it seemed that the greatest menaces on earth were
war, the atomic bomb, and polio.

After our first emotional street meeting, we began to eat
lunch together once a week in a nearby diner, and that's how I
got to hear his story. I turned out to be the first person to
whom he'd ever told the whole of the story, from beginning to
end, and—as he came to confide more intimately with each
passing week—without leaving very much out. I tried my best
to listen closely and to take it all in while he found the words
for everything that had been on his mind for the better part of
his life. Talking like this seemed to him to be neither pleasant
nor unpleasant—it was a pouring forth that before long he
could not control, neither an unburdening nor a remedy so
much as an exile's painful visit to the irreclaimable homeland,
the beloved birthplace that was the site of his undoing. We two
had not been especially close on the playground—I was a poor

athlete, a shy, quiet boy, delicately built. But the fact that I had been one of the kids hanging around Chancellor that horrible summer—that I was the best friend of his playground favorite and, like Alan and like him, had come down with polio—made him bluntly candid in a self-searing manner that sometimes astonished me, the auditor whom he'd never before known as an adult, the auditor now inspiring his confidence the way, as kids, I and the others had been inspired by him.

By and large he had the aura of ineradicable failure about him as he spoke of all that he'd been silent about for years, not just crippled physically by polio but no less demoralized by persistent shame. He was the very antithesis of the country's greatest prototype of the polio victim, FDR, disease having led Bucky not to triumph but to defeat. The paralysis and every-thing that came in its wake had irreparably damaged his assur-ance as a virile man, and he had withdrawn completely from that whole side of life. Mostly Bucky considered himself a gender blank—as in a cartridge that is blank—an abashing self-assessment for a boy who'd come of age in an era of national suffering and strife when men were meant to be undaunted defenders of home and country. When I told him that I had a wife and two children, he replied that he never had it in him to date anyone, let alone to marry, after he was paralyzed. He could never show his withered arm and withered leg to anyone other than a doctor or, when she was living, his grandmother. It was she who had devotedly taken care of him when he left the Kenny Institute, she who, despite her chest pains having been diagnosed as serious heart trouble, had boarded the train from Newark to visit him in Philadelphia every Sunday after-noon, without fail, for the fourteen months he was there.

She was now long dead, but until he found himself in the middle of the 1967 Newark riots—during which a house down the street had burned to the ground and shots had been fired from a nearby rooftop—he'd lived on in their small walkup flat in the tenement on Barclay near Avon. He had the flights of outside stairs to navigate—stairs that he'd once liked to take three at a time—and so, whatever the season, however icy or slippery they were, he laboriously climbed them so as to stay on in the third-floor flat where his grandmother's love had once been limitless and where the mothering voice that had never been unkind could be best remembered. Even though, *especially* though, no loved one from the past remained in his life, he could—and often did, involuntarily, while mounting the steps to his door at the end of the workday—summon up a clear picture of his kneeling grandmother, scrubbing their flight of stairs once a week with a stiff brush and a pail of sudsy water or cooking for their little family over the coal stove. That's the most he could do for his emotional reliance on women.

And never, never since he'd left for Camp Indian Hill in July 1944, had he returned to Weequahic or paid a visit to the gym where he'd taught at the Chancellor Avenue School or to the Chancellor playground.

"Why not?" I asked.

"Why would I? I was the Typhoid Mary of the Chancellor playground. I was the playground polio carrier. I was the Indian Hill polio carrier."

His idea of himself in this role hit me hard. Nothing could have prepared me for its severity.

"Were you? There's certainly no proof that you were."

"There's no proof that I wasn't," he said, speaking, as he mostly did during our lunchtime conversations, either looking away from my face to some unseen point in the distance or looking down into the food on our plates. He did not seem to want me, or perhaps anyone, staring inquisitively into his eyes.

"But you got polio," I told him. "You got it like the rest of us unfortunate enough to get polio eleven years too soon for the vaccine. Twentieth-century medicine made its phenomenal progress just a little too slowly for us. Today childhood summers are as sublimely worry-free as they should be. The significance of polio has disappeared completely. Nobody anymore is defenseless like we were. But to speak specifically about you, the chances are you caught polio from Donald Kaplow rather than that you gave it to him."

"And what about Sheila, the Steinberg twin—who'd she get it from? Look, it's far too late in the day to be rehashing all that now," he said, oddly, having rehashed nearly everything with me already. "Whatever was done, was done," he said. "Whatever I did, I did. What I don't have, I live without."

"But even if it were possible that you were a carrier, you would have been an unsuspecting carrier. Surely you haven't lived all these years punishing yourself, despising yourself, for something you didn't do. That's much too harsh a sentence."

There was a pause, during which he studied that spot that engaged him—to the side of my head and somewhere in the far distance, that spot which more than likely was 1944.

"What I've lived with mostly all these years," he said, "is Marcia Steinberg, if you want the truth. I cut myself free of many things, but I was never able to do that with her. All these years later, and there are times that I still think I recognize her on the street."

"As she was at twenty-two?"

He nodded, and then, to round out the disclosure, he said, "On Sundays I surely don't want to be thinking about her, yet that's when I mostly do. And nothing comes of my trying not to."

Some people are forgotten the moment you turn your back on them; that was not the case for Bucky with Marcia. Marcia's memory had endured.

He reached into his jacket pocket with his unwithered hand and took out an envelope and presented it to me. It was addressed to Eugene Cantor at 17 Barclay Street and postmarked at Stroudsburg, July 2, 1944.

"Go ahead," he said. "I brought it so you can look at it. I got it when she'd been away at camp just a few days."

The note I took from the envelope was written in perfect Palmer Method cursive on a small sheet of pale green stationery. It read:

My man my man my man my man my man
my man my man my man my man my man
my man my man my man my man my man
my man my man my man my man my man

All the way to the bottom of the page and halfway down the other side, the two words were repeated over and over, all of them evenly supported on an invisible straight line. The letter was signed with just her initial, *M*, a tall, beautifully formed capital exhibiting a little flourish in the loop and the stem, followed by "(as in My Man)."

I placed the single page back in the envelope and returned it to him.

"A twenty-two-year-old writes to her first lover. You must have been pleased to get such a letter."

"I got it when I came home from work. I kept it in my pocket during dinner. I took it with me to bed. I went to sleep with it in my hand. Then I was awakened by the phone. My grandmother slept across the hall. She was alarmed. 'Who can it be at this hour?' I went into the kitchen to answer. It was a few minutes after midnight by the clock there. Marcia was calling from the phone booth behind Mr. Blomback's office. She'd been in bed in her cabin, unable to sleep, so she got up and dressed and came out in the dark to call me. She wanted to know if I had received the letter. I said I had. I said I was her man two hundred and eighteen times over—she could depend on that. I said that I was her man forever. Then she told me that she wanted to sing to her man to put him to sleep. I was at the kitchen table in my skivvies in the dark and sweating like a pig from the heat. It had been another whopper of a day, and it hadn't cooled off any by midnight. The lights were out in all the flats across the way. I don't think anyone was awake on our whole street."

"Did she sing to you?"

"A lullaby. It wasn't one I knew, but it was a lullaby. She sang it very, very softly. There it was, all by itself, over the phone. Probably one she remembered from when she was a kid."

"So you had a weakness for her soft voice too."

"I was stunned. Stunned by so much happiness. I was so stunned that I whispered into the phone, 'Are you really as wonderful as this?' I couldn't believe such a girl existed. I was the luckiest guy in the world. And unstoppable. You understand me? With all that love of hers, how could I ever be stopped?"

"Then you lost her," I said. "How did you lose her? That you haven't told me yet."

"No, I haven't. I wouldn't let Marcia see me. That's how it happened. Look, maybe I've said enough." Suddenly, made uneasy by a pang of shame for the sentiments he'd just confided, he flushed deeply. "What the hell got me started? That letter. Finding that letter. I should never have gone looking for it."

With his elbow on the table he dropped his reddened face into his good hand and with his fingertips rubbed at his closed eyelid. We had reached the hardest part of the story.

"What happened to end it with Marcia?" I asked.

"When she came up to Stroudsburg to the hospital, when I was out of isolation, I had them turn her away. She left me a note telling me that her kid sister had only a mild, nonparalytic case and after three weeks recovered completely. I was relieved to learn that, but I still didn't want to resume my relations with the family. Marcia tried a second time to see me when I was transferred down to Philadelphia. That time I let her. We had a terrible argument. I didn't know she had it in her—I'd never seen her openly angry at anyone before. After that, she never came back. We never made contact again. Her father tried to talk to me when I was in Philadelphia, but I wouldn't take the call. When I was working at the Esso station on Springfield Avenue, out of the blue one day he pulled in for gas. That was a long way for him to go for gas."

"Was he there for her? To try to get you to come back?"

"I don't know. Maybe. I let another guy take the pump. I hid. I knew I was no match for Dr. Steinberg. I have no idea what happened to his daughter. I don't want to know. Whoever she married, let them and their children be happy and enjoy good health. Let's hope their merciful God will have blessed them with all that before He sticks His shiv in their back."

It was an arrestingly harsh utterance from the likes of Bucky Cantor, and, momentarily, he seemed to have perturbed himself by making it.

"I owed her her freedom," he finally said, "and I gave it to her. I didn't want the girl to feel stuck with me. I didn't want to ruin her life. She hadn't fallen in love with a cripple, and she shouldn't be stuck with one."

"Wasn't that up to her to decide?" I asked. "A damaged man is sometimes very attractive to a certain type of woman. I know from experience."

"Look, Marcia was a sweet, naive, well-brought-up girl with kindly, responsible parents who had taught her and her sisters to be polite and obliging," Bucky said. "She was a young new first-grade teacher, wet behind the ears. A slight slip of a thing, inches shorter even than me. It didn't help her being more intelligent than me—she still didn't have any idea of how to go about getting out of her mess. So I did it for her. I did what had to be done."

"You've given this a lot of thought," I said. "All your thought, it sounds like."

He smiled for one of the few times during our talks, a smile very like a frown, denoting weariness more than good cheer. There was no lightness in him. That was missing, as were the energy and the industry that were once at the center of him. And, of course, the athletic ingredient had completely vanished. It wasn't only an arm and a leg that were useless. His original personality, all that vital purposefulness that would hit you in the face the moment you met him, seemed itself to have been stripped away, lifted from him in shreds as though it were the thin swatch of bark that he'd peeled from the birch tree the first night with Marcia on the island in the lake at Indian Hill. We had been together one day a week at lunch over a period of a few months and never once did he lighten up, not even when he said, "That song she liked, 'I'll Be Seeing You'—I've never been able to forget that either. Soupy, sappy, yet it looks like I'll remember it for as long as I live. I don't know what would happen if I had to hear it again."

"You'd bawl."

"I might."

"You'd have a right," I said. "Anyone would be miserable, having renounced a true mate like that."

"Oh, my old playground buddy," he said, with more feeling than he'd spoken yet, "I never thought that's how it would end with her. Never."

"When she got angry with you—the time she came to see you in Philadelphia—"

"I never saw her again after that."

"You've said. But what happened?"

He was in a wheelchair, he told me, a glorious autumn Saturday in mid-October, still warm enough for them to go outdoors and for her to sit on a bench on the lawn in front of the Sister Kenny Institute, beneath the branches of a tree whose leaves had turned and begun to fall, but not so warm that the polio epidemic in the northeastern states hadn't finally dissipated and died away. By then Bucky had not seen her or spoken to her in nearly three months, so she hadn't yet had a chance to observe how crippled he was. There had been an exchange of correspondence, not between Bucky and Marcia but between Bucky and Marcia's father. Dr. Steinberg had written to tell Bucky that he had an obligation to allow Marcia to visit him and tell him directly what was on her mind. "Marcia and the family," wrote Dr. Steinberg, "deserve better from you than this." Against a handwritten letter on personalized hospital stationery from a man of the doctor's stature, Bucky, of course, had no defense, and so the date and time of Marcia's visit were set, and the quarrel began almost immediately upon her arrival, when he noticed right off that her hair had grown out since he'd seen her last, making her look more womanly than she had at camp and prettier now than ever. She had dressed with gloves and a hat, just like the proper teacher whom he'd first fallen for.

There was nothing she could say that would change his mind, he announced, however much he would have loved just to reach out with his good hand and touch her face. Instead, he used his good hand to grasp his dead arm around the wrist and raise it to the level of her eyes. "Look," he said. "This is what I look like."

She did not speak, but she did not blink either. No, he told her, he was no longer man enough to be a husband and a father, and it was irresponsible of her to think otherwise.

"Irresponsible of *me*?" she cried.

"To be the noble heroine. Yes."

"What are you talking about? I'm not trying to be anything other than the person who loves you and wants to marry you and be your wife." And then she advanced the gambit that she had no doubt rehearsed on the train down. "Bucky, it's not complicated, really," she told him. "*I'm* not complicated. Remember me? Remember what I said to you the night before I left for camp in June? 'We'll do it perfectly.' Well, we will. Nothing has changed that. I'm just an ordinary girl who wants to be happy. You make me happy. You always have. Why won't you now?"

"Because it's no longer the night before you left for camp. Because I'm no longer the person you fell in love with. You delude yourself if you think that I am. You're only doing what your conscience tells you is right—I understand that."

"You don't at all! You're speaking nonsense! It's you who's trying to be noble by refusing to talk to me and refusing to see me. By telling me to leave you alone. Oh, Bucky, you're being so blind!"

"Marcia, marry a man who isn't maimed, who's strong, who's fit, who's got all that a prospective father needs. You could have anyone, a lawyer, a doctor—someone as smart as you are and as educated as you are. *That's* what you and your family deserve. And that's what you should have."

"You are infuriating me so by talking like this! Nothing in my entire life has ever infuriated me as much as what you are doing right now! I have never known anyone other than you who finds such comfort in castigating himself!"

"That's not what I'm doing. That's an absolute distortion of what I'm doing. I just happen to see the implications of what's happened and you don't. You won't. Listen to me: things aren't the way they were before the summer. Look at me. Things couldn't be more different. Look."

"Stop this, please. I've seen your arm and *I don't care*."

"Then look at my leg," he said, pulling up his pajama bottoms.

"Stop, I beg you! You think it's your body that's deformed, but what's truly deformed is your mind!"

"Another good reason to save yourself from me. Most women would be delighted if a cripple volunteered to get out of their life."

"Then I'm not most women! And you're not just a cripple! Bucky, you've *always* been this way. You could never put things at the right distance—never! You're always holding yourself accountable when you're *not*. Either it's terrible God who is accountable, or it's terrible Bucky Cantor who is accountable, when in fact, accountability belongs to *neither*. Your attitude toward God—it's juvenile, it's just plain silly."

"Look, your God is not to my liking, so don't bring Him into the picture. He's too mean for me. He spends too much time killing children."

"And that is nonsense too! Just because you got polio doesn't give you the right to say ridiculous things. You have no idea what God is! No one does or can! You are being asinine—and you're not asinine. You sound so ignorant—and you're not ignorant. You are being crazy—and you're not crazy. You were never crazy. You were perfectly sane. Sane and sound and

strong and smart. But this! Spurning my love for you, spurning my family—I refuse to be a party to such insanity!"

Here the obstinate resistance collapsed, and she threw her
hands up over her face and began to sob. Other patients who
were entertaining visitors on nearby benches or being pushed
in wheelchairs along the paved path in front of the institute
could not but notice the petite, pretty, well-dressed young
woman, seated beside a patient in a wheelchair, who was so
visibly swept away by her sorrow.

"I'm completely baffled by you," she told him through her
tears. "If only you could have gone into the war, you might—
oh, I don't know what you might. You might have been a soldier and gotten over all this—whatever it is. Can't you believe
that it's you I love, whether or not you had polio? Can't you
understand that the worst possible outcome for both of us is
for you to take yourself away from me? I cannot bear to lose
you—is there no getting that through to you? Bucky, your life
can be so much easier if only you'll let it be. How do I convince you that we have to go on together? Don't save me, for
God's sake. Do what we planned—marry me!"

But he wouldn't be budged, however much she cried and
however heartfelt the crying seemed, even to him. "Marry
me," she said, and he could only reply, "I will not do that to
you," and she could only reply, "You're not doing anything to
me—I am responsible for my decisions!" But there was no
breaking down his opposition, not when his last opportunity
to be a man of integrity was by sparing the virtuous young
woman he dearly loved from unthinkingly taking a cripple as
her mate for life. The only way to save a remnant of his honor
was in denying himself everything he had ever wanted for
himself—should he be weak enough to do otherwise, he would
suffer his final defeat. Most important, if she was not already
secretly relieved that he was rejecting her, if she was still too
much under the sway of that loving innocence of hers—and
under the sway as well of a morally punctilious father—to see
the truth plainly for herself, she would feel differently when
she had a family and a home of her own, with happy children
and a husband who was whole. Yes, a day would come, and
not far in the future, when she would find herself grateful to
him for his having so pitilessly turned her away—when she

would recognize how much better a life he had given her by his having vanished from it.

When he'd completed the story of the final meeting with Marcia, I asked him, "How bitter does all this leave you?"

"God killed my mother in childbirth. God gave me a thief for a father. In my early twenties, God gave me polio that I in turn gave to at least a dozen kids, probably more—including Marcia's sister, including you, most likely. Including Donald Kaplow. He died in an iron lung at Stroudsburg Hospital in August 1944. How bitter should I be? You tell me." He asserted this caustically, in the same tone in which he'd proclaimed that her God would one day betray Marcia and plant a knife in her back too.

"It's not for me," I replied, "to find fault with any polio sufferer, young or old, who can't fully overcome the pain of an infirmity that never ends. Of course there's brooding over its permanence. But there must in time be something more. You speak of God. You still believe in this God you disparage?"

"Yes. Somebody had to make this place."

"God the great criminal," I said. "Yet if it's God who's the criminal, it can't be you who's the criminal as well."

"Okay, it's a medical enigma. *I'm* a medical enigma," Bucky said confusingly. Did he mean perhaps that it was a *theological* enigma? Was this his Everyman's version of Gnostic doctrine, complete with an evil Demiurge? The divine as inimical to our being here? Admittedly, the evidence he could cull from his experience was not negligible. Only a fiend could invent polio. Only a fiend could invent Horace. Only a fiend could invent World War II. Add it all up and the fiend wins. The fiend is omnipotent. Bucky's conception of God, as I thought I understood it, was of an omnipotent being whose nature and purpose was to be adduced not from doubtful biblical evidence but from irrefutable historical proof, gleaned during a lifetime passed on this planet in the middle of the twentieth century. His conception of God was of an omnipotent being who was a union not of three persons in one Godhead, as in Christianity, but of two—a sick fuck and an evil genius.

To my atheistic mind, proposing such a God was certainly no more ridiculous than giving credence to the deities sustaining billions of others; as for Bucky's rebellion against Him, it struck me as absurd simply because there was no need for it. That the polio epidemic among the children of the Weequahic section and the children of Camp Indian Hill was a tragedy, he could not accept. He has to convert tragedy into guilt. He has to find a necessity for what happens. There is an epidemic and he needs a reason for it. He has to ask why. Why? Why? That it is pointless, contingent, preposterous, and tragic will not satisfy him. That it is a proliferating virus will not satisfy him. Instead he looks desperately for a deeper cause, this martyr, this maniac of the why, and finds the why either in God or in himself or, mystically, mysteriously, in their dreadful joining together as the sole destroyer. I have to say that however much I might sympathize with the amassing of woes that had blighted his life, this is nothing more than stupid hubris, not the hubris of will or desire but the hubris of fantastical, childish religious interpretation. We have heard it all before and by now have heard enough of it, even from someone as profoundly decent as Bucky Cantor.

"And you, Arnie?" he asked me. "You're without bitterness?"

"I got the disease when I was still a kid. I was twelve, about half your age. I was in the hospital for close to a year. I was the oldest one on the ward," I said, "surrounded by little kids screaming and crying for their families—day and night these little kids searching in vain for a face they knew. They weren't alone in feeling deserted. There was plenty of fear and despair to go around. And plenty of bitterness growing up with a pair of stick legs. For years I lay in bed at night talking to my limbs, whispering, 'Move! Move!' I missed a year of grade school, so when I got back, I had lost my class and my classmates. And in high school I had some hard knocks. The girls pitied me and the boys avoided me. I was always sitting brooding on the sidelines. Life on the sidelines makes for a painful adolescence. I wanted to walk like everyone else. Watching them, the unbroken ones, out after school playing ball, I wanted to shout, 'I have a right to be running too!' I was constantly torn by the thought that it could so easily have been another way. For a while I didn't want to go to school at all—I didn't want to be reminded all day long of what people my age looked like and of all they could do. What I wanted was the tiniest thing in the world: to be like everyone else. You know the situation," I said to him. "I'll never be me as I was me in the past. I'll be this instead for the rest of my life. I'll never know delight again."

Bucky nodded. He who once, briefly, atop the high board at Indian Hill, was the happiest man on earth—who had listened to Marcia Steinberg tenderly lullabying him to sleep over the long-distance line in the tremendous heat of that poisonous summer—understood all too easily what I was talking about.

I told him then about a college roommate whom I moved out on in my sophomore year. "When I got to Rutgers," I said, "I was given the other Jewish polio victim to room with in the freshman dorm. That's how Noah paired students up in those days. This guy was physically far worse off than I was. Grotesquely deformed. Boy named Pomerantz. A brilliant scholarship student, high school valedictorian, pre-med genius, and I couldn't stand him. He drove me crazy. Couldn't shut up. Could never stifle his all-consuming hunger for pre-polio Pomerantz. Could not elude for a single day the injustice that had befallen him. Went ghoulishly on and on about it. 'First you learn just what a cripple's life is like,' he'd say to me. 'That's the first stage. When you recover from that, you do what little is to be done to avoid spiritual extinction. That's the second stage. After that, you struggle not to be nothing but your ordeal all the while that's all you're becoming. Then, if you're lucky, five hundred stages later, sometime in your seventies, you find you are finally able to say with some truth, "Well, I managed after all—I did not allow the life to be sucked out of me completely." That's when you die.' Pomerantz did great in college, easily got into medical school, and then *he* died—in his first year there he killed himself."

"I can't say," Bucky told me, "that I wasn't once attracted by the idea myself."

"I thought about it too," I said. "But then I wasn't quite the mess that Pomerantz was. And then I got lucky, tremendously lucky: in the last year of college I met my wife. And slowly polio ceased to be the only drama, and I got weaned away from railing at my fate. I learned that back there in Weequahic in 1944 I'd lived through a summerlong social tragedy that didn't have to be a lifelong personal tragedy too. My wife's been a tender, laughing companion for eighteen years. She's counted for a lot. And having children to father, you begin to forget the hand you've been dealt."

"I'm sure that's true. You look like a contented man."

"Where are you living now?" I asked.

"I moved to North Newark. I moved near Branch Brook Park. The furniture at my grandmother's place was so old and creaky that I didn't bother to keep it. Went out one Saturday morning and bought a brand-new bed, sofa, chairs, lamps, everything. I've got a comfortable place."

"What do you do for socializing?"

"I'm not much of a socializer, Arnie. I go to the movies. I go down to the Ironbound on Sundays for a good Portuguese meal. I enjoy sitting in the park when it's nice. I watch TV. I watch the news."

I thought of him doing these things by himself and, like a lovesick swain, attempting on Sundays not to pine for Marcia Steinberg or to imagine during the week that he'd seen her, age twenty-two, walking on one of the downtown streets. One would have predicted, remembering the young man he'd been, that he would have had the strength to battle through to something more than this. And then I thought of myself without my family, and wondered if I would have done any better or even as well. Movies and work and Sunday dinner out—it sounded awfully bleak to me.

"Do you watch sports?"

Vigorously he shook his head as though I'd asked a child if he played with matches.

"I understand," I said. "When my kids were very young and I couldn't run around the yard with them, and when they were older and learned to ride bikes and I couldn't ride with them, it got to me. You try to choke down your feelings but it isn't easy."

"I don't even read the sports pages in the paper. I don't want to see them."

"Did you ever see your friend Dave when he came back from the war?"

"He got a job in the Englewood school system. He took his wife and his kids and he moved up there. No, I don't see him." Then he lapsed into silence, and it couldn't have been clearer that despite his stoical claim that what he did not have he lived without, he had not in the least accustomed himself to having lost so much, and that twenty-seven years later, he wondered still about all that had and had not happened, trying his best not to think of a multitude of things—among them, that by now he would have been head of the athletic program at Weequahic High.

"I wanted to help kids and make them strong," he finally said, "and instead I did them irrevocable harm." That was the thought that had shaped his decades of silent suffering, a man who was himself the least deserving of harm. He looked at that moment as if he had lived on this earth seven thousand shameful years. I took hold of his good hand then—a hand whose muscles worked well enough but that was no longer substantial and strong, a hand with no more firmness to it than a piece of soft fruit—and I said, "*Polio* did them the harm. You weren't a perpetrator. You had as little to do with spreading it as Horace did. You were just as much a victim as any of us was."

"Not so, Arnie. I remember one night Bill Blomback telling the kids about the Indians, telling them how the Indians believed that it was an evil being, shooting them with an invisible arrow, that caused certain of their diseases—"

"Don't," I protested. "Don't go any further with that, please. It's a campfire story, Bucky, a story for kids. There's probably a medicine man in it who drives off evil spirits. You're *not* the Indians' evil being. You were not the arrow, either, damn it— you were not the bringer of crippling and death. If you ever were a perpetrator—if you won't give ground about that— I repeat: you were a totally blameless one."

Then, vehemently—as though I could bring about change in him merely by a tremendous desire to do so; as though, after all our hours of talking over lunch, I could now get him to see himself as something more than his deficiencies and begin to liquidate his shame; as though it were within my power to revive a remnant of the unassailable young playground director who, unaided by anyone, had warded off the ten Italian roughnecks intending to frighten us with the threat of spreading polio among the Jews—I said, "Don't be against yourself. There's enough cruelty in the world as it is. Don't make things worse by scapegoating yourself."

But there's nobody less salvageable than a ruined good boy. He'd been alone far too long with his sense of things—and without all he'd wanted so desperately to have—for me to dislodge his interpretation of his life's terrible event or to shift his relation with it. Bucky wasn't a brilliant man—he wouldn't have had to be one to teach phys ed to kids—nor was he ever in the least carefree. He was largely a humorless person, articulate enough but with barely a trace of wit, who never in his life had spoken satirically or with irony, who rarely cracked a joke or spoke in jest—someone instead haunted by an exacerbated sense of duty but endowed with little force of mind, and for that he had paid a high price in assigning the gravest meaning to his story, one that, intensifying over time, perniciously magnified his misfortune. The havoc that had been wrought both on the Chancellor playground and at Indian Hill seemed to him not a malicious absurdity of nature but a great crime of his own, costing him all he'd once possessed and wrecking his life. The guilt in someone like Bucky may seem absurd but, in fact, is unavoidable. Such a person is condemned. Nothing he does matches the ideal in him. He never knows where his responsibility ends. He never trusts his limits because, saddled with a stern natural goodness that will not permit him to resign himself to the suffering of others, he will never guiltlessly acknowledge that he has any limits. Such a person's greatest triumph is in sparing his beloved from having a crippled husband, and his heroism consists of denying his deepest desire by relinquishing her.

Though maybe if he hadn't fled the challenge of the playground, maybe if he hadn't abandoned the Chancellor kids only days before the city shut down the playground and sent them all home—and maybe, too, if his closest buddy hadn't been killed in the war—he would not have been so quick to blame himself for the cataclysm and might not have become one of those people taken to pieces by his times. Maybe if he had stayed on and outlasted polio's communal testing of the Weequahic Jews, and, regardless of whatever might have happened to him, had manfully seen the epidemic through to the end . . .

Or maybe he would have come to see it his way no matter where he'd been, and for all I know—for all the science of epidemiology knows—maybe rightly so. Maybe Bucky wasn't mistaken. Maybe he wasn't deluded by self-mistrust. Maybe his assertions weren't exaggerated and he hadn't drawn the wrong conclusion. Maybe he *was* the invisible arrow.

And yet, at twenty-three, he was, to all of us boys, the most exemplary and revered authority we knew, a young man of convictions, easygoing, kind, fairminded, thoughtful, stable, gentle, vigorous, muscular—a comrade and leader both. And never a more glorious figure than on the afternoon near the end of June, before the '44 epidemic seriously took hold in the city—before, for more than a few of us, our bodies and our lives would be drastically transformed—when we all marched behind him to the big dirt field across the street and down a short slope from the playground. It was where the high school football team held its workouts and practices and where he was going to show us how to throw the javelin. He was dressed in his skimpy, satiny track shorts and his sleeveless top, he wore cleated shoes, and, leading the pack, he carried the javelin loosely in his right hand.

When we got down to the field it was empty, and Mr. Cantor had us gather together on the sidelines at the Chancellor Avenue end, where he let us each examine the javelin and heft it in our hands, a slender metal pole weighing a little under two pounds and measuring about eight and a half feet long. He showed us the various holds you could use on the whipcord grip and then the one that he preferred. Then he explained to us something about the background of the javelin, which began in early societies, before the invention of the bow and arrow, with the throwing of the spear for hunting, and continued in Greece at the first Olympics in the eighth century B.C. The first javelin thrower was said to be Hercules, the great warrior and slayer of monsters, who, Mr. Cantor told us, was the giant son of the supreme Greek god, Zeus, and the strongest man on earth. The lecture over, he said he would now do his warm-ups, and we watched while he limbered up for about twenty minutes, some of the boys on the sidelines doing their best to mimic his movements. It was important, he said—at the same time as he was performing a side split with his pelvis to the ground—always to work beforehand at stretching the groin muscles, which were easily susceptible to strain. He used the javelin as a stretching stick for many of the exercises, twisting and turning with it balanced like a yoke across his shoulders while he kneeled and squatted and lunged and then while he stood and flexed and rotated his torso. He did a handstand and began walking a wide circle on his hands, and some of the kids tried that; with his mouth only inches from the ground, he informed us that he was doing the handstands in lieu of exercising on a bar to stretch his upper body. He finished off with forward body bends and trunk backbends, during which he kept his heels fixed to the ground while pushing upward with his hips and arching his back amazingly high. When he said he was going to sprint twice around the edge of the field, we followed, barely able to keep up with him but pretending that it was we who were warming up for the throw. Then for a few minutes he practiced running along an imaginary runway without throwing the javelin, just carrying it high, flat, and straight.

When he was ready to begin, he told us what to watch for, starting with his approach run and the bounding stride and ending with the throw. Without the javelin in his hand he walked through the entire delivery for us in slow motion, describing it as he did so. "It's not magic, boys, and it's no picnic either. However, if you practice hard," he said, "and you work hard and you exercise diligently—if you're regular with your balance drills, one, your mobility drills, two, and your flexibility drills, three—if you're faithful to your weight-training program, and if throwing the javelin really matters to you, I guarantee you, something will come of it. Everything in sports requires determination. The three D's. Determination, dedication, and discipline, and you're practically all the way there."

As usual, taking every precaution, he told us that for safety's sake no one was to dart out onto the field at any point; we were to watch everything from where we were standing. He made this point twice. He couldn't have been more serious, the seriousness being the expression of his commitment to the task.

And then he hurled the javelin. You could see each of his muscles bulging when he released it into the air. He let out a strangulated yowl of effort (one we all went around imitating for days afterward), a noise expressing the essence of him—the naked battle cry of striving excellence. The instant the javelin took flight from his hand, he began dancing about to recover his balance and not fall across the foul line he'd etched in the dirt with his cleats. And all the while he watched the javelin as it made its trajectory in a high, sweeping arc over the field. None of us had ever before seen an athletic act so beautifully executed right in front of our eyes. The javelin carried, carried way beyond the fifty-yard line, down to the far side of the opponent's thirty, and when it descended and landed, the shaft quivered and its pointed metal tip angled sharply into the ground from the sailing force of the flight.

We sent up a loud cheer and began leaping about. All of the javelin's trajectory had originated in Mr. Cantor's supple muscles. His was the body—the feet, the legs, the buttocks, the trunk, the arms, the shoulders, even the thick stump of the bull neck—that acting in unison had powered the throw. It was as though our playground director had turned into a primordial man, hunting for food on the plains where he foraged, taming the wilds by the might of his hand. Never were we more in awe of anyone. Through him, we boys had left the little story of the neighborhood and entered the historical saga of our ancient gender.

He threw the javelin repeatedly that afternoon, each throw smooth and powerful, each throw accompanied by that resounding mingling of a shout and a grunt, and each, to our delight, landing several yards farther down the field than the last. Running with the javelin aloft, stretching his throwing arm back behind his body, bringing the throwing arm through to release the javelin high over his shoulder—and releasing it then like an explosion—he seemed to us invincible.

CHRONOLOGY

NOTE ON THE TEXTS

NOTES

Chronology

1933   Born Philip Roth on March 19 in Newark, New Jersey, second child of Herman Roth and Bess Finkel. (Bess Finkel, the second child of five, was born in 1904 in Elizabeth, New Jersey, to Philip and Dora Finkel, Jewish immigrants from near Kiev. Herman Roth was born in 1901 in Newark, New Jersey, the middle child of seven born to Sender and Bertha Roth, Jewish immigrants from Polish Galicia. They were married in Newark on February 21, 1926, and shortly afterward opened a small family-run shoe store. Their son Sanford ["Sandy"] was born December 26, 1927. Following the bankruptcy of the shoe store and a briefly held position as city marshal, Herman Roth took a job as agent with the Newark district office of the Metropolitan Life Insurance Company, and would remain with the company until his retirement as district manager in 1966.) Family moves into second-floor flat of two-and-a-half-family house (with five-room apartments on each of the first two floors and a three-room apartment on the top floor) at 81 Summit Avenue in Newark. Summit Avenue was a lower-middle-class residential street in the Weequahic section, a twenty-minute bus ride from commercial downtown Newark and less than a block from Chancellor Avenue School and from Weequahic High School, then considered the state's best academic public high school. These were the two schools that Sandy and Philip attended. Between 1910 and 1920, Weequahic had been developed as a new city neighborhood at the southwest corner of Newark, some three miles from the edge of industrial Newark and from the international shipping facilities at Port Newark on Newark Bay. In the first half of the twentieth century Newark was a prosperous working-class city of approximately 420,000, the majority of its citizens of German, Italian, Slavic, and Irish extraction. Blacks and Jews composed two of the smallest groups in the city. From the 1930s to the 1950s, the Jews lived mainly in the predominantly Jewish Weequahic section.

1938   Philip enters kindergarten at Chancellor Avenue School
            in January.

1942   Roth family moves to second-floor flat of two-and-a-half-
            family house at 359 Leslie Street, three blocks west of
            Summit Avenue, still within the Weequahic neighborhood
            but nearer to semi-industrial boundary with Irvington.

1946   Philip graduates from elementary school in January, having
            skipped a year. Brother graduates from high school and
            chooses to enter U.S. Navy for two years rather than be
            drafted into the peacetime army.

1947   Family moves to first-floor flat of two-and-a-half-family
            house at 385 Leslie Street, just a few doors from commer-
            cial Chancellor Avenue, the neighborhood's main artery.
            Philip turns from reading sports fiction by John R. Tunis
            and adventure fiction by Howard Pease to reading the
            left-leaning historical novels of Howard Fast.

1948   Brother is discharged from navy and, with the aid of G.I.
            Bill, enrolls as commercial art student at Pratt Institute,
            Brooklyn. Philip takes strong interest in politics during
            the four-way U.S. presidential election in which the Re-
            publican Dewey loses to the Democrat Truman despite a
            segregationist Dixiecrat Party and a left-wing Progressive
            Party drawing away traditionally Democratic voters.

1950   Graduates from high school in January. Works as stock
            clerk at S. Klein department store in downtown Newark.
            Reads Thomas Wolfe; discovers Sherwood Anderson,
            Ring Lardner, Erskine Caldwell, and Theodore Dreiser.
            In September enters Newark College of Rutgers as pre-
            law student while continuing to live at home. (Newark
            Rutgers was at this time a newly formed college housed in
            two small converted downtown buildings, one formerly a
            bank, the other formerly a brewery.)

1951   Still a pre-law student, transfers in September to Bucknell
            University in Lewisburg, Pennsylvania. Brother graduates
            from Pratt Institute and moves to New York City to work
            for advertising agency. Parents move to Moorestown,
            New Jersey, approximately seventy miles southwest of
            Newark; father takes job as manager of Metropolitan
            Life's south Jersey district after having previously man-
            aged several north Jersey district offices.

1952   Roth decides to study English literature. With two friends, founds Bucknell literary magazine, *Et Cetera*, and becomes its first editor. Writes first short stories. Strongly influenced in his literary studies by English professor Mildred Martin, under whose tutelage he reads extensively, and with whom he will maintain lifelong friendship.

1954   Is elected to Phi Beta Kappa and graduates from Bucknell magna cum laude in English. Accepts scholarship to study English at the University of Chicago graduate school, beginning in September. Reads Saul Bellow's *The Adventures of Augie March*, and under its influence explores Chicago.

1955   In June receives M.A. with Honors in English. In September, rather than wait to be drafted, enlists in U.S. Army for two years. Suffers spinal injury during basic training at Fort Dix. In November, is assigned to Public Information Office at Walter Reed Army Hospital, Washington, D.C. Begins to write short stories "The Conversion of the Jews" and "Epstein." *Epoch*, a Cornell University literary quarterly, publishes "The Contest for Aaron Gold," which is reprinted in Martha Foley's *Best American Short Stories 1956*.

1956   Is hospitalized in June for complications from spinal injury. After two-month hospital stay receives honorable discharge for medical reasons and a disability pension. In September returns to University of Chicago as instructor in the liberal arts college, teaching freshman composition. Begins course work for Ph.D. but drops out after one term. Meets Ted Solotaroff, who is also a graduate student, and they become friends.

1957   Publishes in *Commentary* "You Can't Tell a Man by the Song He Sings." Writes novella "Goodbye, Columbus." Meets Saul Bellow at University of Chicago when Bellow is a classroom guest of Roth's friend and colleague, the writer Richard Stern. Begins to review movies and television for *The New Republic* after magazine publishes "Positive Thinking on Pennsylvania Avenue," a humor piece satirizing President Eisenhower's religious beliefs.

1958   Publishes "The Conversion of the Jews" and "Epstein" in *The Paris Review*; "Epstein" wins *Paris Review* Aga Khan Prize, presented to Roth in Paris in July. Spends first summer abroad, mainly in Paris. Houghton Mifflin awards Roth the Houghton Mifflin Literary Fellowship to publish the novella and five stories in one volume; George Starbuck, a poet and friend from Chicago, is his editor. Resigns from teaching position at University of Chicago. Moves to two-room basement apartment on Manhattan's Lower East Side. Becomes friendly with *Paris Review* editors George Plimpton and Robert Silvers and *Commentary* editor Martin Greenberg.

1959   Marries Margaret Martinson Williams. Publishes "Defender of the Faith" in *The New Yorker*, causing consternation among Jewish organizations and rabbis who attack magazine and condemn author as anti-Semitic; story collected in *Goodbye, Columbus* and included in *Best American Short Stories 1960* and *Prize Stories 1960: The O. Henry Awards*, where it wins second prize. *Goodbye, Columbus* is published in May. Roth receives Guggenheim fellowship and award from the American Academy of Arts and Letters. *Goodbye, Columbus* gains highly favorable reviews from Bellow, Alfred Kazin, Leslie Fiedler, and Irving Howe; influential rabbis denounce Roth in their sermons as "a self-hating Jew." Roth and wife leave U.S. to spend seven months in Italy, where he works on his first novel, *Letting Go*; he meets William Styron, who is living in Rome and who becomes a lifelong friend. Styron introduces Roth to his publisher, Donald Klopfer of Random House; when George Starbuck leaves Houghton Mifflin, Roth moves to Random House.

1960   *Goodbye, Columbus and Five Short Stories* wins National Book Award. The collection also wins Daroff Award of the Jewish Book Council of America. Roth returns to America to teach at the Writers' Workshop of the University of Iowa, Iowa City. Meets drama professor Howard Stein (later dean of the Columbia University Drama School), who becomes lifelong friend. Continues working on *Letting Go*. Travels in Midwest. Participates in *Esquire* magazine symposium at Stanford University; his speech "Writing American Fiction," published in *Commentary* in March 1961, is widely discussed. After a speaking engagement in Oregon, meets Bernard Malamud, whose fiction he admires.

1962   After two years at Iowa, accepts two-year position as writer-in-residence at Princeton. Separates from Margaret Roth. Moves to New York City and commutes to Princeton classes. (Lives at various Manhattan locations until 1970.) Meets Princeton sociologist Melvin Tumin, a Newark native who becomes a friend. Random House publishes *Letting Go*.

1963   Receives Ford Foundation grant to write plays in affiliation with American Place Theater in New York. Is legally separated from Margaret Roth. Becomes close friend of Aaron Asher, a University of Chicago graduate and editor at Meridian Books, original paperback publisher of *Goodbye, Columbus*. In June takes part in American Jewish Congress symposium in Tel Aviv, Israel, along with American writers Leslie Fiedler, Max Lerner, and literary critic David Boroff. Travels in Israel for a month.

1964   Teaches at State University of New York at Stony Brook, Long Island. Reviews plays by James Baldwin, LeRoi Jones, and Edward Albee for newly founded *New York Review of Books*. Spends a month at Yaddo, writers' retreat in Saratoga Springs, New York, that provides free room and board. (Will work at Yaddo for several months at a time throughout the 1960s.) Meets and establishes friendships there with novelist Alison Lurie and painter Julius Goldstein.

1965   Begins to teach comparative literature at University of Pennsylvania one semester each year more or less annually until the mid-1970s. Meets professor Joel Conarroe, who becomes a close friend. Begins work on *When She Was Good* after abandoning another novel, begun in 1962.

1966   Publishes section of *When She Was Good* in *Harper's*. Is increasingly troubled by Vietnam War and in ensuing years takes part in marches and demonstrations against it.

1967   Publishes *When She Was Good*. Begins work on *Portnoy's Complaint*, of which he publishes excerpts in *Esquire, Partisan Review*, and *New American Review*, where Ted Solotaroff is editor.

1968   Margaret Roth dies in an automobile accident. Roth spends two months at Yaddo completing *Portnoy's Complaint*.

1969   *Portnoy's Complaint* published in February. Within weeks
          becomes number-one fiction best seller and a widely dis-
          cussed cultural phenomenon. Roth makes no public ap-
          pearances and retreats for several months to Yaddo. Rents
          house in Woodstock, New York, and meets the painter
          Philip Guston, who lives nearby. They remain close friends
          and see each other regularly until Guston's death in 1980.
          Renews friendship with Bernard Malamud, who like Roth
          is serving as a member of The Corporation of Yaddo.

1970   Spends March traveling in Thailand, Burma, Cambodia,
          and Hong Kong. Begins work on *My Life as a Man* and
          publishes excerpt in *Modern Occasions*. Is elected to Na-
          tional Institute of Arts and Letters and is its youngest
          member. Commutes to his classes at University of Penn-
          sylvania and lives mainly in Woodstock until 1972.

1971   Excerpts of *Our Gang*, satire of the Nixon administration,
          appear in *New York Review of Books* and *Modern Occa-
          sions*; the book is published by Random House in the fall.
          Continues work on *My Life as a Man*; writes *The Breast*
          and *The Great American Novel*. Begins teaching a Kafka
          course at University of Pennsylvania.

1972   *The Breast*, first book of three featuring protagonist David
          Kepesh, published by Holt, Rinehart, Winston, where
          Aaron Asher is his editor. Roth buys old farmhouse and
          forty acres in northwest Connecticut, one hundred miles
          from New York City, and moves there from Woodstock.
          In May travels to Venice, Vienna, and, for the first time,
          Prague. Meets his translators there, Luba and Rudolph
          Pilar, and they describe to him the impact of the political
          situation on Czech writers. In U.S., arranges to meet
          exiled Czech editor Antonin Liehm in New York; attends
          Liehm's weekly classes in Czech history, literature, and
          film at College of Staten Island, City University of New
          York. Through friendship with Liehm meets numerous
          Czech exiles, including film directors Ivan Passer and Jiří
          Weiss, who become friends. Is elected to the American
          Academy of Arts and Sciences.

1973   Publishes *The Great American Novel* and the essay
          "Looking at Kafka" in *New American Review*. Returns to
          Prague and meets novelists Milan Kundera, Ivan Klíma,
          Ludvik Vaculik, the poet Miroslav Holub, and other
          writers blacklisted and persecuted by the Soviet-backed

Communist regime; becomes friendly with Rita Klímová,
a blacklisted translator and academic, who will serve as
Czechoslovakia's first ambassador to U.S. following the
1989 "Velvet Revolution." (Will make annual spring trips
to Prague to visit his writer friends until he is denied an
entry visa in 1977.) Writes "Country Report" on Czechoslovakia for American PEN. Proposes paperback series,
"Writers from the Other Europe," to Penguin Books
USA; becomes general editor of the series, selecting titles,
commissioning introductions, and overseeing publication
of Eastern European writers relatively unknown to American readers. Beginning in 1974, series publishes fiction by
Polish writers Jerzy Andrzejewski, Tadeusz Borowski,
Tadeusz Konwicki, Witold Gombrowicz, and Bruno
Schulz; Hungarian writers György Konrád and Géza
Csáth; Yugoslav writer Danilo Kiš; and Czech writers Bo-
humil Hrabal, Milan Kundera, and Ludvik Vaculik; series
ends in 1989. "Watergate Edition" of *Our Gang* published,
which includes a new preface by Roth.

1974   Roth publishes *My Life as a Man*. Visits Budapest as well
as Prague and meets Budapest writers through Hungarian
PEN and the *Hungarian Quarterly*. In Prague meets Va-
clav Havel. Through friend Professor Zdenek Strybyrny,
visits and becomes friend of the niece of Franz Kafka,
Vera Saudkova, who shows him Kafka family photographs
and family belongings; subsequently becomes friendly in
London with Marianne Steiner, daughter of Kafka's sister
Valli. Also through Strybyrny meets the widow of Jiří
Weil; upon his return to America arranges for translation
and publication of Weil's novel *Life with a Star* as well as
publication of several Weil short stories in *American
Poetry Review*, for which he provides an introduction. In
Princeton meets Joanna Rostropowicz Clark, wife of
friend Blair Clark; she becomes close friend and introduces Roth to contemporary Polish writing and to Polish
writers visiting America, including Konwicki and Kazi-
mierz Brandys. Publishes "Imagining Jews" in *New York
Review of Books*; essay prompts letter from university
professor, editor, writer, and former Jesuit Jack Miles.
Correspondence ensues and the two establish a lasting intellectual friendship. In New York, meets teacher, editor,
author, and journalist Bernard Avishai; they quickly establish a strong intellectual bond and become lifelong friends.

1975   Aaron Asher leaves Holt and becomes editor in chief at
            Farrar, Straus and Giroux; Roth moves to FSG with Asher
            for publication of *Reading Myself and Others*, a collection
            of interviews and critical essays. Meets British actress Claire
            Bloom.

1976   Interviews Isaac Bashevis Singer about Bruno Schulz for
            New York Times Book Review article to coincide with pub-
            lication of Schulz's *Street of Crocodiles* in "Writers from
            the Other Europe" series. Moves with Claire Bloom to
            London, where they live six to seven months a year for
            the next twelve years. Spends the remaining months in
            Connecticut, where Bloom joins him when she is not act-
            ing in films, television, or stage productions. In London
            resumes an old friendship with British critic A. Alvarez
            and, a few years later, begins a friendship with American
            writer Michael Herr (author of *Dispatches*, which Roth
            admires) and with the American painter R. B. Kitaj. Also
            meets critic and biographer Hermione Lee, who becomes
            a friend, as does novelist Edna O'Brien. Begins regular
            visits to France to see Milan Kundera and another new
            friend, French writer-critic Alain Finkielkraut. Visits Israel
            for the first time since 1963 and returns there regularly,
            keeping a journal that eventually provides ideas and ma-
            terial for novels *The Counterlife* and *Operation Shylock*.
            Meets the writer Aharon Appelfeld in Jerusalem and they
            become close friends.

1977   Publishes *The Professor of Desire*, second book of Kepesh
            trilogy. Beginning in 1977 and continuing over the next
            few years, writes series of TV dramas for Claire Bloom:
            adaptations of *The Name-Day Party*, a short story by
            Chekhov; *Journey into the Whirlwind*, the gulag autobi-
            ography of Eugenia Ginzburg; and, with David Plante,
            It Isn't Fair, Plante's memoir of Jean Rhys. At request
            of Chichester Festival director, modernizes the David
            Magarshack translation of Chekhov's *The Cherry Orchard*
            for Claire Bloom's 1981 performance at the festival as
            Madame Ranyevskaya.

1979   *The Ghost Writer*, first novel featuring novelist Nathan
            Zuckerman as protagonist, is published in its entirety in
            The New Yorker, then published by Farrar, Straus and Gi-
            roux. Bucknell awards Roth his first honorary degree;
            eventually receives honorary degrees from Amherst,

Brown, Columbia, Dartmouth, Harvard, Pennsylvania, and Rutgers, among others.

1980   *A Philip Roth Reader* published, edited by Martin Green. Milan and Vera Kundera visit Connecticut on first trip to U.S.; Roth introduces Kundera to friend and *New Yorker* editor Veronica Geng, who also becomes Kundera's editor at the magazine. Conversation with Milan Kundera, in London and Connecticut, published in *New York Times Book Review*.

1981   Mother dies of a sudden heart attack in Elizabeth, New Jersey. *Zuckerman Unbound* published.

1982   Corresponds with Judith Thurman after reading her biography of Isak Dinesen, and they begin a friendship.

1983   Roth's physician and Litchfield County neighbor, Dr. C. H. Huvelle, retires from his Connecticut practice and the two become close friends.

1984   *The Anatomy Lesson* published. Aaron Asher leaves FSG and David Rieff becomes Roth's editor; the two soon become close friends. Conversation with Edna O'Brien in London published in *New York Times Book Review*. With BBC director Tristram Powell, adapts *The Ghost Writer* for television drama, featuring Claire Bloom; program is aired in U.S. and U.K. Meets University of Connecticut professor Ross Miller and the two forge strong literary friendship.

1985   *Zuckerman Bound*, a compilation of *The Ghost Writer*, *Zuckerman Unbound*, *The Anatomy Lesson*, with epilogue *The Prague Orgy*, published. Adapts *The Prague Orgy* for a British television production that is never realized.

1986   Spends several days in Turin with Primo Levi. Conversation with Levi published in *New York Times Book Review*, which also asks that Roth write a memoir about Bernard Malamud upon Malamud's death at age seventy-two. *The Counterlife* published; wins National Book Critics Circle Award for fiction that year.

1987   Corresponds with exiled Romanian writer Norman Manea, who is living in Berlin, and encourages him to come to live in U.S.; Manea arrives the next year, and the two become close friends.

1988   *The Facts* published. Travels to Jerusalem for Aharon Appelfeld interview, which is published in *New York Times Book Review*. In Jerusalem, attends daily the trial of Ivan Demjanjuk, the alleged Treblinka guard "Ivan the Terrible." Returns to America to live year-round. Becomes Distinguished Professor of Literature at Hunter College of the City University of New York, where he will teach one semester each year until 1991.

1989   Father dies of brain tumor after yearlong illness. David Rieff leaves Farrar, Straus. For the first time since 1970, acquires a literary agent, Andrew Wylie of Wylie, Aitken, and Stone. Leaves FSG for Simon and Schuster. Writes a memoir of Philip Guston, which is published in *Vanity Fair* and subsequently reprinted in Guston catalogs.

1990   Travels to post-Communist Prague for conversation with Ivan Klíma, published in *New York Review of Books*. *Deception* published by Simon and Schuster. Roth marries Claire Bloom in New York.

1991   *Patrimony* published; wins National Book Critics Circle Award for biography. Renews strong friendship with Saul Bellow.

1992   Reads from *Patrimony* for nationwide reading tour, extending into 1993. Publishes brief profile of Norman Manea in *New York Times Book Review*.

1993   *Operation Shylock* published; wins PEN/Faulkner Award for fiction. Separates from Claire Bloom. Writes *Dr. Huvelle: A Biographical Sketch*, which he publishes privately as a thirty-four-page booklet for local distribution.

1994   Divorces Claire Bloom.

1995   Returns to Houghton Mifflin, where John Sterling is his editor. *Sabbath's Theater* is published and wins National Book Award for fiction.

1997   John Sterling leaves Houghton Mifflin and Wendy Strothman becomes Roth's editor. *American Pastoral*, first book of the "American Trilogy," is published and wins Pulitzer Prize for fiction.

1998   *I Married a Communist*, the second book of the trilogy, is published and wins Ambassador Book Award of the English-Speaking Union. In October Roth attends three-day international literary program honoring his work in Aix-en-Provence. In November receives National Medal of Arts at the White House.

2000   Publishes *The Human Stain*, final book of American trilogy, which wins PEN/Faulkner Award in U.S., the W. H. Smith Award in the U.K., and the Prix Medicis for the best foreign book of the year in France. Publishes "Rereading Saul Bellow" in *The New Yorker*.

2001   Publishes *The Dying Animal*, final book of the Kepesh trilogy, and *Shop Talk*, a collection of interviews with and essays on Primo Levi, Aharon Appelfeld, I. B. Singer, Edna O'Brien, Milan Kundera, Ivan Klíma, Philip Guston, Bernard Malamud, and Saul Bellow, and an exchange with Mary McCarthy. Receives highest award of the American Academy of Arts and Letters, the Gold Medal in fiction, given every six years "for the entire work of the recipient," previously awarded to Willa Cather, Edith Wharton, John Dos Passos, William Faulkner, Saul Bellow, and Isaac Bashevis Singer, among others. Is awarded the Edward McDowell Medal; William Styron, chair of the selection committee, remarks at the presentation ceremony that Roth "has caused to be lodged in our collective consciousness a small, select company of human beings who are as arrestingly alive and as fully realized as any in modern fiction."

2002   Wins the National Book Foundation's Medal for Distinguished Contribution to American Letters.

2003   Receives honorary degrees at Harvard University and University of Pennsylvania. Roth's work now appears in 31 languages.

2004   Publishes novel *The Plot Against America*, which becomes a best seller and wins the W. H. Smith Award for best book of the year in the U.K.; Roth is the first writer in the forty-six-year history of the prize to win it twice.

2005   *The Plot Against America* wins the Society of American Historians' James Fenimore Cooper Prize as the outstanding historical novel on an American theme for 2003–04. On October 23, Roth's childhood home at 81 Summit Avenue in Newark is marked with a plaque as a historic landmark and the nearby intersection is named Philip Roth Plaza.

2006   Publishes *Everyman* in May. Becomes fourth recipient of PEN's highest writing honor, the PEN/Nabokov Award. Receives Power of the Press Award from the New Jersey Library Association for Newark *Star-Ledger* eulogy to his close friend, Newark librarian and city historian Charles Cummings.

2007   Receives PEN/Faulkner Award for *Everyman*, the first author to be given the award three times. Wins the inaugural PEN/Saul Bellow Award for Achievement in American Fiction and Italy's first Grinzane-Masters Award, an award dedicated to the grand masters of literature. *Exit Ghost* is published.

2008   Roth's seventy-fifth birthday is marked by a celebration of his life and work at Columbia University. *Indignation* is published.

2009   Honored in program at Queens College, "A 50th Anniversary Celebration of the Work of Philip Roth." Receives the Charles Cummings Award from the Newark Preservation and Landmarks Committee, the sponsor of semi-annual tours of "Philip Roth's Newark." Publishes *The Humbling*. Wins the annual literary prize of the German newspaper *Die Welt*.

2010   Receives *Paris Review*'s Hadada Award in April. Publishes *Nemesis* in September.

2011   In March receives the National Humanities Medal at the White House. Wins the Man Booker International Prize.

2012   Receives Library of Congress Creative Achievement Award. In October, wins Spain's Prince of Asturias Award for Literature.

Note on the Texts

This volume contains the four novels of Philip Roth's "Nemeses" tetralogy: *Everyman* (2006), *Indignation* (2008), *The Humbling* (2009), and *Nemesis* (2010). At the author's request, and because corrections were made to the texts of the novels when brought out in paperback, this volume prints the versions published under Random House's Vintage International imprint.

Roth began working on *Everyman* the day after attending the funeral of the novelist Saul Bellow in April 2005. The novel was published in New York by Houghton Mifflin and in London by Jonathan Cape in May 2006. The text of *Everyman* printed here is taken from the Vintage paperback edition, published in April 2007.

Indignation was published in New York by Houghton Mifflin and in London by Jonathan Cape in September 2008. The Vintage paperback edition, published in November 2009, contains the text printed here.

The Humbling was published in September 2009 by Houghton Mifflin Harcourt in New York and by Jonathan Cape in London. The text printed here is taken from the Vintage paperback edition, published in October 2010.

Written from August 2008 to August 2009, *Nemesis* was published in New York by Houghton Mifflin Harcourt and in London by Jonathan Cape in October 2010. The Vintage paperback edition, published in October 2011, contains the text printed here.

This volume presents the texts of the original printings chosen for inclusion here, but it does not attempt to reproduce nontextual features of their typographic design. The texts are presented without change, except for the correction of typographical errors. Spelling, punctuation, and capitalization are often expressive features and are not altered, even when inconsistent or irregular. The following is a list of typographical errors corrected, cited by page and line number: 145.20 World War I; 392.7, and half; 400.29, died?; 423.9, named.

Notes

In the notes below, the reference numbers denote page and line of this volume (the line count includes chapter headings). Biblical quotations are keyed to the King James Version. Quotations from Shakespeare are keyed to *The Riverside Shakespeare*, ed. G. Blakemore Evans (Boston: Houghton Mifflin, 1974).

EVERYMAN

1.1   EVERYMAN] Title of anonymous fifteenth-century English morality play, in which the title character is abandoned by all his companions except one (Good Deeds) on his journey to death.

8.27–28   worked for . . . company] At the factories of the Singer Manufacturing Company and the Burry Biscuit Company in Elizabeth.

14.8   *Li'l Abner*] Comic strip (1934–77) by Al Capp (1909–1979), featuring a cast of boisterous hillbillies in the fictional town of Dogpatch.

14.28   Hasidic Jews] A movement in Judaism emphasizing mysticism and spiritual enthusiasm, founded in the Polish-Lithuanian Commonwealth by Israel ben Eliezer (1698–1760), known as the Baal Shem Tov (Master of the Good Name).

17.2–3   *Swiss Family . . . Kim.*] The popular adventure novels *The Swiss Family Robinson* (1812) by Swiss writer Johann David Wyss (1743–1818); *Treasure Island* (1883) by Scottish writer Robert Louis Stevenson (1850–1894); and *Kim* (1901) by English writer Rudyard Kipling (1865–1936).

17.20–21   body of a seaman . . . German U-boat.] From January to July 1942, German U-boats (submarines) waged a devastating campaign against Allied tankers and other merchant ships off the U.S. eastern seaboard.

19.38   the tolling bells] Cf. Meditation XVII in *Devotions upon Emergent Occasions* (1624), prose work by English cleric and poet John Donne (1572–1631): "Any mans death diminishes me, because I am involved in Mankinde. And therefore never send to know for whom the bell tolls; it tolls for thee."

21.36   Marquis de Sade] French libertine and writer Donatien Alphonse François, Marquis de Sade (1740–1814).

26.3   City Athletic Club] Club and athletic facility, 1908–2002, on 54th Street between Fifth and Sixth Avenues, established by Jews denied membership in the New York Athletic Club.

26.22   EKG] Electrocardiogram.

28.16   the Wharton School] Prestigious business school of the University of Pennsylvania.

32.23   *anni horribili*] Latin: horrible years.

36.27   angioplasty] Technique used to increase arterial blood flow by mechanically widening narrowed or occluded blood vessels.

45.37   Parkinson's tremors] Parkinson's disease is a degenerative neurologic disorder. Early symptoms include shaking and rigidity of movement.

46.28–30   Chuck Close's having said . . . go to work] Cf. the 2006 statement by American artist Chuck Close (b. 1940), a version of a remark Close has often made: "Inspiration is for amateurs, the rest of us just show up and get to work," in interview collected in *Inside the Painter's Studio*, ed. Joe Fig (2009).

49.5   a little Cessna] A small piston-driven private plane.

59.5   Art Students League] The Art Students League of New York, founded in 1875, known for its liberal curriculum in the fine arts, catering to amateurs as well as professionals.

63.19   de Gaulle] Paris-Charles de Gaulle airport.

63.36   demantoid garnets] Rare and valuable green gemstones.

64.21   *une femme choyée*] French: a pampered woman.

66.35   Cassandra] In Greek mythology Cassandra, King Priam's daughter, has the power to foretell the future.

72.35   Varga Girl] One of the voluptuous models featured in *Esquire* magazine's pinups of the 1940s, created by Peruvian painter and illustrator Alberto Vargas (1896–1982), who signed his work for *Esquire* as "Varga."

78.14   a myocardial infarct] A heart attack.

78.36   Four Seasons] Famous restaurant in the Seagram Building on Park Avenue.

79.25–27   Savoy . . . Connaught] Two London luxury hotels.

80.13   Turtle Bay] Neighborhood on New York's East Side.

80.15–17   "Smile . . . Cole record] From "Smile," hit record in 1954 for singer Nat King Cole (1919–1965), with title and lyrics added by John Turner and Geoffrey Parsons to music written by Charlie Chaplin (1889–1977) for his film *Modern Times* (1936).

91.5–6   High Holy Day period] The ten days from Rosh Hashanah (Jewish New Year) to Yom Kippur (the Day of Atonement).

95.25   With Jewish people we only get a day's notice] Jewish law requires that a Jew be buried within twenty-four hours after death.

INDIGNATION

107.28   Panzer] Panzer College of Physical Education and Hygiene, which in 1958 merged with Montclair State Teachers College, now Montclair State University.

110.5–6   Bill Stern's . . . sports roundup] American sports broadcaster Bill Stern (1907–1971).

111.27–28   Winesburg] Winesburg, Ohio, is the eponymous fictional setting of a 1919 short story cycle by American writer Sherwood Anderson (1876–1941).

115.23   Mama Aurelius] Reference to Roman emperor and stoic philosopher Marcus Aurelius (121–180 C.E.).

118.10   ROTC] Reserve Officers' Training Corps, college program training officer candidates for the United States military.

119.15   Chinese nationalist troops in Korea] Troops from the Republic of China, the Chinese Nationalist regime established on Formosa (Taiwan) after the Communist victory in China in 1949.

119.22–24   Senator Joseph McCarthy . . . Communists] Joseph McCarthy (1908–1957), Republican U.S. senator from Wisconsin, 1947–57, chaired a Senate subcommittee investigating purported Communist infiltration of the federal government.

119.33   M-1 rifle] Semiautomatic rifle issued to U.S. Army infantry, 1937–57.

120.9   Anzio . . . Battle of the Bulge in '44.] Beachhead thirty miles southwest of Rome between the towns of Anzio and Nettuno, site of fighting between Anglo-American and German forces, January 22–May 23, 1944; the German offensive and the Allied counteroffensive in the Ardennes, December 16, 1944–January 25, 1945.

144.29   Seabees and the WACs.] Seabees, common name for those serving in the U.S. Naval Construction Battalions; WACs, members of the Women's Army Corps.

144.30   national anthem of our Chinese allies] See 100.2–8 in this volume.

157.26   Nietzsche or a Schopenhauer.] German philosophers Friedrich Nietzsche (1844–1900) and Arthur Schopenhauer (1788–1860).

165.25–26   drop kick, the old vintage drop kick?] Play in football, now rare, when a player drops the ball and kicks it off the bounce through the uprights at the end of the playing field to score a field goal or point-after-touchdown.

169.29–30   "I shot an arrow . . . where"]   First two lines of "The Arrow and the Song" (1845) by American poet Henry Wadsworth Longfellow (1807–1882).

175.4   ration stamps]   Government-issued coupons redeemable for commodities in short supply during World War II.

189.4   Fisher Ames . . . "Jacobin" President]   Federalist politician Fisher Ames (1758–1808), U.S. representative from Massachusetts, 1789–97, supported President John Adams in his unsuccessful reelection campaign in 1800 against Thomas Jefferson, whom Ames derisively called a "Jacobin," after the most radical French revolutionaries.

196.6   Marty Marion of the Cards]   Professional baseball player and manager Marty Marion (1916–2011), nicknamed "Mr. Shortstop," who played most of his career for the St. Louis Cardinals.

203.33   John Barrymore]   American stage and film star (1882–1942), known for his many marriages and love affairs.

203.36–37   *School for Scandal*]   Comedy (1777) by Irish-born playwright Richard Brinsley Sheridan (1751–1816).

209.27–28   college deferments]   The Universal Military Training and Service Act of 1951, an amended version of the 1948 Selective Service Act, allowed local draft boards to defer the military service of full-time college students on the basis of either current academic standing or satisfactory performance on a standardized test.

210.14   named for the French explorer]   Robert de La Salle (1643–1687), explorer of the Great Lakes and Mississippi River.

215.12   Old Baldy area]   Old Baldy Hill (Hill 266) and its surrounding area in west-central Korea, including Pork Chop Hill (Hill 255).

219.15   BAR]   Browning Automatic Rifle.

221.26–27   Our Folly, which art in Heaven.]   Cf. the opening of the Lord's Prayer, Matthew 6:9, from Christ's Sermon on the Mount.

THE HUMBLING

227.16   Falstaff and Peer Gynt and Vanya]   Sir John Falstaff, from Shakespeare's two *Henry IV* plays and *The Merry Wives of Windsor*; eponymous antihero of *Peer Gynt* (1876), by Norwegian playwright Henrik Ibsen (1828–1906); Ivan Petrovitch Voynitsky, title character of *Uncle Vanya* (1897) by Russian playwright and short story writer Anton Chekhov (1860–1904).

228.32   Prospero]   Protagonist of Shakespeare's *The Tempest*.

230.12–14   Our revels . . . air]   *The Tempest*, IV.i.148–50.

230.36   Balanchine's]   Russian-born American choreographer George Balanchine (1904–1983).

240.9   The Guthrie]   Renowned repertory theater company in Minneapolis, Minnesota.

240.9   *Long Day's Journey.*]   *Long Day's Journey into Night* by American playwright Eugene O'Neill (1888–1953), written in 1940–41, first produced and published in 1956.

240.15–16   James Tyrone.]   Aging patriarch in *Long Day's Journey into Night*, who had abandoned his ambition to become a great Shakespearean actor and instead became rich and famous for a role in a popular play he had bought the rights to.

240.33–38   John Gielgud . . . Olivier.]   British stage and film actors John Gielgud (1904–2000) and Laurence Olivier (1907–1989).

241.27   *The Family Reunion*]   Play (1939) by American poet and playwright T. S. Eliot (1888–1965).

244.8   watched Vincent work.]   Roth notes on the copyright page of *The Humbling* that Daniels's teaching technique is borrowed from *How to Stop Acting* (Faber & Faber, 2003) by Harold Guskin.

246.14–19   plays . . . *Our Town*]   *Hedda Gabler* (1890) by Ibsen; *Miss Julie* (1888) by Swedish playwright August Strindberg (1849–1912); *Hippolytus* (428 B.C.E.) by Greek playwright Euripides (c. 480–406 B.C.E.); *Oedipus Rex* (429 B.C.E.) and *Antigone* (c. 441 B.C.E.) by Greek playwright Sophocles (c. 497–406 B.C.E.); *Death of a Salesman* (1949) and *All My Sons* (1947) by American playwright Arthur Miller (1915–2005); *The Iceman Cometh* (1939) by Eugene O'Neill; *Our Town* (1938) by American playwright Thornton Wilder (1897–1975).

246.22–23   *Awake and Sing! . . . Seagull*]   *Awake and Sing!* (1935) by American playwright Clifford Odets (1906–1963); *Ivanov* (1887) and *The Seagull* (1896) by Chekhov.

246.29–31   *Deirdre . . . Electra*]   *Deirdre of the Sorrows* (1910) by Irish playwright John Millington Synge (1871–1909); *The Wild Duck* (1884) and *Rosmersholm* (1886) by Ibsen; *Mourning Becomes Electra* (1931) by O'Neill.

249.8   *Playboy of the Western World.*]   Play (1907) by Synge.

254.17   Brendel]   Classical pianist Alfred Brendel (b. 1931).

278.35   Clytemnestra]   In Greek myth, Clytemnestra commits adultery while her husband, Agamemnon, king of Mycenae, is at the siege of Troy, and upon his return murders him.

285.32   god Pan]   Greek god of hunting, fertility, and pastoral music.

287.7 myelogram] An x-ray procedure in which contrast dye is injected into the spinal canal to identify nerve damage.

298.21–22 Actors Studio] Theatrical organization founded in 1947 known primarily for its training in "method acting," a technique based on the teachings of Russian actor and director Konstantin Stanislavski (1863–1938).

NEMESIS

306.39 iron lung] A negative pressure ventilator or "iron lung" is a heavy steel cylinder that enables a patient without normal muscle control to breathe.

313.22 *Life Can Be Beautiful*] Radio drama on NBC and CBS, 1938–54.

315.12–13 Polish Galicia.] Region in the southeastern part of present-day Poland and the southwestern part of present-day Ukraine.

316.1 4-F] Selective Service designation for a registrant judged mentally, physically, or morally unfit for military service.

326.11 V-mail letters] Letters on forms that were microfilmed and sent overseas, then enlarged and delivered.

327.17 victory garden.] As part of the war effort Americans were encouraged to maintain vegetable gardens on their own property or in larger community plots.

328.14 shul] Yiddish: synagogue, school.

329.35 "I'll Be Seeing You,"] Popular song (1938), lyrics by Irving Kahal (1903–1942), music by Sammy Fain (1902–1989), which provided the title for a 1944 film, in which it was sung by Bing Crosby.

333.18–22 Joseph Lee . . . gaining of life."] From "Standards of Children's Play" (1919) by Boston recreation advocate Joseph Lee (1862–1937).

339.6 Louis Pasteur] French chemist and microbiologist Louis Pasteur (1822–1895), creator of the pasteurization process that prevents milk and other foods from causing illness.

340.31 Kaddish] Hebrew mourning prayer.

352.20 blackout shades.] Black window coverings that prevented light from escaping from inside buildings. They were installed along the eastern seaboard to prevent ships from being silhouetted against the coastline, thereby becoming more vulnerable to German submarine attack.

377.14 Ernest Thompson Seton] Naturalist and nature writer (1860–1946), cofounder of the Boy Scouts of America and an enthusiast of American Indian woodcraft and folklore.

413.1–2 Arno River . . . invaded Guam] British and New Zealand troops crossed the Arno near Arezzo, about thirty-five miles southeast of Florence, on July 16. The first American landings on Guam occurred on July 21, 1944.

413.27   "Till We Meet Again,"] Popular song (1918), lyrics by Raymond B. Egan (1890–1952), music by Richard A. Whitting (1891–1938).

425.25–26   a Sister Kenny Institute] One of numerous medical clinics treating polio with techniques developed by Australian nurse and public-health advocate Elizabeth Kenny (1880–1952), who lacked formal nursing training. Although medical opinion was divided about the efficacy of the treatment, the National Foundation for Infantile Paralysis endorsed her approach in 1941.

429.32   1967 Newark riots] Rioting in Newark began on the evening of July 12, 1967, spreading from the black Central Ward to other sections of the city. After six days 23 people were killed, with 725 injured and 1,500 arrested.

430.14   Typhoid Mary] Mary Mallon (1869–1938), Irish immigrant cook who carried the organism causing typhoid fever without manifesting symptoms of the disease. Vehemently denying that she was infected, Mallon spread the disease to at least fifty-three people (three fatally) while working in New York City and Long Island. After spending 1907–10 in quarantine, she continued to work as a cook and to transmit the disease. In 1915 she was returned to quarantine, where she remained for the rest of her life.

431.26   Palmer Method] A widely adopted method of handwriting developed by Austin Norman Palmer (1860–1927).

438.24–25   Gnostic doctrine . . . Demiurge.] In Gnostic thought, which developed in early Christianity and was condemned as heretical, the material world was created by an intermediary figure, the Demiurge, rather than God.

This book is set in 10 point ITC Galliard Pro,
a face designed for digital composition by Matthew Carter
and based on the sixteenth-century face Granjon. The paper
is acid-free lightweight opaque and meets the requirements
for permanence of the American National Standards Institute.
The binding material is Brillianta, a woven rayon cloth made
by Van Heek-Scholco Textielfabrieken, Holland. Compo-
sition by Dedicated Book Services. Printing and
binding by Edwards Brothers Malloy, Ann Arbor.
Designed by Bruce Campbell.